THE JACKET

Richard Baran

TotalRecall Publications, Inc.
1103 Middlecreek
Friendswood, Texas 77546
281-992-3131   281-482-5390 Fax
www.totalrecallpress.com

Copyright © 2014 by: Richard Baran
Edited by William R. "Will" Barshop
All rights reserved
ISBN: 978-1-59095-566-6
UPC: 6-43977-45668-7

Printed in the United States of America with simultaneous printings in Australia, Canada, and United Kingdom.

FIRST EDITION
1   2   3   4   5   6   7   8   9   10

This is a work of fiction. The characters, names, events, views, and subject matter of this book are either the author's imagination or are used fictitiously. Any similarity or resemblance to any real people, real situations or actual events is purely coincidental and not intended to portray any person, place, or event in a false, disparaging or negative light.

For Carol Ann—The love of my life and girl of my dreams.

To My Daughters
Cheryl and Lisa

Author Richard Baran

holds a doctorate and two masters' degrees besides his bachelor's in business. A Navy veteran, he taught and coached for forty years at the secondary school and collegiate levels. Besides publishing a book about coaching football, he's published a short story and several dozen articles in professional journals. Dick and his eighth grade sweetheart, Carol have twenty grandchildren and they divide their year between Franklin Park, Illinois, Phoenix, Arizona and Minocqua, Wisconsin.

Visit www.richardbaran.com for more information.

Acknowledgment

Thanks to Rebecca Pratt of the Pratt Literary Group and my agent, Jeff Lovell for his creative right brain, impersonations of Max Bialystock (although not as good as Duke Mongan) and pretending to be gluten-free at Portillo's Hot Dogs.

Thanks to William Barshop for his editing prowess. I haven't heard the term, "non sequitur" used by someone who is seventeen in fifty years.

My very special thanks to, Carol Ann Capuzzo Fredrickson for her convoluted inspiration and right-to-the-point comments on my writing especially, "Blah-blah-blah."

Oh, yeah, and to Denny Toll. You were in "Coaching Football's Polypotent Offense." If I left you out of this one, you'd never pop for another one of Chuck Romano's pizzas in Rosemont.

Everyone needs a computer guru. I have Mark Puck. He's a bloody genius.

I was lucky to have several inspirational teachers who encouraged me to write. Thank you, Sister Mary Helen, B.V.M., Perry A. Guedry, Ph.D., and Colonel Charles Stribling.

Joseph T. Baran, Chicago, Illinois, (1894-1953), Entrepreneur and Public Servant. My idol and role model. Thank you, Grandpa.

About The Book

Tidge Mackiewicz, new patriarch of his family, received several orders from his dying father, Kid Scream. One order stated that Tidge should quit believing in Santa Claus and stop acting like every day was Christmas. Tidge should also abandon his belief that the Luftwaffe shot down Santa Claus on Christmas Eve in 1944 and Santa survived. Approaching fifty, Tidge still wears a scuffed and stained Army Air Corps flight jacket given to him as a young boy by his late uncle, a Navy aviator and Korean War hero, who claimed it belonged to Santa Claus. His uncle also believed that the jacket possessed a special magic. It is "The Jacket" and the spirit of Christmas that brings eighteen family members to Tidge and his wife's magnificent log chalet located in Wisconsin's Northwoods on Lake Namakagon for the Christmas holidays. Tidge can now carry out his father's final order of unscrewing his screwed up family and much more.

List of Characters

Tidge Mackiewicz, —the protagonist. Approaching fifty, he is the oldest of four brothers and the father of three daughters from a prior marriage. Handsome and tough his loves include his wife who he calls Willy, his three daughters, nature photography and Santa Claus.

Wilhelmina Schneider Mackiewicz, —Tidge's wife. She is fourteen years his junior, a widow, former grammar school teacher, budding novelist and victim of spousal abuse from her first marriage.

Ignacy Mackiewicz, —father, patriarch and tyrant known by his four sons as "Kid Scream" because of his enthusiastic love of boxing. He is an Archie Bunker type bigot who, on his death bed, places three demands on his oldest son, Tidge.

Margret Mary Mackiewicz, —Ignacy's wife and mother of the four boys. She is known lovingly by her sons as "Mother Mary May I" because of her insistence of the proper uses of the words "Can" and "May."

Peter, Paul and John Mackiewicz, —Tidge's three younger brothers. Peter is married to an African American; Paul to a Chinese American and John to a Native American. Their father had referred to the wives as "The Natives." Each of the brothers has two children, a boy and a girl.

Harold and Gert Schneider, —Willy's parents. Harold is a retired millionaire having made his fortune in the Men's girlie magazine business of the late 40's and early 50's. He fled Germany near the end of World War II as a young teen along with his mother. His father was a Luftwaffe pilot. Gert was a pin-up model for the same girlie magazines who retired and became a professional lady wrestler.

Carol, Carm and Martha, —Tidge's daughters from youngest to oldest. Martha carries an angry grudge against her father for his divorcing her mother. Carm supports and loves her father. Carol, the youngest, is in her teens and was the matchmaker who originally brought her father to meet her grammar school teacher, Wihelmina Schneider Jones (Willy). Carol brings her new boyfriend to Wisconsin to spend Christmas with her family.

Ronald Paul Mackenzie "Mackie" Johnston, —Carol's boyfriend, is an overly polite high school senior attending military academy who is Carol's surprise Christmas guest at her father and stepmother's house in the Northwoods.

Don and Norma Miller, —along with their son, Kenny who is in his late teens are neighbors of Tidge and Willy. They live on a dairy farm across the bay from Tidge and Willy.

Humper and Bean Head, —are Tidge's long-time friends from his early days in grammar school.

Chapter 1

Almost every word Kid Scream ever said to his oldest son combined a gruff command and shouted warning that pierced the core of Tidge's soul. Not this time. What had been gravel coated, frightening threats now oozed out as cough punctuated gasps. The Kid's shriveled mouth, set in what had once been a square tough jaw, forced out each word. Even Kid Scream's last words to Tidge emerged as commands, the once feared bark and bite absent, a trinity of frail warnings. His father's right hand made a twitching motion and Tidge moved closer. His father gasped and his hard, steel blue eyes flickered as he pronounced the first of his orders, "Get your head out of your ass and toss Brew's goddamned jacket into the trash."

Tidge nodded.

The second order followed, sounding like a giant exhale. His eyes didn't flicker. "There ain't no Santa Claus," he wheezed. "So stop acting like every day is goddamn Christmas." His father emitted a deep, raspy phlegm coated cough. His breath, a mix of decay and the cheap *wodka* that sustained him through life, collided with the revolting antiseptic aroma that permeated the hospital room.

Tidge swallowed hard and shut his eyes. "Yeah, Dad," he whispered, the rancid odors gagging him. He grabbed at the disfigured side rail of his father's bed. His father's chest heaved, lungs struggling for a last breath of air. The Kid's eyelids opened. Tidge bent closer. Kid Scream choked out his final words. "The screwed up Natives are yours now," he managed. "Unscrew them."

Tidge understood. Now compassion replaced–too late–the dread Tidge felt for his father. Sometime before, he realized that he feared his father more than he loved him. He nodded to the skeleton lying on the hospital bed. Then he saw his father's eyes close again, heard a relieved sigh and knew the torch had been passed.

Tidge straightened, his hands slipping off the hand rail as he backed away a few steps, still staring at his father's body. He understood why Kid Scream referred to his son's family as screwed up. His father and his bigotry had screwed it up. The Kid had estranged his sons and alienated Tidge against his brothers. Kid Scream could never comprehend why three of his sons couldn't marry girls just like the girl he had married. "Look at those goddamned kids of yours," he once said to his wife.

Mary Rose Callahan Mackiewicz could have been Maureen O'Hara's older sister. She had been dubbed "Mother Mary May I" by her children; a term of deep respect because of her constant correcting of their use of the word *can* and *may*. Her long red hair spent most of its time curled in bobby pins. It framed her calm look of disapproval which, when aimed at her husband's language, always stopped his tirades in mid-sentence. She would permit none of his demeaning comments about any of her daughters-in-law whom she cherished as if she had gone through the pains of child birth with each. "Your sons are good husbands and fathers who married beautiful women who are loving mothers," she would say in a brogue that could thicken when necessary.

Tidge resented his father's bigoted imprecations about his sons' wives. Bits and pieces of his father's comments chipped off to include Tidge's wife, Sissy. Then there was the rubble of his divorce and Tidge joined his brothers in banishing Kid Scream from the family. The Kid called his daughters-in-law *natives*, though never to their faces. He, however, never considered his hurtful comments as bigotry. One of his daughters-in-law came from Native American heritage, another descended from Asian-Americans and another from African American parents. When Kid Scream wanted to specify one of the women, he used the names "Squaw", "Slant" or "Spade". He did not understand why his sons found these sobriquets offensive.

His father regarded Tidge as the only one who married a real American even though he disliked the black haired, self-centered fashion plate at first sight. "I can't believe he's going to marry that stuck up broad," he said to Mother Mary May I, then dodging her look of disapproval. Kid Scream garnered more looks over time from Mother Mary May I describing Tidge's wife, Sissy. Among other things, he said, "She's lazy, useless as tits on a nun, and stopped being a mother to our three granddaughters about the time the afterbirth appeared."

Over time, Tidge came to agree with his father even though he loved Sissy, at least in the beginning. Then the love vanished along with the marriage.

Tidge looked down again at his lifeless father and, to his surprise, began to cry. He didn't weep for his father. Tidge wept because he didn't want the responsibility that his father had passed to him.

He understood his three brothers resented him for being his father's favorite and he knew they wouldn't want him to be the Mackiewicz family patriarch. Even before the anointing, they ignored almost everything he said to them including polite questions and expressions of concern such as, *how ya doin'*, *how's the wife* and *take care of yourself*.

If his mother had been alive, he would have been spared his siblings' animosity. Mother Mary May I would have forced her sons to respect all courtesies. If her sons deviated one step from what she often described as the path the Lord's sandals trod on, she would give them a gentle though firm reminder that they had been named after saints, each word smothered in her gravy thick brogue. Reminders changed to warnings when a second step went awry. Her brogue would thicken and with stern looks of disapproval her words of warning became spicier and filled with censure as she would say, "You boys will certainly get the what for from Saints Thomas, Peter, Paul and John if you don't mend your ways."

Mother Mary May I never handed the gravy ladle to Kid Scream. Nonetheless the boys lived in fear of their father's tyranny even after their mother's death and they were adults. When Kid Scream died *what for* didn't matter. What mattered to Tidge was that not one of his brothers bothered to be with their father at the hospital when he passed away. He knew that Mother Mary May I would have been so incensed if she knew her gravy ladle would have been in splinters.

Over the next several years Tidge's failure to reconcile with his family nagged at him. His father's final orders became a debilitating burden. Tidge, however, never stopped believing that every day was Christmas, and his belief ruled every stage of his life.

After his father's death he continued to embrace the total spirit of Christmas. Despite an incident at age six when Tidge reviled a department store Santa, calling him a "fat bastard", he hoped that Santa Claus would someday leave him a special present that would help him unscrew his screwed up family.

Tidge waited and believed, but he had no intention of following one of his father's last commands. His late Uncle Brew had passed an old aviator's jacket on to him and the jacket became his coat of arms. Tidge believed the jacket possessed a magic that would one day provide the solution to carrying out his father's three demands. The story his Uncle Brew attached to the jacket acted as Tidge's shield and sword: The German Luftwaffe had shot down Santa Claus over Germany on Christmas Eve of 1944 and, according to his uncle and several other eye witnesses, Santa survived.

Mother Mary May I even believed the story of Santa's war heroics. Her brother-in-law, a Navy pilot and Korean War hero himself, once possessed Santa's flight jacket. Now her son wore it. She however saw Christmas as sacred, not jolly.

Tidge's mother taught him that Christmas decorations should adorn every square inch of table space with religious figurines nestled in layers of surgical cotton. The Infant Jesus was her favorite. She displayed with reverence statues of the Christ child in a variety of poses throughout her house. Baby Jesus statues outnumbered his closest competitors, Santa and Frosty, by twelve to one.

Tidge, without a trace of disrespect, reversed his mother's priorities. He had an Infant Jesus or two, but his Santa collection, and conglomeration of snowmen, Rudolph and the other reindeer, Uncle Mistletoe, Aunt Holly, Mrs. Claus and Suzy Snowflake, overwhelmed his mother's religious figurines. His demoting of his mother's blessed iconic statuettes turned out to be not so great a reduction in rank.

Mother Mary May I had her favorite decorations, but so did her first born son. His centerpiece, spotlighted in the front window of his house, portrayed the Nativity scene with antique hand-carved figurines. Carvings of tiny, curious children, heralding angels, snoozing cows, bored goats, grazing sheep and visitors' camels graced the front window. His grandfather shipped the set from Poland to Tidge's father and his new wife about the time Hitler was putting on his hob nail boots to crush Poland. The battered cardboard carton was the last the Mackiewicz newlyweds in America ever heard from *Dziadziu*. The Mackiewicz children of Ignatius and Mary Rose only knew their grandfather, who they called, Ja-Ja from several cracked photographs, the square jaw and stern eyes replicated in their own father.

Tidge saw Christmas as giving and giving and giving. He always completed his Christmas shopping by the Fourth of July. He stacked boxes of Christmas decorations in closets one day exactly after the official end of the Christmas season the way his mother did. He recalled her coming home after Sunday Mass at St. Ferdinand's and announce to he and his brothers: "Get out the boxes, boys. Christ has been baptized and Christmas is officially over." The boxes wouldn't appear again until the day after Thanksgiving according to Mother Mary May I's edict.

When Tidge and his brothers were carefree kids and life was a happy sand pile, Christmas almost always meant presents of all types. Mounds of festive wrapped packages jutted out from under their Christmas tree, the tree almost hidden by ornaments, strings of lights– half burned out, silver, recycled tinsel and spirals of colored paper loops each son had made in kindergarten and saved by Mother Mary May I. There was always a toy or a game or a ball that represented a sport. Even receiving an item of clothing was a delight though no one's favorite.

However, a Christmas or two had been sparse. Once their father had been temporarily laid off from working on the shipping and receiving dock at a meat packing company across the street from what remained of the Union Stock Yards. No packages bulged out from under the tree on that Christmas morning, but each of the boys received a present thanks to a frugal Mother Mary May I. She had gone into her contingency savings account, the currency and coins stashed away in one of several cracked tea cups that had belonged to her mother who had died in Ireland. The cups were stashed behind two chipped oval serving platters in the back of two cabinets above the kitchen sink.

Each Mackiewicz boy got to open a festive package thanks to Mother Mary May I, the queen of recycled Christmas wrapping. Her first words to them after wishing them a Blessed and Merry Christmas were, "Be careful not to tear the paper or ruin the ribbons and bows." One Christmas morning Tidge opened a package that had his name on the front of the name tag and, written on the back, *To: Iggy. From: Bruce.*

Recycled Christmas wrap never stopped Tidge from believing in Santa Claus. His divorce and the resulting fallout may have dampened his spirit, but he still believed. Even his father's bigotry couldn't get in the way of his getting excited about Christmas. Excitement was what Christmas was all about. Little had changed for him during the brief interlude starting the day after Thanksgiving to Christmas morning. Still he and his brothers missed searching the family house for hidden presents weeks before Christmas. Like intrepid archeologists they sifted through every inch of their tiny Cape Cod house and never found a thing: nothing in the attic, nothing in the garage and nothing in their parent's bedroom closet. Christmas morning found them dejected, but still optimistic, as the four of them rolled out of the two single beds they shared. After a stumbling race down the stairs to the living room, the sight that greeted them banished all traces of dejection. The Mackiewicz boys always found something under the tree for them.

One morning the something under the tree was Santa Claus. As they discovered, it wasn't Santa but, instead, their Uncle Bruce. Uncle Brew, as he was also known because of his voracious thirst for anything alcohol, had passed out Christmas Eve and spent the night snoring under the tree, still wearing his, stained, faded red suit and hat. Joining the snoring was their father, Kid Scream who was nestled in his favorite chair, his body twisted in a geometric curve that gladdened the hearts of chiropractors. The Mackiewicz boys didn't care. They extricated their presents from under the tree without disturbing Santa and their father.

Christmases came and went. Then Uncle Brew, their Santa Claus, was gone. He was followed by Mother Mary May I who almost took the spirit of Christmas with her. Kid Scream departed soon after, his final orders to Tidge gathering dust along with the Natives staying screwed up.

Tidge's belief in the magic of Christmas stood solid even though he developed an earnest desire to shed the mantle of family leadership. Through it all, he clung to an optimism that refused to die thanks to his second wife, Willy whom he married less than two months before his father passed away. If his special present didn't come from Santa Claus this Christmas, next year awaited. At one tick-tock past midnight to start December 26th, he would swallow the bile of his disappointment like he had in the past, tell himself he understood and started waiting all over again.

As October gave way to November, Tidge's hopes heated up from a simmer to a low boil. Thanksgiving to him transcended gluttony and televised football. It was time to once again pass underneath the archway to the start of another Christmas season. This Christmas, he was convinced, would be the one.

Chapter 2

"I'll betcha this is the year," Tidge said to Willy, as they took their daily walk. "I know it." They savored the late fall afternoons of the Northwoods and walking along the black top county road surrounded by a canyon of pine and birch of the Chequamegon National Forest. Inhaling the incredible fragrances of the crisp and clear air seemed to accelerate the coming of Thanksgiving and, finally, Christmas.

Tidge had been married to Wilhelmina Schneider-Jones going on three years. She was fourteen years his junior, his youngest daughter's former eighth grade teacher, a widow, and the love of his life. He adored her. His devotion to her nosed out his affection for the Yule Time, Santa Claus and his aviator's jacket, but not by much.

Willy looked up at him, her head surrounded by the fur halo of her hooded parka, and said, "This is the third time I've heard you state that this is the year Santa Claus will bring you your special present." She tried to be sympathetic, her near arm looped with his, as they strolled together shuffling their feet through the October leaves that grudgingly lingered as Thanksgiving approached. "I still can't believe how disappointed you get, and then how philosophical you become about being let down by your hero, idol and role model, Kristopher Kringle."

"Into each life some leaves must fall," he said, acting philosophical. "A man's got to believe," he continued, his optimistic enthusiasm crackling like the delicate sound of the leaves under their hiking boots. "He's got to have a dream."

"Even if your dream is what my father used to call a pipe dream," she said, then wishing she could reach out with her deer skin, fur lined mittens and snatch her words back.

"A dream by any other name," he said, a cherubic smile twinkled back at Willy. "I dream therefore I am," He loved the way her frosted brown hair blended with the hood's fur trim and how her sugar brown eyes, his description of them, seemed to flash a continuous message telling him he was her one and only. His head did a dance as if he were listening to Gene Autry singing about a red nosed reindeer. "Santa's a busy dude at Christmas," he continued. "There are lots of little kids on his list who also have dreams." His optimism climbed like a psychedelic colored hot air balloon at a summer Wisconsin art festival. "Once he takes care of the kids, he'll bring my special present."

"You're the biggest little kid I've ever seen," she replied, her voice now lacking any signs of sympathy. "Just don't walk around here down in the mouth until Easter because Kris the Dude let you down again."

Tidge smiled at her, his mischievous blue eyes sparkling, and then pointed at himself. "Me? Down? No way, dearest wife."

He saw her squeeze at his arm with her mittens, but felt only a gentle pressure through the padded thickness of his layers of a wool lumberjack shirt, ski sweater and the scarred World War II Army Air Corps leather jacket he wore with pride as if he had flown in combat over the ack-ack filled skies of Europe. "Santa's my main man," he said, an impish grin teasing her. "If you believe in him, he believes in you." The expression on his face underscored his statement. "This is the year he makes my dream, pipe or otherwise, come true."

She gave his arm another squeeze and looked straight ahead. "If your main man doesn't make your dream come true, are you going to stop believing in him?" she asked, the sing-song lilt of her voice sounding like elevator music punctuated with a Brubeck rondo. "I feel bad about mocking hallowed grounds," she continued, then pausing for several seconds before going on. "Honey, I wasn't being sarcastic when I questioned the possibility of your dream not coming true." She turned and looked into his eyes that never showed any signs of disappointment, at least not for more than an instant. "I do hope, from the bottom of my heart, that your dream doesn't become a gruesome nightmare. I'd hate to see my big little kid drown his sorrows after Christmas by eating too many fermented sugar plums marinated in juniper berry juice."

Tidge laughed and patted her mitten. "You know," he said,

trying to be serious. "I've never seen a sugar plum, only heard about them." He paused as if looking for an answer. "Do they really dance?"

Willy stopped in her tracks as if not believing what she just heard. "Surely you jest," she said, then looking into his almost sincere eyes, knowing that they always gave away what he would say next.

"Nope," he said, a Buster Keaton look-a-like dead pan plastered across his face. "I never jest with anything related to Santa Claus and Christmas."

"Did you ever hear of the Nutcracker?"

"Come on," he said, sounding like he had just been insulted. "Of course I've heard of nutcrackers."

"Not a nutcracker," she said, placing the emphasis on the "A" and sounding like the grammar school teacher she had been when she first met him. Her eyes seemed to go from brown to red as she waited for her husband to add another twist to her nutcracker question. "Did you ever hear of the ballet?" she asked, being careful not to step into one of his nonsensical traps camouflaged with philosophy.

"Yeah. So?"

"Sew buttons," she said, using one of her favorite expressions when she began feeling annoyed. "I'm talking about Tchaikovsky's *Nutcracker, The Dance of the Sugar Plum Fairy*, Mother Ginger and wooden soldiers and mice. It's my mother's favorite."

"Yeah. So?" he repeated, knowing he could rile her with his repetitious comments. "Your mother, the former professional lady wrestler, likes tutus." He pointed at himself. "And, me, I like my Uncle Brew's old aviator's jacket. You have a point you'd like to make?"

"My point," she repeated, her exasperation evident as she pushed back the hood of her parka. "You dream too much."

"No way."

She stooped down, picked up a twig, stood back up and pointed it at him. "Do you intend to deny that you're always dreaming about Santa Claus bringing you a special gift?" She thrust the twig at his chest. "Or that you're always dreaming of a *White Christmas*? If you're not dreaming, then you're constantly singing about it." She was gathering momentum. "Or hallucinating about all the money you were going to make for us selling your photographs of Wisconsin's flora and fauna?"

He gave a shrug and sidestepped a second thrust of her twig with the grace of a lame reindeer.

"I bet you even fantasize about that *Sugar Claus* pin-up above the left pocket of that Goodwill Box reject you insist on wearing?"

"Speak with reverence about my Uncle Brew's jacket," he said, his voice indicating that she indeed trespassed on hallowed ground. "The man was a war hero and besides, I still don't see your point."

She smiled at him and tossed the twig back to the ground.

"I told you why I wear the jacket," he said, and then tempered his own changing mood. His right index finger zeroed in above the left breast pocket of the leather jacket pointing at, but not touching, what remained of the once colorful handmade insignia. "According to my Uncle Brew, every crew member of the B-25 Mitchell bomber, called *Sugar Claus,* wore jackets with that insignia on every mission including the last one on a fateful Christmas Eve in 1944."

He stopped and looked at the only female who could get his dander up and make him laugh at himself at the same time. His finger tip gently touched the jacket's insignia, landing on the hat the faded pin-up girl was wearing. "That's a classic Santa Claus hat she's wearing if I ever saw a classic Santa Claus hat." He cocked an eye at her and his finger moved down a fraction. "And those are sugar plums if I ever saw sugar plums." His index finger went back and forth under the artist's rendition of the pin-up girl's pointed breasts and he gave Willy a smug look. "I wear this jacket because my late Uncle Brew told me Santa Claus wore it." He crossed his arms over his chest. "That's a point that even my mother couldn't refute."

She wrinkled her nose at him, her message that he was talking too much. "Maybe you should make a wish on your jacket to insure that Santa will really bring you your special present." A teasing smile popped across her face. "It's becoming very apparent to me that your rotund friend in the red suit is going to have you tossing and turning the night before Christmas." She gave him a sad shake of her head. "Maybe you should ask your dude to bring the real Miss Sugar Claus with him along with your special gift." She gave another very light shake of her head. "On second thought, maybe Santa and Sugar would be better off sending your special present by Fed Ex." Her mittens latched onto his arm again.

Willy had more than crossed the line into sacred territory with her slap at Santa, but he knew that now was not the time for angry reprimands. "Oh, ye of little faith," he said, as if preaching. His square dimpled face lit up. "I did know a girl who was named Claus."

"Oh, sure," she said, her mittens slipping off his arm again as she stepped back.

"Of course, sure," he said, offering his arm back to her. "Marietta Claus was her name and her parents moved to our northwest side neighborhood from a town called Mexico, Missouri. She was in the eighth grade with me at St. Ferdinand's." He winked at her. "I danced with her at a Christmas party in the school's basement." He held his opposite hand as high above his head as he could. "She towered over me." He gave Willy another wink. "She was very pretty and had the nicest set of sugar plums any naughty Marietta could have." His eyes danced. "We dated all through high school. I even took her to my senior prom at the same hotel we had our wedding reception."

Willy ignored his extended arm as she shook her head from side to side. "Knowing you, I bet you checked to see how naughty Miss Marietta was and how ripe her sugar plums were."

"Not me," he said in all innocence. "Respect is my middle name. Besides, at that eighth grade Christmas dance we were surrounded by nuns."

Her head still wagged from side to side. "Spare me."

"Honest," he said, crossing his index finger over his heart. "If the nuns weren't tough enough, she had a mean stepfather named Wolfgang. Honest," he said again, his index finger adding to his crosses. "If Wolfie thought I even considered taking a quick squeeze of his little girl's plums, he would've beaten me senseless. Then he would've given me a Hiel, Adolph, and goose stepped over my body until he turned me into a bloody pulp. After, when there was no more pulp to bloody, he would've told my dad. Kid Scream would have done ditto, only substituting a Polish Hop while my mother did an Irish jig on my groin." He struggled to keep from laughing. "No plums are worth that much punishment." Laughter beat the struggle. "Well, except yours."

They continued their walk along the sand and gravel shoulder of the road, each taking random kicks at leaves while enjoying the accompaniment of fine loose gravel under their boots and anticipating the approaching holidays. "Talk about tossing and turning," she said to him, her eyes still downcast on the leaves, "all you needed to do was tell me again how you quit your job two years ago and purchased Henry David Thoreau's log cabin on Walden Namakagon."

"That's Lake Namakagon, my dearest Wilhelmina," he said, using her given name, something he rarely did, to show his displeasure at her poking fun at a decision that ended up making them more than happy.

"I didn't know that when you first told me," she said. "I tossed and turned so bad that night I thought I was going to end up rolling off the balcony of our condo."

Tidge took a deep breath and recalled the scene after he announced his decision to her.

"A what?" she had asked, after hearing about his resigning from his job and buying a cabin somewhere on another planet. She remembered wondering why she couldn't breathe and why she had no sense of feeling, a numbing sensation having taken over her body. "Where?" she had asked, her question coming out as if by the dashes and dots of Morse Code. "Where in God's name is Cable, Wisconsin?" She choked, "Why?" and then started crying, blubbering out her next question that came in four jumpy words. "You quit your job?"

Tidge never thought twice about buying the massive chalet of polished logs and floor-to-ceiling glass. He saw it the first time by mistake, the designer log home smiling at him from his computer screen like Sugar Claus on the nose of the Mitchell bomber. A phone call from his office the next morning to a realtor in Cable, Wisconsin produced a check for the earnest money. The realtor was thrilled, but tried to get him to think about what he was doing, to not make a mistake. Tidge knew he wasn't making a mistake even though he never saw the house in person. The only mistake he made was the night before when he coughed, sneezed and passed gas all at once confusing his index finger that rested on his computer mouse. The mouse jumped as if avoiding the wire death of a sprung trap and his Internet search for Immanuel Kant ended on Kenosha, Wisconsin.

Philosophy had fascinated him since he minored in it at Loyola University Chicago. A series of frustrated computer mouse twitches introduced him to northwestern Wisconsin. Then the town of Cable popped up on his screen. Another quick twitch transported him to a lake called Namakagon. Curiosity brushed aside his mistaken mouse prods and he ventured into real estate.

Several clicks later, he spotted his dream house nestled on the shore of a lake with a strange sounding name surrounded by eight acres of birch, oak, hemlock and pine punctuated with maples. The scene brought back memories of the family vacations he and his brothers went on with their parents to Sven's Muskellunge Resort on Squirrel Lake just west of Minocqua, Wisconsin. They considered those annual summer vacations the best times of their lives, a present for which their father scrimped and saved all year.

He remembered those vacations while his eyes stayed glued to the computer screen, memories of Sven's Muskellunge Resort on Squirrel Lake flashing by, those snippets convincing him, along with a subliminal prod from the North Pole, to buy the log chalet. He didn't tell Willy about his purchase at first. That was to be a surprise. He had a second surprise that turned into more of a shock. Quitting a lucrative job with a stock brokerage firm to follow one's dream can have that effect on a certain other concerned party known as a wife. He never imagined that his two surprise announcements would almost bring an end to their brief marriage, especially after he prefaced his good news with a dozen long stem roses and a bottle of champagne.

"You did what?" she had asked again, aghast, her body turning numb from her toes to her tonsils.

"You'll love it," he had said, as if buying a log chalet, moving from Chicago's Lake Shore Drive and living in the middle of a forest was something that happened every day. He had no idea that the scent of his purchase had a school of divorce attorneys swimming around him, jaws open, his assets and his ass triggering their feeding instinct.

Her repeated questions, based on variations of *Why* and *What* and containing words like sanity, insanity, sense, and lack of sense didn't seem to faze him. Hysteria soon followed and, then, a first for them both. She began beating on his chest with tiny fists as more questions spilled from her along with a flood of tears. Then she shook him even more by launching a rapid fire of concerned sentence fragments involving their condo, her class of eighth graders and his giving up everything, using her sarcastic words, "to photograph weeds, dead fish and Smokey the Bear." All the while she continued pounding on his chest, the tears not letting up.

Tidge was too surprised to feel a thing. When the shock ebbed for them both, and she no longer had any tears left, they made a pact. Tidge agreed to everything Willy wanted. All she had to do was to drive with him to Cable, Wisconsin and see their new Garden of Eden. After that, if she was still not receptive, he would take her on a shopping spree at another of his surprise mouse clicks, the Mall of America across the Mississippi in Minnesota. He would pick up the tab. Price limits were to be determined first by how much she hated "that tree house where Cheetah made do-do" and, two, how much she felt he had squandered. The final part of the pact had him selling the tree house and then crawling back to his employer.

She never spoke during the eight-hour drive north. Her only words were to the waitress at the Norske Nook off the Interstate in Osseo where she ordered a piece of lemon meringue pie that turned out to be almost as big as her head. "Is this really a slice?" she had asked the waitress.

Tidge had been thrilled to hear her voice, but those were the only words she spoke until his car had stopped in front of the massive architectural creation of polished logs and the biggest windows either of them had ever seen. Skepticism and possible mayhem flipped one hundred and eighty degrees. Thoughts of a shopping spree vanished. Willy's soul comprehended why Tidge did what he did. Her heart jumped and she fell in love with the house. That had been two Christmases ago.

Willy's love blossomed for *Henry's Hut,* as she now called it. She embraced the peace and tranquility of the Northwoods to such a degree that the mosquitoes considered her their patron saint. Tidge, on the other hand, was always slapping and swatting at the creatures he called, "those damned blood sucking vampires."

Above all, Willy loved the solitude of their first Christmas in the Northwoods. She couldn't have been happier. Her happiness, she thought, would go on forever. Then forever took a hike when Tidge made a suggestion during their walk that caused her toes to curl up in her hiking boots.

Tidge's suggestion was preceded by a conversation centered on the approaching Thanksgiving and his derailed plan for preparing a turkey dinner for two. His dream of the aroma of turkey cooking on Thanksgiving morning vanished with an invitation from their neighbors across the tiny bay from where they lived.

Don and Norma Miller formally met their new neighbors, "those two Chicago people," according to Don Miller, by accident. Actually, two accidents, both taking place before approaching Thanksgivings. The first accident, one involving gun fire, two shots aimed in their direction, happened during Tidge and Willy's first year in their new home. That's when they informally met Don Miller for the first time. The second meeting was less dramatic and frightening than the first, but still an accident. Tidge and Willy had emerged from the woods at the back of the Miller's property one late November afternoon a week before Thanksgiving. Don's farmer's face, beaten by years of rough Wisconsin winters, looked like he used sandpaper for a wash cloth, showed no emotion. He said to Norma without taking his sad, Basset Hound eyes off the couple who had bounded out of the thick timber, "I think our city slicker neighbors may have taken a wrong turn, eh?"

Tidge and Willy had followed one of their two usual courses along the cracked black top surface of Highway County M that day, this time heading east. Tidge felt an adventurous urge and turned explorer. Into the woods he went with Willy in tow. "Geez isn't this great," he said, looking over his shoulder at Willy who was at least twenty yards behind him. His stride shortened and his pace cut in half when he realized that his explorer's security blanket, the constant sight of the road, had vanished. A lucky turn here, a correct veer there and, after a nervous hour, they cleared the timber onto the Miller's pasture.

Willy and Norma Miller clicked without saying a word. She accepted Norma Miller's invitation for an old fashioned family thanksgiving before Tidge could formulate an excuse and Don's Basset Hound eyes could blink. Before Tidge realized what happened, the two organized wives had supplemented the dinner menu and made plans to finalize the details of the Thanksgiving meal over coffee the next morning at Henry's Hut.

Tidge pretended to be appreciative, but groused on the walk back home. "I'm still cooking a turkey," he announced. His statement sounded like it was etched in a massive, jagged slab of northern Wisconsin granite.

Willy didn't say a word.

"We have to have the smell of turkey in the house on Thanksgiving," he continued, making sure that both Willy and the trees on both sides of the road could hear him. "The smell coming from Mother Mary May I's kitchen on Thanksgiving when I was growing up was the greatest."

"You'll have the aroma of turkey cooking at the Miller's," she said, her words way too sensitive. "And, I'm sure, a delicious dinner."

"The Millers can have their aroma but I want mine," he said, his grousing not letting up. He kept walking, his pace increasing. "Did you ever hear of leftovers?" he asked, without trying to insult his wife, something he knew better not to do. "If the Millers can have leftovers, so can the Mackiewicz household."

"Leftovers sound reasonable," she said, tempering the tone of her voice with a gentle softness she had learned to use on him when she wanted him to feel that he was getting his way. It always worked.

"Okay," he said the authoritarian in him draining away and his chiseled slab of granite now no bigger than a head stone in a pet cemetery for a red-winged black bird. "I'll do the cooking and the cleaning up after."

She looped her arm through his. "Once again I know why I married you."

Their current conversation now focused on Christmas and Tidge felt the time was right to spring his idea on her. He seldom applied the old adage about being sure the brain was engaged before the tongue moved. After all, he had thought, this was about Christmas and what could he say about the approaching Yule that could provoke any form of negativity from his wife? He overlooked two things as he introduced his idea to her by saying, "It sure is beginning to look a lot like Christmas."

"What happened to Thanksgiving leftovers and you snoring like one of those noisy lumberjack saw things after eating yourself into a coma?" she asked.

Thanksgiving holiday leftovers, football on television and naps couldn't come close to what he was about to dump in Willy's lap and his reply to her was an indifferent shrug. He took a deep breath, held it in his lungs until he could feel his temples pounding and then let it out along with his idea for Christmas. His brain and tongue were nowhere synchronized when he blurted, "I think we should invite the whole fam-dam-ily up here for Christmas."

Her toes cramped and her tongue felt six inches thick. She tried to speak, her facial expression seen over the decades by readers of *Mad Magazine*.

"We'll invite the natives, my kids and your parents," he said, his brain and tongue grinding and stripping gears, a rancid smoke coming from his ears. "The more the merrier. Deck the halls. Tis the season. Holly jolly. Jingle bell rock. What do you think?"

Her look said everything there was about what she thought.

"Whoa," he said, stopping in his tracks almost skidding on a soft spot of fine gravel. "What did I say to deserve your notorious laser look of loathing?" he asked, a seasoned veteran of her looks of disapproval, her laser look the fiercest in her arsenal. The laser look combined pertinent questions, matching facial expressions, all bordering on mean, some with the intent to kill. Fire shot from her eyes. When he saw the beam, he realized that his status of being her one and only was in jeopardy. So was his existence on Earth.

"May I ask a question," she said the laser beam and the tone of her voice coming from two different humans?

Tidge nodded.

"Are you out of your mind?" she screamed.

A meek, "No" came from him.

"May I ask another question," she said, the laser and tone now linked to the same human being? "Were you born brain dead?" Before he could reply, she asked: "Do you really want to see Jesus?"

Tidge always had answers to her questions and looks. They were never correct. He knew when to keep his mouth shut and when to take his medicine like a big boy. Docility and meekness always worked. Not this time.

"How would you enjoy spending Christmas at the hospital clinic up in Ashland?" she asked. "Then I'll arrange for you to spend New Year's Eve on a vacant iron ore boat. Norma Miller told me that's how she keeps her husband walking the straight and narrow path. Reminds me of what you once told me about your mother and the path Jesus walked on."

He knew this additional barrage hadn't been triggered by fermenting sugar plums dancing in her head. A realization hit him that perhaps his idea might have been presented with a more logical, sensitive approach. Logic and sensitivity had no bearing on what followed.

"You're really serious, aren't you," she said, without looking at him. She had also skidded to a halt, her mind creating what Tidge often called her zany scenarios. "Have you lost what few remaining marbles I thought you had left?"

"Marbles all present and accounted for," he said, trying not to rile up his wife more. "And, yes, I am serious." His eyes did a Mother Mary May I jig.

"Are you sure?" she asked, no sing-song present in her voice.

He nodded. "Not quite as sure the day when I asked you out for the first time," he said, his hands nervously toying with the hood of her parka, pushing it down and pulling it up, his throat making up and down sounds with each playful push and pull. "If you haven't forgotten, I stopped by to see you at your school every day for almost two months after that first parent teacher conference. Surely, you didn't think I was being an overly concerned parent wanting to know how my youngest daughter was doing in your class." His foot lashed out at an unsuspecting leaf and he looked at Willy.

She didn't look back.

"Do you know how scared I was coming back day after day to your classroom after dismissal trying to get up enough nerve to ask you out?" he asked, hoping for some type of reaction. "When I finally stopped acting like a nervous adolescent fearing rejection it was the start of your Christmas break and me, Mister Smooth Operator, picked New Year's Eve for a first date."

She still didn't respond. Head remaining down and mitten-covered hands forced into the pockets of her parka, she started walking, kicking at any leaf that got in her way.

Tidge felt uneasy. He hadn't seen her like this since telling her he bought what eventually became *Henry's Hut*. Out of frustration, he began acting like the little kid Willy had called him. He began skipping after her tracing the crumbling black top shoulder of the road that ran west from their entrance lane towards the town of Cable and east to Clam Lake.

"The nieces and nephews will love spending their Christmas vacation here," he said, breaking the silence with his sales pitch. "Can you picture them bounding out of bed Christmas morning, storming down the stairs and seeing a mountain of presents under the tree in our Great Room?"

Willy stopped, stooped down and picked up a large, fiery red maple leaf and held it up in front of her eyes. She squinted, her upper lip pursing up making her nose appear to be creased. The leaf filtered out a misty, downward moving sun fighting to stay visible through the trees across the lake. "Beautiful, isn't it," she said, as if he never spoke.

"Not as beautiful as Christmas," he said, relieved that her laser switched off and the threat of his impending doom had disappeared. His eyes jumped back and forth from Willy to the leaf that seemed to enhance his calling her the girl of his dreams. "Christmas is for kids," he said, his unleashed mind erupting with ideas generating a mental list that included what they would need to entertain her parents, his three brothers, their wives and six kids, and his three daughters.

She placed the leaf back on the ground as if it were a single rose being laid to rest on a grave. "Oh, God," she said, feeling sick.

"Honey," he said a nervous caring in his voice. "Are you okay?"

She looked up and saw the top of a rickety, rotted wooden platform. A guillotine hung over the platform. Then it hit her. Tidge, the man she loved, had placed her on the first sagging step. "All of them here?" she asked, while the guillotine's ugly stained blade, not quite bright enough to reflect the sunlight that was being painted over by grey clouds, grinned at her. "For Christmas?" The faint sound of a snare drum's dirge didn't belong with her husband's season to be jolly as she asked: "Even my parents?"

"Absolutely," he said his twinkling eyes ready to beam out answers and explanations to all of her questions.

An extended family Christmas in the Northwoods called out to him when he first soaked up the beauty of the massive log chalet home sitting on the shore of Lake Namakagon. His mind spun out of control spewing out images that were far from her writer's creative ones. "A Bing Crosby *White Christmas*, Dad," he had said to himself and the memory of his father. "You couldn't pick a better place to unscrew this screwed up family, with or without Danny Kaye." He began envisioning walking with the girl of his dreams in their exclusive winter wonderland. His mind conjured up scenes from watching reruns of the old Hollywood musical from the forties and fifties. "Oh, man, what beautiful love we could make by a delightful fire," he said.

She picked up another leaf. "My parents here?" she asked again, interrupting the dirge of the snare drum. "And your daughters, especially Martha?" she continued, appearing to be talking to the leaf. "Unimaginable."

"Imagine away, my wife," he said, as he stooped down to join her. He placed his hands on her shoulders and felt the parka's insulation compress until he was feeling her. "Your parents and the Kid's natives are what novels are based on." He let go of her, stood up and resumed his skipping looking like a kid playing a form of *Hop Scotch*, jumping in a circle around her. "My budding novelist wife, the Jacquelyn London of the Northwoods, should be thrilled with the opportunity to do literary research for her next book." He stopped and landed on his right foot, teetered from side to side before catching his balance and stated, "You could call your new novel, *Return of the Natives.*" He came off his right foot with a twisting turn that had him facing her.

"Native," she said, sounding disgusted. "Singular and already been done."

He continued his circular course around her, jumping as if he were on a pogo stick. After several jumps he stopped, faced her and said what he shouldn't say, "If you don't think Mama and Papa and my first born will like it here, cross all of them off the invitation list. We'll go to Chicago and join them for New Year's Eve." He thought for a moment. "That's what we did our first Christmas together when we drove down to Chicago for the holidays. Remember?"

"How could I forget?" she said, appearing frustrated. "Count your mental marbles again, Mister Non Compos Mentis," she said, a warning attached to her frustration. "Christmas is a time for family togetherness no matter how dysfunctional family members might be." Her statement told him he had said something that was beyond dumb. "My parents and your Martha are family," she said, standing and watching him walk toward her, but then using a simple sidestep to avoid his embrace. Kneeling back down on one knee, she replaced the leaf on the ground. She glanced up at him and asked in almost a whisper, "Did your parents ever leave you alone at Christmas?"

He let out a laugh. "The Kid and May I never let us out of their sight," he said, his hand coming to rest on her shoulder as she continued to kneel, her eyes finding the leaf. "Willy, my love and life, you told me all about your parents not being able to get home from a trip to Germany," he said, surprised at her unearthing a Christmas childhood memory that haunted her. "They most certainly didn't leave you alone with your German grandmother on purpose. Those things the Wright brothers invented don't like fog, and your father's homeland most certainly has its fair share."

She looked up at him and smiled. "For one of the rare times in our relationship you're correct."

He grinned at her and offered his hand to help her stand up. "I'm always correct," he said. "You just have a hard time seeing my logic."

She released his hand and brushed off the knees of her jeans.

He saw her give him a look that he never saw before. "Okay," he said cautiously. "Drop whatever it is you're going to drop on me."

"Did you know that all parents hurt their children?"

"What," he blurted out, his first instinct telling him to shred her question. He didn't. He thought about her question, his mouth open a sliver, no words forming. He knew his divorce from Sissy hurt his daughters. He didn't know the extent. Visions of his childhood marched by. A vivid picture of a frustrated Ignacy Mackiewicz molting into an ugly Kid Scream stared back at him as Tidge heard his father say, "Put up your dukes."

Tidge's sometimes out-of-work boxing fanatic father never talked to his sons unless he was giving an order or a threat. His instructions were identical to the orders they had grown to fear but obey. Once again they obeyed and assumed the classic boxing pose Kid Scream had taught them albeit with reluctance. Crouched and ready, their dukes up, they waited for the inevitable.

There were playful slaps in slow motion at first blocked with little effort by their own hands and arms. Their limbs looked puny dwarfed by their father's biceps that resembled nail kegs. His calloused hands, toughened by his work, made them quiver, but not on the outside. Playful always ended. Ears stung. Faces reddened. But there were never tears, never after the first time. The four sons learned that lesson.

"When you say hurt," he said to Willy, wanting clarification, "you're not limiting that to the physical are you?"

Her head went from side to side as she removed her mittens, placed them in the pockets of her parka and rested her hands on the shoulders of his leather jacket. "In all my years in the classroom, I never did meet a perfect parent," she said, her hands sliding around his neck.

"Not even me?" he asked, trying to look surprised.

Willy pursed her lips. She moved them in a counterclockwise direction, pausing, the returning in the opposite direction before she said, "This family Christmas thing," she said, then pausing just long enough to know it would drive him crazy. "How many will I be cleaning up after?" Her arms tightened around his neck.

"Not quite a dozen and a half," he said, his optimism joined by the excitement in his voice that stampeded away all of his doubts.

"The more natives the merrier," he almost shouted.

She loosened her grip and stepped back without breaking eye contact, embracing the magnetic blue that seemed to hypnotize her and made her feel as beautiful as the leaf she had been holding. Her head shook slowly from side to side. "How can you get so excited about having a house full of people for four days?" she asked, feeling her doubts growing by the second as they started walking again. She paused giving herself a chance to place a giant net around the butterflies in her stomach. "Now you want to invite your brothers for Christmas when all you do is argue with them." She felt like she was shopping barefoot in the Co-op Market in Hayward on a floor totally covered with fresh eggs. "And then we have my parents to contend with. I just know they won't like it here."

"What's not to like," he said, answering her concerns as he turned onto the rut road leading back to their house?

She stopped and grabbed at his arm. "Could we keep walking?" she asked, trying not to show the panic she felt.

"Where to?" he asked, responding to the tug on his arm and coming toward her.

"Maybe we could walk toward Lakewoods," she said, referring to the resort about a mile to the west on the way to Cable. "Or, we could go past the Miller's and make our way toward Clam Lake. We've never walked that far before."

"Lakewoods it is," he said, knowing he would have walked on his knees all the way to Sven's Muskellunge Resort about ninety miles to the east and south if his wife agreed to his idea for a family Christmas. He wasn't the least bit curious about why she wanted to keep walking. He learned early on not to ask, replying to her suggestions, "Mine is not to reason why."

His surprise about Christmas had rattled her, but not enough to dampen her own surprise for him. Giving him his Christmas present early, she surmised, would minimize the let down she knew he would experience again this year after Santa left leaving him another empty bag. She inched along now, poking, trying to buy time, and not wanting to get back home before the workmen had left. Her top secret plans to surprise her husband had been arranged weeks earlier. She had even formulated a list of clever things to say titled, *If Tidge*

Gets Suspicious. He didn't.

"Your parents are going to love Christmas here," he said, his voice showing more than its usual excitement. "I'll even have chestnuts roasting on an open fire for mama and papa."

"My mother's allergic to nuts," she replied, giving him an *I thought you knew that* look.

"Okay, then I'll have some corn for popping." He felt beyond proud of his creative reply. "I'll even use that antique corn popper alongside of our fireplace." He smiled, gave her a wink and said, "Now, what's not to like?"

"What's not to like?" she repeated, drinking in the beauty of the leaves spread over the ground like a faded, fiery quilt. "How about my parents spending Christmas somewhere north and west of where Moses lost his sandals?" she asked. She took a right footed kick at some innocent leaves in front of her. "The Magi couldn't find this place if they had Captain Kirk and the *Enterprise* guiding them. My parents only know a Chicago Christmas. They love the lights along the Magnificent Mile, going to see *A Christmas Carol* at the Goodman and *The Nutcracker*, the real one, not your version." She sighed. "Mother loves having lunch in the Walnut Room at Marshall Field's even though the Field's name is no more," she said. "My father is enthralled like some other little kid I know by the decorated windows on State Street." She paused and then continued on, "Daddy puts a silver dollar in every Salvation Army kettle he sees."

"Harold can afford to put a silver dollar into every kettle in every house in Chicago," Tidge said, a touch of envy evident. His head was down as they continued to walk. "Our wedding reception at the Pump Room must have set him back a bundle."

She didn't say a word and kept on walking feeling she was still tip-toeing on the Co-op's egg covered floor.

Silence now accompanied them on their walk. Willy kept trying to judge the time while Tidge visualized Christmas with their combined families. There would be his brothers, their wives and six kids, the ages in sequence from five to twelve. Then there would be Willy's parents and his three daughters from his first marriage.

Tidge had a premonition when the first leaf fluttered to the ground to welcome in the fall season. He was convinced a family

Christmas in the Northwoods was the key to guiding his family back on the straight and narrow path his mother loved, the one trod on by Jesus. His mind kicked into its whirling mode again and he said to himself, "How can Santa Claus not bring me my special gift this Christmas?" He knew his time had finally come. His soul told him that this was going to be his year and his soul never lied. The disappointments were over. Patience and perseverance had won out. If he had added prayer to the other two *P's*, his mother would have shouted hallelujah from the heavens. Then his wife said something that hit him even harder than one of Kid Scream's slaps during a not-so-playful boxing lesson.

"Do you think any of them will accept our invitation?" she asked, sounding way too serious.

His grand plan did not address that one, some or all of the invitations would be rejected. He tried to be cavalier, acting as cool as a cucumber, but feeling like the cucumber had been in the refrigerator several weeks too long. He was scared. "They'll all be here," he said, sounding the way he was acting, but not the way his gut was feeling. Before he could say another word, Willy stopped in her tracks, turned, and nodded that they should be heading back. He wanted to hug her for interrupting the show-or-no-show conversation. Even one rejection of their Christmas invitation would crush him, and rejections were real and possible. His family wasn't referred to as screwed up for nothing.

They walked back east in silence, both glad to return to their respective concerns. The sun continued its downward path and they knew it would be close to dark about the time they got back to their house.

"Here we are," he announced about a half hour later, as if telling her something she didn't know. "The Henry David Thoreau Memorial Drive welcomes you." He leaned up against their metal mail box with a hand painted loon decorating each side. The mail box was topped with his handmade cedar sign of *Tidge and Willy*. He had cut out the sign on his band saw in the garage and it was one of his prized accomplishments. He had ignored Willy's remarks pertaining to his taking several trips to town to the lumber yard to buy more cedar. "Care to join me for a stroll to David's Dump?" he asked, standing proudly alongside the mail box. "I know the owner."

She looped her arm through his and they started down the leaf-covered road. It was just wide enough for a single car leaving an inch or two to spare on each side before leaves, tiny branches and blackberry briars brushed at the car's finish. Tire ruts had been worn into the sand and gravel so deep in spots that even their pickup truck had to straddle the deep furrows or end up with a critical part on the ground.

As they walked up the slight incline of the hill, his dream of a family Christmas continued to simmer. His gaze turned to the last of the sun's faint red fading glow peeking through the dense timber and giving a final tip of the hat to Lake Namakagon. Sunset was his favorite time of day, more so in the summer when the sky seemed to blossom in shades of reds and gold's for hours. The sun wasted no time in disappearing during the winter months. It would drag a blanket of clouds along for the ride and make nights darker than any he had ever known in Chicago.

Tidge thought he found total peace in the Northwoods. Hundreds of miles to the south and east lay his father's last wishes as did feuding with his brothers. His daughter, Martha was also back in Chicago. "Coiled and ready to strike," he said to himself. Kid Scream's last wishes, brothers and an angry daughter didn't gnaw on Tidge now. He had a forest and a lake called Namakagon. There was the moat he built around his castle and a draw bridge. He was safe and secure. Nothing upset him, not even memories of an infatuated indiscretion he later called it when his first marriage had gone beyond sour. He felt Willy's arm grabbing for support as she momentarily lost her balance, her outside leg dangling over the tire rut. "You okay?" he asked.

"How can I be anything but," she replied her head down as she concentrated on where she was stepping? "I have a manly lumberjack with a double digit I.Q. to protect me."

He laughed knowing he never had anyone to protect him from falling into ruts like he protected Willy. He had his jacket and his belief in Santa Claus, but they didn't prevent his life from once resembling the ruts in his bumpy driveway. The jacket and Santa didn't keep his brothers from perpetuating a war of jealousy against him. Even more painful was his oldest daughter, Martha, launching her own attack against him. Martha's timing was impeccable. She came at her father with all of her verbal guns blazing, a blitzkrieg of anger and resentment. Choosing the night of his and Willy's wedding reception to attack surprised Tidge more then what happened on December 7, at Pearl Harbor.

Willy and Tidge never forgot the attack. Most of the guests, fortified by a cocktail hour that approached two in duration, applauded and laughed at what they thought was an act provided by the bride's parents. Both Willy and Tidge knew it wasn't an act. They stood dumbfounded like the miniature bride and groom atop their three tiered angel food and strawberry wedding cake.

Thanks to her father's creative thinking, his handful of twenty dollar bills and the intervention of Tidge's boyhood friend and best man, Humper the attack became a humorous anecdote.

Humper knew something wasn't right when he saw Martha approach the bridal table with an uncorked bottle of champagne in each hand. He had been talking to Willy's father when he saw the expression on Martha's face. "Oh, crap," he managed to say, as Martha positioned herself in front of the bridal table ready to launch her first salvo. Humper looked at Willy's father and he looked back. Without a word they headed in different directions trying to minimize casualties. Martha's initial blast, a sarcastic toast laced with profanities and several obscenities ended with her main target, her father and new step mother, stunned and demoralized.

Humper, a jolly smile beaming from his red face, made a beeline to Martha. He had known her since the night she was born. He and her father had celebrated her birth at a neighborhood bar. Humper watched her grow up mostly from afar because Tidge's wife Sissy had banned him from their house.

Humper still saw Martha and always had a birthday card and a present for her. Tidge, worried about his wife's reaction, disguised Humper's gifts as being from one of his late mother's Irish relatives. Humper watched her go through the stage of little girl temper tantrums, a stage carried into young adulthood. He attended dance recitals arriving a minute late, sitting in the back of the school auditorium and leaving just as the last metal cleat of her tap shoes hit the floor. He gradually became a surrogate parent to Martha since Sissy never had time for her or any of her children. He was the only one who could calm Martha down when she threw a tantrum.

Humper or, "Missa Billys," as Martha called him with her slight girlish lisp, would speak Polish to her. He had learned the language from his father who came to America from Poland via England after World War II had ended.

Humper's favorite technique for calming Martha was to imitate a baby elephant's walk. Martha always giggled and clung to his leg as he dragged her along. The same baby elephant escorted a fuming Martha into the lobby of the Ambassador East Hotel to cool off. This time she didn't giggle or cling to his leg. Instead she sobbed on his shoulder, swearing like her late grandfather, Kid Scream.

Willy's father's beeline took him to the quartet of strolling violinists he had hired for the reception. Twenty dollar bills and orders with a German accent had the musicians serenading the stunned wedding couple with several choruses of *Happy Days Are Here Again*.

It was two different perceptions of Henry's Hut that brought tranquility into the lives of Willy and Tidge. Their wedding photo album was a collection of smiles and happy, attacks and baby elephants missing. A serene peace had embraced Willy instantly when she saw Henry's Hut. She embraced it back. Tidge said to her when the subject of Martha came up: "Out of sight, and almost out of mind."

Tidge's perception of tranquility, boosted by a continuous fragrance of pine scented air and a beer commercial's sky blue waters, began to creep into his soul with a series of computer mouse clicks. Peace managed to circumnavigate Martha and eventually engulf Tidge. Shrouded in peace, however, didn't erase the pain of that night. A father hurt, but so did a daughter. In his heart and soul he knew he was responsible. What hurt him more was that Willy was an innocent victim.

Tidge's idea for a family Christmas in Wisconsin's Northwoods had turned his mind into a pinball machine. As lights blinked and bells rang, he found himself frantic, grabbing at a million loose ends, missing all but two or three.

One of his worries was trying to convince his soon-to-be-invited guests that the distance from Chicago to Cable, Wisconsin was a walk around the block. That's how he planned on wording a direction's sheet he would insert in his invitations. In order for him to unscrew the natives, he needed them under his roof. Only then, he hoped, could Kid Scream rest in peace.

"I know most of your thoughts aren't worth a penny," Willy said to him, as she shuffled through the leaves that came over the tops of her hiking boots. Her careful steps were a reminder of how she tripped and slid into one of the deep ruts of their road the first week after they had moved in resulting in a sprained ankle. "But, what else is on that warped little mind of yours?"

He forced a smile. "What's on my warped little mind?" he repeated. "I was just thinking about your parents."

"What about them?" she asked, the tone of her question told him that his answer had better be coated with kind, respectful sensitivity.

"Instead of all that Christmas time in the city stuff you mentioned, they might enjoy a change this year."

"Change," she repeated. "Try culture shock. Try cardiac arrest. There's not enough gin in this state to convert my mother's image of Christmas from The Loop to the Land of the Loon." Her words seemed to pound on the door of his luck like her tiny fists once did on his chest. "Notice that loon was singular."

Tidge tried to ignore her verbal pummeling on his chest. "Christmas for them this year could be snow up to their behinds, seeing deer feeding in our back yard and our friend the eagle circling overhead." His eyes twinkled. "Oh, I almost forgot and me playing Santa."

She stopped, her right toe toying with several fragments of broken leaves breaking them further into infinitesimal pieces. "Snow, deer, and eagles I'll accept." She glanced at him and then returned her attention to the leaves. "But, you in that relic of a Santa Claus suit you dragged up here," she paused, her hood twisting from side to side. "You look more like a Magi of Ebenezer Scrooge, Bozo the Clown and Uncle Fester than Santa."

"Gert and Harold will love me in that Santa Claus suit," he said his enthusiasm growing as he referred to his in-laws. "So will my brothers' kids," he said, as they continued up the incline that would take them to the top of the hill of their driveway. "They'll eat it up."

Willy's head continued to go from side to side. "Provided the moths haven't beaten them to it," she said. Her eyes turned serious as she looked at him. "On second thought, moths wouldn't be interested in that foul smelling Santa Claus suit. Ugly relics leave a bad taste in their little mouths."

"Moths don't have tastes," he said, taking her by the hand as the roof to the front entrance of their house appeared. "They do, however, have respect for war heroes, Santa and Christmas."

"If you say so," she said, trying to curb her excitement while enjoying the sight of their house trimmed in colored lights that Tidge had strung the day before. He had outlined their pitched roof, entranceway and the front of the house while testing the limits of a rickety extension ladder. He even put the lights on a timer and was both pleased and surprised when they lit up with a noon test. Now was the first time he saw the lights in the dark and any feelings of guilt he had about violating Mother Mary May I's sacred rule of: "Nothing Christmas until after we give thanks for Thanksgiving," were null and void.

As they reached the crest of the drive, he began to glow like the lights and kept saying to Willy, "Geez! Look at that!"

"It's beautiful," she said, slipping her hand out of her mitten and taking his, giving it a tender squeeze. "If only that Santa Claus suit had as much charm."

"Me and my brothers loved it when our Uncle Brew wore that suit and played Santa," he said, his eyes never leaving the outline of colored lights as he squeezed her hand back.

"That's exactly why I have very little faith," she said, her feet settling into one of the tire ruts until the top of her head was even with his sternum. Then she spotted her early Christmas present to him. At that moment, she wanted to jump up and down and yell, "Merry Christmas" so that every living soul in Bayfield County clear up to Madeline Island on Lake Superior heard her. "Oh, Thomas," she said, her other hand coming around to grab his arm for balance as she maneuvered for the opportune moment to point out her surprise. "Are you sure we'll have room enough for our families?"

He looked down at her. "We've got plenty of space, Shorty." He attempted to muss up the top of her hair and almost fell into the opposite rut from her. His attention turned back to the house. He still hadn't noticed the small satellite dish that had been mounted off to one side of the roof.

"We do?" she asked, biting her cheeks to keep from exploding into laughter.

"Of course," he said, engrossed in the outline of lights that got brighter as night gave the sun one final push behind the horizon. "Geez, we've got four extra bedrooms, the loft and a sofa bed in the den. There's space in your writing room where I can set up those fold up military cots I got from my dad via Uncle Brew," he continued, his excitement growing. "We can put my girls in there and we've got blow up rafts coming out of our ears stashed in the garage. We can use those for mattresses for the nieces and nephews, and there's also a tent." He glanced down at her then held out his hand and helped pull her up out of the rut. "I'm joking about the tent." His mind had shifted into high gear. "You know, honey," he continued, his excitement bubbling, "we can turn our kitchen and Great Room into one of those cheap all-you-can-snatch-and-grab Las Vegas buffets." He paused, thought, then added, "The Apostles and natives love buffets."

She latched onto his arm, almost ready to spring her surprise on him. "I'm sure they do," she said, trying to sound sarcastic, but her dancing eyes gave her away. "But you don't have to sugar coat your imperfect brothers by calling them apostles."

"Okay, okay," he said, knowing he was being condescending. "My brothers have faults, lots of them. Like you said back there, no parents are perfect, and neither are their kids." He caught her eye just before she looked back toward the colored lights outlining their house. "You, my dearest, darling wife, are the exception."

"Thank you for your astute observation," she said, a glee in her voice she couldn't contain. "I'll be sure to convert your cheap Las Vegas buffet into one worthy of the Four Seasons." She winked. "I'll also serve up a breakfast to compete with the one served by the Cable Volunteer Fire Department that we enjoyed during our fist summer here." She paused and winked again. "My pancakes will be as good as theirs."

"My old man loved pancakes," he said, a smile crossing his face for a moment and then disappearing. "There weren't many things in his life besides my mother that he loved," he continued. He had his Polaroid camera, pancakes, his summer vacation to Minocqua to fish and, his true love, pugilism." He paused to assess his Christmas lights yet again. "The Kid forced us to watch real boxing on television with him."

"Forced," she repeated, turning to position herself so that she was facing him and the house and that his back was to his surprise. "He forced you?"

"Force was The Kid's middle name," he said, unable to take his eyes off the multiple of colors lighting up the house.

"Do you intend to force our families to come up here to celebrate Christmas with us?" Willy asked. "Kind of perverse if you ask me."

His answer was calm. "It wasn't perverse. It was the Gillette Cavalcade of Sports just before it went off the air." He bent down into a boxer's classic pose. "The Kid loved the fights. His favorite boxer was a guy called Kid Gavilan. He was called The Cuban Hawk and was famous for his Bolo punch." Tidge's head began dodging imaginary punches. "That's one reason why we called our father, Kid Scream." He lashed out with a series of his own punches. "The Kid got so worked up he spent the entire fight on his feet screaming vulgarities at the television.

"Are you telling me this is what I have to look forward to when your family comes to spend Christmas?" she asked, not letting a word he was saying bother her. "I can't wait for the privilege of hearing you and your brothers swearing at some sporting event when you're not swearing at each other."

"No need to fret." He gave her a playful hug. "The Gillette Cavalcade of Sports has been off the air since your Moses was a lad and Captain Kirk is no longer the skipper of the Enterprise. Besides our TV reception here is like watching a snow storm. Even my brothers' spoiled kids wouldn't want to watch television here."

"Ah," she said, stepping away from him, stretching her arms out and up as she tilted her head back and shouted, "I do believe there is a God." She fought to keep from once again jumping up and down and started to count not quite at the top of her voice: "Five! Four! Three!"

"What's with you and the count down?"

"Two! One!" She bent down, scooped up a handful of leaves and tossed them at him, a couple finding his face, the rest floating off the front of his Air Corps jacket. "Surprise!" she shouted.

Tidge was at a loss.

Then she began to sing: "I wish you a Merry Christmas," putting an emphasis on *I* until ending with wishing him a Happy New Year. Then she waved both mittens in the direction of the house.

"And you have the nerve to tell me I'm short on my marbles," he said, turning, looking at where her mittens were going through a series of thrusting motions toward the house. "Is the eagle sitting on our roof again or is there a bear up there?"

She continued to point, but was now jumping up and down like an excited child. "Look," she squealed. "Are you blind?"

"Me blind?" he asked, pointing at himself. "You're wishing me a Merry Christmas and it's not even Thanksgiving yet," he said, sounding confused. He stopped short, turned, looked at her for a moment and then focused his attention back to the roof of the house. "What the . . . ?"

"What the what?" she asked. Her tiny arms tried to wrap around him from behind to give him a bear hug. "What the what?" she repeated, teasing him and squeezing her arms as tight as she could.

"That," he said, pointing and then starting toward the house dragging her behind him as if she were being towed.

"What's a what, and what's a that?" she asked, enjoying the moment as she re-wrapped her arms around his neck in a strangle hold, her feet barely skimming the ground, creating two new tiny grooves through the leaves.

He stopped and stared at the dark outline of a satellite dish. If it hadn't been for his Christmas lights, he would have never seen it. "Is that what I think it is?" He turned toward her and cupped her tapered chin in the *V* formed by the palms of his hands.

"Now you won't have to watch television through a snow storm."

After convincing him that he didn't need to take out the ladder from the garage and climb up on the roof to examine his present, they went inside. "You can look at it all you want in the daylight tomorrow morning," she said, grabbing his hand and pulling him into to their Great Room where she came to a jumping stop, both arms extend, her hands pointing as a stream of tears spilled onto her grin. "Ta-Da!"

His arm went around her waist for the third time since they came in from their walk. The other two times he had dashed out the front door to be sure that what he had seen mounted on the roof was really what he had seen. Now he stared. His mouth hung open. His jaw muscles were as limp as the Musky wind sock in a morning mist he flew off a pole at the end of their boat pier. The second part of Willy's surprise Christmas present stared back. He wanted to say, "Thank you," but couldn't dislodge the words sticking sideways in his throat. His own versions of *What* questions and *Why* questions and *How* questions peeled and cored his Adam's Apple. When he could finally speak he used an expression he had learned from his father, one he had never said in her presence. "Look at the size of that son of a bitch," he managed to say in awe.

Her arms encircled his neck while the worn leather collar of his jacket collected more of her tears.

He was dragging her along with him again until he stopped in front of the big screen television. Hiding next to it, dwarfed and looking out of place like some poor relation fallen on hard times, sat the beat up television set he salvaged from his first marriage. He cautiously reached out as if he were trying to pet a porcupine.

"It won't bite," she sniffled, her hands sliding down the front of his jacket.

He Brailled the top of the new gleaming black frame that embraced the biggest screen he had ever seen, touching it as if it were a priceless fragile art object. "Does this thing work?" he asked, without taking his eyes off his present and not knowing what else to say.

"I think so, my big little kid," she said, her heart beat almost drowning out her words. "I paid enough to rid your life of snow storms."

His arms wrapped around her and he gave her a hug. "Geez," he said, his own eyes fighting a battle to stay dry, "Christmas before Thanksgiving." He stepped back slightly from her, winked and said: "Somehow I get the feeling that Mother Mary May I would approve of your surprise."

They inched back to the front of the television like a couple of curious, timid fawns on shaky legs. With one nervous hand and then two, Tidge began to fondle the top of the television again. "My, God," he said, in an uncharacteristic quiet voice, "I'm more nervous than when I asked that tall German girl with the nice sugar plums to dance at that eighth grade party." Then, like asking for that dance, he shoved his nerves aside, reached down and found the power button. The screen came alive greeting him with a menu that made him blink then grin. He wondered if Edison had felt the same thing when he turned on his first switch. "Geez, Willy, look at how clear that is."

"I know," she said, marveling at the lifelike picture that she first saw demonstrated to her in the appliance store in Superior. "Do you like it?"

His eyes rolled up as if he had just heard the dumbest question of all time. "My coat hanger days are gone forever," he said.

She looked at him puzzled by his statement.

He started to grin, but never took his eyes off the giant screen. "When us kids watched our old black and white television with the Kid and May I," he paused for a moment, feeling the lump return to his throat. "My father would assign each one of us a show where we would have to stand alongside the television and hold his homemade coat hanger antenna."

"A coat hanger what?"

"My father got the coat hanger antenna idea from a *Popular Mechanics* magazine. The Kid took an old coat hanger, snipped it in the middle, bent down the cut end on each side, attached a scrap piece of cable and he had his TV antenna. He hooked it up to the back of our little television and we had a picture."

"I don't believe you," she said, her own excitement still churning merrily away. "The first antenna I remembered was a set of what were called rabbit ears. My father was always adjusting them."

Tidge laughed. "No need to adjust our coat hanger. The Kid discovered that having one of his sons hold his homemade antenna made the picture come in crystal clear thanks to our little bodies."

"You're kidding."

"So help me, it worked," he said. "Wait until my brothers see what you bought me for Christmas. Geez, are they ever going to be jealous."

"Is that good?" she asked, a sudden fear clawing at her that her Christmas gift could possibly blow up in her face depending on his brothers' reactions.

"They'll go crazy over it," he said, standing almost mesmerized by the menu options.

She became very serious. "I'm sure they'll like the size of the screen and those four hundred channels I got with that silly dish on the roof, but will they like watching television here," she said, placing the emphasis on *here*. She looked at him almost pleading. "Will they like Henry's Hut the way we do?"

"Here we go again," he said, his eyes never leaving the screen. "They'll all love it here." A building courage took a swat at his nerves and his eyes latched onto the manual waiting for him alongside the television on the hardwood floor. "If they don't, Henry will put a curse on them," he said, as he opened the manual. "There. Your worries are over."

Willy's worries were just starting. "Your Martha, as I recall from our wedding reception, is more of a curser than a curse recipient," she said, knowing that her husband never recovered from his daughter's outburst. She hadn't either.

Visions of Martha with an uncorked champagne bottle in each hand waving, alternate slurping sips and shouted slurs didn't erase easily. Willy found her eraser leaving ugly smudges across her efforts to eradicate Martha's screaming at her father: "You were never home for us, you bastard!" Champagne splashed out of both bottles, most of it running down her chin. She staggered to her left, caught herself then pointed both bottles at the newlyweds. "You were out screwing that bimbo of yours!" Another drooling sip of champagne ran off her chin disappearing into the cleavage of her dress. "Now you married this teeny bopper," she said, the bottle in her right hand pointing, the one in her left finding her mouth. "You cradle robbing son of a bitch!" The bottoms of both champagne bottles pointed at the newlyweds as champagne splashed from each on Martha's shoes.

Tidge took his eyes off the instruction manual. "I recall too," he said. "Never forgot a word she said."

"Nor I," she said, being careful what she was about to say, "I think curses of all kinds should be stored in your den closet along with all of those boxes you keep your cache of Christmas decorations in."

"Curses will be sealed away and Martha will be here," he said, his attention focused on the instruction manual for his new television set. "It's Christmas and my first born will make a grand entrance, hands and arms open, expecting Santa to heap presents on her." The next page of the manual made its appearance, a series of confusing diagrams. "One thing about Martha, when it comes to the Yule time, she's the greediest kid in the neighborhood."

Willy knew that if only one person showed up from their Christmas invitation list, Martha would make it a total success for him even if her last words to him were, "I hate you."

Chapter 3

Willy's early surprise Christmas gift to Tidge surpassed the size of her heart. The few people who really knew her, her parents and her late Mitty, understood Wilhelmina Schneider's generosity. Tidge was learning about his wife's core of basic needs. Everything she did was spurred on by well-planned and calculated motives. There were no knee-jerks in her life.

Her motive for Tidge's television viewing package was twofold. The television and dish system would bring him warmth and comfort during the bone chilling, teeth chattering sub-zero winter nights of the Northwoods. That was obvious to her. A second motive, this one more primary than secondary, was based on her assessment of her husband's own basic core of needs. On the outside, Tidge was even more simplistic than the big little kid label she stuck on him. Inside, she likened him to the can of worms he dug for fishing the second day they lived at Henry's Hut.

"Look at these beauties," he had said to her, the can held about six inches from her nose. He had laughed when she backed away, a look of disgust on her face that he hadn't seen since. "We'll have us a fish fry tonight," he continued, the can still extended toward her.

There was no fish fry. He had spent the entire afternoon casting out a worm baited hook suspended from a red and white plastic bobber. The rod and reel, bobber included, had belonged to one of his brothers and last used on a family vacation to Sven's Muskellunge Resort. He had no idea how the fishing gear ended up with him at Henry's Hut. He caught fish, dozens of them, all Blue Gills and all but three about the size of his middle finger. He hadn't cared. He had crossed the bridge into another life. His oldest daughter's venom, a deceased father's trinity of orders and his brothers' taunts lay far to the south. He was at peace with the girl of his dreams on the shore of Lake Namakagon.

Willy didn't understand her husband's behavior at first. His actions defied logic. He was like the tangled ball of worms in his fishing bait can. Pull on one and you always came up with something. The worms had their reasons for being in a ball. Tidge had his. One moment he appeared to stalk an ugly weed with his camera, the shutter clicking from angles that saw him standing on his toes to being sprawled on his belly. The next moment he was on all fours kneeling on their boat dock wearing a snorkel and looking at fish. Then Willy realized her husband knew exactly what he was doing even though he looked like the can of worms. The worms, however, displayed more logic, but her husband was happy.

Willy knew that a Sunday brunch buffet at the Lakewoods Resort Lakeside Restaurant had almost as many selections as Tidge's television dish package. Lakeside didn't have more channels than any human being could watch in a lifetime. Tidge did. His menu would provide the basis for the compassion she knew she had to give him on the day after Christmas.

Willy had but a handful of experiences watching Tidge's brief free fall into an abyss of disappointment after his special Christmas stocking dangled limp and empty on December the twenty sixth. She was amazed at his resilience. Before his breakfast coffee turned cold that fateful morning where even a lump of coal would seem like a treasure, he was singing the entirety of, "We Need A Little Christmas."

Willy didn't believe in Santa Claus the way Tidge did. The spirit associated with the holiday season bolstered her total being. She was too much of a realist and much more logical than her husband to believe in a person bringing joy to the world once a year. Facts dictated that, yes, there had been a Saint Nicholas, and that person became a legend and a storybook character with many variations. There was Sinter Claes, Father Christmas, The Starman, her husband's Polish, *Wesolych Swiat* for Merry Christmas, the mention of *Jul* by his Aunt Bessie who wasn't really an aunt and Willy's own father dictating in German that the holiday was called, *Weihnachten.* Yet, her interpretation of Santa Claus had her comparing him to magic or hocus-pocus. He was an illusion.

The first sight of seeing Tidge in his World War II Army Air Corps flight jacket was more than an illusion. She likened the vision to hearing her father relate what happened to his native Germany during Hitler's rampage.

As each day in her life with Tidge began anew, Willy marveled at her husband's resilience and perseverance. She had heard about the sport of boxing from her husband too many times. The spectacle of human carnage, as she referred to it, disgusted her. Yet, she understood. Once-upon-a-time in her life carnage had come a calling. There was no smiling Santa face etched into the canvas floor where she found herself. There was no smiling face period. She needed help to get up from her canvas floor. Tidge did it all by himself. That scene bruised her heart as much as her husband's battered spirit. Still she rooted for him pledging her undying support to the man she loved. He was, after all, the man she trusted to give her a second chance at life.

There was one common denominator between Willy and Tidge when it came to Christmas. Giving was that denominator. They were as far apart as the penguins at the South Pole were from Santa Claus at the North when it came to shopping. Her world was filled with extensive, detailed lists. Those details included price ranges, retail and wholesale outlets and their locations, hours of operation, discounts offered, the duration of the discounts and any disclaimers and even the first names of some of the clerks. Her eyes never missed an item of merchandise on display. Her hands touched almost every item she saw.

Tidge's shopping was based on one of the few Latin phrases he remembered from high school: "Veni, vidi, vici." He bought on impulse, never looked at a price tag or examined a piece of merchandise.

Willy never forgot a gift. Copies of her shopping lists wouldn't let her. She had lists displayed in several locations. There was one on her desk in a designated spot while another waited in their pickup truck's glove box. She kept at least one in each purse she owned and posted a master list on the refrigerator door with a plethora of magnets depicting famous authors.

Her memories of Christmases past differed from her husband's. As a child, for the most part, she experienced gala times at Christmas. She could distinguish between Christmas and the rest of the year by the colorful decorations in her parent's apartment and the continuous sounds of Christmas carols, mostly in German, that started in the morning and continued until her bed time. The decorations made an appearance on December the first and disappeared promptly on January the third, her parents, especially her mother, needing the extra time to recover from New Year's Eve.

Willy, by her own admission, was spoiled by her adoring parents, a grandmother who had fled Germany during the end of the war who cherished her and a cast of characters that her parents entertained on a weekly basis. She had a life other children couldn't fathom. Her Christmases exceeded what the store windows along Michigan Avenue and State Street dangled in front of disbelieving young eyes.

Then, as a newlywed with Christmas sneaking up over the horizon, her child memories got trampled. Gone were the nights snuggling with her Mitty. Gone were the talks she had with Grizelda, her doll about what Santa would bring her. Gone was the awe of sitting between her parents watching Tchaikovsky's dancing sugar plums. In its place was an introduction to physical abuse.

Wilhelmina Schneider-Jones, the new bride of Chicago Police Officer, Robert Jones discovered how spoiled brats, worthless bitches and two-bit whores were treated. Her husband seemed to turn from Casanova to Conan overnight. She didn't know why. Her questions were answered by more violence. "Why?" she pleaded. "What did I do?"

Other answers arrived the following day in the forms of candy, flowers, cards adorned with hearts and angels and apologies. Some of her husband's apologies were even tearful. Then their first Christmas together came. Her gift to him was to be a surprise. She was expecting a baby. She didn't get the opportunity to deliver her surprise. Her husband literally beat her to it. His surprise had no fancy gift wrap, no pretty ribbons and bows and no tag with written words of love.

The beating ended her pregnancy and any chance of her conceiving again. The tokens of apology came but tokens couldn't heal the wounds festering inside Willy. She knew all men weren't like her husband. Her father, the epitome of love and respect, wasn't. Then she met Tidge. He may not have dressed as dapper as her father, but she had never been worshiped before.

Willy had limited experience when it came to men. Dating consisted of her senior prom where her date, the co-captain of the football team, tried to force her to drink a half pint of cheap bourbon in the hotel parking lot. She refused. He got mad, pouted and then drank it himself. In the middle of the hotel's grand ballroom dance floor he puked down the front of his tux and splattered her golden slippers. There had also been a debutante ball where she was introduced to the crème de la crème of society. She experienced a similar routine the brand of liquor was more expense, the bottle bigger. No vomit this time, her escort passing out cold on the staircase he had escorted her down earlier. Harold and Gert came to her rescue whisking her away, acting as if nothing had happened.

In her world and that of her parents, an individual's character was judged by a gown or tuxedo. There was no formal attire to help her judge the character of the police officer she literally bumped into while shopping with her mother. She saw a handsome, Elvis type in uniform moonlighting as a security guard in Bonwit Teller. He had a warm smile, black, intriguing eyes and had asked her for her phone number before she knew what hit her. Her judgment failed her again.

Willy's first impression of Tidge was guarded. He didn't look like the kind of man who would vomit on himself or hang draped over a polished banister railing like a discarded overcoat. She later learned that he didn't know a cummerbund from a cumquat. Her initial glance of who was to be her future husband took place during an Indian Summer evening when she saw him stroll into her classroom for a parent-teacher conference during his youngest daughter's eighth grade year.

Willy fought to keep from staring. "Oh, my God," she said to herself, wondering if she should summon the sole security guard on duty to help her get rid of a vagrant who had entered her classroom. No parent of any of Miss Schneider-Jones's students ever came wearing what she saw that night. No one had ever worn a beat up, brown leather jacket on a balmy fall evening, the jacket appearing to have been trampled by a horde of crazed Christmas shoppers on the day after Thanksgiving. "Surely," she thought, losing her battle of trying not to stare, "this man doesn't know where he's at."

"Hi," said the man who was indeed a parent of one of her students. "I guess you have the honor of being my daughter's teacher."

"Honor," she remembered repeating, aghast at seeing the parent in faded Levi's, black, high top Converse All Star basketball shoes and a white t-shirt with the words, *Santa Lives* written across the front of the shirt in cracked, faded red lettering.

Willy removed her slim line reading glasses perched on the end of her nose, her once perfect vision altered by her late husband. She never said a word, her eyes asking a single question.

"Carol," said Tidge, as if there was only one student in the entire world named Carol.

Tidge's daughter, Carol, in this case, was a bubbly ball of energy just shedding her gangly growth stage of skinny legs and arms and too large feet and hands. She also fantasized about her divorced father marrying her favorite teacher, Miss Schneider-Jones.

Tidge, after Willy introduced herself with a polite, professional indifference, surprised her by asking: "What's with you having two last names? You have a hyphen fetish?"

Those are my maiden and married names," she said, a slight chill coating her reply to the parent who looked like he should be holding up a homemade cardboard sign stating: "Got Any Spare Change?" Curiosity and the bluest, kindest eyes she had ever seen smiled at her.

"Jones is your married name," he said, sounding disappointed. "Lucky guy." He saw her nod no trace of emotion on what he thought was the prettiest face he had ever seen in spite of a slight droop of her right eye lid. He was intrigued by the way her thin lips curled into an almost sexy flair. Her mouth reminded him of a calendar girl pin-up he found hidden under a pile of old newspapers stacked on his father's cluttered work bench in the family garage. He gave a slight shrug and said: "You know you're the first hyphenated woman I've ever known." He paused then repeated her name.

"Wilhelmina Schneider hyphen Jones." His head went from side to side. "Well, my Carol thinks you're cool, punctuation mark and all."

"Thank you for sharing that with me, Mr. Mackiewicz," she said, butchering the Polish pronunciation of his name making it sound like Mackie-whiz.

"Call me Tidge," he said. "Those are the first initials of my first, middle and Confirmation names. T-I-J. Thomas Ignacy Joseph. It's easier than muddling through Ma-ke-vitch." He paused then quickly added, "Ignacy's Polish for Ignatius." There was no response. He saw her captivating smile disappear and watched her check his daughter's progress in her grade book. "I bet you went through adolescence with Kaiser as a nickname," he said, then laughing at his creativity.

She didn't share in his humor not getting the connection between her name and Kaiser Wilhelm. "My colleagues call me Mina," she said, now sounding way too professional for the both of them.

Really?" he asked his question void of humor. "The only Mina I ever heard of was the one Bram Stoker wrote about in *Dracula*. You aren't a vampire, are you?" he asked, his question coated with an impish grin.

"Hardly, Mr. Mackiewicz," she said, getting the pronunciation correct. "However, it is nice to know that a parent of one of my students does read."

"On occasion," he said scrambling to project an image he thought was suave and to hang onto something he wanted to hang onto, but didn't know why. "Mostly philosophy," he said, feeling he was losing his scramble. "Immanuel, Machiavelli, Rene and the old guys," he continued. You know, I think, therefore I'm cool." He looked at her hoping to see approval, but saw polite indifference. He then realized he was the cover boy for a book titled, *Stupid*. "And, what does your husband call you?" he asked, pressing ahead.

"I'm divorced," she said. Then her professional demeanor stumbled when she stammered, "And a widow." Her index finger rested on his daughter's name in the middle of her grade book and her face started to show a faint shade of pink. "That doesn't make sense, does it," she said, her composure back in check. "A divorced widow?"

"Divorced hyphen widow," he said, pleased with himself. "It makes sense to me." He looked at her, but her eyes were focused on the grade book. "Me? I only have one name. Call me divorced. Like you."

"I know."

"You do?" he asked, caught off-guard.

"Your daughter has made it a point to give me a daily, in-depth progress report of her sisters, mother and father."

"Oh, God," he said, his upper and lower lips folding inward so they seemed to vanish. "I'm in trouble." His eyes went from the grade book to hers and back again as a new series of feelings lined up in front of his heart waiting for marching orders. "I noticed an "I" in your book. What's that for?"

She examined the grade book for a second, her finger tracing the date in question. "Carol still owes me the results of her science experiment."

He burst out laughing. "No problem," he said, the echoes from his laugh finding the hall. The heads of several waiting parents appeared in the doorway. "She did it." His index finger crossed his heart several times. "Honest. I swear on a stack of bibles, Catholic and the King James versions."

She looked at him, questioning, trying not to laugh. "You didn't really eat her experiment, did you?"

His index finger made several more repeat traces over the area of his heart. "Guilty as charged."

She stared at him in disbelief. "I've heard all kinds of excuses from students for work not being done on time, but your daughter's was by far the most original." She paused, eyes questioning. "It really is true?"

"Cross my heart and hope to die," he said, his index finger pointing at the center of his chest. "After I ate her experiment, Carol led me to believe that I poisoned myself."

She looked at him, trying not to laugh and said with all innocence: "One of these days I would love to hear the entire story."

"Today works for me," he said, grinning as he sat down in a high back, cane chair alongside of her desk. He folded his hands in his lap. "My fine dining episode happened when I spent a weekend baby-sitting my daughters," he said sounding serious and looking the same way. "Actually, it wasn't so much baby-sitting, but being sure my three girls observed their curfews." He continued to relate how he spent a weekend with his daughters while his ex-wife was away visiting her mother.

"I had been watching the tube waiting for the girls to return home on Friday night when a hunger pang struck during a re-run of the Tonight Show," he said, rambling on while assuming Miss Schneider-Jones was interested. "I got up and went to the kitchen looking for something to eat." He didn't repeat what he had said to the kitchen walls after finding an empty bread box. "I finally stumbled on two plastic bags, each containing a slice of white bread. The bread found the toaster. Another scan of the refrigerator turned up a single slice of American cheese sitting like an abandoned orphan on the bottom of one of the door shelves. The cheese found the toasted bread." He smiled. "I fell asleep on the couch and never did hear any of the three come in. The next morning I was having a cup of coffee when Carol bound down the stairs. She tossed me a, 'Good morning, Daddy-kins,' stopped at the refrigerator, opened the door and stared. Then she stared at me and asked, 'Dad, did you see my science experiment'?"

He looked at Carol's teacher, trying not to act like a comedian or be flippant. "The moment I said, what experiment, she knew she had me. By the time I got through asking her what her experiment was, what it involved, and finally, was it dangerous, as in harmful to human beings," he said, then stopping and pointing at himself before continuing. "This human being. She knew she had me."

"So, you really did eat her mold experiment," Carol's teacher said, the pin-up calendar girl smile appearing, the smile turning to a grin so cute he wanted to hug her. "Oh, my," she giggled.

"I at least toasted it," he said, trying to act indifferent and innocent. He watched as Miss Schneider-Jones took a tissue from an open box on her desk and dabbed at her eyes. Her smile was too broad to dab.

"I'll talk with Carol tomorrow about her incomplete grade," she said, then inhaling and trying to regain her composure while dabbing at her eyes again. "Oh, my," she said again, this time minus the giggle. "Dad eats his daughter's science experiment. The faculty lounge will never be the same after this."

"I won't eat her make-up experiment," he said, holding up his right hand and two fingers. A third finger followed. "How many fingers in a Scout's honor salute?" He wanted to burst out laughing, but was too scared. He forced a smile while trying to ignore feelings that wouldn't be ignored. His head bowed for a moment so she wouldn't see him staring. He had never seen frosted brown hair like hers, the incredible perfect lips and, what he called, sugar brown eyes, a slight droopy lid that was like a spider luring him into her web. He felt the tangled snare of the web, unfolded his hands, gripped the seat of his chair and fought to keep from running away from what he knew was finding his impossible dream.

Parent-teacher conference over, Tidge started to drive home to his garden apartment in Norridge. The conference had lasted its allotted time of seven minutes and he felt he had known Wilhelmina Schneider-Jones his entire life. "Damn," he muttered to his empty car, as the palms of his hands banged against the steering wheel. He felt the urge to go back to school and ask his daughter's teacher if she'd like to out with him for a drink, or a cup of coffee or for a pizza. "You are too stupid for words," he continued, knowing he had been deliciously engulfed by the ultimate impossible dream. "Nice going, numb-nuts," he cursed. "You really blew it."

Glaring tail lights had his right foot jamming his brake pedal almost through the floor boards of his new, burgundy Sebring convertible temporarily ending his dream. "Be careful, Tidge," he said to himself, the screech of brakes snapping him out of his trance and his comment not related to his driving. "She doesn't need some old fart like you in her life."

Tidge could count the impossible dreams he had experienced before meeting Wilhelmina Schneider-Jones with the same number of fingers in his Scout salute. One of those dreams was his three daughters who he adored. Another of his dreams, one that he cherished, was his college degree. That impressive engraved piece of paper with the Loyola University name embossed across the top in maroon letters was in and out of his grasp countless frustrating times. Tidge had also entertained dreams and fantasies of meeting women. Outside of Sissy and Barbara Ann, none of those dreams materialized. A father like Kid Scream and his three brothers made women, real or imagined, skip his address. Besides, his life was one of scrambling to get by. Whatever Tidge accomplished in life, whatever dreams did get fulfilled, he worked for. His hands were calloused just like his father's, only his calluses had toiled along with his brain and his backside as he worked his way through college, a hitch in the Navy prefacing the grind of higher education.

He ground away to meet the minimum graduation requirements for his degree from Loyola. He celebrated his impossible dream of sorts at a party in his honor, an impromptu gathering at the Sunset Inn a neighborhood saloon where he had drank since turning sixteen. He had discovered at an early age that alcohol helped him cope with his father. Then Sissy became his excuse. Then he ran out of excuses, looked at himself in the mirror and switched from buying half gallons of *wodka* at the liquor store to half pints of diet root beer at a convenient gas mart store.

Helping him celebrate his dream of earning a college diploma were his friends, Humper and Bean Head. His two neighborhood boyhood buddies had continued on with school while Tidge was in the Navy. They were a year from graduating when Tidge got his discharge. When Humper and Bean Head graduated they went out and got drunk together. Now the three friends got drunk again, Tidge considerably drunker than the others.

Humper and Bean Head managed to get Tidge home and inside without waking The Kid. Mother Mary May I heard the three coming from a block away and greeted them at the front door. She reassured William and Robert, (she would have nothing to do with their vile nicknames that insulted two Catholic saints) "I'll take care of my first born, boys."

Tidge's two friends apologized to his mother and staggered home. Humper teetered his way next door and Bean Head waddled down to the end of the block stumbling off the curb twice. That night Tidge slept with his degree, the protective simulated leather folder covered with beer stains from the Sunset Inn, tucked safely under his pillow.

Tail lights flashed in front of him and his right foot jammed down again. He heard the screech of his tires. There was no sound of a collision. Nothing was making sense to him. "A father doesn't fall in love with his eighth grade daughter's teacher," he said, lecturing himself. "At least not one with a hyphenated name, and not the first time he lays eyes on her." But, as much as he tried, he couldn't erase the divine vision of Wilhelmina Schneider-Jones from his mind. His heart wouldn't let him. It kept saying to him, "She's a keeper, Tidge. Don't screw this one up."

That night, two lives began to change along with the spirit of Christmas and gift giving. Five years later they were celebrating their third year of marriage and planning a family Christmas that she was dreading and made him feel both elated and scared to death.

Chapter 4

Tidge's blood started icing over the moment he realized that his oldest daughter could nix his invitation for a family Christmas at Henry's Hut. The possibility of Martha giving him thumbs down hit him harder than Kid Gavilan, his father's favorite, battering him with a series of his Bolo punches. Realizing that others might also toss his Christmas invitation into the trash had him hearing the Cuban Hawk spitting Feliz Navidad at him through his mouth piece with the whip of each punch.

Willy calling his name ended his deflecting punches and dodging crumbled up holiday invitations being hurled at him by sneering family members. He stared at the sleek television, the operating manual's pages reflecting the tremor of his quivering, sweaty hands. He hadn't been so nervous since a long ago boy/girl Christmas party in the basement of Janice Koester's parent's house when he was an eighth grader. There were no nuns chaperoning that night even though word of the party leaked out. Sister Mary Gertrude Beatrice, the principal at St. Ferdinand's had called the Koester residence to dissuade the family from creating a possible occasion of sin for impressionable young people. "After all," started the principal's gentle warning, "we are celebrating the birth of Christ."

Janice Koester's father, who had been drinking at a Christmas office party that afternoon, took the call. Sister Mary Gertrude Beatrice was informed that no one sinned in the Koester house except him.

That night, accompanied by the urge to partake in what he had heard referred to as sins of the flesh, Tidge somehow corralled his nerves and once again asked a tall, gangly and incredibly pretty Marietta Claus to dance. She was more exciting than a Christmas morning snow fall in her white taffeta party dress and jet black hair tied back with a festive, red ribbon. He couldn't imagine that sinning with her would really be a sin. He remembered that he had to look up slightly into eyes so blue that made him feel he was in a trance. They both barely shuffled their feet to one of Janice Koester's father's favorite records, a scratchy version of Kay Starr's *Wheel of Fortune* coming from an old phonograph. A frugal Mr. Koester, like Kid Scream, never discarded anything. Kay's husky lyrics engulfed all of the barely moving nervous adolescents. Palms sweating, a periodic muffled giggle, kisses attempted, a few succeeding and only one tongue bitten, that followed by, "Wahcha do dat for?" being interjected into Kay's lyrics in the flickering candlelight darkness. An epic occasion of sin smoldered like Krakatoa while Janice Koester's parents sat upstairs in the living room, her mother sipping her third Stinger while her father guzzled the last beer from his new six-pack.

"Tidge," said Willy in a concerned whisper. "Are you okay?"

He felt his head move in her direction as his eyes absorbed the most beautiful face God, Mother Nature and genetics ever created. "Why wouldn't I be?" he said, as if her question lacked merit. His eyes shifted back to the intimidating television and then to the manual, his sweaty hands making the crisp, new pages damp and limp. He pretended to study the maze of diagrams. After a frustrating minute of silence, he turned to Willy again, his eyes asking if he was seeing what he was really seeing.

"It's real," she said, stroking his arm. She looked into the warmth of his eyes and saw a first. Her husband resembled a deer frozen by the headlights of their pickup truck. She grinned and said: "Can you believe the size of that son of a bitch."

The manual cleared the polished log beams of the Great Room's ceiling before plopping down in front of Tidge's feet. He stared at her in shock, half of his face being swallowed by his own grin. His arms went around her in a bear hug and he said softly in her ear, "That's the first time since we've met that you used bad words, Miss Potty Mouth." He squeezed her harder. "And you taught young, impressionable children, especially my baby?"

She squeezed him back, pulled slightly away, her love for him radiating from her eyes and said: "Well, it is the biggest son of a bitch I've ever seen." She felt his arms relax and he pulled away just enough to project a face filled with adulation.

"The biggest for me too, Wilhelmina Mackie Whiz," he said, his voice choked as his eyes pooled up making him look like a bug eyed frog wearing giant contact lenses. He reached up with the knuckle of his curved right index finger and took a swipe above each cheek.

She hugged him again and whispered in his ear: "I thought Christmas was the season to be jolly, you big cry baby." Her arms tightened around him.

"It is," he whispered back. "There's jolly, holly, a lot of ho-ho-ho, but no big son of a bitch." He choked back a sniffle.

Her arms slowly slid to her sides, her hands taking hold of his. "So, my jolly, holly, ho-ho-ho love, what's on your agenda for today?"

"My agenda," he repeated, his watery eyes going back and forth between the television and the beauty of her face, "should begin with my leading you to the kitchen sink, take a bar of soap and wash your mouth out for saying words I never heard you say before." he said, nodding in the direction of their kitchen.

"Are you forgetting something, Saint Thomas?" she asked, her lush brown eyes turning syrupy.

He gave a shrug.

"You're the one who taught me those bad words."

He shrugged again. "Oh, and you never heard any bad words from your parents?"

She didn't miss a beat. "Only from my father, but those were in German."

He gave her a hug. "As for my agenda, love of my life, I'm going to my workshop and then the den to prepare for Santa Claus. Call me if you need me," he said.

"Workshop?" she asked, taken back. "Den?" Her husband's words sounded as if receiving a big screen television and a satellite dish system was a daily occurrence. Disappointment hit her like the angry Lake Michigan waves she used to watch from the twenty third floor of her Lake Shore Drive condo as they pummeled the Montrose Harbor breakwater.

He pulled her to him again and held her tighter than before. When he thought their bodies would become one, he let her go and winked. "I've got to create our Christmas invitations so I can get them into the mail."

"Invitations?" she asked, wondering what was going on in her husband's mind. "We're just getting ready for Thanksgiving."

"Heck, I know that," he said, looking at her as only a man who adores a woman can, his eyes continuing to pool up. "And Christmas comes right after Thanksgiving, doesn't it?" He smiled trying to choke back a tardy sniffle. "Didn't you just give me an early Christmas present?" His head went up and down. "Then it's only logical that I give more than enough time to our families to prepare for their trip north for Christmas."

Her head did a slow side to side move and she said softly: "If you say so."

He rested his hands on her shoulders. "I like early presents," he said, his fingers stroking at her shoulders lighter than the humming birds that would surround their feeders lining the back porch when all signs of winter disappeared. "And that's why I'm giving our families plenty of advanced notice to get ready for their Christmas trek to the Northwoods." His fingers slid to both sides of her cheeks and he winked at her. "Am I logical or am I logical?"

"Well," she managed to say before he interrupted.

"If I liked my early surprise, don't you think the natives would also like an early surprise?"

"Tidge!"

"Sorry," he said, knowing that he had slipped and became his father if only for one innocent statement. "I didn't mean that the way you thought," he continued, not giving her time to level one of her politically correct warnings to him. "I used the native expression in the generic, like in old movies where someone comments about the natives being restless." His hands formed their familiar *V* and cupped the point of her chin. "I just want to give everyone enough time to make their plans." He kissed her on the nose, let her go and started for his basement workshop, imitating Alvin and the Chipmunks with their Christmas Chipmunk Song.

The next morning, bleary eyed and looking like a squinting owl from using his calligraphy pens under a neon desk lamp most of the night, he handed his stack of invitations to Willy. "Here, Teach," he said, his words looking like how he felt. "Don't waste your time critiquing and grading, just give me your seal of approval."

Her nose wrinkled as she slid an invitation from the middle of the stack. "It's not that I don't trust you," she said, without looking up. "I've just heard too many stories about how you stacked a deck."

"No way," he replied. "Heck, I hate playing cards." He watched the tip of her index finger do a serpentine motion down the page. Then he saw her look at him and knew he was in trouble.

She pulled a red pen from her Shakespeare mug of pens and pencils gave him her sternest of stern teacher looks and said: "Wisconsin is not spelled with three *n*'s."

"My baby brother thinks so," he said, meekly picking up his stack of invitations. "The three *n*'s are for him. He turned without a word and headed for his den saying: "If John believes the state should be pronounced, Winsconsin, then that's how I'm going to spell it."

Willy continued planning for seventeen possible guests. Her preparations, like everything she did in life, were organized and included a host of options. One option included a plan of condolences for her husband if one or, heaven forbid, all rejected his invitation.

Tidge's feeling of being overwhelmed by the size of the television couldn't compare to how he felt about Willy buying into his plan for a family Christmas. Their combined families together in Henry's Hut at Christmas was like adding a second satellite dish to the roof, this one specifically designed by NASA engineers for tracking Santa's sleigh. If it had been possible, he would have had the B-25 bomber, *Sugar Claus* escort Santa for a safe touch down at Henry's Hut.

Willy had never seen her husband so hyper. When he started for his workshop imitating the Chipmunks singing their Christmas song, she couldn't help shake her head at his optimism.

As Tidge started down the stairs to his workshop, the volume of his vocalizing increased with an emphasis being placed on his wanting a Hula-hoop. Her initial expression of emotions came out in a simple, muttered statement to the television. "He wants a hula-hoop instead of you?" She looked at the closed door to his workshop and yelled: "Alvin!"

Self-pity wasn't a part of Willy's make-up, but it walked with her as she went up to the second floor to the converted bedroom she called, *Boss Turf*. This was her sanctuary, her private space. Tidge had his workshop, actually three. One was in his small den on the first floor, another in the basement and the third in the garage. She had her studio. It was where she wrote. It was where inspiration fueled her creative juices. Above all, it was neat and orderly.

When she wasn't simultaneously engaged in working on three novels, she sat curled up in her stuffed floral patterned chair like a comfy kitten and crocheted. She would gaze out the large rectangular window of her *Turf* mesmerized by a view of the lake that put her life into perspective. Now each glance seemed to be accompanied by more than a perspective. She felt an almost eerie but comforting feeling. At first, she likened it to being cradled in her Mitty's arms. Those arms, she remembered, provided comfort. She still felt comfort, but now there was more. Comfort began to nudge her, attempting to steer her in directions she questioned. The nudges only seemed to come when she had even the faintest thought, good or bad, about the approaching Christmas season. Then it dawned on her. The first time she noticed a nudge was about the time she made her decision to surprise Tidge with an early Christmas present.

Willy turned off the lamp on her roll top desk and soaked up the night winter view. She anticipated being greeted by a sky filled with more stars than she ever knew existed and wasn't disappointed. Instinctively, she got up and removed the afghan her late grandmother had knitted for her from the back of her chair. She sat back down, curled up in the afghan and wondering if the eerie feelings of being nudged would return. She didn't wait long.

The instant her thoughts turned to the satellite dish and television her afghan seemed to generate warmth that belonged to her Mitty. She knew she did the right thing. Her decision was more than the giving of a Christmas gift to the man she loved. It was her attempt to cushion the giant let down she knew her husband would feel when his on-going dream of Santa Claus bringing him his special present vanished like the spring morning fog surrounding their Camelot. She wanted desperately for her husband to finally open his ultimate Christmas gift. He had waited, hoped and prayed for that gift. What had Willy totally amazed was that not even a Neiman-Marcus Christmas catalogue could fulfill Tidge's dream.

She reached up, switched on the floor lamp next to her chair and picked up one of her legal pads from a perfect pile stacked on an antique drop leaf end table next to her chair, the table purchased on a summer Monday visit to the Hayward Ice Arena flea market. The first several pages contained scribbled notes for her writing projects. Ready fingers flipped over the pages and her mind began to take stock of what needed to be accomplished. She lifted a Number Two yellow pencil from a stack sticking out from a coffee cup sporting a picture of William Shakespeare, each pencil's point sharpened like a deadly weapon. If her husband's natives got restless and decided to venture north, she would be prepared. Like her mother, she was anal retentive, organized and a neat freak, and her house would be a show place several days before their guests arrived. Like her father who had taught her, she was also a gourmet cook as Tidge discovered on their first date.

Her first pencil filled up line after line and page after page of the legal tablet with possible meals. When the point was worn beyond her specifications, the pencil found its way into a box sandwiched between Shakespeare and a temperamental electric sharpener that needed coaxing not to bite off the point. She plucked out a second pencil and another page began to fill up with ideas for table center pieces. Each would be coordinated with a particular meal. That meant her table on Christmas Eve and Christmas Day, as well as the days before and after, would have to be tasteful, unique and festive and that included the breakfasts, lunches, dinners, mid-day snacks and late night sweets. Several more dull pencils later and a dozen filled pages, both sides, she stopped. Another pencil was laid to rest in the box and she flipped the yellow pages back to the beginning. She scanned her list. As she got to the third page she said, "Dearest, God, why did you allow me to agree to this?" She felt the afghan give her a reassuring hug.

The lined, legal sized pages snapped back and forth creating a breeze in her *Turf* and another wooden pencil was placed into action. She jotted numerous additions and clarifications. Ignoring the eraser, she made a few deletions by shunning neat and blackening out the items that had made her nose crinkle up. Satisfied, she set the legal pad in her lap and felt exhausted. She glanced at the digital clock blinking at her from her antique, blond oak roll top desk and was surprised to see that almost three hours had gone by. She pulled her afghan around her until it hugged her cheeks. Then she heard the door to Tidge's workshop open. Before she could unwrap herself, he was in the doorway beaming.

"How about we watch the ten o'clock news on my new Christmas present." he said. "I can't wait to see a picture without a blizzard." He winked, turned around and headed for the stairs and the Great Room.

She placed the legal pad on the table, slid out from her chair, folded her afghan, replaced it and followed him.

They both nestled into their designated spots on the sofa in front of the new television. He held the television's remote in one hand and the instruction manual in the other. A button on the remote went down and then up. Nothing happened. More buttons did their down and up dance. Still nothing came on the screen. "I'm so used to seeing snowy characters in hues of greens and reds that it'll take me well into next year to get used to a real television picture." His index finger punched the remote buttons even harder, but brute force didn't change the blank screen.

"Why don't you read the directions," she suggested.

"Oh, directions," he said, a tinge of frustration in his voice. The pages flipped in one direction and then back in the other. He picked up the remote, studied it, looked at the front and then at the back. No more quick glances from him that were borderline frantic.

"Duh," he muttered his discovery evident in his hand. The remote needed batteries. He was in and out of his workshop in less than a minute, packages of three different sizes in his hand. When the local ten o'clock news came on from Duluth they both sat in silence not believing that living color humans looked live and in color. Most nights saw them dozing off and ready for bed after the weather report that always looked like rainbow streaked snow. Tonight was different. Weather and sports looked like weather and sports. After the news, Tidge experimented making two complete circuits of channel selections with the remote. "There's got to be at least ten thousand channels on this thing," he said, a look of wonderment beaming at the girl he adored.

"At least that many," she said, then yawing. She stretched, got up, gave another stretch, this one accompanied by a bigger yawn and blew him a kiss. "Some of us have a need to push buttons," she said, her eyes smiling at him. "Me? I need my beauty sleep." She turned and headed for the stairs. "Too bad you don't like the present," she said, expecting a reaction from him. None came. "I'll call the store tomorrow to take it back." She smiled as she watched him as if he were an ice sculpture; the only part of him moving was his right index finger on the remote control. "Good night, my love." She heard him grunt as she headed up the stairs to bed.

Tidge couldn't believe what came on the screen. He clicked through talk shows, cooking shows, and shows featuring antiques, pawn shops and junk yards. His index finger rested just above the buttons when an array of women, some in lingerie, other's in bikinis and a few nude flashed on. Most had blond hair, black roots evident and countless shapes of black eye brows. They all winked at him from the screen. He caught glimpses of commentaries, more women in various stages of undress, comedy shows, country music shows, and, the farther up the numeric channels he climbed, more nude women. One, he thought, could have been a twin of his once illicit love, Barbara Ann Lindstrom. "Nah," he said. "Couldn't be."

Shows flashed on the screen as if shot out of a high-powered *T.V. Guide*.

- Fishing shows.
- Alligator hunters.
- Gold diggers.
- Cartoons.
- Men missing most teeth catching catfish bare handed.
- Wives cheating on husbands.
- Husbands cheating on wives.
- Binge drinking.
- Biographies from A-Z.

Those shows were interspersed by a nude exercise show from Great Britain where two small breasted white women wearing sneakers were sandwiched between a tall, skinny black man who genetics had blest. He also wore sneakers. Nothing else. The three did side-straddle hops.

The Russians had a topless news anchor. She too was blond with black eye brows, the eye brows shaped like a hammer and sickle seeming to keep with the trend.

Talking heads, male or female, screamed at Tidge. Bible pages beat the air. Somewhere in Asia, on a theatre stage, he saw the re-enactment of a couple's wedding night, close-ups and all. He gave a nervous glance to the area on the sofa where Willy would be curled up and felt relieved. An Asian version of a marriage being consummated within the Great Room of Henry's Hut would not have pleased her.

His index finger moved again and he was staring back at Danny Kaye and Bing Crosby in *White Christmas*. "Too soon," he muttered, as he pushed a button and the screen went blank. "Mother Mary May I's law said nothing Christmas until after Thanksgiving and that's the way it is." He smiled. "Well, I'm looking at the one exception to her law."

His excitement drove away sleep. He dropped the remote on the sofa and headed for his den and the stack of invitations. "Like it or not, dearest Wilhelmina, three *n*'s is the only way to spell Wisconsin according to Mackiewicz family tradition," he said aloud. He plopped down on the rickety wooden swivel chair at his own beat up desk, the roll top only working when he talked nice to it. "This will definitely get the natives restless," he said, picking up the box with his calligraphy pens. He stayed up most of the night, meticulous penmanship in Old English script replacing the original hand written invitations.

He recalled how his brother, John, at the time, would get so worked up about the family's coming vacation to Sven's Muskellunge Resort in Minocqua, Wisconsin, that he would repeat over and over, "I'm goin' to Winsconsin." Then John would add, "I'm gonna catch me a giant Muskellena."

Tidge felt pleased with his creativity. He also felt his head nodding and eye that were losing their fight to stay open. He stacked the invitations on his desk, flipped off the tarnished brass goose neck light with three golf ball size dents in the metal shade and headed for the stairs and bed.

As Tidge handed her one of his new invitations, Willy's nose went into a crinkle. He knew why, but didn't care. He envied her, knowing she had graduated from Loyola, Cum Laude saying, "Well, I got my degree Magna Come Lousy." Her writing classes and Jesuit demands for perfection had her ready to forgo her morning coffee for a trip up the stairs to her studio to get her trusty red pen. She wasn't about to be embarrassed at Christmas, or at any other time, by any form of illiteracy, eye catching or not. "Misspelled words are inexcusable," she said to him, then took a sip of steaming coffee.

Tidge sloughed off her warning by trying to convince her that his family would recognize his attempt at levity. "My brothers will enjoy my intentional slip of the calligraphy pen," he said to her. "Especially my brother, John." He tried to glare at her. "You just don't like the fact that my pen is mightier than your corrective red ink covered sword."

"Mea culpa," she said, the two words coming out in a reverent prayer as the wrinkle from her nose expanded, working its way across her forehead. "Do the Jesuits still say a Mass of Thanksgiving every year at Madonna della Strada Chapel in honor of your finally leaving the University?"

Tidge was too tired to spar with his wife, his body operating on explosions of nervous energy. After breakfast, his aching, blood shot eyes took a glance at his Christmas present from Willy and he was back in his den addressing and stamping the envelopes to his invitations. Winsconsin stayed.

Before Willy had finished dressing and putting on what little make-up she wore, she heard a downstairs door open and a shout: "Back in a flash!" By the time she got downstairs, she looked out one of their massive floor-to-ceiling front windows to see their pickup truck disappear over the rise of their rut road drive. She sighed and started mouthing the words to *Run, Rudolph, run.*

Tidge had taken no chances with his invitations getting in the mail. He trusted no one, not even Morty the mail carrier, who had been on the job for twenty seven years. The obese Morty waddled when he walked, and wore a grey train engineer's cap and a full salt and pepper beard year round. He had covered the rural routes of the Cable area making sure that the mail got through when nothing or no one else could. Appreciation for his efforts came in the form of assorted homemade baked goods left in the mail boxes. Morty never met a cake or cookie he didn't like.

Tidge joked with Morty almost daily, making it a point to be at the mail box about the time Morty drove up. "You eat any more of those chocolate chips those horny old widows on your route leave you, and you're going to be fatter than Santa Claus," Tidge said to him.

"Damn the United States Postal Service," said Tidge, to the empty cab of their pickup truck, as he drove west to town and the Cable Post Office. He damned his wife's mania for perfection and her good-natured jokes about his academic achievement. None of that mattered, not even memories of the hangover he had after his graduation celebration at the Sunset Inn. Then he damned Morty several dozen more times because that seemed appropriate, though not logical, and he threw in a curse or two at the Jesuits for no good reason. "Santa's bringing my special present to Lake Namakagon this year and it'll be wrapped and tagged, Patriarch," he said to the road noise filtering into the truck. "Dearest wife," he said to the continuous bumpy hum of the remaining spots of packed snow on the road, "I'm saying a prayer of thanksgiving for the yearly Mass in my honor at Madonna della Strata Chapel. Then, I'm taking Loyola's motto, *Ad Majorem Dei Gloriam,* and stenciling it on the side of Santa's sleigh underneath the pin-up picture of Sugar Claus."

Willy anticipated a problem getting Tidge to go for their walk the day after she gave him her surprise Christmas present, but he was raring to go. He stayed in his revved-up mode until after Thanksgiving dinner at the Miller's.

Their daily walks were filled with conversations that started with the topic of turkey and progressed into tending to the details and finalizing of their plans for Christmas. Tidge couldn't wait for the day after Thanksgiving. Outside of Christmas, Willy's birthday and their anniversary, that was next most important day in his year. The morning after Thanksgiving, the boxes with all of his Christmas decorations emerged from the den closet ready to go on display.

After his mother's death, Tidge took great care with her religious figurines. Death, coupled with his family's growing rebellious attitude toward him, presented Tidge with the premonition that his mother wanted her Infant Jesus collection to take a religious hiatus. He felt that was the respectful thing to do and, for several years, even with his marriage to Willy, that's what he did.

This year he knew was the time and the place to remove the three beer cartons from his closet and join the other awaiting boxes. An army of the Infant Jesus nestled in not quite a ton of surgical cotton was about to descend on Henry's Hut.

Tidge stared at the stack of cardboard boxes that stood at perfect attention, awaiting his orders, but couldn't open the first box. Something didn't feel right to him. "Mom," he said, his empty den listening. "Can I?" He thought he heard his mother's stock reply to any question she heard that contained the expression, "Can I?"

"Thomas, you may if you think you can."

Tidge continued to stare at the cardboard beer cases, each sporting a brand his father once drank. Like Kid Scream, all of the breweries were no longer in existence. After what seemed an eternity, he said: "Mom, I've got to make this Christmas perfect."

"Thomas, perfect it will be," he heard his mother say. "You're the only one of my sons who believes in the true spirit of Christmas."

"Will it be perfect, Mom?" He thought he heard the faint sound of his mother's rare chuckle.

"Thomas, you can count on it."

"Can I?"

"Can you what?'

Tidge blinked and saw Willy standing in the open door of his den. She was dressed for their daily walk.

"I can be ready in a minute." he said, followed by a copy of his mother's chuckle. He took the top three cartons containing most of his mother's figurines and replaced them in the closet.

They hiked through the woods, a dusting of snow changing the landscape. Their walk took them east onto the land of their neighbor's farm where they stopped by to once again thank Don and Norma Miller for Thanksgiving dinner. Willy had baked a loaf each of banana, raisin and cranberry walnut breads to show the Millers how much they appreciated an old fashioned farm-style Thanksgiving. Thanks to the Millers' seventeen year old son, Kenny, it was a Thanksgiving dinner they doubted they would ever experience again.

Kenny was tall and awkward, had a slight lisp and sprayed saliva on everyone within six feet when he talked. He was border line handsome with a swatch of freckles on one cheek and a head of dark blond curls that looked as if they could be used to scour pots and pans. Kenny had invited his high school girlfriend, Mickey and her parents for dinner. Mickey nudged five feet in heels. She was sweet sixteen, and showing signs of converting baby fat into real adult flab. Mickey's father was a tall, strapping dark haired man of Finnish decent who Tidge felt shaved with Paul Bunyan's axe and could tear off one of the ornate wooden legs from the Millers' massive, walnut dining room table and use it for a toothpick. Tidge thought he had eyes that flashed one continuous message, *I wanna stomp your ass into the ground.* His message seemed to be aimed at everyone seated at the table. Mickey's mother was as tall as her daughter, but had given up counting calories after her daughter was born. Where Mickey had straight auburn hair that hung to her waist, her mother's was streaked with grey and in tight pin curls. Bright red lipstick adorned her lips, the top one almost invisible with the lower one puffy and appearing to roll down her chin.

Before dinner Mickey had gone outside with Kenny, the two of them disappearing into the barn. During dinner, Mickey kept picking strands of straw from her hair and dropping them on Kenny's plate. Kenny would blush and a bubble of saliva would form at the corner of his mouth before popping. Then, with her plate almost empty, Mickey put down her knife and fork and reached into her blouse. The outline of fingers could be seen moving under the material, sliding and picking before reappearing and holding several pieces of straw. Her new find joined the others on Kenny's plate. Somehow, more straw sprouted from Mickey's clothing, each stem added to Kenny's collection. As the harvest became more bountiful, Kenny's complexion turned redder while Mickey's father's eyes got scarier, the message now flashing: *I'm really gonna enjoy stompin' your ass.*

Norma Miller, her grey hair twisted behind her in a single, tight pigtail hanging half way down her back, and without any signs of make-up, was plain and pretty. Where Tidge had always prided himself on his Thanksgiving turkey and stuffing, (he would never call it dressing) Norma Miller introduced him to Thanksgiving aromas and tastes that he never knew existed. Even Willy, a gourmet cook, salivated. They listened as Norma Miller joked about the straw and how, as a youngster, she would play games in their family barn with her brothers and how straw would be thrown about and dumped on heads. "We played in the straw so much that I would find it in my underpants." Mickey's father gave a grunt and the expression on his face was now flashing, *I'm gonna take that little drummer boy son of yours and shove his drumsticks, one up each nostril, and then make sure all he wants for Christmas are his two front teeth.*

Norma continued on. She laughed and said, "I sat down once and a piece of straw stuck me in the backside. I must have jumped three feet off my chair. It was so funny." There was another grunt that sounded more like a growl. Tidge's butt slid back and forth on his chair several quick times and Kenny turned so red he almost exploded. Everyone at the table laughed except Mickey's father who Tidge now thought resembled a cross between the Grinch, the Grim Reaper and an old time Italian boxing favorite of his father's, Primo Carnera, who had been known as The Ambling Alp. It was Tidge who then noticed Mickey's left hand disappear under the table cloth. A full minute later it reappeared with several pieces of straw concealed in her palm. Tidge was convinced that Mickey had no sense of discretion as the straw dropped onto Kenny's plate. Bubbles popped in rapid fire from both corners of Kenny's mouth. His head went down and his fork kicked into supersonic speeds, the new straw additions being consumed with his mashed potatoes. Tidge was sure he felt the dining room table vibrate. He knew a minor earth quake had not struck the Lake Namakagon area. The vision of Mickey's father almost blocking out the view of the back wall of the Millers' dining room was answer enough.

With their cakes delivered and the walk back home through the woods in front of them, they once again thanked the Millers and retraced their footsteps in a light snow cover. They now felt like hiking experts having walked through the woods several times to the Millers'. Fallen limbs were stepped over, hanging branches that wanted to shave an ear or a nose off their faces were sidestepped and decayed stumps blocking their path navigated. Experience had taught them to be cautious. Talking while walking in the woods had been minimized after a lesson learned on their first venture off their driveway and the county road. Tidge had pushed away a sapling from his path and it sprang back hitting Willy face high. She had been wearing a baseball cap at the time, a blue Chicago Cubs hat with the red C that belonged to Tidge. She was looking down at the ground when the whip affect of the branch hit her. Off flew the hat, the branch knocking it further than some of Tidge's boyhood Cub heroes could ever hit a baseball. Now they knew that a misstep could lead to an ankle sprain, the snap of a human limb, a fall, or even worse. Christmas on crutches was only for Dickens and Tiny Tim.

Willy almost always wore a baseball cap after that experience even if it clashed with the hood of her parka. "I can't believe we're doing this," she said, sounding out of breath, her hood down and mittens stuffed into the pockets of her parka as she followed in his footsteps. "Last Christmas was so beautiful," she continued. "Just the two of us and Henry comfy cozy in a setting that all of the Christmas cards ever printed couldn't capture."

"And two dozen phone calls interrupting our peace on earth," he said, recalling how the phone rang and rang and rang. Each call had been greeted with a, "Merry Christmas," and ended with, "Happy New Year." Hopes for a joyful new year never made it to his brothers. His Christmas conversations with Peter, Paul and John ended like the first summer tornado they experienced, cutting a howling swath through the timber, snapping trees in half. His youngest brother, John really infuriated him and Willy relegated her husband to the den that night. Tidge was so irate after John called him a Cheese Head and the illegitimate son of an abusive tyrant who played favorites and a goody two shoes, guilt ridden Irish Catholic mother, he launched the portable phone. Seeing it bounce off the mantle and drop behind the fireplace screen saw him calm down in an instant. Willy's famous laser look of loathing made him even calmer. Apologies spilled from him as he used the fire place tongs to slide the singed phone from the flames. Each time Tidge used the portable phone, the charred ear piece and several burned off numbers and letters reminded him of the incident.

"Christmas was still beautiful even with the phone calls," she said, cherishing every detail of her first Christmas alone with her husband in their wooded Eden blanketed with the whitest snow she had ever seen. The year before, when they had just finished moving in and getting situated, pages on the calendar in their mud room began flapping. Christmas was marching at them across a newly frozen Lake Namagakon and being preceded by a new holiday season they weren't familiar with: Deer Hunting.

They decided to drive south to Chicago to spend Christmas Eve with his brothers and their families and Christmas Day with her parents. Christmas Eve had always been for the Mackiewicz family ever since he could remember. His mother's side of the family got the actual day. Her side was small, just two antique relatives from Ireland. There was a senile uncle in adult diapers pushing ninety (he claimed one hundred) and a second cousin who had a brogue so thick Merry Christmas sounded like Tidge's sister-in-law's Cherokee tongue. They were both too generous and drank Tullamore Dew out of juice glasses. Half of a fifth of Irish whiskey later, the ninety year old ended up sound asleep in the Kid's favorite chair just before presents were handed out. He left a urine stain behind as a sign that another Christmas Day was over and thanked the Kid and Mother Mary May I with, "Thanks to ye for a Happy St. Patrick's Day" while being ushered to a taxi to take him back to the Assisted Living Home.

The other cousin's presents were many, expensive and needed. His mother cried at the generosity. The Kid, his pride beat up like some of his boxing heroes, silently cursed with envy. Tidge and his brothers didn't care. Two days worth of presents and two great meals were sandwiched between the nine o'clock children's Mass at St. Ferdinand's. After Mass, Tidge would meet with his friends, Humper, Bean Head, Zamboni and other eighth grade classmates as they described and compared their presents. Each present was always prefaced with the statement, "And I got . . ."

The decision for them to head back to Chicago for the Christmas holidays that first year in their new home had been made easier, thanks to being shot at several days before Thanksgiving.

They were taking their daily walk, ducking in and out of the woods to explore, but not too far in where Tidge could lose sight of his security blanket—the road. Both of them were oblivious that Wisconsin's national pastime, deer hunting season, was in full salvo. Tidge, with Willy on his heels, cut a path through the timber just east of their house when they heard two noises, one loud, sounding like a gunshot, and the second, less than an instant after the first, a rotted tree having its rot and bark turn into splinters and wood dust. There was a second gunshot and Tidge, spinning around, tackled a surprised Willy to the ground. Before she could say a word, visions of her first marriage coming alive, Tidge was smothering her with his body. A string of obscenities echoed from him in decibels equivalent to that of a fleet of snowmobiles racing across Lake Namakagon. Each was a creative statement containing the expression that had accompanied his throwing the portable phone into the fireplace preceded by, "You stupid fuckin'!" No one ever showed their face. Tidge, still on top of a shaken and confused Willy, kept yelling from his prone position behind a fallen tree. "Do we look like fuckin' Bambi?"

The next day they curtailed their walk opting to rake leaves, these covered with a dusting of fresh snow. They ventured no farther than their garage doors. During a break in raking, Willy asked, "Did someone really think we were deer?"

Tidge laid his rake over the pile of leaves they had gathered. "I guess."

A second question followed. "Did you learn to yell and use language like that from your father?

"I guess."

"Thank you for protecting me," she said, looking at him, her eyes barely visible under her baseball cap.

"You're my girl," he said.

"And you're my hero," she said, her head tilted back, eyes now visible. "But please don't use words like that again."

He picked up the rake, looked at her and said, "Even if we get shot at?"

She smiled. "If that happens again, I'll use those words."

The walks started up again several days later after a phone call from a neighbor they hadn't met. Don Miller introduced himself then apologized for the shooting even though he had nothing to do with it and didn't know who did. All of Bayfield County heard about it, but nobody owned up to knowing who the trigger-happy culprit might be. Then Don Miller explained that deer season in northern Wisconsin bordered on fanaticism. "It's a family ritual," he said. "Even the high schools close opening day, eh. Most of students, boys and girls, the principal and many faculty members go hunting, eh." He reassured them that hunting season had ended and it was safe to walk in the woods.

Bright and early the next morning, a faded black, rusted pickup truck, circa 1950's with, "Don Miller and Son, Cable, Wisconsin" stenciled in white on both doors, pulled up to their three car garage. "When another deer season comes around," said Don Miller without getting out of the truck, "wear one of these." He held up a road worker's orange vest and stuck it out the window. "Baseball may be the national pastime in Milwaukee and across the Mississippi in that other state, eh." He nodded towards Minnesota. "Up here, deer hunting is more sacred than the Lutheran religion and the Green Bay Packers." He handed Tidge a second vest.

Tidge thanked him, offered to pay for the vests, but Don shook his head, put the pickup's grinding gears into reverse and drove away. On their next trip to town, Tidge bought them matching orange scarves and knit stocking caps to go with their plastic vests.

They did more than enjoy their walks, becoming kindred spirits with the woods, she more than he. The daily walk through the dense timber became Willy's addiction. She would pull Tidge away from whatever occupied his undivided attention saying: "Come on, Nature

Boy, time to get your old heart rate elevated and drain the nastiness out of your cranky old system." Her daily reminder sounded like one of his father's commands when she would add, "Hup-two-three-four."

"Okay, Sarge," he would reply, his head doing a slow motion right to left movement and then back. "By the way, what's this nastiness stuff and cranky old system?"

"If you don't know by now, I'm hiding your orange vest."

They became more adventurous during their walks since Don Miller's reassuring talk that hunting season was over and the addition of bright colors to their hiking ensembles wouldn't be necessary until next November. That made Tidge happy. He didn't like wearing anything that would cover up his old flight jacket. Then he recalled listening to his Uncle Brew tell how a bright yellow Mae West became blood stained during his rescue from a Korean countryside. He began to shuffle his feet through the floor of leaves in the woods. "I wish Don Miller was around to give me, Humper and Bean Head orange vests when we were kids."

"You're not going to tell me you were shot at before," she said, her usual skepticism present when her husband alluded to his boyhood days.

"No," he said, breaking into a grin. "But we came close to getting beaten within an inch of our early adolescent lives by some guy who looked like Kenny's girlfriend's father."

"Tell me more," she said, smiling, then adding, "Especially the part about getting beaten."

"Figures," he said, laughing. "One time me, Humper and Bean Head went to the forest preserves," he began. "It was over Christmas vacation from grammar school. We were bored and looking for something to do. You know, like the old movie, *Marty*."

"Is this going to be another one of your long, drawn out stories about the sociopathic behavior of you and your friends?"

"We were not juvenile delinquents," he said, giving a flip of his right hand as if shooing away an annoying insect. "It was a mild day for the end of December, and almost all of the snow we had at Christmas had melted away," said Tidge, sounding like he was narrating a saga. "We had taken the Belmont bus to the end of the line at Cumberland and were hiking the bridal path that paralleled the Des Plaines River and joking around," he continued, his hands becoming more animated with his words. "Not wearing orange, I might add." He grinned. "Then Humper spots a couple of horses tied to a tree. The horses had to be from one of the nearby riding stables. There was also what looked like a blanket with a large mound bulging up and moving. Humper goads Bean Head into going over to check out the mound. Humper could make Beanie do anything. Bean Head wasn't very coordinated and kind of waddled like a pregnant penguin. He does his Willy Lump-Lump walk over to the blanket, that turns out to be a canvas tarp and lifts it up. Lo and behold, there's some guy doin' it with his girl."

"Doin' it?" asked Willy, stunned.

"Exactly," said Tidge, the vivid scene of western wear in disarray, cowboy boots kicking in the air, the girl letting out a yell, and not enough available hands to cover way too much exposed flesh. "The guy leaps off her," he continued, "his jeans around the tops of his boots while Bean Head is standing there frozen in place holding the end of the tarp. He had a look on his face as if Sister Mary Benevolence, our eighth grade nun caught him looking out of the corner of his eye at Jumbo Jugs Janice Koester who sat next to him.

"Doin' it," Willy repeated again.

Tidge's head went up and down. "Humper yelled to the startled, but growing real angry guy, 'Hey, how far is the Yule Log Inn?' The guy hesitated long enough from wrestling with his jeans to ponder Humper's statement for directions. Then Humper yelled out two more profound statements. The first was intended to save Bean Head from a sure death. 'Run!' he screamed at Bean Head. Beanie didn't budge. He just stood there like some lawn jockey holding a tarp instead of a lantern and staring at a panic stricken woman trying to pull on her jeans while her bare bottom is bouncing up and down on the damp, soggy grass. Humper's second profound statement made reference to his original question, and he answered it by saying, 'looked like the Yule Log was pretty far in.' At that point, the naked girl gave up on her jeans, grabbed the opposite corner of the tarp and rolled herself up in it. Her lover, his pants now up and his zipper following took a step towards Beanie who still hadn't moved. Suddenly, the guy lets out an agonizing scream. Something like

Kenny Miller would have let out if his girlfriend's father had his way. Actually, there were two screams. The first came from the guy who had gotten his manhood caught in his zipper. That had Humper laughing, his hee-haw cackle really upsetting the guy wrestling with his zipper. The second scream came from Bean Head. 'Ma!' thundered from his lungs almost sending them up through his throat. He dropped the tarp and tried to run. He really did look like a pregnant penguin. Then Beanie trips, goes flying forward out of control and collides with the guy who was trying to free himself from his zipper. The guy falls on the girl and Bean Head on top of both of them. She lets out a yell calling them morons. Only she used one of those bad words you didn't like me using to describe Bambi. I don't know how or where Bean Head became so agile, but he jumps up like a gymnast, looks at the guy and then says something totally out of character. He repeats what the girl had just yelled. I don't know where he got the speed, but he passed me and Humper as if he had been shot out of a circus cannon."

Willy looked at her husband her arms folded across the front of her parka, her skepticism now entrenched. "How would someone your age know what that couple was doing?" she asked.

"Humper was well versed in the human anatomy," said Tidge, his eyes asking, "You do believe me, don't you?"

Willy started walking, Tidge joining her after several paces.

"It's true," Tidge said, after he got alongside of her. "Humper heard the original Yule Log Inn story from listening to his dad and uncles talk during some family get-together." He kicked at a small stone peeking out from under an oak leaf. "Heck, listening in on our elders taught us all kinds of lessons about life, liberty and the pursuit of the female anatomy."

"Chasing after females I can believe," she said, her eyes focused on the shoulder of the road. "Yule Log Inn, I don't think so."

Three weeks later they drove to Chicago in their new pickup truck sporting Wisconsin license plates to spend the Christmas holidays with their families. They arrived early choosing not to give out the date and stayed at her unsold Lake Shore Drive condominium. The condo had been on the real estate market since Willy fell in love with Lake Namakagon. Their trip had been filled with surprises they could do without. After Christmas Eve arguing with his brothers, and a Christmas Day with her parents, they craved Henry's Hut and left ahead of schedule for a quiet New Year's Eve.

Willy said to Tidge as they took the elevator up to the twenty third floor of her building: "I provided the dine once before, and you provided the wine. What are you doing New Year's, New Year Eve?"

As the elevator door opened, Tidge walked out ahead of her, stopped, turned and said: "Providing the wine like last time. Do you think Henry would like to join us?"

Their first New Year's Eve was anything but quiet. It was also their first date. "How 'bout we paint the town red," he had said to Wilhelmina Schneider-Jones in her class room, trying to cover up his gaffe of a New Year's Eve first date. "Heck, I think a bit of the old wine and dine would be nice way to say adios to this year and *witam* to the new one."

She gave him a questioning look.

"Witam," he said. "That's a formal Polish way of saying hello."

The teacher had surprised the parent with her own versions of hello and good-bye. "You bring the wine and I'll provide the dine," she countered from behind her desk as she got ready to leave school for the long Christmas vacation. She sounded as if she expected his invitation. "New Year's Eve is absolutely the worst night of the year to go out," she continued, sounding as if she were an entertainment critic. "Any restaurant, no matter how posh or how many stars it has in its rating is the last place any sane individual would go on New Year's Eve."

He was taken back with her knowledge of restaurants ignoring reservations, having a limited menu, charging obscene prices and waiters and waitresses vaguely attempting not to be surly on the last day of the year. He listened to her explain that her parents always entertained at home to bring in the New Year. Willy's mother, he had quickly learned during courtship, enjoyed the finer things in life. Those finer things were emphasized with manners, appropriate behavior and etiquette. Tidge always thought this was a strange value system for a former lady wrestler and pin-up girl.

Tidge made sure he provided the finer things for Willy's New Year's invitation. Not knowing what Willy drank, or if she even drank, he decided to bring it all. He showed up at her door with a liquor carton containing expensive brand name bottles of bourbon, gin and vodka. He liked a martini, but didn't know if she did. He heard her mention something about her mother drinking Gibsons. Not knowing what a Gibson was, he almost panicked until he discovered that the cause of his distress was a cocktail onion. He included a jar of onions and one of olives and another of maraschino cherries in the carton. A bottle each of Beaujolais, Chardonnay and champagne were also in the carton, the champagne having been chilled by his putting it in an ice filled, cracked Styrofoam cooler in the trunk of his car. All he knew about champagne was that expensive was supposed to be good. Thirty nine ninety nine was what he could afford after depleting his budget on the other liquors and wines. Also packed in the carton were two quarts of tonic, a bottle of Rose's Lime and a small bottle each of dry and sweet vermouth. In his right hand suit coat pocket was a lemon, a lime and even a box of toothpicks. His left hand pocket contained a cork screw. He prided himself on being prepared. He was not.

Willy had learned how to be a cook and a hostess, the hostess part coming from her mother. The cook part came from her father who, as a middle aged man, watched Public Broadcasting cooking shows on Saturday afternoons for his entertainment. Her New Year's Eve dinner would have made her father proud. Tidge had only heard of medallions, reductions, drizzles and foie whatever's. His culinary expertise was beneath minimal. When he and his first wife were dating he ordered escargot to impress her. He almost gagged when he discovered snails sitting in front of him.

Willy's dinner more than eclipsed Tidge eating his daughter's science experiment. After dinner they ventured onto her balcony to sip champagne and watch the New Year's Eve fireworks from downtown. The Windy City's notorious icy wind, known as the

Hawk, moved their champagne sipping back inside. The fireworks continued outside while a surprise sexual crescendo of assorted sky rockets and star bursts took place inside.

The next morning, passions cooled, the alcohol dispersed and a New Year's Day sunlight designed for the wearing of sun glasses, they both sat in silence, sipping coffee and feeling like two naughty children.

Tidge inhaled the steaming vapors of his coffee, swallowed a wave of nausea and realized that his New Year's Eve preparations were inadequate. Whatever they had done saying, "witam", whatever they discovered welcoming in a new year, didn't matter. Tidge, with Willy's help, started moving some of his clothing and personal items out of his garden apartment in Norridge later that afternoon. He never looked back.

Willy felt guilty about cutting short their Christmas trip to Chicago and heading back to her new home in Wisconsin. Mothers crying on Christmas Day can make daughters feel that way. Besides, her mother never cried. Intelligent, sophisticated, former professional lady wrestlers who sloshed down Gibsons were like big boys. Emotion to Gert had once been getting an expression on her face that flashed out mayhem as she was about to enter the wrestling ring. Her flash was accentuated by a series of grunts laced with screams as she bent her opponent into a grotesque anatomical shape that defied basic skeletal configurations. It was her *See 'em Hold* that had brought her notoriety after her earlier modeling years.

Willy was used to seeing her mother drunk, but never saw her cry. She could never understand how she always appeared a walking edition of Emily Post's book on manners while carrying on a dignified and intelligent conversation. But the sophisticated platinum blond hugged her daughter and sobbed when she knew her only child was getting ready to head back north after that first Christmas time in the city. "Your mother misses you," Willy heard her mother say. "I wish you weren't so far away." Willy didn't know how to react. She had never experienced the emotion of being close to her mother. It was her grossmutter who she sought out and clung to when she was a little girl.

The only new experiences for Tidge during that first Christmas trip to Chicago was hearing his sisters-in-law chastising his brothers for their language on Christmas Eve. He also witnessed his three daughters heaping presents and Christmas spirit on Willy. Carol, the youngest, had always adored Willy and considered herself the maven of matchmakers. Carm, his middle daughter, who had accepted Willy in the beginning with a chilled, polite demeanor, had joined her younger sister, doting over her. Martha had mellowed after her verbal lambasting of her father and Willy at their wedding reception. She now picked up her middle sister's original feelings. She was friendly, but acted as if guilt was trying to work its way out of her.

The ultimate experience interrupted their early departure for Cable. Willy's realtor phoned the morning they were leaving informing her that she had three prospective buyers for the condo. They were a whirl of arms and blur of legs putting her once-prized cocoon into mint condition before the telephone connection had been terminated. Three prospects came and looked. Three prospects made their bids. The condo had been sold that evening before Tidge and Willy realized what happened.

Christ's presence that Christmas was as frequent as angels' appearances and rarer than the sighting of Wisconsin's state animal, the Badger, much to the disappointment of the deceased Mother Mary May I. The second Christmas, however, with just the two of them, had Mother Mary May I blushing from her place in Heaven. All of Heaven blushed after Willy kissed Santa Claus underneath the mistletoe that Tidge had hung from one of the giant, polished cross beams running across the ceiling of their Great Room. Tidge would never forget Willy's impersonation of Eartha Kitt's, *Santa Baby*.

"Not bad for a preppie white chick," he said after, feeling a euphoric exhaustion that only true lovers knew.

"Did you mind my wearing my *CFMP's* to bed?" she asked, snuggled next to him.

He gave her a curious look and repeated, "CFMP's?"

"Come Fulfill Me Pumps," she replied with a teasing smile. Then she told him that fulfill was a substitute word she felt more comfortable with even though the actress Joan Crawford had allegedly used another *F* word in a book about her life.

Tidge almost choked. "Your pumps are definitely that," he said, a relaxed smile warming his face. "I can't believe an old movie star would use, according to you, such a naughty word to describe her shoes." He looked at the outline of his wife under the sheet, her legs exposed from the knees down, a pair of black, patent leather high heels sticking out and asked, "Did Joan Crawford really say she was putting on her *CFMP's* when she was in the mood for some physiological gratification?"

Willy's answer was her snuggling closer to him and whispering in his ear, "That's what I remember reading."

"Don't get nervous if I start drooling like Kenny Miller the next time you wear those alphabet shoes of yours in my presence," he said.

Now, as they continued their routine of trudging through the woods, he found himself shouting, "Watch it!" A tree limb had brushed off his old leather flight jacket and was rushing for her face.

Willy, the experienced hiker, had anticipated the branch, caught it and then guided it back to where it came. Millions of enemies lurked in the woods. She also learned that those enemies could be her friends. She was surprised at how she adapted to the woods, learning the types of trees, the ground cover, and what to touch and what not to. She even joined a local Mushroom Club, *The Fungi Finders*, taking walks without her husband with a group of year round residents. They always culminated their trek with a stop at a nearby coffee shop, restaurant or country tavern, as long as there was a daily special. She took pride at not being classified as a *Snow Bird*, those seasonal residents who would vacate Bayfield County for warmer climates when the north winds could blow snow through a snowmobile suit into one's underwear.

Tidge often went into the woods without Willy, his photographer's eye in search of the unique, the composition, the one of a kind. But, most times, they walked together doing more than talk, their other senses joining in to help them embrace what realtors call the three most important aspects of buying a home: Location,

location and location.

They blended in, they thought, quite well with their new environment. Neither became complacent or bored with what greeted them each day. Not many people could wipe the sleep from their eyes and then admire the beauty of an eagle riding the air currents high above their end of the lake.

Willy had developed more of a respect for nature than her husband. She always stepped around or over, returning, replacing, or repairing what might have been disturbed. Tidge, on the other hand, seldom practiced what he once preached to his wife when they first moved north. Most times he was the proverbial bull in the china shop. When he went into the woods, branches snapped, tree limbs popped, and what had gone undisturbed for decades in the decaying process was trampled or kicked out of the way. He saw himself as a trail blazer, Tomasz Ignacy Jozef Mackiewicz, The Polish Daniel Boone of the Northwoods.

Walking with Willy meant they would head out in one direction from Point A, their house, with him leading the way. After one half to three quarters of an hour heading for Point B, that in either an east or west direction, Tidge the Trail Blazer would turn them around and head back to Point A. Point B's varied the only restrictions put on their direction came from the meandering shore line of Lake Namakagon.

Points on the compass didn't limit their topics of conversation, neither had the presence of assorted skeletons rattling in their respective closets. They were two open books. When they talked nothing was sacred. Not family, friends, or one's faith in a Supreme Being. The *Three F's* Tidge called them. According to him, Santa Claus was the exception to the sacred rule, having been elevated to a position a fraction of an inch below the Almighty, but never on the same level. Mother Mary May I, he knew, would have none of God the Father, God the Son, and God the Holy Spirit being given second class citizen status to some saint dressed up in a gaudy red suit. Experiencing her drunken brother-in-law wearing a soiled and tattered Santa Claus suit he brought back from Korea when he was a Navy pilot was not Mother Mary May I's idea of keeping Christ in Christmas. Neither was hearing her husband and brother-in-law arguing and almost coming to drunken blows every Christmas Eve. Jolly fat men dressed in red soured her. The Infant Jesus away in the manger didn't.

Mother Mary May I heard her brother-in-law unearth the memories of Korea only once. That was enough. Her mind had painted a gruesome scene of a baby faced first class petty officer attempting to rescue a frightened young, bruised and slightly wounded Lieutenant Junior Grade Bruce Mackiewicz who had been shot down. Her mental canvas had captured the splattered, grotesque colors of slaughter. She could see the sad picture of her brother-in-law sitting at the bunk side of his rescuer in the USS Princeton's Sick Bay watching a hero die. Mother Mary May I was both sympathetic and empathetic toward her brother-in-law. She thought she knew what he had gone through. She didn't. She tried to understand. She couldn't. All she heard were sentences filled with *gunning down Chink fuckers, bombing Commie sumbitches* and *blowin' the shit out of dem slant eyed pricks.* Her soul cringed. When her brother-in-law wished out loud to his brother, Iggy, her husband, *I wish I could've killed more of those Russian backed dirty Chink fuckers* the conversation became too much for Mary Rose Callahan Mackiewicz. Listening to nightmares of the wholesale killing of human beings, for whatever reasons, was something she couldn't tolerate, especially at Christmas. The Commandment stated that thou should not kill and Mother Mary May I was a staunch believer in all Ten, and even some extra ones she thought should have been included with the originals. Her heart had gone out to the family of the young sailor who died saving her brother-in-law. Nicholas she remembered him being called. She felt even worse knowing that two lives from the same family had been lost over a leather aviator's jacket and a Santa Claus suit. Those had to be the most traumatic, Hell-filled moments children of God had to endure.

Traumatic moments experiencing Hell weren't restricted to men in combat as Tidge could attest. His trauma came during his childhood and lasted six months, culminating on Christmas morning. His experience signed, sealed, and delivered his unwavering belief in Santa Claus and discovering that his mother's oft used warning about God knowing all was for real.

He had shared his traumatic experience with Willy after surviving what he felt was the insanity of Christmas shopping. They had driven to Lincoln Park for a bowl of French onion soup and a salad bar at R. J. Grunt's after spending what he thought was an agonizing torture Christmas shopping along the Magnificent Mile. It had been her doing, the shopping for her mother and father and trying to pry information from him on what she should buy for his brothers, their wives, and the nieces and nephews on their first Christmas together as husband and wife.

Tidge loved Christmas. He despised Christmas shopping. Willy loved it. He had dutifully followed her like a sad, shaggy dog on a leash, sniffing at every food court, salivating at every food vendor's counter they passed while anticipating a stop for lunch that didn't come. As four o'clock and the evening rush hour neared, Tidge expressed his feelings. "I'm starving," he barked. "I want food. I need food. I want and need it now!"

His last statement drew the attention of other shoppers. They were all women and they all gave him the same look. At that moment, he was convinced that starvation would be the cause of his demise.

Tidge had lost all feelings of a jolly season. His hunger pangs were exacerbated by crowds. Stores were crowded. Sidewalks were crowded. Cars wanted to run him over. Riding in his car with Willy was like crawling on his hands and knees. Chicago's rush hour traffic didn't budge. His salvation, after an hour of crawling, was valet parking. His neck ached from too many tugs on his leash and following his wife into yet another store that looked the same as the one they just left. His patience teetered on empty and he knew he had set a record for the number of store aisles walked during a given day. He wasn't close.

Willy kept asking him what he thought his brothers might like for Christmas. "How should I know," he had said to her, his reply void of enthusiasm as he watched her scrutinize gloves and scarves beneath a lighted counter in one of the chic Water Tower shops on Michigan Avenue. "Since my mom and dad died, the last time I saw them was at our wedding."

Her head moved closer to a glass case and then pulled back as if she were adjusting a microscope in a science laboratory for a better view. "Heavens, for someone who still believes in the spirit of the season, you certainly have your ugly Charles Dickens moments."

Tidge shrugged and said, "Just like my brothers have their pick-a-part-Tidge-the-despised-patriarch moments." He saw her wrinkle her nose and knew that they would be moving along to the next section of lighted counters. "By the way, I know that teachers don't like being corrected, but it's not the spirit of the season."

She straightened up from where her face had been pressed within inches of the glass counter top and looked at him. "Well, then, what would you call it?"

"It's the Christmas season," he said, making his correction then punctuating in with an emphatic, "Peace on earth and goodwill toward men."

"That's what I alluded to," she said, defending her choice of words.

"Then so state," he said, annoyed with generic holiday greetings. "Leave that season garbage for the bleeding heart nit-wits who want to make the world one big, legal happy family." He ignored her head going slowly from side to side as his hands went behind his back where he squeezed them in a near death grip. "My Uncle Brew didn't get his butt shot at by a bunch of nutty Chinese commies in Korea so his beloved Christmas could be desecrated by big business, spineless politicians and talking heads on TV controlled by money." He looked at Willy the way his Uncle Brew once looked at him when he told him the story behind the aviator's jacket. "Non-believers use expressions like you just used, stuff about happy holidays and season's greetings." He gently rapped his knuckles on top of the glass counter top. "Listen carefully. The holiday is called Christmas. It's named after one of the most famous men, if not the most famous, in the history of man."

"Oh." She held back the urge to carve him to pieces with words. "What about Hanukkah or Kwanza? What about people who aren't Christians?"

"Ah ha," he said, appearing as if he had just beaten his boyhood friend, Humper in a yo-yo contest, his rock the cradle two rocks better. "You teachers only think you know it all." His arms were folded across his chest and he made sure his smirk was exaggerated.

"Kwanza doesn't have a thing to do with Christmas." He paused, gloating, loving the way he felt. "It's a time to reflect on and pay tribute to family among other things."

"Isn't family important to you?"

He let out a sigh.

A smile joined the wrinkle on her nose.

"And I'm well aware there isn't a baby Jesus during Hanukkah." he said, surprised at how calm he was. "And there's no Santa Claus either."

She looked at him as if she were lecturing to one of her students who needed lecturing. "They have their holidays, their holy days, I might add, and they should be respected and included when saying, happy holidays."

"Do their holidays have names?" he asked, digging in for a war of words. He didn't give her time to answer. "Do the politically correct, bleeding heart nit-wits tell them to sterilize their holiday names so they don't offend others who might not believe? Do they conform? Do they give up their beliefs?"

"For someone who claims to read philosophy and have minored in it in college, you are the most illogical person I know," she said, her eyes returning to scrutinizing the contents under another glass display case.

"Illogical," he repeated. "I, my darling, am the consummate logician." He waited for a reaction from her, but got her moving to another counter instead. He followed her. "Are you aware that learned philosophers refer to me as Syllogism the Superb? Syl for short."

Willy kept examining potential gift purchases, never looking up. Her only reaction was to take her right hand, raise it up to shoulder level and rotate her index finger in slow, tiny circles.

"Mock me," he said. "See if I care."

Her finger continued in its circular pattern.

"At least I believe." His voice was loud enough to be heard for several aisles around them. "I, Syl, nee, Syllogism the Superb, the omniscient and omnipotent, have the courage and conviction to speak up and defend what is right, what is respectful and to give reverence where reverence is do. I'm not some advertising agency greedy lackey selling his soul for the almighty buck by keeping Christ buried until December twenty fifth and then giving society the okay to say, 'Merry Christmas'."

"I'm impressed," she said, still not looking at him and moving on to the next counter. Before he could reply, she looked up at him and said, "I'm so lucky to be in the company of Loco Logician the Bilingual Loon," she said, her eye brows inching up. "Is this your first holiday season furlough away from the funny farm in Warsaw?" Her nose wrinkled. "What's the word for loon in your native tongue?"

He didn't have an answer. "I can accept holiday season," he said, sounding almost ashamed. "Just don't legislate it and ram it down my throat." Then in a whisper he said: "One time I almost gave up believing in everything." He gave her a sheepish look. "I even gave up on Santa Claus."

His statement caused her to suspend her shopping, her lips pursed, eye brows on the rise again. "You mean you doubted the existence of your hero, idol and role model?" she asked. "How could you question Santa's existence after seeing lighted plastic replicas of jolly Saint Nick standing in front yards throughout Chicago?" she asked, her attention returning to the counter's treasures. "You didn't have to be a looney logician to surmise that Mr. Plastic Santa and Mrs. Plastic Santa resided at the North Pole with plastic elves and plastic reindeers."

"Very funny ha-ha," he said, his exhale causing a rack of gold chains displayed on a counter across the aisle from them to rustle like wind chimes.

"I thought so," she said, as she moved down the glass counter top. "A plastic Santa is much jollier than your real one, don't you think, Syl? It is, Syl, isn't it?"

"Mock away, Sugar Brown Eyes," he said, finding himself way too serious. Santa wasn't plastic when he wore my jacket. He wasn't plastic when he brought me my Red Ryder BB Gun when I was a kid," he said, primed to do battle with the love of his life.

Willy straightened up as if she had popped out of a jack-in-the-box. "I hope that you're not going to tell me about how you wanted a BB gun for Christmas and your mother told you, no because you could shoot your eye out."

His head made a slow reluctant trip from side to side, his hands pressed deep into the aviator's jacket pockets. "I've seen the movie too. It's one of my favorites." There was no trace of humor evident in his words or demeanor. "And, besides, my name's not Ralphy."

Her head jerked as if she had a spasm. A sound resembling a subdued groan came from her as she turned her attention back to the attractive displays beneath the glass counter.

"Groan all you want, Miss Skeptic from the planet Skeptonia, a satellite of Uranus," he said, surprised that she didn't look up. "Santa did come to me back then. I think he was checking out the courage of my convictions, testing me, seeing if I really believed."

Tidge could still see the advertisement on the back page of an old comic book he had saved. Every word was in bold black supporting the sequence of colorful boxes with his illustrated heroes Red Ryder and Little Beaver. All he had to do, according to Red Ryder and his smiling Indian companion, was sell flower and vegetable seeds. "Sell my seeds and I'll send you a genuine copy of my lever action carbine, pronto," said Red, a toothy grin indicating that he was serious. "It's easy."

Tidge knew he could sell the seeds. If Red Ryder guaranteed it would be easy, then it would be easy. "I can sell those in a snap," he said to himself, as he took the small scissors from his school pencil box and clipped the coupon from the back page. He printed his name and address, pressing extra hard on his pencil while muttering to himself. "The seeds are a lousy ten cents a pack. I'll sell those easy as pie." He found an envelope and stamp, walked down to the corner mail box and watched his dream disappear into the slot that clanged shut. He went home and waited. When the seeds came he told his mother he had a job because he wanted to earn some money. He neglected to tell her that the money was in the form of an air rifle. Off he went, hundreds of packages of seeds stuffed into his pockets and a paper lunch bag. He pushed every door bell on every house in a six block radius of his own home. His efforts the first day brought in a dollar and forty cents and a realization that BB guns did not come easy, especially Red Ryder, lever action BB guns. Undaunted, he moved on fearing that the tip of his right index finger would be worn down past the second knuckle. The right index finger was, as all Red

Ryder BB gun aficionados knew, the trigger finger. He pushed on, believing he could sell all of the packages. Doorbell buttons were pushed until he thought he could distinguish round buttons with buzzers from rectangular buttons and the sound of chimes. His knuckles rapping on doors brought either silence or threats of bodily harm. Persistence paid off and he was down to his last ten seed packets. Then his market dried up. July had ended and he was running out of August. No one in Chicago wanted to buy seeds when a growing season was almost over. No one, that is, except his mother.

He had told her his plan, the whole plan and nothing but the plan, so help him God. Mother Mary May I listened nodded and went to the kitchen cabinet above the sink where she kept her series of chipped coffee and tea cups lined up. Each cup held her designated budgeted amounts of coins and currency, most for the month, a few for future dreams.

"If you'd like," she said, very characteristic May I, "I'll buy some of your seeds." She gave him a dollar for the last ten packets. He, in turn, gave her all of his earnings. The next day she presented him with a money order and he sent it off with the proper documentation and waited.

Tidge waited and waited and waited. No Red Ryder BB gun came. He told his mother and she, in turn, told him to be patient. And patient he stayed. September went by. No Red Ryder BB gun. October soon vanished and Red Ryder hadn't been seen or heard from. He couldn't conceal the heaviness he felt pressing down on him. "Don't stop believing," Mother Mary May I said to him, while kneading the back of his shoulders for a moment, driving away his end-of-the-world tension. The vision of his believing was slowly disappearing over the horizon along with November.

Tidge told Humper and Bean Head about what happened. Bean Head's too small eyes peeked out from the sockets of his too big head and he said, "God, Mackiewicz, you sure are a dumb shit." Humper put a different spin on Tidge's situation, his remarks preceding what Tidge's father would end up telling him a number of years down the road. "Man, you must've really had your head up your ass when you sent in that money. Red Ryder and Little Beaver took your dough and blew it on themselves."

That was the only time his buddy and next door neighbor, Humper, had been critical of him. When Tidge's future bride, Sissy, said she didn't want Humper as best man or any other role at their wedding because, as she put it, "I don't want some imbecile who looks like Alfred E. Neuman ruining my special day," Tidge defended his friend and choice for best man. His defense lasted about as long as it took Sissy to stick her right index finger a fraction from his nose. "I don't want that stupid Polack near my wedding, period." She glared at him. "Make your choice. Him or me?"

"But, I'm Polish," he said to her, not comprehending then trying to explain to her that this was his wedding as well and that Stanislaus Thaddeus, William, his Confirmation name, Biganski was his best friend and had been since kindergarten. She didn't care.

Humper wasn't critical. He might have been had he known that Sissy didn't want him, as she put it, at or even within a mile, of her wedding reception. Tidge never told Humper about Sissy's anger when she saw Humper show up at the wedding reception. She was under the impression he hadn't been invited. The only thing that saved Humper from Sissy's wrath was that he was carrying an elegant store wrapped wedding present from C. D. Peacock's, the exclusive jewelry store. Sissy had sighed and reluctantly said, "Okay, the dumb Polack can stay. Just be sure you sit him back in the corner with your idiot brothers."

When Tidge told his best friend about his affair with Barbara Ann Lindstrom, Humper wasn't critical saying only, "Are you sure you're not letting the little head control the big head?" Even when Tidge got divorced, Humper listened and picked up their bar tab that night at the Sunset Inn. He had limited himself to the first three letters of the alphabet in describing how he felt about his friend's ex-wife.

Tidge never let go of his dream of owning a Red Ryder BB gun. He did, however, vow never to sell another package of flower or vegetable seeds or to believe in another comic book advertisement again. Tidge never stopped believing. His Uncle Brew had told him to write a letter to Santa Claus asking for the air rifle. His Uncle Brew always told Tidge and his brothers to believe. Each year he would have each of the four boys write a letter to Santa Claus. They wrote their letters giving them to their mother who would wait for the rare moment when her brother-in-law was sober before turning them over to him. Santa always delivered, in person. Why Santa made a personal appearance to their house on Christmas Eve and not their friends didn't matter. Santa had what they asked for in their letters.

The Christmas Eve of the BB gun was the only time Tidge doubted that there was a Santa Claus. He never completely lost hope, his believing a flicker, but he came close. Even on Christmas morning, in his pajamas, sleep still cemented to his eye lids, he almost went head first down the stairs, stumbling, breaking his fall and ending up in the living room on his hands and knees.

Presents were stacked under and around the tree as if they were on display in the Goldblatt's Department Store windows along Belmont Avenue just west of Central. He knew the size and shape of the package he wanted, but there was no package that size and shape. Had Santa failed him? Was his friend, Humper, right about where his head was at? His world was on the brink of collapse when he saw it. Peeking at him from under the tree, buried beneath several packages, was his dream. He only saw the butt end of the Red Ryder BB gun stock, but that was enough. His BB gun wasn't even wrapped. There was no display of a ceremonial ribbon. Red Ryder didn't even send him an apology for making him wait so long. Little Beaver didn't even attach a note telling him to be a straight shooter. He didn't care. Santa had come through and he would never doubt his existence again.

Tidge's mother had intercepted the seed company's delivery to their house two weeks after the mail had gone out. Like all mothers, she did fear he would shoot his eye out or, even worse, the eye of one of his younger brothers, maybe all three. Mother Mary May I wasn't one to take chances. She stashed the BB gun under her side of the mattress in her bedroom.

"That's how I got my Red Ryder BB gun," he said to Willy, who had long since given up on the contents under the counter for the contents of his story.

"And, the little boy who I married is still believing," she said, as a tinge of emotion brought a moist film over her eyes.

"A little boy is to believing as Santa Claus is to living," he said, his hands worming their way into the leather jacket's tattered pockets. "That's according to your looney logician and his theory of believing in a Mister Claus," he continued, as his cautious fingers were careful not to poke holes in the fragile material that had experienced two men dying and a near miss with Santa Claus.

Tidge's Uncle Brew had believed. Tidge discovered that fact at a way too early age. He had accompanied his father who wanted to stop and visit his brother, Tidge's Uncle Bruce. His father went into the drab, dark brown brick two-flat and Tidge stayed outside to play. Boredom, not seeing any other kids and a feeling that he was being grabbed by the hand and led to the front door, had him inside. He tip-toed up the long flight of stairs to the second floor until he found himself sitting on the thread bare carpet in the hall leading to the kitchen, his knees tucked under his chin. He listened until he felt pins and needles attack his behind. Antsy, he was ready to head back outside and play. Then he realized something wasn't right. His dad and uncle weren't arguing. There was no swearing. The sensation that led him inside pushed down on his shoulders and kept him seated. His arms tightened around his knees and he pulled them tighter to his chin again. He listened without breathing.

Tidge knew his uncle had been in the Navy. He saw the framed picture of him in his uniform that Aunt Bessie kept on the mantle of the false fireplace in their apartment. Tidge never paid attention to the gold wings on his uncle's uniform until he discovered that his uncle had been a pilot who took off and landed planes on aircraft carriers. His attention rocketed when he learned that his uncle had been shot down on a mission over Korea after firing rockets from his Panther jet at the enemy. His uncle always stayed mum about his combat experiences when he was around others, telling only his older brother, Iggy, Tidge's dad, pieces and fragments.

Tidge could tell by the conversation going on at the kitchen table that shots of *wodka* and cans of beer were involved. That was always the case when his dad and uncle talked at the kitchen table. Tidge heard a mention of a *May Day* and not being able to get back to the *Princeton*. There was a description of a crash landing, a plane sliding, skipping and bouncing until the nose buried itself in a drainage ditch filled with *human excrement. Honest, Iggy they used gówno for fertilizer.* Then different kinds of shots were mentioned. They were shots fired at his uncle by whoever those *Commie Chink Fuckers* were with whatever *Burp Guns* were. There were lots of shots. His uncle had fired shots back from his own *Burp Gun* he taken from the severed hand of a *Chink Fucker* his plane had crushed. Shots were fired back and forth, lots of shots from lots of *Burp Guns.* One of the shots had hit his uncle, a glancing slice across his right hip. The *Princeton* was mentioned again, but now his uncle kept referring to the ship as *She.* A helicopter, *Angel* he heard it called, came to rescue his uncle. By then, a horde of those *Commie Chink Fuckers in quilted uniforms were charging at his uncle. There were bugles blaring and Burp Guns spraying bullets everywhere.* His uncle had picked up another *Burp Gun. My plane must've slammed into a bunch of those crazy bastards, Iggy. Parts of them were everywhere covering the ground like ants. I don't know how many got crushed and tore apart when I crash landed. There were arms and legs, even heads scattered all over the place. I saw one of those commie bastard's arms sticking out from under the aft part of the fuselage. It was attached to the damned tail hook. He still held his Burp Gun.*

Tidge listened to how his uncle had sprayed bullets back, emptying the gun in seconds. About that time, two Panther jets from the Princeton came in low strafing everything that moved. His uncle had picked up two more Burp Guns as the Angel maneuvered its way in to the bloody arena to save his uncle. The Panthers made a second pass, pock marking the earth with machine gun fire and sending quilted body parts every which way. Then the Angel set down near and behind his uncle's crashed plane. Impatient rotors beat at the air as a side door slid open and a crew man jumped out. *The kid had on a Mae West covering this beat up brown leather jacket. Iggy, I remember it like it was this morning. Baby faced son of a bitch stood out like a sore thumb and didn't get a half dozen steps towards me before that yellow life jacket ended up sporting a couple of punctures. The impact of those bullets sent the kid flying back. I saw red form around those punctures, Iggy. Blood, Iggy. The kid's blood.*

More Burp Guns blazed as Tidge, fighting the urge to urinate, continued to listen. He heard his Uncle Bruce stammer on, telling his father what a young, but getting older way too fast, Lieutenant Junior

Grade Bruce Stanley Mackiewicz had experienced. *The kid was still alive when I got to him. I emptied another damned gun in the direction those Fuckers were coming. They were like damned fanatics hell bent on filling me full of holes as well. Thank god for the Panthers. They blew the livin' shit out of those commie bastards. That's when I had a chance to grab the collar of the kid's Mae West and haul him to the helicopter. I don't remember much after that except catching a glimpse of a couple of our prop driven fighter planes following our Panthers and firing rockets into those pricks. Our guys did a number on those bastards. I still don't know who we were fighting, Iggy. It was supposed to have been the North Koreans, but the Chinese and the fuckin' Russians were also shootin' at us. Whoever we were fighting over there around the 38th Parallel a young kid paid for it.*

A petrified but comprehending Tidge listened to how the Angel hugged a hilly terrain leaving behind the devastation before seeking the heavens and, eventually, the deck of the Princeton. He heard about *She's* sick bay. There were words that mentioned valor, Purple Heart and the Navy Cross. He also heard two beer cans being opened. Then there was the mention of Santa Claus. What did Santa Claus have to do with chopped off arms and heads, shooting, blood, explosions and rockets he thought? He wanted to creep closer, but didn't dare. If his father knew he was eavesdropping, he'd be experiencing devastation of a different kind at the hands of his father. He had only moved his head a fraction of an inch when he saw his uncle looking at him.

"Actually," Tidge had said to Willy when relating the story, "I only saw his right index finger summoning me."

To Tidge's surprise his uncle took him to the kitchen table, pulled over one of the chairs with the scratched chrome legs and nodded for him to sit down.

"He even gave me a sip of beer," he said to her. "My father, however, never said a word. He seemed to ignore me."

So help me, Iggy that shot up kid asked me if I believed in Santa Claus. Here he is in a bunk in Sick Bay fighting for his life, and he's asking me if I believe in Saint Nick.

Tidge watched his father sip his beer, an admiration in his stern eyes he had never seen before. *Hell, yeah, I said to the kid. Why wouldn't I? Any man who believes in Santa Claus believes that all of this shootin' and killin' has got to stop so we can have peace on this earth of ours. The kid's eyes kept fluttering like sometimes he was there and sometimes he wasn't, and he had this ashen grey color to him. There was plasma and more stuff dripping into him from so many tubes I didn't know the human body had that many veins. He was barely able to nod at his belongings stacked next to the bunk and he told me to take it. I didn't know what I should take, so I picked up the leather jacket. It wasn't Navy issue. I knew that. It was World War II Air Force. They called themselves the Air Corps back then. The jacket was beat up, slightly charred across the chest, and it had an insignia sewn above one of the breast pockets. It was of some pin-up girl wearing a Santa Claus hat. I saw traces of what looked like old dried blood on it and a couple of jagged slits going through both of those breast pockets. The kid's blood was also there.*

Tidge watched his uncle reach for the bottle of vodka that was sitting in the middle of the chipped, silver streaked Formica table top and refill two shot glasses. He held the bottle under Tidge's nose, his face asking, laughing as his nephew made a face. Uncle Brew and the Kid nodded at each other and the glasses were empty.

Iggy, the kid told me that the jagged slits in his jacket were from shrapnel. Muttered something about an older brother, a Captain, last name of Claus, same last name as his, getting killed by the Krauts. For a minute I thought the kid was pulling my leg. Then he told me how a Chaplain had sent him the jacket and a beat up, blood stained Santa Claus suit. I really got shook when I figured out that a kid brother of a dead Air Corps hero had saved me. The kid then told me his brother had worn the Santa suit on a bombing mission over Germany on Christmas Eve, the day he was killed. Then he went into unconsciousness. I sat there like I was made of stone.

Tidge saw his uncle reach for the bottle again and his father's hand seem to float over the two shot glasses covering them up. He could see that the look on his father's face kept going from awe to confused compassion. There was a sad film over his father's eyes that made Tidge nervous. It was a look he had never experienced before.

When the kid comes to again, he's trying to tell me about his older brother. His brother was married, had a kid, same age as your Tommy back then. Hell, Iggy, he was fighting to stay alive long enough to let me know how important that damned jacket was. The Hospital Corpsman was trying to get him to take it easy, but the kid was on another mission.

Tidge sat glued to the silver colored vinyl covered kitchen chair with a slight tear on the back listening about someone's older brother who flew a B-25 bomber during World War II. Tidge knew about the B-25 bomber. He had seen *Thirty Seconds Over Tokyo* on television with a parade of other old war movies. He had devoured pictures of the Mitchell bomber from just as many books to formulate an understanding of heroes and heroics from generations that preceded him. War, death and dying were harder concepts to grasp.

The kid tells me that his older brother volunteered for another mission after he had completed his required twenty five. Can you belief that? He could have gone home to his wife and kid. War's over for him. Kiss Europe, Lilly from Piccadilly and the Krauts bye-bye. Instead, off he goes into the wild blue yonder to have a German fighter plane damn near tear off the nose off his plane with machine gun fire. Then the ack-ack came. How's that for a Merry Christmas? Tore holes in the B-25. Chunks of that ack-ack hit the brother, two pieces going into his chest and another chunk shredding his foot. His navigator somehow crawled on his belly and lay alongside the kid's brother, making a tourniquet from his white scarf and managing to keep the foot intact. The kid's gutsy brother brought what remained of the plane and his crew home safe to an RAF base in England.

Tidge watched an unsteady hand pick up the bottle, another unsteady hand slide one of the shot glasses into the open and pour a shot. The unsteady hand with the shot glass lifted it and the vodka disappeared in an instant. His father's hand still rested over the top of his own glass in such a manner that wasn't insulting to his brother.

The kid who came to save me related a story about his brother making the Chaplain, who was giving him the Last Rites, promise to be sure his kid brother got his jacket and the Santa Claus suit he had been wearing. There was silence at the table as two beer cans found their way to mouths and then were set back on the table without a sound. *Get this, Ignacy, the older brother's fading fast and he tells the Chaplin to pray for him. He tells the Padre to say a prayer to Santa Claus to remind him to bring a gift of peace to a world gone crazy. Then he wished the priest a Merry Christmas and to please pray for his kid brother, Nicholas was his name. He was from a little town in Missouri. Mexico I think it was called.* Another shot of vodka was swallowed up by his uncle as a respectful silence settled over the kitchen. *That's how I came to get this beat up old jacket, Iggy.*

Two brave kids dying for this and that damned Santa Claus suit that carves a piece of my heart and soul out every time I wear it.

Tidge could never forget seeing the tears streaming down his uncle's cheeks and the sounds of his sobs coated with sorrow and pleas for peace. He remembered how his father made no effort to do or say anything, his hand still resting on top of the shot glass.

This jacket means more to me than all of the money in the world. I'm humbled and honored to be wearing what two brave young kids wore when they died for their country.

Tidge heard his father tell his uncle that he too was a brave man, doing what he did and how he did it. He watched as his uncle kept crying, feeling he too should be crying, but then he saw his father's eyes and knew that others' tears at the table weren't necessary. There was a feeling of helplessness that engulfed him, making him feel only the way a young child can feel when seeing someone else, an adult, his uncle suffer.

I know there's going to be a time, Iggy, when I'm going to have to part with this old leather rag I wear. I've thought about it a lot lately and I've got a pretty good idea who I'll pass it on to.

Tidge never forgot that afternoon at his late Aunt Bessie's kitchen table with Uncle Brew and the Kid, discovering that Santa Claus had been his uncle. He didn't believe it at first, his mind concocting one of the first of his many logical problem solving solutions to what life both offered and, way too often, dumped in his lap. Tidge had figured that if Santa Claus was old, older than his mother, father, aunt and uncle combined, then his uncle had somehow been selected to carry on Santa's good works. It made sense, just as it now made sense to him to tell the girl of his dreams about his jacket.

Tidge watched Willy turn away and return to her shopping for their first Christmas together with both of their families. He couldn't have been happier. Fortunes, he knew, came wrapped in different packages. He had two fortunes. One fortune did her Christmas shopping in front of him and he was wearing the other. Now, for the first time, Tidge thought about his uncle's words from so many years ago and he began to realize who he would pass the jacket along to when the time was right for him.

The gift wrapping process for Tidge always consisted of too much cellophane tape, paper cut too short, too long, wrinkled and spliced or in some combinations reflecting disarray. His attempt at ribbons and bows followed along with what he did to paper. His efforts made his presents look like they had gone over the river and through the woods being drug behind the sleigh for miles before arriving at grandma's house, grandma having been run over by a reindeer along with his gifts. Kind of like his past. That realization unearthed a long buried part of his life as he made a return trip to the salad bar at R. J. Grunt's.

In between deciding whether beets and cottage cheese would win out over coleslaw and potato salad topped with a spoon of garbanzo beans, Tidge saw a major portion of his past adult life looking up at him. He also saw a black cardboard sign covered in mold, two large letters painted in blood: *BW*. He didn't need his Uncle Brew telling him to write a letter to Santa Claus for the initial's meaning. It was obvious, *Before Willy*.

Sitting back down at their table for two against the wall, his salad plate on the brink of spilling over from too many selections, he said to Willy: "Thanks."

"You're welcome," she said, no question from her as to why she was being thanked. Her warm eyes teased, almost seducing him.

"I'm not thanking you for leading me around like a dog on a leash today," he said, poking carefully at the salad items about to spill off his plate with his index finger, scooping them on the pile and not concerned with mixing the selections. "I hate Christmas shopping," he continued.

Her brown eyes twinkled at him while the tip of her tongue made a teasing journey across the tines of her fork. "My women's intuition is telling me I'm being thanked for feeding you and getting you another step closer to home and our bedroom."

He licked his index finger, wiped it on his napkin, picked up his fork and said:

"You know, we had names for girls like you when I was in the eighth grade."

Her eyes continued to tease. "Really," she said, her napkin finding the corners of her mouth.

Tidge picked up his fork and shoveled a mound of his mixed salad selection into his mouth. His left cheek puffed out. "Actually, we didn't use a name," he said, filtering his words through the puff. He waited for a moment to get her reaction. Her tongue tracing her lower lip was all he got. "We used initials."

She continued playing her coquette game while placing her fork and knife at a perfect twelve to four position across her plate. "What initials were those?" she asked.

He told her, taking time to elaborate on each of the initials, P and T.

Her coy demeanor continued as she folded her hands in front of her resting them on the table. "How many of those two initial girls did you know back in the eighth grade?" she asked, her eyes shifting easily into overdrive, "and, in high school? Oh, and in the Navy, and college and," she pointed at herself, "Before little ol' me?"

"I can't remember," he said, telling a white lie. "Marietta Claus wasn't one. Neither was Janice Koester. At least I don't think she was one of those two initial girls. Humper would've never married her. What I do know is that there's this girl I really worship and adore who thrives on the alphabet. She's especially fond of, almost a slave to, two initials."

A soft, inquisitive, "Oh," came from Willy.

"The letter, O isn't one of them," he said, his fork stabbing at his salad. "I'd put her on a pedestal if she didn't insist on being called, PC."

"Lucky me," she said, each word still dripping with her brand of tease. Her tongue returned to making another slow circuit of her lips which had been formed into a pouting, seductive oval.

"Definitely lucky you" he said, going on the offensive. "I may have known one or two girls in my lifetime who played the *PT* game, but only one who was politically correct. Anyway, guys don't tease."

Her tongue retreated behind her lips again, her eyes laughing at him. "You mean you never picked on or made fun of your friend Humper?"

"That's not teasing," he snapped back so fast it caught her off guard. "It's friends having fun with friends. Guy friends do that to guy friends. *PT's* ain't friends. That's why they're *PT's*. A true friend can share anything with a true friend. A *PT*, well she just gets her jollies by teasing *P's*. Kind of sick if you ask me," he said, swallowing a lump of salad. "Sounds like it may have been the basis for your feminist movement stuff."

"Oh, spare me," she said, having learned from early on in their relationship not to try to become too logical with him.

"Seriously," he said, another mound of salad mixture finding his mouth, this time being shifted to the right cheek. "One time Humper showed me some dirty books he found in his old man's dresser drawer. They were illustrated joke books with cartoon characters. We called them eight pagers. No teasing then. No questions about why his father had them. We were more interested in when that part of our male anatomy would grow to the size of the characters in the dirty books."

"And did it grow?" she asked, suppressing an urge to laugh.

"Well, I'm not known as Super Stud Syllogism Syl for nothing."

"Oh," she replied, sounding surprised, "when did the Super come in? "Was there something I missed on our honeymoon?"

"I expected that," he said, a deep sigh escaped from him as his fork poked at the diminished mound of salad. "Well, we kept secretly waiting and hoping," he said, covering is mouth with his left hand to suppress a burp. "I even found some pictures in my dad's drawer once."

"Really," she said, startled then becoming curious. "Like what was in those awful men's magazines my mother posed for?"

"I wouldn't call them dirty or awful," he answered. "Not like today's leave-nothing-to-the-imagination garbage. The eight page joke books Humper found in his dad's dresser drawer were definitely dirty." He swallowed a chunk of beet smothered in cottage cheese. "Dirty in a funny way."

She waited for him to continue, but he didn't. Then her curiosity got the better of her. "Tell me about the pictures."

"After Humper's discovery of buried treasure under his dad's underwear, I decided to do my own dresser drawer treasure hunt."

"Find any pieces of eight?'

"Cute," he said, setting down his fork across his salad. "However, I did find this business size manila envelope hidden under some neatly folded undershirts. Of course, inquiring adolescent minds wanted to know, right?"

"So your dad really did have dirty pictures?"

"Well, I can't say that they were dirty," he said, having trouble keeping his voice under control before turning it into a whisper. "They were of my mother."

"Your mother?" she blurted out, her hands hitting her water glass and spilling the contents onto the remainder of Tidge's salad.

He nodded.

"Pictures of your mother?" she whispered, as she blotted up the water spill with her napkin. "In the nude?"

"Yep," he said, his napkin joining hers. His awkward explanation was choppy at best. His father, an assistant foreman on the loading dock of a meat packing plant had few interests and even less money to pursue those interests. Outside of his annual summer vacation to Minocqua and Sven's Resort, Tidge's father enjoyed photography. It had been his passion although he wasn't good at it, and he never had enough money to invest in his hobby. He had a secondhand box camera that needed to be wound after each picture. His prized camera was a Polaroid. That was as close as he ever came to having a dark room. "Most of his pictures," he said to Willy, feeling a burden being taken from him, "had people with their heads cut off. The only way you could recognize anyone was by the shoes they wore." He laughed, glanced down at his water logged salad and made a face. "The Kid splurged once and bought a sixteen millimeter movie camera from a guy at work who sold them out of the trunk of his car. Along with his headless subjects, my father took what seemed like thousands of feet of sixteen millimeter movie film of nothing but the shoreline of Squirrel Lake at Sven's."

"He photographed your mother nude?" asked Willy again, her voice still a whisper, her salad blotting continuing.

His head went up and down. "Photographed Mother Mary May I in the altogether even kept her head on. She was complete and unabridged."

"I don't believe it."

"I didn't either," he continued, a somber tone to his voice that seldom appeared. " I was numb. This was my mother. Mothers don't pose in the nude. Not Mother Mary May I. Heck, me and my brothers didn't believe we were the result of the Kid and May I ever copulating."

"At that age, a parent is all we see," she said, her words filled with compassion. "I'm still trying to admit that my mother strutted around a wrestling ring in a bathing suit attempting to cripple people. I still can't believe that my father made his money promoting magazines that my mother once posed for in lingerie, sprawled out in risqué, seductive, sometimes almost comical poses."

"It boggles my mind that my father popped off flash bulbs in the privacy of their bedroom while us kids were asleep." He paused, still feeling at a loss. "I told Humper. Showed him the pictures my dad had taken. He didn't say anything. We just looked at each other, not quite comprehending."

"How could you show those pictures to anyone else?"

"Humper was my best friend and I didn't know who else to turn to."

"Did those pictures change the way you felt about your parents, especially your mother?"

"Not really," he said each word still serious. "I kind of put the whole thing out of my mind. Didn't think about it again until Mom died and Dad spent every day after that with a blank stare on his face until he just gave up the will to live. I'm now convinced he wanted to join her from the very moment she left him." His eyes closed for a moment. When they reopened the happy blue had turned sad. "Even though the two of them had their share of battles, May I always winning, they couldn't stand to be apart."

"As different as my parents are they can't stand to be apart either. They do everything together. Everything, that is except drink. Dad used to. He was once like my mom, a sophisticated souse. Now he's just sophisticated, has a sip or two of wine during the holidays, works crossword puzzles and watches inane sitcoms. Mom . . ."

"Kills brain cells like my Uncle Brew."

"Such a waste," she said, feeling angry, annoyed and ashamed.

"I seldom saw my Mom take a drink. Sometimes she'd have one at Christmas. But the Kid, well, he was a different story. He'd go out to the neighborhood tavern after supper to, in his words, buy the evening papers. Two hours later he would return, red faced, staggering, and reeking of booze. Me and my brothers used to say that our father was out playing *na zdrowie* with his friends at Harry Dungan's Saloon."

"That's the Polish toast, correct."

He nodded.

"See, I do listen to you," she said with a smile. "Not often. But I do listen."

He laughed. "If you ever heard my father yell, you'd listen." He suddenly turned serious. "One time he didn't yell. I was a sophomore in high school. Thanks to an unfair English composition given to me by Brother James Virgil," he said, smiling, thinking about his favorite teacher. "I was up late and the Kid comes home incredibly loaded from Harry Dungan's. He sits down across from me at the kitchen table where I was trying to write this stupid paper. The smell of booze and cigarette smoke was enough to gag a maggot. Then, for whatever reason, he starts reminding me about how I'm the oldest in the family and if anything happens to him, I'm the one who will have to look out for my mother and brothers. His message was short and sweet. He said something about passing a torch and being a patriarch. Hell, I didn't know what he was talking about. Then he told me to stop acting like a jerk with my friends and start taking life seriously." He paused, smiled and said, "His actual words to me were that I should get my head out of my ass. That was probably his favorite expression." His head went from side to side. "He kept harping about my getting an education so I could get a real job. Not one like his where he was treated no better than the cattle that were slaughtered into steaks for someone's plate."

"Obviously you listened to him."

"Not at first," he said, a shrug tacked on. "Besides, I didn't think I was being a jerk, and I knew my head wasn't stuck up my butt." He continued to be way too serious, his part of the salad plate napkin blotting abandoned. "I didn't believe for an instant that my old man was going to die. Parents don't die on their kids." He could see his father back then and said, "Any man who loved his wife, taking pictures as a hobby and herding his family to the same resort in northern Wisconsin summer after summer isn't a candidate for the grave."

"Was your father a good parent?" she asked, then elaborating on her question. "Even if he went to the corner playground to play Polish *na zdrowie* with his friends?"

"My father was a father," he said, feeling himself get upset again because his father had made him patriarch. "He wasn't my buddy. He wasn't my pal. He was my father. He worked his butt off providing for my mother and us kids and, along with his giving us his version of boxing lessons, that's how he showed his love to us."

She gave a slight nod trying to show him that she understood. "Every now and then I envy you."

"Envy me?" He appeared taken back.

"You have so many friends," she said, the envy evident. "When I was growing up I never had anyone I could talk to. You had your friend, Humper. You had your favorite teacher, Brother James Virgil. You had your family vacations at that resort in Wisconsin. I had Grizelda."

"Who?"

"A doll I made out of an old sock," she said.

"Grizelda?"

"That's the name I gave her," she said, still feeling the warmth she had for the doll with black Crayola eyes and a mouth strategically located because of the hole in her father's sock. "I had the best conversations with her."

"I hope she didn't talk back to you," he said, wanting to tease her, but thinking the better of it.

"She was like your friend, Humper."

"A listener," he said, trying to understand how his wife might have felt as a child. "Humper was a good guy. Still is." He felt a sadness creep through him. "Brother James Virgil's gone, but I don't think I could've talked to him about some of the nightmares that made up my adult life."

"But he was someone you knew who had an ear you could bend." She could feel a lump in her throat. "The time my parents went away two weeks before Christmas on a trip to Germany and were supposed to return Christmas Eve and didn't, I only have my Mitty who was baby-sitting for me."

"Your Mitty?"

"My grossmutter," she said. "That's grandmother in German. She used to sing lullabies to me in German, like Brahms Lullaby." She turned reflective, almost in another world. "I only remember a little. Guten Abend, gute Wacht, Mit Rosen, bedacht. I think that's how it went."

"Geez, in German," he said. "That's cool."

"My father once told me that his mother was born in Switzerland and was Jewish." She paused. "Mitty also sang to me in Yiddish, holding me on her lap, me and Grizelda, and I wouldn't be afraid of a thing." She closed her eyes and thought about that Christmas of being alone so long ago. Even to this day I wonder if she knew how I felt."

"She knew," he said, a warm smile attached to his reassurance. "Humper, well, he might not have known how you felt, and I don't think he would've sung any lullabies to you in his native Polish tongue, but he would've listened without being judgmental." He looked at his wife, the sadness gone replaced by the happy blue of love and the adoration he felt for her radiating from his eyes. "Now that's a rare trait for any adolescent."

"I wish I had a Humper when I was growing up." Suddenly she found herself not being able to talk, surprised at a feeling that surged through her, a soggy napkin draped over her husband's salad plate.

"You've got one now."

Christmases past were filled with memories for them both, most cherished, a few tarnished. The tarnished parts didn't ruin Christmas. They had long since been relegated to the closets of their souls.

There were no closets with tarnished memories or skeletons to contend with now as they sorted through the mail. The Lake Shore Drive Christmas was in the past and so was the serenity of their first Christmas alone as husband and wife in their new home in the Northwoods. What surprised them both with Thanksgiving having bowed to December was how fast the responses came back on their invitations. Willy's parents were the first to RSVP sending a note, written and signed by her mother, and then a phone call several days later. Two of his brothers said they would make it with John, the youngest, writing in a comment that he was going to *Winsconsin*. His comment also wished that Mrs. Sven from the resort they used to go to on their family vacations would be there in place of his mean, much older brother. Carol, his youngest daughter and match maker, had replied with a single word response, *YES* written on a separate sheet of paper. On the back she wrote to her father telling him to be sure and to take good care of her favorite teacher of all time. "She's my Brother James Virgil," she added in her curly-cue hand writing. Then there was a post script with her writing: *Be prepared for a big surprise!*

"She better not be knocked up," he had said to Willy when he showed her Carol's reply.

Willy wrinkled her nose. "What was that I said about I never met a perfect parent?"

"Love is to the knocked up as a slow, agonizing death is to the knocker upper."

"Ah, my illogical loon," said Willy as she watched her dream of a second private peaceful Christmas with her husband float off towards the North Pole along with her contingency plan for no-shows. She was about to be invaded by, according to the words of her late father-in-law, Natives. How would she cope with the children? Six from near five to not quite teenagers and none in the eighth grade like her former students. Then she added Tidge's three daughters. "Oh, Lord," she muttered. "Why hast Thou forsaken me?"

The pending family invasion elated Tidge. Christmas would be the greatest since the very first one happening in a stable under the brightest star ever witnessed by poor shepherds. He was in his basement workshop, his dark room all but abandoned by computer technology, experimenting with several printing techniques, but unable to maintain his concentration. No logic could correct the jumble of fragmented thoughts that darted through his mind. Sleeping arrangements for an estimated seventeen out of town guests had been no problem. Willy had aired her contingency plans to him that covered topics ranging from gifts to guilt. Each day and every night Christmas was the only thing on their minds.

Tidge surprised her one night turning off the news and shifting the topic of conversation away from Christmas. They were sitting exhausted in front of his new Christmas present, an almost life size image talking to them about how, "His and Her snowmobiles can enhance your lives in the north country." He picked up the remote, pointed it at Willy and pushed the power button. "Much better," he said a blank screen and quiet sending snowmobiles, weather forecasts and tips on how to prevent frostbite into the cold December night. "I'm worn out from preparing and worrying about Christmas."

She'd wrinkled her nose at him. "Poor baby," she said no attempt at sugar coating her sarcasm. "Preparing? Worn out?" she asked, lines forming across her nose. "Well, Buster, you're going to discover preparing the Wilhelmina Schneider Mackie-whiz way. Then you'll know what worn out is."

"You're all heart," he said, his own heart pleading with him not to go where he was intending to go. Then he dug into a tiny private crypt in his soul, opened the rusty, creaking door and rationalized to her why his father's last wish was still a last wish.

Two simple words summed up Tidge's logical conclusion. Barbara Ann. Those two words made him feel that God, Santa and Mother Mary May I were making him pay the price for his sins. So was Barbara Ann, The Sweet Swede he had nicknamed her, the innocent party to his promises given from the heart, but not from his soul.

Willy had heard his attempt at untying the knots in his stomach and airing out the guilt in his soul, at best, two times before, but only in bits and pieces. She felt a relief when he would end his confession by hearing him say, "Everybody knows I was a crap husband in a crap marriage and a crap father who did a crappy job raising his daughters."

Her response to his bits and pieces on those two occasions had been almost identical. "Do you have anything relevant to say?" she asked, several creases coming and going across her forehead in rapid succession.

"Didn't you hear a word I said?" he asked, expecting to be wrapped in a blanket of sympathy.

"If you had said something that wasn't coated in self-pity, something that had substance and meaning, I would have really listened."

"Didn't I do that?" he asked frustrated. Didn't you hear a word I said?"

"The first two times I heard," she said. "And we talked afterwards. Did we not?"

"We did."

"What did we talk about?" The eyebrow of her right eye cocked indicating he was in trouble and that her laser look was forthcoming.

"I'm not quite sure." He thought for a moment. "I do remember you telling me to get off the pity pot. That I remember."

"And did you?"

He looked at her and then at the floor. His looks kept going back and forth several times. "I thought I did."

"Think again, Buster."

"Tell me this," he said, not letting go even though he knew Willy had. "Does Martha ever talk to me?" He couldn't believe how serious he sounded. "Geez, she's the oldest. How's she going to take over the family when I croak?"

That statement of his pending demise and passing the family torch to the next in line always got her dander up and had her reprimanding him. "Thomas Ignacy Joseph," she said, using his three names the way his mother used to do which meant he was in trouble, "you're not going to die so don't even talk about it."

"Carol, our little matchmaker, talks to me," he continued, sounding almost proud. "She loves you more than she loves me, but at least there's some love there for her old man." He noticed Willy roll her eyes and his mood changed. "As for Carm, I have my doubts. Every time I see the kid she's got a new boyfriend. Can't she hang on to a guy?"

"Maybe they don't measure up to Dad," Willy said, trying to ease the pressure.

"Why would they want to?" he asked, a self-loathing in his question. "I most certainly wouldn't want any of my daughters going out with a loser like me." His thumb and index finger formed a letter L that he centered against his forehead.

"Lucky me," said Willy. "I married a loser. So much for graduating with honors from college." Willy knew more than she wanted about Barbara Ann. "You can't forget her can you?"

"I can't forget what I did to her."

"That wasn't your fault."

"That's easy to say," he said, his expression showing that he was drifting back in time. There had been the look on her parents' faces he could never erase as he ran into the emergency room at Swedish Covenant Hospital. The ER doctors were working to save their baby, their Barbara Ann, and he was there with them, the cause of their look.

Tidge never believed that cheating on an exam would lead to real cheating. Barbara Ann never did. She took every word Tidge ever said to her as Gospel. From his casual, "Cheat off me to your heart's content," at the start of class, to his subdued, almost asinine, "I'm thinking about getting separated," to, "I love you," she believed him. Then, too many I-love-you vows, coated with an equal amount of unfulfilled promises and a string of delays and excuses for getting divorced, found Barbara Ann no longer believing, not even in her own life.

"Do you still love her?" asked Willy, fearing she would get the answer she didn't want.

"You're the only lady I love," he said, sincerity smothering every word. "Barbara Ann was back then, like The Regents." He remembered every word to that song, words that came back time and again to haunt him. *Bar bar bar, bar Barbara Ann. Oh, Barbara Ann, take my hand.* And she took his hand and his heart and his soul without ever once trying to cheat off of him on an exam. He, on the other hand, found himself taking frequent glances at her paper during a mid-term test. The other times his glances were at her legs. Then there were more than glances that put the fragile, spun glass sculptures of the lives of three daughters in the palms of his hands waiting to be crushed or caressed. He swallowed hard, cursed fate and himself and released his grip on Bar-bar-bar, bar-Barbara-Ann's hand.

"No one can go back and recapture those times," he said, sometimes wishing he could. "I just want to be a better husband to you, a better father to my kids and a patriarch who can somehow unscrew a screwed up family."

"Don't worry about being better," she said relieved. "Just be you."

"That's what got me into trouble in the first place."

"I'm not talking about that you. I'm talking about the you that you are now, the you I love."

"You, you, you," he repeated, saying the words to the song. "That's an old Ames Brothers record. And don't go asking me who the Ames Brothers were."

"The Regent's grandfathers?" she asked, without a smile.

Their conversation came to a halt as he switched the television back on and they were greeted by the sports results. "If you don't stop feeling sorry for yourself," she said, as she tucked her legs under her. "I'm going to get up, go out to the garage and bring in that old television."

"You're going to do what?"

She wiggled her feet into a more comfortable position under her. "Do you see how clear this picture is?"

He nodded.

"That's the life you have now, stupid," she said, again no sympathy in her voice. "Keep acting like you're acting and you'll be looking at a blurred screen again." There was a slight turn of her head. "Get my drift, Mr. Logician?"

Another day vanished and their guests' arrival drew uncomfortably close for Willy. Cleaning and organizing continued, each room of Henry's Hut receiving the extra special attention reserved only for visiting foreign heads of state. Willy knew what had to be done, each item on her extensive list receiving a small, neat pencil check mark upon being completed to her satisfaction. Tidge's satisfaction didn't count. He knew that fact and didn't argue. The long last fulfillment of his Christmas wish danced over the pines across the lake on Paine's Island. Knowing how he worked, she gave him one job at a time before giving him the next one, but when mid-afternoon rolled around, caps snapped on the aerosol cans, towels for washing windows were hung up on a clothes line he had strung up in the basement for her and the vacuum cleaner carted off to the first room on the agenda of the next day's list. Their daily walk together sat atop her job list.

They were both out of breath after trudging through the woods. Holding hands, they began to skip across the light snow cover of their backyard when Willy put on the brakes and stopped. She gave Tidge a strange look. "Now I know where the expression, 'roll in the hay' came from."

"Are you talking about Mickey?" he asked.

"I'm talking about Mickey."

Tidge laughed along with her then said, "God, that risqué kid should be called Little Miss Mickey without the curds and whey."

Willy nodded.

"And her old man was one of the biggest meanest looking human beings I ever saw. He kind of reminded me of a James Bond character, the one with the steel teeth and jaws."

He stopped and thought for a moment. "On second thought, he was jaws, a Great White shark from Finland who used his teeth to chop down trees. I wanted to tell the Millers to keep Kenny from going out with them to Friday night fish fries at the local supper clubs because, if Mickey's father had his way, their son might be on the menu, served with or without tartar sauce."

"Like always, you exaggerate," said Willy. She flashed a smile that seemed to dance like ginger bread men in her sugar brown eyes. "He was just being a protective father and keeping an eye on his spunky teenage daughter."

Tidge let out what sounded like a huff. "Spunky," he repeated, looking at her like he knew something she didn't. "You didn't see her reach under the dining room table cloth after Norma Miller mentioned having once had straw in her underwear."

"She didn't."

"Oh, she did, my dearest lover," he said, his eyes joining in the dance with hers. "The innocent little cherub brought up a handful. Probably had a pubic or two mixed in with the straw."

Willy's eyes stopped dancing. "You are such a gross pig," she said, emphasizing the last two words of her comment. She let go of his hand and started walking, pretending to cross country ski only without the skis.

Tidge stood there for a minute watching the parallel trail she was making and started to jog to catch up to her. Taking her hand he said, "Did you ever hear of a roll in the leaves?"

She kept up her skiing motion heading for their back deck. "You're still a gross pig," she said, shaking her hand free and starting to run for the mud room door that was at the back of the deck, the room doubling as a heated air lock and receptacle for hanging coats, jackets, hats and placing snow covered boots.

He caught up to her in several quick strides and grabbed her arm bringing her to a stop. "See," he said, pointing to the area behind their house between the steps that led up to the deck and the back of the house.

"See what?" she asked, her breath coming in uneven puffs disappearing into the frigid, mid-December air.

"That inviting pile of leaves I raked and lovingly positioned by our house in your honor," he said with a smile.

"In my honor," she repeated then stopping, looking up at him and realizing what was on her husband's mind. "You want me to roll in that pile of leaves with you?" She pointed at him. "Here?" Her finger moved in the direction of the leaves. "Now?" she asked. "Here in broad daylight?"

"Now is the time for all good lovers to come to the aid of their patriarch," he said, his smile beginning to show a trace of lust. "Santa likes girls who have been nice and naughty."

"Nice play on words she said," her head going from side to side a couple of times. "You're trading hay for leaves?"

"Don't knock it if you haven't tried it."

Chapter 5

They sat at their massive, round pedestal oak table in the cedar planked kitchen, shoulders and souls touching. They had bought the cumbersome antique at an estate auction south and west of town in late spring their first year. Estate was a misnomer. Ragged tar paper encircled a dilapidated side-by-side that tipped at a precarious angle. The rusted hulk of a Hudson Hornet, buried up to its door handles by dead weeds, stood guard over the estate from what was once a front yard.

"Are you really going inside?" Willy had asked, after the auctioneer made mention of treasures to be found.

They both ventured into what was once the home to a pair of octogenarian spinster sisters, Willy glued to Tidge's back. They were greeted by jagged water stains decorating the interior ceiling. A dozen more tentative steps had them surrounded by peeling wall paper and bundles of neatly stacked and tied newspapers and magazines. "Geez," Tidge had said, "it feels like were a couple of rats caught in a maze." They inched their way ahead until they entered what was once a kitchen.

The sisters, it was rumored, had died from asphyxiation, hypothermia or both while sitting in the kitchen at the oak table that now belonged to Tidge and Willy. They had been inches from a wood burning stove during one of the coldest spells in Wisconsin history. Their bodies hadn't been discovered until Bleeding Heart Roses began to poke their heads above ground around the Hudson Hornet.

Willy's heart all but flew out of her body when she saw the table. She ended up outbidding Tidge for the table, endearing her to the heart of the auctioneer. After writing a check, she said to husband: "That table is us. I can feel it."

Tidge looked at her in disbelief. "And I can feel our bank account two hundred dollars heavier if you hadn't got caught up in a bidding frenzy with your one and only," he said, pointing at himself while his head went slowly from side-to-side, his unbelieving eyes asking.

Now his eyes radiated love as he asked Willy, "Warm enough?" He could feel his own body temperature still clinging to the passion of their outdoor love making.

"Since I'm re-zipped, re-buttoned and re-buckled I think most of the frost bite has left," she replied, a trace of a smile giving away her poker face. "At least I'm warmer than those two sisters who used to sit at this table."

Tidge let out a sad laugh. "I still can't believe there was still a decorated Christmas tree in that living room," he said. "Do you think Santa paid them one last visit?"

Willy's hands were clamped over the top of her mug absorbing the heat. "I don't know about them, but I do know that if your lame brained scheme for a family Christmas here blows up you'll be joining those sisters."

Tidge's eyes danced. "You're a hard woman, Wilhelmina Schneider Mackiewicz," he said. "One minute you're enjoying a late afternoon roll in the leaves and the next you're warming your hands on a coffee cup and planning my demise."

Their drowsy eyes said all that was needed between them until Tidge muttered, "Damn," and made a disgusting face after trying for one more sip of coffee that had joined the outside temperature. He looked at Willy and started to grin.

She saw his impish smile and asked, "What's so funny?" She noticed his eyes appeared to be focused at the top of her head.

His head went down, his smile becoming a grin. He lifted his right hand and extended his index finger in her direction.

"I'm funny?" she asked, sounding not at all pleased as she watched his index finger do a gentle bounce up and down as he raised its aim. "Keep making fun of me, Buster and it'll be December a year from now before you get to play in the leaves again."

Tidge's laughter echoed throughout the house as his finger stayed locked at the top of her head.

Her own right hand took a slow, cautious course to her forehead and crept upward. Then she knew. Sandwiched between her hand

and her hair was a small pine cone. She removed the pine cone, twisting it between her thumb and forefinger. Her eyes traveled slowly back and forth between the pine cone and Tidge's. "At least it's not straw."

"You must admit it is a nice souvenir," he said, his laughter transforming into a look that told her he wasn't finished teasing her. "I bet your corsage from the senior prom doesn't hold the memories that pine cone does."

She continued to hold the memento between in her thumb and forefinger giving it a slow critical twist one way and then back the other. "I'm betting that you're not going to find out either."

"You're no fun," he said, faking a pout, his adoring eyes giving him away.

"I was on your pile of leaves," she said, gently transferring the jagged cone to the table top like she had transferred trusting dragon flies from the gunnels of their canoe to her forefinger during sunny August afternoons.

Tidge blinked several times, let out a yawn and said: "Before our heads come to rest on this table, I think we should reinforce our assurances about Christmas and family by fueling us with a plate of assorted cheeses, celery sticks, sliced apple wedges and crackers. How does that sound, girl of my dreams?"

"Yummy," she said, with a serious look. "Could we savor said delicacies with a glass of wine?"

"My feelings exactly," said Tidge, as he took their coffee mugs, gave them a quick rinse and filled them with what remained from a bottle of Chablis they started several days earlier in the week.

The cheeses were favorites of theirs: a foil wrapped wedge of Wisconsin Blue from downstate, a block of aged cheddar they had picked up in late summer on a trip north to Bayfield and the Apostle Islands and a circle of imported Brie.

Willy loved the Blue on celery, enjoying lady like bites while sipping her wine. Tidge, according to Willy, looked like he used a shovel instead of a fork to eat. "You are such a slob," she said, as she watched him match a chunk of cheddar with an apple wedge, balance it all on a cracker and slide same into his mouth. Then he washed all of it down with a gulp of wine that came out with a loud slurp.

With the Chablis gone, the plate empty and two souls filled with reassurances, Willy slid her mug away with a display of proper manners, sighed and got up from the polished oak table. She walked to the portable phone mounted on the kitchen wall, lifted it off the receiver and held it out for him. "Since this was your brainstorm, Thomas Hardy, you get the honor to push your buttons first."

Tidge looked puzzled. "What's with the Thomas Hardy and honors?"

She began to wave the phone back and forth in slow motion. "Everyone returned their RSVP cards in the mail," she said, her voice full of resignation. "Your firstborn, Martha even said she'd attend. The next step is for you to confirm their reservations and give them the particulars." The phone was still waving back and forth as her eyes called him to it. "If I were you, I'd leave your oldest for last. She's the one native you wanted to return, so, I'd make all of your other calls first." She paused. "By then, you'll be too tired to start a fight."

"I never start fights," he said, jumping up. "But, before we send our long distance phone bill through the ceiling, there's something I want to show you." He headed to the basement door yelling over his shoulder, "I've been experimenting with what I think will be a money maker."

It's about time!" she hollered back, looking at the phone in her hand and feeling apprehensive.

He returned in seconds waving an eight by ten photo in his right hand. "I printed this out on our computer." He laid the picture down in front of her. "Cool, huh."

"Did you hear what I said?" she asked, giving the phone a slight wave in his direction.

"About money?"

"The one and only thing that doesn't fall off the trees around here," she said. She examined the photograph, her lips pursed. "I thought you were through creating fancy W's surrounded by outlines of hearts," she said, not looking up. "I think we have one in every room in the house, including the bathrooms."

"It's only because I'm trying to show you how much I love you," he said, reaching for the picture, his eyes focused on the W. "I can use any letter in the alphabet." He stopped, his eyes lighting up like the colored lights trimming their house. "I could make custom Christmas presents for the ladies," he said, beaming. "How does a *G* for Gert sound?"

"My mother?" she asked, with more than surprise in her voice. "You're kidding."

"Nope," he said, his excitement growing. "You know me, the truth, the whole truth and nothing but the truth, for better or for worse." He paused, eyes now twinkling like silver tinsel hanging from a Christmas tree's branches. "I might even etch in the outline of a ballerina for your mom." Then, never knowing when to keep his mouth shut, he added, "I could glue on a variety of cutout pictures of that old, flamboyant wrestler from her era, Gorgeous George to remind her of the good old days."

"Don't you dare make fun of my mother," she warned.

"I'm not," he said, trying to act like a choir boy. "I've never known a lady wrestler before." He stopped cold when he saw her eyebrow go up. "Now let me see." His right hand, four fingers extended, added a thumb and his left hand showed two fingers. "I'll also need three more for the brothers' wives." He thought for a minute. "That'll be another *C* and two *L's*. Add two more *C's*," he said, his explanation of his Christmas present project taking shape. "One each for Carol and Carm." He looked at her, his face like a little child peering into the window of a downtown State Street department store absorbing the Christmas displays. "Oh, yes, must not forget an *M* for you-know-who." He waved the seven digits at Willy. "Man, this is too cool for words."

"Cool," she repeated. "Are you giving a weather forecast or predicting the reactions of afore mentioned female family members when they look upon your art work with indifference?"

"Indifference?" he asked. "The ladies will adore me even more than you do."

"You are beyond help."

"And, do you know what else?" he asked, while holding the picture at different angles as he turned it in his hands. "I've ordered a fancy digital camera. It has all the bells and whistles. So much better than that old relic I've been using."

"Oh, you mean that old relic I gave you for our first Christmas together?" she asked. "And where, may I ask, is the money coming from? We're lucky we can buy bread."

"The money I make from being able to create all kinds of pictures on our computer will be enough to buy you your own bakery," he said, his excitement growing and eyes reaching saucer status. "I could illustrate the cover for your first novel." He smiled. "And your main character's head would not be chopped off."

"How about you illustrate this," she said, her arm extended out so the phone almost touched the tip of his nose. "It's time to see how many of our invited guests will want to spend over eight hours on treacherous winter roads to get here."

"Maybe treacherous in Illinois, but not up here," he said, taking the phone and pointing it at her. "It's only a seven hour drive here from Chicago," he said, correcting her while giving a chivalrous bow so that his forehead came in contact with the table top with a gentle thud. He looked up, made a face and said, "Just be sure you do your part and make it sound like it's just a walk around the block when your parents ask you how long the drive will take."

"About eight long, boring, almost grueling hours," she said, gently rubbing the end of the phone across the tip of his nose. "Maybe they'll all decide not to come." She smiled at him. "How about if I tell them it's just a teeny-weeny bit less than nine? Longer if it's snowing as in I'm dreaming of a white one."

"Ha-ha," he said, pushing the phone back at her. "Ladies first," he said. "Funny ladies."

"Coward," she said in a huff, gently pushing the buttons of her parent's phone number.

The phone stayed busy until the late news came on at ten. Then, sitting on the sofa, legs stretched out with their wool stocking covered feet on the coffee table, toes wiggling at the TV that made them feel they were in the news studio with the reporters, they dozed off before the weather report.

They had prepared for Christmas by staying out of the other's way when the situation dictated, but working as a team most of the time. A week before their families were to arrive they were sitting in the kitchen savoring their morning coffee. They had just finished a light breakfast of cereal, hers a multi-grain type mixed with vanilla yogurt and his, sugar coated generic corn flakes he called, *Tony*, drowning in milk. He picked up his bowl drinking the last of the milk with a gulp and a slurp and then looked at her over rim and asked, "Are you sure you're ready to be hostess to the invaders from the south?" He paused, his eyes teasing her. "You do have a master's degree in psychological counseling, don't you?"

"Have you forgotten that I'm a woman for all seasons," she said, while trying to find a subtle way to correct his lack of table manners. "I also have an advanced degree in Etiquette and Appropriate Social Behavior and another in TV Weather Forecasting. You'll be happy to know that I'm also guaranteeing our guests a white Christmas."

"Big deal, dearest wife," he said, as he set down his bowl and took one final lick of his spoon. "Anyone can guarantee Jack Frost nipping at their noses and singing Yuletide carols in front of our fireplace." He smiled. "You could also get on a snowmobile, if we had one, and ride over the hills and through the woods so fast that Mother Nature would frost that luscious brown hair of yours." He wanted to laugh. "At least I wouldn't have to look at you walking around the house wearing that silly plastic bag over your head and stinking of that pasty hair coloring slime the day before our guests get here."

"Don't be critical of my hair coloring or weather forecasting," she said, her coffee mug hiding lips turned up at the corners. "I'm as good as that guy with the bad rug you poke fun at when we watch the weather on the late news. Now there's someone who definitely needs a bag over his head."

"True," he said, reaching for his coffee mug. He took a slurping sip knowing her nose would wrinkle. "As for forecasting the weather, I'm sure you'll create an ideal Christmas for our families and have them dressed up like Eskimos the entire time they're here."

"I'll be sure to make the weather outside absolutely frightful upon their arrival," she said, pointing as she tossed out her challenge. "And what will your contributions be for our idyllic Yule? Showing the children how to popcorn in that blackened rusted old popper you insist on keeping alongside the fireplace."

Tidge shrugged his shoulders. "My contributions, darling wife, will be a fire that is so delightful along with said popping of corn. I am also pleased to be adding to the icing on my Christmas cake the clatter up on our roof that will have all of our guests springing from their beds."

"Clatter?" she asked. Her lower lip rolled down in a curl that made her upper lip disappear. "Is that the same clatter that's related to your brothers and their discarding of empty beer cans?"

"Not that kind of clatter," he said, trying to assure her. "Mine will be officially sanctioned reindeer clatter."

"What are you going to do when parents start punching, brothers begin beating, wives wind up whipping and the children all huddled in a corner cowering after your popcorn burns; the icing melts on your Christmas cake and your brothers ignore your official sanctions?"

"When the maids stop their milking and the lord's start leaping, hopefully not landing in the milk pails, I won't have a thing to do," he said with a straight face. "If that doesn't work, then I'll referee the punching, whipping, beatings and cowering."

She inhaled what remained of the vanishing wispy vapors of her breakfast coffee rising from her cup. "I'm starting to have second thoughts about this white Christmas stuff with your brothers, the Dysfunctional Magi and their lovely wives who your late bigoted father called the natives." She lowered her mug to the scratched oak table top. Her head turned just a fraction to one side. She fluffed at the front of her short hair with a nervous index finger and said, "Please tell me that you've abandoned your idea of playing Santa Claus in that relic of a costume of your late uncle what's-his-name?"

Tidge lowered his mug to where it rested in the palms of his hands. "The last I heard was that Santa was coming to town and he would be wearing his traditional red suit."

"I know all of that," she said, hoping he would not propel himself into the subjects of war, alcohol and his jacket. "It's just that your uncle's old Santa Claus suit is hideous."

"Agreed," said Tidge, his reply catching her off guard. "But, what you're forgetting, Wilhelmina is that Uncle Brew believed in the magic of that suit." He paused ready to strike. "And my jacket and a guy named, Santa Claus."

"I didn't forget," she said, digging in her heels. "Sometimes you allow magic, your uncle's memory and Saint Nick to shove aside, even bury, your so-called logical approach to life."

Tidge smiled. "Several weeks before Christmas Uncle Brew would always ask me and my brothers if we believed in Santa Claus. He also asked us if we had been good. He had a way of looking at us that we couldn't say anything but the truth. Then, before we could answer, he'd nod his head, smile a sober smile and tell each of us to write a letter to Santa telling him what we wanted for Christmas."

"And, of course, you'll carry on the tradition of saying the same things to your nieces and nephews when they're here." She had made her comment sound like *I really hope that's not going to be the case.*

"You bet I am," he said, his short statement an edict. "Traditions might come and go," he said. "Some might even be suspended or made against the law, but letters to Santa will be a part of this coming Christmas."

"You're really not going to listen to what I have to say, are you."

"I always listen," he said, knowing that he would resurrect the letter writing to Santa. He had vivid memories when writing those Christmas letters had stopped. Family Christmases started to unravel about the time he graduated from high school and Marietta Claus told him she would like to date others.

Numb and bewildered, Tidge found himself at Great Lakes in Boot Camp. Marietta had changed her mind, but the Navy couldn't be bothered. Tidge found himself heading for San Diego and the Miramar Naval Air Station. That was his first Christmas away from Mackiewicz traditions. Southern California sunshine and getting drunk on margaritas in Tijuana failed as a substitute. The next year he made up a lame excuse not to come home for Christmas. He lied about being temporarily assigned duty to load rockets on planes at a tiny base in Fallon, Nevada. He couldn't be bothered with celebrating Christmas, not even attending Mass. His final Christmas away from home included sea duty on the aircraft carrier, Ticonderoga, launching devastation to a country in the Far East he never knew existed. He got more of a sense as to how his Uncle Brew must have felt being launched from the flight deck of the Princeton years earlier.

An early discharge came as a surprise and he was on his way home, a DD-214 tucked safely in his carry-on bag, Loyola University Chicago, Humper and Bean Head waiting. That's when he learned that Uncle Brew's liver was about to give out, Mother Mary May I was ailing from what the doctor's couldn't find and that Kid Scream's blows had disintegrated into nothing more than being pummeled by a marshmallow.

Tidge tried to light a fire under the old Christmas Eve traditions his first Christmas back at his old house. His mother had just passed on the day before Thanksgiving, taking the once wonderful aromas emanating from her kitchen with her. Christmas Eve dinner had been purchased that afternoon from a local deli. Tidge bought what appeared to be everything in the store's meat counter. He even picked up a Christmas tree from a vacated tree lot, the seller pulling up stakes that morning. It didn't matter. Christmas Eve wasn't. For the first time in Mackiewicz family history, the Infant Jesus was a no-show and Santa Claus didn't bother to stop.

Kid Scream sat in a trance barely touching his dinner. He went to his room to take a nap after eating, not wanting any part of Christmas. Tidge lit match after match, but his Christmas fire coughed, sputtered and fizzled out without a puff of smoke. He wore his uncle's Santa Claus suit with its collection of tears and a faded blood stain on the right leg. He tried not to inhale, the suit reeking of body odor laced with alcohol and nicotine. It was almost as if his uncle had died wearing that suit, his body not discovered for a month.

Tidge's brothers were at the old house for that Christmas Eve. Peter and Paul were accompanied by their fiancées, his brother John, with his girlfriend and her mother and Tidge's new girlfriend, Sissy. He had met her at a young adult dance at the neighboring St. John Bosco church. All of them were red faced, boisterous and telling jokes that Kid Scream wouldn't have uttered to his buddies on the meat packing company's loading dock. The alcohol flowed and they all poked fun of Tidge wearing the Santa Claus suit. Sissy seemed to poke harder. She was more mean-spirited, her barbs shocking Tidge. He thought he was dreaming. This wasn't the same girl he had met two weeks earlier. This wasn't the chic model look-a-like with the jet black shoulder length hair, several strands toying with covering her right eye, which made him laugh during the dance at St. John Bosco. They had slow danced and he was surprised at how quick he got aroused. Her right eye peeked out from behind the curtain of hair while the lower half of her anatomy made several brushing contacts with his lower half before pulling away. Then, agonizing moments later, she would sway and brush again. He knew immediately she sported two initials, but didn't care. The dance had been fun, even more fun after with her in his car parked down the block from her house. There was nothing funny now.

Mean spirited joking hitched up to behaviors that were almost evil, the spirit of Christmas ignored. At first, Tidge warned them like Mother Mary May I would have. His warnings were ignored. Then he turned into Kid Scream, but his brothers didn't fear him. He asked them to remember how Christ and Christmas were important to Mother Mary May I. Their comments ranged from, "She's dead" to "Christ who" to John's girlfriend's mother sitting on Tidge's lap, cupping her right breast in her hand and asking, "Would Santa like a little milk with his cookies?"

Tidge lost his temper, stood up thereby dropping John's girlfriend's mother and his potential source of calcium on her butt, grabbed a reluctant Sissy by the hand and left the house. He was still wearing the Santa Claus suit and screaming obscenities as he pulled a kicking and scratching Sissy to his car.

It was hardly the behavior of a soon-to-be responsible patriarch, but one that both God and Santa Claus noticed and tried to understand, God saying to Santa: "Our boy's headed for a stretch of rough seas, Kris."

Santa nodded at God. "Rough might be an understatement," he said. "The lad's really got his hands full now," Santa said. "Too bad that cute Marietta kid didn't give him more of a chance. I liked her."

"I did too, Kris." God thought for a moment then said, "I don't think we have to worry about him. He's a tough one. I think all those boxing lessons his father gave him will pay off."

The following Christmas Eve was somewhat subdued. Peter and Paul no longer had fiancées. John, who had ended up in a mother-daughter love triangle, received a surprise education in Life 101.

John thought he had what no other man could or would ever have, the mother, in her late thirties, and her daughter, nineteen. He had driven his father to the brink of insanity when he would show up at a family function, mother on one arm, daughter on the other, both indeed stacked and showing off those stacks. The entire time John would gloat. Then John woke up one morning and experienced an excruciating burning sensation as he began to urinate. His love for triangles vanished with the removal of his rose colored glasses and a shot of penicillin.

The Mackiewicz boys always attracted beautiful women. They fell in love, usually after a first kiss, and, like their parents had preached to them, respected that member of the opposite gender. Red cheeks brought back the lesson in respect for women taught by Mother Mary May I. She once said to each of her sons, hands folded in her lap, her worn rosary beads intertwined through her fingers: "The apple of your eye may produce blessed fruit." For whatever reason or reasons, the Mackiewicz boys' relationships with the opposite gender always ended up as a plot for an Edgar Allen Poe creation instead of reaping a golden harvest.

Peter, for example, was the first married and the first divorced, setting a record for one of the shortest marriages in the history of Holy Matrimony. The apple of his eye turned out to be rotten. So did her lover who was also her girlfriend. Peter forgot all about the lessons in respect his parents taught him.

Paul had life simpler, having been told by his fiancée, "Get lost, you colossal bore. You're no fun and I'm keeping the ring."

John had his experience with a social disease and Tidge, in spite of Sissy, reaped a golden harvest of three daughters.

All of Mother Mary May I and Kid Scream's boys were eventually blessed even though three of their sons' apples were something their father could not comprehend. Three daughters-in-law, one a Native American, another an Asian American and the third an African American were not cast in the image and likeness of the Irish Catholic colleen he had married. The Kid's comments about his daughters-in-law made him sound like a bigot, which he wasn't, at least not to him. He had worked in meat packing houses all of his life, starting in the Stock Yards and finding work in a smaller packing house after the

Stock Yards became history. The Kid had labored alongside a collection of the original rainbow coalition. "I work with Spics, Spades, Chinks, Beaners and Rag Heads," he had often boasted, but not at home, at least while Mother Mary May I was alive. "That's what I call them," he said, sounding like a carbon copy of his once favorite television character, Archie Bunker. "And they call me every slang expression they got for Polack white guys."

His family didn't know that the Kid went out and drank with his rainbow coalition after work, their politically incorrect names bantered about whatever neighborhood bar they frequented. The sons never heard about the wakes and hospital visits their father had made to coalition members, offering comfort to hurting families. They never saw the hugs, handshakes and back slapping. All they ever heard was his references to their brides. That was enough to distance them from him and to be wary of their older brother. Not too much later, the Kid passed away and that first Christmas Eve without both of their parents was a quiet, alcohol induced time filled with reminiscing about the Kid, Mother Mary May I and Uncle Brew. It was also a Christmas Eve that their uncle's Santa Claus suit didn't appear and one that gave Tidge a full realization of the down side of being a patriarch.

During their first Christmas together, Willy had opened the door to her closet. "Are you sure you want to look inside?" she asked, her body trembling.

"Ain't nothin' this beat up old patriarch can't handle," he said, masking his curiosity.

"Are you sure?" she asked, hoping he would change his mind.

He didn't and wished that he had. "That no good son of a bitch," he muttered, trying desperately to keep his rage bottled up. He held her close, feeling her body tremble, her explanation awash in tears. He listened until he could somehow smother the useless rage and revenge that tried to take him over. "Geez, Willy, he didn't," he said, trying to wipe the tears off her cheeks with trembling index fingers.

She nodded.

He knew tirades and tantrums were useless and, for one of the rare times in his life, kept his big mouth shut. Words couldn't make her whole again. Her days of conceiving were gone. Punches, well aimed kicks and an intentional push at the top of the stairs to her apartment by her then husband took care of that. A slight droop in an eye lid was a bonus.

"That gutless bastard," muttered Tidge, knowing there would be no children in the new marriage of Wilhelmina Schneider and Thomas Mackiewicz. Any children to scare, frighten and petrify by seeing someone in an old Santa Claus suit would be the children of others.

Tidge had three daughters from his first marriage, a divorce from Sissy and nagging memories of a voluptuous, cow-eyed grad student, Barbara Ann Lindstrom to remind him of a life before Willy. His brothers finally found their own forms of happiness with the likes of their native wives named, Chareese, Lilly, and Lucy, and a pair of children from each.

"I still can't believe that your parents accepted our invitation," said Tidge to Willy.

"My parents are enthused about coming," she said, still looking at him, almost studying him. "Mother's called every other day wanting to know what she should bring."

Tidge could sense something was wrong. When his wife stared at him the way she was doing now he knew that a question and a pat answer would make an appearance. "Is there something bothering my best girl?" He saw her head tilt to one side and what had been on her mind make an appearance.

"That Santa Claus outfit," she said.

"You never let go, do you," he said, his head shaking his answer. "No," he said, having found various creative ways to dodge an honest answer. "There's no need."

"Oh."

"I'm counting on the real Santa to make his appearance on Christmas Eve," he continued. "Just the way he does for all the good little girls and boys. I have faith. I believe. So, you better not shout and you better not pout because, girl of my dreams, the man in the red suit with the big bag is definitely coming to town. It is also rumored that he's parking his sleigh on our roof. I do hope you'll have some milk and cookies for him because I've made and arrangements with Kenny and Mickey to provide all the fresh hay Rudolph, Dasher and the boys will need." He grinned at her. "And, whatever hay is left over . . ."

There was a slow, exasperated exhale from her. "That's what I thought, she said. "It's bad enough I have to get ready for a house full of Christmas guests, but I have to be Santa's care-giver as well."

"Willy," he said, pretending to be serious, "my wife, my life, my love. I've heard that Santa craves a good kolachke."

"Spare me." She got up and went to the sink with her almost empty cup, turned and said: "What your friend Santa won't crave is you making fun of him dressed up like you came out of the eighteenth century." She let out a sigh. "I bet that Santa Claus suit is older than the man himself."

"Santa Claus doesn't concern himself about being on the cover of *Vogue* or *GQ*," he replied, appearing to be insulted by her comment. "Santa never looks foolish."

"Promise?" asked Willy, sounding nervous.

His eyes didn't flinch as he said, "If I don't?"

"What was that you told me about teasing, Mister Mackie Whiz," she said her warning cut short in mid-sentence to aim her laser look at him. "Keep it up with your T for teasing and your P will be spending the entire holiday season, and every single day thereafter, living in that pile of leaves out back. A pile I'll fill with reindeer poop." She smiled. "Did you just notice my creative use of the letter P?"

"You're beautiful when you're mad," he said, trying to tease her and loving the fact that he was succeeding.

"And when I get mad like this, thanks to you, I also develop an incredible backache and headache." She paused for a second. "And those aches need at least a month to go away. Right now they could take until well after our families return home after celebrating the birth of Christ." She cocked her right eyebrow, her left eye almost closed and wrinkles burrowing deep across her forehead. "I'm talking about Christmas a year from now."

He walked to the kitchen doorway, stopped, turned and said, "Stay right where you are."

She had given up trying to figure out what her husband would do when he would ask her to stay put. Most times it related to his photographs or an idea for selling same. Other times it was just some nonsense he would concoct. Nonsense, concoctions and jokes took an early holiday hiatus this time. He reappeared in the doorway with something long, dark and luxuriant black hanging from his right shoulder.

"If you can give a good little boy his Christmas present before Thanksgiving," he said with a cavalier smile, the long, black object now being stretched out hanging in front of him from his chin almost to the floor, "then Santa Claus can give a good little girl her present early." He didn't give her a chance to answer. "Merry Christmas, love of my life and girl of my dreams. Hope you like the mink coat."

She saw the coat. Then she didn't. She could make out Tidge's silhouette and the blurred image he held in front of him. All she could think to say was, "Where's are next loaf of bread coming from?" Then she started sobbing.

Tidge didn't move. "Oh, you big cry baby," he said, still holding out the coat. "At least you could've said it's the most beautiful son of a bitch you've ever seen."

Chapter 6

Their families began trickling in the day before Christmas Eve. Willy's parents arrived first. As noon approached, Tidge, his nose glued to one of the front windows saw their twenty year old Lincoln, the size of a small cruise liner, navigating the coral reef ruts of the driveway like a cautious lumbering tortoise. They were greeted by lazy snow flurries appearing to have no interest in dusting the ground. The picturesque snow's sole function was to escort Willy's parents to a safe docking in front of the center door of the three car garage.

Tidge, more excited than he used to be as a small boy on Christmas morning, dashed out the front door without his jacket and sprinted across the asphalt drive. He had the driver's side door opened before the Lincoln came to a full stop. "Did you folks fly?" he asked.

"Left before five this morning," said Willy's father, Harold, his German accent still evident even after coming to America at age fifteen. "We made it in slightly less than seven hours, Thomas. Just the way you said." He glanced toward the garage. "Am I okay parked here?"

"Perfect for now," said Tidge, reaching out his hand. "Welcome and Merry Christmas," he said, shaking Harold's hand. Tidge beamed even though he was always caught off guard at his diminutive father-in-law's crushing grip, reminding him of the Kid's brute strength. "I'll pull your chariot into the garage after you two get settled." His eyes swept over the car. "I don't want Mother Nature to get any silly ideas about covering this beauty with ice and snow." He stepped aside so Willy's father could get out of the car and then leaned into the cavernous, plush interior and smiled at Willy's mother. "Merry Christmas, Gert," he said, to the stunning platinum blond Amazon with fashion model features, perfect make-up and wearing a winter ensemble that screamed expensive. "Your daughter's beyond excited about your spending Christmas with her."

"We're both delighted to be spending the holiday season with our daughter and favorite son-in-law," she said, her voice border line sultry with a touch of raspy, the result of too many Gibsons over the years and a kicked cigarette habit. "My, but you certainly are isolated out here in God's country." She gave a slight wave of her hand across the front of the windshield. "Do you own all of these trees?"

Tidge nodded. "Only eight measly acres," he said politely, as he backed out of the car. The cold air made him shelve his mother-in-law's comments about holiday seasons and his being her favorite son-in-law. He glanced at Harold who was drinking in the wooded surroundings and noticed that the flurries were entering flake status. "Harold, I think we should get your car out of the elements," he said, pushing the opener button for the garage door buried in his right front pocket.

Harold got back in behind the steering wheel giving an understanding nod. He guided the sleek, massive car inside faster than it took the garage door to go up. Tidge opened the passenger side door for Gert. "Merry Christmas again," he said, extending his hand to assist her out. "I'm guaranteeing that this Christmas season will be the best ever for you both."

Gert swung her long, shapely legs out of the car in a perfect, lady-like move and stood facing her son-in-law, her intriguing deep emerald eyes an inch higher than his. "We've been so looking forward to this day since we received your personalized, hand written invitation." She let go of his hand. "Are there really three *n*'s in Wisconsin?"

Tidge let out a nervous laugh. "That was a special joke for my baby brother, John." He gave her a cautious hug expecting to have several ribs broken for his efforts. Her hug surprised him, no stronger than a single floating snow flake drifting into the open garage. "I see the boss coming," he said, referring to Willy walking across the driveway. "I'll get your luggage."

Willy covered her case of the jitters with her mink. The top of her head was barely visible poking out from the mink's collar as she strolled inside the protection of the garage. "Merry Christmas, Mom and Dad," she said beaming, her head emerging from the collar of her coat. She gave her mother a duplicate of the hug she had gotten when leaving Chicago after their first Christmas, a crushing, emotional embrace filled with love and her mother's tears hidden behind her Gucci sun glasses. She stepped to her father, held out her arms and gave him a hug, her lips making a caressing peck on his cheek. "Oh, Daddy," she said, feeling an excitement she hadn't experienced since being a little girl curled up next to her *grossmutter*. "It's wonderful you're both here for Christmas." Trepidations of three combined families together in Henry's Hut for Christmas drifted off with the snow that had shifted gears. An increasing wind had her saying to her parents: "It's too cold to chit-chat out here." Her shoulders were hunched exaggerating the cold and she rubbed her bare hands together. "Come," she said, nodding toward the polished log home, the lighted outline stating a warm welcome.

"Listen to your daughter," said Tidge, his statement sounding like a military order. "I'll unload the car. Your tour guide will lead you."

Willy stepped back from her parents and turned to the open garage door. "I'm anxious to show you our log cabin," she said, all signs of jitters gone. "We call it Henry's Hut."

"What a stunning coat," said Gert, folding her arms across her chest in a sign of approval as she admired the full length mink.

"An early Christmas present from your favorite son-in-law," said Willy.

"A most exquisite early present," said Harold, handing his car keys to Tidge without taking his eyes off his daughter. "Thomas, may I assist you with the luggage?"

"Got it under control," said Tidge. "Go with your daughter. The noon hour tour is about to start." He ushered his wife and guests out of the protective garage and into the increasing snow fall with another polite order. "Off you go into the Northwoods yonder," he said, his head giving a nod in the direction of the chalet. "Henry's Hut eagerly awaits your presence." He watched his wife and her parent's waste no time traipsing toward the security of the house. "Baby, me thinkest it's getting colder," he said, rubbing his hands together as he went back into the garage. He opened both doors to the Lincoln Continental that appeared and smelled showroom new inside.

"Geez' he said, a whistle followed when he saw the cardboard containers filled with Christmas packages in the back seat. He found the correct key for the Continental's trunk on Harold's key ring. The key went into the trunk lock and the lid popped open. "Christ, how long are they planning on staying?"

Willy's parents were taken in by the sheer size of the two storey five bedroom, three bathroom glistening log chalet where their only child lived. "Henry's Hut is so cozy," said Willy, stretching out the word, so that it sounded like something to snuggle up with during a cold winter's night. "This is the Great Room, she said, trying not to boast.

Harold gave a knowing nod to Willy and said to his daughter, "Great Room is indeed an apropos name."

Outside, Tidge wrestled the luggage to the front door occasionally sliding a piece over the black top drive in front of the house that was now showing signs of becoming an annex to the ice arena in nearby Hayward. The snow's intensity continued to mount. "You sure about this family Christmas stuff," he carped, his words outlined by his breath. "My back in traction and a case of double pneumonia wasn't in my letter to Santa."

Gifts that filled the Lincoln's back seat beckoned to him after he half walked and half skated back to the garage. He stared into the back seat counting the number of cartons and was impressed at how uniform each carton had been packed. Tidge glanced outside. The snowflakes were now on a mission that included entering the garage. "Best get my butt in high gear," he said, noticing that each box sported the label of *Bombay Gin*. His head did a quick side to side motion, his estimate telling him that Santa Claus could very well spoil the family this Christmas. "This is starting out better than I hoped," he said, overcome by the number of gaily wrapped packages. He shivered, feeling a combination of awe and chill topped by the return of a strange sensation he recalled experiencing when his computer mouse click introduced him to Lake Namakagon. He said to the increasing snow: "My in-laws ain't cheap skates."

With the luggage and presents stacked at the front door, he glanced up at the grey sky and then to the circular thermometer mounted to the left of the front door, a picture of a proud buck looking back. Tidge didn't need the red needle on the circular thermometer to tell him the temperature dropped in the short time since Willy's parents arrived. The snowflakes morphed, flexing their muscles and indicated they wanted more than to stick to the ground. Spearing it appeared to be their goal. The once lazy flakes cast aside their ability to float, melded together and tumbled from the sky as if each carried an exercise dumb bell. Several of them struck him on his eye lashes causing him to mutter, "Ouch." He shaded his eyes and tried to look up. "Keep 'em safe on the road," he said his request to whoever it was in the sky that was the target of his patriarchal order.

Tidge, his shivering joined by chattering teeth, opened the oversize oak front door with the half-moon leaded glass covering the top fourth and glanced inside. He could see Willy and her parents standing at the foot of the staircase leading to the second floor. "Have your tour guide take you upstairs to your room," he said, welcoming the warmth of the house. He slid the luggage and the boxes of gifts inside as fast as he could and then banged the door closed. The feeling of being chilled to the bone finally registered with him. He felt thankful that Harold and Gert had taken the time to be so neat and uniform in packing the gifts, the elegant wrappings flashing: *Only the Best.*

Tidge thought about how his father didn't care about wrapping Christmas presents, saying to his mother: "Why bother. The kids won't care. They'll shred every present in sight once they get their greedy little lunch hooks into them."

"Follow me, Mom and Dad," Tidge heard his wife say. "Our bell hop will take your things to your room and we can continue our tour." She sounded peppy and took the steps like a real tour guide, stopping at every third stair with an explanation.

"Now I'm relegated to bell hop status," he muttered, his right foot nudging the nearest box six inches toward the Great Room and the Christmas tree. The warmth of the house reminded him that his jacket would be part of his welcoming committee attire when the others arrived. Frost bite would take a back seat to enthusiasm.

"Your cathedral ceiling is truly breathtaking," Tidge heard Harold remark from the top of the stairs just before Willy's parents followed their daughter down the hall to the biggest of the guest bedrooms where they would be staying. "The span and circumference of those impeccably polished logs is architecturally hypnotic."

"How about those floor-to-ceiling windows," Tidge hollered after them. "Cool, huh. And the views ain't bad either."

Harold poked his head around the corner of the hall. "Magnificent, Thomas," he said. "Truly magnificent."

"You know something, Harold," said Tidge as he started up the stairs carrying two suitcases under each arm, one small resting on a bigger one, "They are truly magnificent." He stopped to rearrange the weight of the luggage. "Just like you and Gert being able to spend Christmas with us this year."

Tidge had just set down his first load of suitcases in the guest room that had a full bath complete with a marble hot tub when he turned and saw Willy's mother in the bedroom doorway.

"Thomas," she said, his name coming out soft and polite, a contrast to how she once shouted at her opponents in her days as a professional wrestler. "Do you think I might have a small libation?"

"By all means," said Tidge, another birch log being tossed on his burning enthusiasm. He savored playing his role as host to the hilt. "Traveling does have a tendency to give one a parched throat," he said to Gert, looking at her and finding it hard to believe that his mother-in-law was once known as *Filly Full Nelson, Mistress of Pain and Minister of the See 'em Hold.* "What tickles your taste buds at noonish?"

"Would a small Gibson be too much trouble?" she asked, sounding as if she had once been a diction instructor for the world's rich and famous. "Up, if possible."

"Up, down, in, out, any old way you like, Gert," he said, sounding as if he could have used some of her diction lessons. "It's Christmas time in the Northwoods and you can have whatever your heart desires." His wide-eyed smile concealed his amazement with his mother-in-law's impeccable appearance. Whenever he saw her, no matter where or what time of day or night, she looked as if she stepped out of a fashion magazine wearing the latest creation of a world famous designer. Tidge saw Gert hold up her right thumb and index finger, the space between allowing a ray of light to squeeze through and he said: "Wee it tis durin' this season to be jolly. And

I've stocked up on cocktail onions."

Unlike her daughter, Gert had no need to frost her hair. She had been platinum blond as a pin-up model, the page boy style carrying over to the wrestling ring years later and she wasn't about to change the image. With the exception of her hair and her physical stature, Gertrude, Gert, or Trudy as she was known when she posed for risqué, cheesecake pictures in nylons, garter belt and heels, could have been an older twin sister to her daughter. Age and exercise, not the pharmaceutical industry or surgery had been good to her. A trace of lines by her eyes and a chin just starting to give way to the force of gravity only added to her stature. Gert could still climb back into the ring as *Filly* or present a seductive pose to the lens of a Zeiss Icon as Trudy.

Tidge put his arm around her shoulder and gave her a hug. "Merry Christmas again, Gert," he said. A few minutes later, as Harold and Gert unpacked, Tidge came down the hall with a Gibson in his hand singing, "He knows if you've been bad or good." He knocked on the oak frame of the open door, walked into Harold and Gert's room, and announced, "A wee libation for our very first and honored guests to Henry's Hut." He placed the long stemmed glass on the dresser. "A little nip, Harold?" he asked, the cordial host ready to serve.

"Perhaps later, Thomas" said Harold. He was a dignified, polite man, barely five six with no evidence of a spare tire that most men his age sported. Like his wife, his manners were flawless and he radiated sophistication. He reminded Tidge of watching old black and white movies on television where William Powell and Myrna Loy would be attired in formal wear in the middle of the afternoon; chain smoked and drank martinis straight up like a doe and a buck gulping water from the bay behind Henry's Hut in the heat of summer. Harold's sophistication showed no trace of his having fled from Nazi Germany with his mother during World War II, his father, a Luftwaffe pilot, staying behind to die.

"Thank you, Thomas," said Gert, discretely sliding the tooth pick with the impaled onion to the side of the glass, taking a delicate sip and returning the glass to the dresser.

Tidge wanted to like Gert more than he did, but his mind built an

invisible wall that wouldn't let him. He didn't dislike her, just feared
her. Gert's physical size, her being taller than him when she wore
high heels, which she always did because Harold loved her wearing
them, intimidated Tidge. From the first time he met Gert he asked
himself: "How in the hell can I love my mother-in-law when I feel
I'm going to go best out of three falls with her?"

Tidge liked Harold immediately. Harold's hint of a German
accent and his demeanor fascinated Tidge. Willy's father exuded a
faint aura of arrogance and an attitude he could do anything better
than anyone. That sometimes annoyed Tidge even though he knew
Harold could, and he did. Harold was a millionaire and married to
the only woman he ever fell in love with and, to him, the most
beautiful girl in the world. Tidge didn't envy him, having found his
own heaven and being married to the perfect girl, their daughter. He
would never reach Harold's tax bracket, but didn't care. Henry's Hut
was paid for; he had some savings and worked hard at his dream of
nature photography.

"How's the picture business?" Tidge heard Harold ask, as they
both watched Gert unpack and meticulously hang their clothes. She
took another lady like sip of her Gibson as she moved from the open
luggage on the bed to the closet and the dresser.

"Slow," said Tidge, hoping the conversation would take a
different direction. "Like all start-ups, a man needs at least three
years to get going."

"Quite true," said Harold, his interest more than curious.

"Lots of good art fairs and festivals across the state take place
from before Memorial Day to Columbus Day," continued Tidge,
hoping that the subject of how much money he was making wouldn't
come up. "By then, I'll have enough framed inventory to rent a space
at a fair or flea market and test the waters."

"Very wise," said Harold, nodding his approval. "I admire you,
Thomas. If I had your guts back when I was your age, I would've
loved to have done the same thing."

"Go into nature and wild life photography?" asked Tidge
surprised.

"Oh, no," said Harold, shaking his head from side to side, a
chuckle following his comment. He gave a quick glance at Gert and

said, "You might surmise that I did have a photographer's eye and that my particular line of economic endeavor paralleled that profession." A smile replaced the chuckle. "Not behind the lens, mind you, but during my tenure I did observe numerous variations of what could be interpreted as beauty in both au natural and unbridled depictions," he continued, the smile now gone. "I did well financially from the promotional and sales aspects of the business. Mind you, I never realized the staggering sums of money spent by adult males to view provocative, photographic depictions of the female gender in bathing attire and lingerie." Harold paused as if pursuing his own dream. "I would've loved to have had, how should I put it, the genitalia to extricate myself from toiling for a superior to toiling for me." Harold stopped and pointed at himself. "The only posterior I would have to plant my lips on would be by own." He stopped and glanced at his wife. "Sorry, darling." He looked back at Tidge. "You get my drift. Be your own man, your own boss."

"What would you have done?" asked Tidge, openly expressing his curiosity about the past of his father-in-law.

"I would've liked to had my own bookstore," he said, a touch of excitement going off like an old flash bulb from the photography he remembered. "Specialize in rare books. Deal in first editions, things like that." He gave a slight evidence of a sigh. "Too late now, I fear."

"Never too late," said Tidge, enjoying what he could remember as his first real conversation with Willy's father. "Find a location and I'll come down from Cable and help you set up, do all of the grunt work for you. Your daughter can come along and visit with her mother."

"I wish I had your optimism and energy," said Harold, appearing to start a laugh. He connected with Tidge again. "I've made my money and had my time in the arena." He paused, looking at his wife. "Not the same type of arena where I first met Wilhelmina's mother." There was another pause. "Actually, my entrepreneurial obligations brought me in contact with Gertrude during her days in cheesecake photography, her pseudo fashion modeling career, but never in person. Only photographs of her. She was, like she is today, stunning and I could see why men would spend money to buy a magazine with her in it."

Tidge nodded his approval to Harold while Gert appeared only interested in continuing to unpack and sip her Gibson.

"You might hypothesize," he said to Tidge, smiling. "My daughter has told me that philosophy is a special bailiwick of yours, therefore I'm sure you follow me when I say that I harbored two loves at first sight," he said, a slight chuckle interjected. "My second sight, however, was my true first and, indeed, a unique example of love at first sight." He stopped as Gert handed him a navy blue blazer and nodded towards the walk-in closet.

"Love at first sight or first fight?" asked Tidge, unable to keep from smiling and totally unaware as to the accuracy of his question.

Harold first became aware of Gert when he saw her name on a marquee. She was billed as Filly Full Nelson. He met her for the first time that evening in a smoke filled arena. Filly and her chunky opponent with an out-of-control henna crew cut came twisting and slithering through the wrestling ring ropes. There was a hair tug-o-war being waged between the two adversaries coupled with shrill screams equated with the end of human life. Harold saw only Gert and heard only his heart. Human life did not come to an end as Filly and her opponent, Boomer Bonnie spun across the space separating the ring from the first row of fans. There sat Harold Schneider. He was more than enthralled by the platinum blonde who looked anything but sophisticated. He believed he had seen her before. Then Filly ended up in Harold's lap. Boomer Bonnie, also known as the, Buxom Brute was tipped upside down, her head resting in Filly's crotch. She was like an inverted totem pole tied in a grotesque knot, her eyes inches from examining her own genitals. The crowd loved it and so did Harold. He fell in love with Gert at first sight or, if their future son-in-law had known, first fight.

Harold found himself acting most undignified as he watched the referee escort the two wrestlers back to the ring. His two index fingers had been inserted in his mouth and he was whistling loudly the way his father had taught him as a boy. He joined the ringside audience's applause, adding raucous shouts of, "Bravo!" until he thought he would lose his voice. Before the match ended he propelled himself out the main door and headed to the back entrance of the arena. On his way he bought out a street vendor's entire inventory of flowers. Then he waited. Filly noticed the sincerest, sophisticated eyes she had ever seen looking at her from behind a mountain of flowers as she exited the arena's back door. She bought a small bunch to liven up her studio apartment that she shared with Boomer Bonnie. "How much?" she asked.

"Best out of three falls?"

Tidge saw his wife standing in the bedroom doorway. "Your tour guide is back," he said, appearing to startle Harold. "The Henry's Hut noon tour is only half over." He snapped his thumb and middle finger together. "Oh, and wait until you see the sumptuous buffet your daughter has created."

"Henry's Hut," repeated Harold with a laugh. "First sight and first fight," he said, his laughter growing. "Oh, my, Thomas, your sense of humor is truly *wunderbar*."

"If there's anything you need, give a holler," said a cheerful Tidge. "Your tour guide is also our resident sugar plum fairy and your wish is her command." He glanced at the dresser and saw Gert's empty glass and then his eyes met hers. "Actually, any wish is both our commands."

"Yes, thank you, Thomas," said Gert, as she watched him take her empty glass.

"Coming right up, Gert," said Tidge, as he rolled the stem of the empty cocktail glass back and forth between his thumb and forefinger. "Santa will have a Gibson for you before Rudolph can plug in his nose to get it glowing for his Christmas Eve journey tomorrow night." He gave Willy a wink and a quick pat on her butt as he walked out the door. The pat went unnoticed having been absorbed by the plush, luxurious pelts of the mink. Another log went on his enthusiasm fire as he bounded down the stairs, saying to himself, "Two checked in, a bunch more on the way and all's right with the world provided there's no blizzard."

All wasn't right with the world when Tidge took a look out the floor-to-ceiling windows in the Great Room on his way to the kitchen to make another Gibson for Gert. The snow, now whipped by an Edmund Fitzgerald maelstrom, erased Tidge's fears of Christmas turning into the Gillette Cavalcade of Sports. This was worse. He knew blizzards, snow-packed roads and automobiles didn't mix. Factoring in memories of how his daughters managed to obtain drivers licenses, created a new set of fears. He looked at Gert's glass in his hand then headed to the kitchen. "One Gibson coming up," he said, giving more than a glance out the kitchen window and seeing only white. "Ain't nothin' this old rejected patriarch can do now," he said, seeing horizontal sheets of white streaking by. He studied the empty cocktail glass, gave a shrug and said: "Maybe I'll try one of these things. What the heck, it's Christmas."

Tidge saw the glow emerge from the woods at the end of their driveway from his post at the edge of one of the Great Room's windows. He had been like a sentry on guard duty waiting for his next guests. A pair of bouncing dim headlights poked out from the swirling blizzard and Tidge yelled out, "Another one's here!" His hand was on the front door knob before Willy and her parents heard him.

Tidge's brother, Paul led a three car caravan of snow covered and road dirt splattered cars each bounding off the rut road and skidding onto the snow buried driveway. His brothers arrived with their families at a time when the sky should have been at the tail end of waving good-bye to the remains of a fading golden ball. White obliterated gold and black. It also buried the remains of colored leaves lingering on the driveway or anywhere else.

Tidge was prepared for the weather this time, his leather jacket zipped and a Chicago Bears stocking cap pulled over his ears. Fur lined mittens and a pair of rubber Wellington boots keeping his feet warm and dry added to his protection.

The snow bludgeoned the ground at wicked, angry angles and edged up to ankle depth as he shuffled toward the faint glow of the headlights while waving and pointing frantically in the direction of the garage. Each car sported a luggage rack, the tie straps groaning against their loads. Add a rocking chair to the top of each and the cars would have resembled a convoy of Beverly Hillbillies. They parked in front of the three closed garage doors, the front bumpers inches away from the snow pocked doors each car etching matched slushy tire paths in the snow.

Tidge and Willy's pickup truck sat snug and safe inside the garage alongside of Gert and Harold's Lincoln. Tidge's fiber glass canoe rested on two wooden saw horses beside his aluminum fishing boat out of trouble on its trailer. His riding mower, fitted with a snow plow blade, prevented any more cars from being protected from the storm.

Tidge tried to look through the dirt and snow streaked windows, but could only make out four silhouettes in each car. He wanted to rub his heavy leather mittens into his eyes to be sure he wasn't suffering from snow blindness. His brothers really came.

He bounded in and out of the spaces between the cars waving like an eager child trying to get Santa's attention in a Christmas parade along Chicago's Magnificent Mile. His brother, Peter's door cracked open jarring loose a crust of ice and snow and Tidge yelled out, "Welcome and Merry Christmas!" Before Peter could say a word, Tidge had sloshed through the snow to Paul's car, opened his door and yelled, "Welcome!" Then he yanked open John's door and yelled, "Merry Christmas! What took you so long to get to Winsconsin?"

Aching adult bodies emerged from the cars. Stretching punctuated with quick exchanges of, "Merry Christmas" followed. The exchanges got blown away by the blizzard that had no sense of Christmas spirit and didn't care. The world's fastest group hugs and back slapping followed. Reality was close behind introducing the weary travelers to how much pain blowing snow could cause.

Willy emerged from the blinding snow wearing her parka and mukluks Tidge bought her when they first moved north. She left her parents sitting by the fireplace staring in a toasty awe at the hypnotic flames while she trudged through the snow to join her new family now shivering in the driveway. The novelty of standing in a blizzard vanished about the time they left the cramped warmth of their cars.

"Ladies, follow me," said Willy, foregoing any time consuming Christmas pleasantries. Her arms moved like a downtown Chicago traffic cop at rush hour. "You'll all end up turning into Frosty the Snowman if you stand out here any longer." She corralled her three sisters-in-law and started toward the house in a combination shuffle slide. "Let the men tend to the kids and unpack the cars.

"Listen to the boss!" hollered Tidge, the screaming wind drowning out his order. He slipped off his right mitten, put his hand in his pocket and pushed the garage door opener three times. The programmed signal lifted the garage door where no cars were parked, his boat and canoe having the honors as they waited for the spring thaw. Without hesitating, he opened the back door of John's car and looked into the eyes of two shy faces. "Merry Christmas," he said to his brother's two kids, Frankie and Star. "And welcome to Santa's backyard." He pointed to the open garage. "John," he hollered. "You got coats and boots for your kids?" He repeated the process twice more, wishing Merry Christmas to Natasha and Nathan, Peter's two children, and then to Pauline and Paul, Jr., all still buckled up.

Chareese, Lilly, and Lucy, oldest to youngest of the wives, and tallest to shortest, broke into their own versions of the shuffle slide. They resembled a tip toe race following in the trail Willy left for them. Each stomped their feet on the welcome mat outside that showed a snoozing black bear appearing to ignore the elements. Inside, they wiped their shoes on a second welcome mat that sported a picture of a humming bird feeding on a red flower.

Willy wasted no time getting the door closed. Shuffle slides and shivers disappeared replaced by disbelieving eyes that scanned the Great Room in detail. None of Willy's sisters-in-law anticipated a drive through a blizzard that lasted a shade over nine hours to be embraced by the warm opulence of Henry's Hut. None of them said a word while Willy absorbed every admiring expression and questioned how Tidge's father could ever refer to them as *Natives*. The expression riled her just as her husband and his brothers calling their father, Kid Scream, did. She loved her new family even though her mother-in-law had passed on almost two years before Tidge came into her life.

Peter's wife, Chareese was African American. Her father, a

personal injury liability lawyer, and her mother an anesthesiologist, lived in an elegant stucco home in the Chicago North Shore suburb of Kennilworth, Lake Michigan visible at the end of their street. She had met Peter at a Glow in the Dark bowling fund raiser for Notre Dame High School for Girls. The introduction came when, during her back swing on her very first ball, the ball slipped from her hand and cracked into Peter's right shin. The only color he saw when he looked at Chareese was a brief flash of painful orange followed by a zap of aching yellow. Black was beautiful and so was love at first sight. His shin didn't show black until two days later.

After several dates, one consisting of meeting Peter's parents in their tiny Cape Cod house, Chareese, at the insistence of her parents, invited Peter and his family to their home for dinner. It took The Kid and Mother Mary May I a week to get their jaws closed after seeing where and how Peter's girlfriend lived. Her being black in color didn't matter to them. Her parent's wealth humbled them. That evening they dined in elegance, seated at a dining room table that couldn't fit in the combined kitchen and living room of their Cape Cod. Mother Mary May I only saw opulence like that in movies and on magazine covers. The next day at supper in their cramped kitchen, the Kid said to his son: "Pietr, you're in over your head. Those folks are from the filet mignon sector of society, not like us." He paused and could see his son getting agitated. "Love her if you must, but remember all you can afford are chitlins and, maybe, kielbasa for Sunday lunch."

Kid Scream's perceived bigotry didn't hinder his other two sons from marrying other species of Natives. Working with the Kid on the loading dock of a meat packing plant were two of his closest friends, Harry Wong and Sid Stooping, Sid a full blooded Cherokee. Theirs was a unique relationship filled with colorful nicknames, most making sense only to them. They shared brown bag lunches, and stopped for a single drink at a local bar together after work. The Kid was known most times as *Ski* because of his Polish heritage. Other times he was called *Polack*, the name preceded by descriptive terms ranging from mental defectiveness to crude sexual innuendos. Harry responded to *Charlie, Charlie Chan, Chop,* as in chop sticks, or *Chink.* Sid was called *Chief, Cherokee Kid,* after Will Rogers, *Will,* or *Skins* because he was an avid Washington Redskins fan. It was Harry Wong's accidental death on the loading dock, crushed by a fork lift truck, that brought Tidge's brother Paul and his future wife together.

The Kid did more than insist his entire family attend the wake, he threatened them. They went. There, among the mourners, The Kid unable to stop sobbing, Paul met Lilly the deceased's youngest daughter. At the funeral the next day, attended by Mackiewicz family with a still sobbing Kid Scream, Paul exchanged pleasantries with Lilly. His round eyes never left her almond shaped ones. Like his brother, Peter, he fell in love, this after second sight.

Sid Stooping attended both the wake and funeral for his friend, Harry, who he kept referring to as, Charlie. His daughter, Lucy, had accompanied him to the funeral. She saw John at the funeral and couldn't take her eyes off him. John never saw her. For her, it was love at first sight followed by a contrived phone call to the Mackiewicz home looking for her father, a widower, who had not followed his usual routine of coming home after work. Skins and Ski made their usual stop for a drink after work. Sid, a recovering alcoholic, drank ice water with a lime wedge from an on-the-rocks glass and only The Kid knew it. During this stop, in honor of their late friend, they each had three drinks. After several, futile embarrassing tries on the phone, Lucy took it upon herself to go to the Mackiewicz home in search of her father. Seeing John Mackiewicz in a controlled environment, she thought, might be a bonus.

John opened the front door and saw Lucy Stooping. Her bonus became his bonus as Cupid's arrow hit John in the center of his heart. Gone forever was John's fetish for mother-daughter combinations.

Still outside in the hollowing northern Wisconsin storm, Tidge's brothers slipped and slid in snow that had inched over their ankles. "Where do you want our stuff?" yelled Peter to Tidge, his words being whipped by the wind into something more like the Chipmunk Song.

Tidge pointed several times in the direction of the house and got a "thumbs up" gesture from Peter. Several more emphatic points at the house saw Paul and John open the hatch-backs of their vehicles. Tidge rounded up his three nephews and three nieces and herded them out of the snow into the garage. "Do you guys have boots and gloves?" he asked the kids. The kids looked in the direction of their fathers.

"Hey," yelled Tidge at his brothers who looked like three white blurs. "You guys got boots, hats and gloves for your kids?" The blizzard distorted his words into gibberish that Alvin and the Chipmunks wouldn't understand. He took off one of his gloves and waved it at his brothers who were now wrestling with uncooperative tie-down straps. His three brothers, hands feeling the razor sharp cold and showing signs of turning both blue and numb, disappeared into the hatch backs of the three SUV's. Bits and pieces of winter wear arched through the air, his brothers sounding as if they belonged on the same Christmas song as Tidge. Hats landed on the garage floor along with gloves that were minus their mates. Thuds were heard coming from boots bouncing off the hull of the aluminum boat as the blizzard roared and tried to enter the open garage. Tidge sorted through the collection of assorted boots, gloves, stocking caps, scarves and jackets scattered throughout the garage. His nieces and nephews appeared not to notice the cold, their attention, instead, fixed on a canoe, a boat with an outboard motor and a riding lawn mower that had a small snow plow blade attached.

"Uncle Thomas," said Peter's son, Nathan, his shyness nudged aside by an emerging curiosity coupled with a touch of bravery, "could I plow your driveway?"

An explosion of five enthusiastic, "Me too, Uncle Thomas. Me too," followed the request.

"Who needs help getting on their boots?" asked Tidge, seeming not to hear the request for snow removal and not noticing that the older children were helping their younger siblings get winterized. When all of the kids were bundled up and passed Tidge's inspection, he called out to his brothers: "Hey, guys, your children are accounted for and dressed for action. Get inside the house before your *dupas* come down with frost bite!" He didn't know if his brothers heard him, but he pushed the remote mounted inside the side access door to the garage and the door settled gently down.

Tidge took a quick glance at his nieces and nephews. Then, acting like John Wayne as a U.S. Calvary officer, he raised his right hand, pointed it forward like the Duke on location in Monument Valley and yelled out, "Yo!" The kids looked at him and didn't move. He looked back at the kids. "That means follow me on a short cut to the world's best snow for making snowmen, and good packing for a snowball fight." The kids looked at each other, some shy, others curious and then followed their uncle through the garage and out the side access door closest to the house not knowing what to expect.

At the outside entrance to the back of the house, Tidge flipped on a wall switch. Four flood lights lit up the back yard as six variations of, "Awesome," got swept away by the howling wind. In minutes, the sounds of kids screaming and yelling, oblivious to the angry, pelting snow and the effects of hours being cooped up in a car, never noticed their uncle's two heavy leather mittens brush at the corners of his eyes.

Tidge's brothers grunted and groaned as they hauled, pushed and slid their miscellaneous luggage across the snow covered driveway, their ankles measuring the depth of the snow. Bulging duffle bags, an assortment of backpacks in a variety of colors, cardboard boxes and miscellaneous sizes of paper and plastic bags plowed through the blinding snow to the protective overhang of the front entrance. None of the brothers wore a coat and each had an inch of snow crowning their heads. Trails to and from the house and cars resembled a visit by a stampeding herd of frightened elk that wandered too far south. The front entrance to Henry's Hut could have easily been mistaken for a display at a Cable sidewalk sale.

The near frozen brothers stomped their feet at the front door while bare hands brushed, wiped and shook off snow. The snoozing bear never stirred. Stomping, brushing, wiping and shaking gave way to a luggage brigade. Duffle bags, school backpacks, Chareese's four piece matched set of designer luggage and an array of wrapped Christmas presents protected in several plastic lawn and leaf bags, three paper shopping bags and six cardboard cartons got passed through the front door. Three almost frozen fathers wasted no time stepping inside and closing the door, John saying: "Now I know that the cry of the Key-key Bird is for real." His brothers nodded with Paul delivering the punch line to the old joke: "Key-key-key, Christ its cold!"

Willy left her still silent, appraising sisters-in-law to greet Tidge's brothers. She managed four steps in their direction when she saw the same silent facial expressions. Her feet froze to the carpet runner spanning the front door to the stairs, a wave of emotion ready to pounce like a poised lynx, the tell-tale arched brows accentuating the stalking eyes. Her husband's brothers looked like marble statues under a spell. Nothing moved. "Are you three frozen stiff?" she asked.

"Only key-keyed," answered Peter, an impish grin being flashed. His arms returned to slapping warmth and circulation into his upper body.

The sound of a sophisticated, "Merry Christmas, divine family," made six pairs of eyes blink and focus on Harold, a cut crystal punch cup extended in a toast to the new arrivals as he said in German, "*Wie geht's?*"

"How delightful to see all of you again," added Gert. She was by her husband's side, a Gibson held delicately in her hand. "I believe the last time Harold and I had the pleasure was at Wilhelmina's wedding reception."

Willy's parents were dressed in corduroy sports jackets and gabardine slacks. Harold's jacket was burgundy in color, his trousers a Christmas green. Gert's ensemble reversed. They both wore white wool turtleneck sweaters and his and hers matching deer skin ankle high slippers lined with white lamb's wool fleece. Long green and red stripped woolen scarves hung down from their shoulders making them appear like priests ready for Baptisms. "I see you're admiring the lavish accommodations," said Harold, taking a sip of a steaming, dark purple liquid. "Wilhelmina, darling, do get each of your guests a cup of this marvelous elixir your most thoughtful husband procured from Sweden."

The brothers exchanged glances as did their wives. Then they exchanged glances with each other. Peter appeared to stare at Willy for a full minute before he said: "My brother lives here? With you? Inside? And you allow it?"

Willy blushed.

Paul let out a soft whistle. "Willy, if this is the Great Room, what names do you have for the rest of the rooms in this castle of yours?"

"Is that for us?" asked John, nodding at the dining room table.

Willy smiled.

"A magnificent culinary display," said Harold, his hand doing a single sweeping motion in the direction of the lavish buffet. "My Wilhelmina could give Julia and, of course, myself competition in the kitchen."

"Indeed she could," said Gert.

"Enough already," said Willy, pointing at Tidge's brothers and then at the pile of luggage jamming the front entrance. "The children will be sleeping in the second floor loft," she said, her right index finger aimed at the double wide polished stair case. "Your rooms are down the hall behind me." Her orientation and orders continued. "We'll have a small bite to eat after my front entrance is cleared." She looked at her sisters-in-law. "Ladies, I think we should put the presents under the Christmas tree." Then she gave a look to her brothers-in-law and pointed again at the stairs. "The loft!"

"Gee, Harold," said Peter, to Willy's father. "Your daughter's one tough cookie."

Harold held out his punch cup in a toast, his eyes saying, "I know." He gave them a friendly nod and said: "Gets that from her mother." A look of melancholy washed over him. "And, if I were a man who placed wagers, who I'm not, I'd say her strength also came from both my late parents." He glanced into the purple of the glogg. "Especially my father," he whispered.

Tidge's brothers nodded then returned to grunting and groaning as they hauled their kids' duffle bags and backpacks up to the loft on the far end of the second floor. The six kids would have their choice of two single mattresses, two matching box springs, one double blow up mattress, and two blowup floats that were used during the summer for swimming. There were stacks of blankets suitable for Roald Amundsen's polar expedition and pillows to accommodate a dozen more sleepy heads. Soon after, another series of grunts and groans echoed from the first floor hall as adult bags and baggage disappeared into three bedrooms. Wives, along with Willy and her mother put the final touches on arranging Christmas gifts that surrounded the tree while Harold contributed as overseer.

About then, Tidge escorted his three nieces inside from playing in the snow, the girls tired of being picked on by the boys. Multiple complaints entered the room with them. "Ma, Frankie threw snow in my face," was the first. Another sibling got blamed for shoving snow down his sister's neck. "Ma, I hate Paul." Her statement didn't need a junior attached to it as she added, "He's a brat." Natasha, the oldest of the girls said, "Oh, mother, Nathan is a disgusting Cretin."

Tidge herded the girls back into the mud room where they hung up their coats, kicked off their boots and left their stocking caps and gloves in a hodge-podge pile on top the clothes dryer.

It didn't take the kids long to warm up sprawled out on the Great Room floor fascinated by the mesmerizing dance of a blazing fire in the field stone fireplace. A twelve foot Christmas tree, surrounded by the gaily wrapped presents, stood at a proud attention, glistening in its sparkling glory in a corner opposite the dining room table. "Your Uncle Thomas chopped that down himself," he said to the girls, making him sound like a professional lumber jack. He left out the part that Don Miller finished a botched job with his chain saw and that Kenny Miller helped Tidge drag the monstrous tree from the woods, across the yard and driveway and into the Great Room. There was also no mention made of the Miller family helping get the tree upright and into the homemade stand Tidge made. That night Tidge and Willy awoke to a crash from the Great Room. The tree had toppled over.

The girls didn't say a word, their wide eyes saying all that needed to be said. "As soon as your Aunt Mina gets in here, we'll all have a snack and then she'll give you girls some of the best cookies you will ever eat," said their Uncle Tidge. "She made them herself." They looked at him with eyes about to fall out of their sockets. "And, I'm also going to show you how to make popcorn on an open fire."

"Without a microwave?" Star, the youngest asked.

Tidge picked up the long handled metal corn popper, the container blackened by years of flame. "Meet your Northwoods style microwave corn popper."

Tidge's daughters arrived after midnight and well after the estimated driving time his etched invitations had stated.

The blizzard had moved out after making a preliminary White Christmas statement. Tidge knew his girls would be late. Getting out of work with the rest of Chicago and suburbs, going home, loading their cars and heading north in rush hour traffic would add at least an hour or more to their trip. He hadn't anticipated a blizzard. After numerous nervous trips pacing to the front door window, he felt relieved when he saw two sets of headlights piercing the inky black velvet blanket that had replaced the blizzard. A sky filled with speckled bragging stars appeared to have guided them on the final leg. The two cars plowed up the slope of the driveway, axle deep snow making tires spin and hum. A greeting from a roof trimmed with glowing colored lights peeking out from a cover of snow had both cars heading for the house. A jogging figure, waving and pointing, solved the dilemma and the cars pulled up alongside the three giant snow mounds in front of the garage doors. Tidge's brothers' cars resembled igloos.

Before two ignition switches clicked off, Tidge was standing in between the cars. His beat-up leather jacket was inside, warm and toasty, hanging from a coat hook. "Merry Christmas," he said, his grin bigger than his snow covered property as he looked at Carm and Carol. Then his snow covered drive and his eight acres of white, Christmas card trees got a shock.

Carol and Carm drove together and, as Tidge remembered from his youngest daughter's RSVP note, she bought a surprise. "Daddy," said Carol, a touch of pride coated with a shield of protection, "I'd like you to meet my boyfriend, Mackie."

Suddenly, Tidge wished for the warmth and protection provided by his missing jacket. "Merry Christmas, Mackie," he said, reaching into the car across his daughter to the driver and shaking his hand. "Welcome and Merry Christmas." Just as quickly he spun around and saw the window of the other car rolled down. "Merry Christmas, Martha," he said, placing his hand on the fur collar of her chocolate brown leather coat.

"Merry Christmas, Dad," Martha said, turning, looking up, a soft smile joining her long black hair that cascaded over her left eye making her look like her mother. "After the ride up that road of yours and seeing all those lights I can't wait to see what a real tundra looks like in the daylight."

"You'll love it," said Tidge, standing between the two cars and shivering as he listened to Carm from the back seat say: "We accidentally met Martha at a truck stop off the Interstate in a place called Osseo."

"I know where it's at," said Tidge, his teeth starting to chatter. "You can get a huge slab of pie there in a café called the Norske Nook."

"We didn't see any pie, Dad, but that's where we saw Martha at the gas pump looking like a human popcicle," continued Carm, no trace of being a weary traveler. "The snow was so thick we were lucky we could see. That's when we decided to follow each other."

Tidge kept looking at Mackie. "Where'd you meet my daughter?" he asked the suspicion of an overly protective father evident. "Boyfriend was not a term he hugged to his bosom."

"We met at the roller rink," Carol interrupted, her beaming smile disarming her father as did her black ponytail sticking out of the back of a Chicago Blackhawks cap she wore. "He was home from military school in Missouri for Thanksgiving vacation," she continued, her bubbly personality filled with pride and excitement. "He drove from that pie place of yours and got us here all safe and sound." Her hand rested on the sleeve of Mackie's maroon and gold letterman's jacket. "We wouldn't be here right now if it wasn't for him."

Tidge leaned in the passenger side window and kissed Carol on the cheek. "Thanks for getting my girls here in one piece, Mackie. I can imagine that driving was no picnic." He reached across his daughter and shook hands again with the young man who had a matching maroon and gold stocking cap pulled down over his ears.

"You're welcome, Sir," said Mackie, his military demeanor evident.

"That sir stuff isn't necessary," Tidge said to Mackie. "Just call me Tidge."

"A pleasure to meet you, Mister Tidge, Sir," said Mackie in a polite drawl that had too much Chicagoeze spilling out: "Drivin' wasn't all *dat* bad if *ya'll* concentrated on what *ya* were doin'. It's kind of like drivin' a car on *da* icy ruts of *Chacaga* streets. If you can drive on *dem*, you can drive *anywherez*."

Eau Claire, Wisconsin's driving conditions were not the same as

Chicago's icy ruts, as Mackie learned, and their speed was soon cut in half. "I just wanted to apologize to *ya'll* for gettin' here so late."

"You're all here and that's the important thing," said Tidge. The cold, now in total control of him, had him saying: "Time to unload." His breath had ice crystals on it. "There's a fire roaring inside, plenty of food and even a relaxing beverage or two."

"Did you say food, Mister Tidge, Sir?" said Mackie.

"I did," said Tidge bending down and looking at Carol's surprise again. His name Tidge later learned was Ronald Paul Mackenzie "Mackie" Johnston, and Tidge began to doubt his idea of a family Christmas. Not even Willy and her extensive list of contingency plans had allowed for a Mackie.

When the three sisters and Mackie finally got inside, they were greeted by the backs of six worn out children. The younger kids were stuffed with popcorn and cookies packing down on their aunt's buffet supper. Each displayed their own unique reluctance at trudging up the polished staircase to bed. Star bringing up the rear, stopped and turned. "Merry Christmas, Aunties," she said, the batteries of her innocent child's voice run down to a flicker of energy. "Will you come and tuck me in?"

"Merry Christmas," came a chorus of the newly arrived voices aimed at the backs of five heads and the face of one fresh, but very tired little girl. Mackie's booming voice carried an enthusiastic spirit that almost drowned out the others. "I'll tuck you in!"

The front door opened and a wave of frigid air filled the entry way along with Tidge. He pushed a pink duffle bag into the house with his right foot while carrying in Martha's and Carm's luggage. Tidge looked in Mackie's direction. "Your stuff is on the front porch," he said with a nod as he closed the door.

"Thank you, Sir," said Mackie. He was outside and back in before the cold had a chance to enter the house.

Tidge pushed and carried his daughters' bags to the foot of the stairs saying to himself, "I'm still not liking this kid under my roof for Christmas." He went up the stairs to Willy's Boss Turf carrying seven assorted pieces of travel bags.

A weary welcoming toast, in the form of two empty extended glasses belonging to Harold and Gert, greeted the late arrivers. Two drowsy heads feeling an early morning departure from Chicago's Gold Coast, coupled with Gert's steady flow of Gibsons and Harold enjoying several cups of Tidge's homemade Swedish Glogg, finally caught up with them. "We're not being rude," said Harold, his polite demeanor refusing to yield to sleep. "Both Mrs. Schneider and I beat the birds out of bed this morning and we are both feeling fatigued after our arduous journey to this Christmas card environment." He glanced at his wife who was sitting on the edge of her chair, back straight, ankles crossed in a lady like manner, her long stem cocktail class still extended in a toast and eyes smiling. She was sound asleep. Harold placed his right hand under her left arm and said: "Come, my *liebchen*, we need our rest so we might give a proper *wellkommen* to Christmas Eve morning." They both smiled and walked up the stairs to the second floor, Gert sashaying like a fashion model on a Nordstrom's runway.

Tidge's brothers had welcomed their nieces with the slight wave of hands executed from sprawled positions coming from comfortable chairs. His sisters-in-law had no problems getting their collective broods ushered up the stairs and settled in place. The intriguing, pitched loft ceiling giving each child a feeling that they were exploring a cave. The explorers were sleeping before their mothers turned off the light.

Tidge's sisters-in-law tip toed down the stairs to greet Tidge's girls with hugs and a series of Merry Christmases.

Mackie, his military buzz cut of red hair exposed, managed to utter a muffled, "Merry Christmas," through a large chunk of ham, turkey, corned beef and American cheese sandwich held together by two slices of cranberry walnut bread, stone ground mustard oozing out the sides staining his fingers. The buffet sidetracked his tucking in of tiny Star.

Tidge looked at Mackie and said to himself: "If that red headed fart looks at my little girl even cross eyed, he's going to find himself sleeping in that snow covered pile of leaves by the back deck."

Willy continued playing her role as the energetic hostess applying the lessons learned from her mother. The do's and don'ts, the ins and outs and the ups and downs of entertaining were carried out. It didn't matter whether stomachs stuffed with food and alcohol and brains intoxicated by pure fresh air felt content. She would not be content until all her guests had received the prescribed welcome, Wilhelmina Schneider Mackiewicz style. She would relax when she was finally convinced that not even the din from grandma getting run over by a reindeer would wake her guests. That wouldn't happen until everyone had started back home.

Tidge's daughters, like the other adult family members who arrived earlier in the day, went silent, the aura of the Great Room holding them spellbound until Willy worked her magic. "The buffet is open and waiting, ladies," she said, her invitation excluding Mackie. He appeared to be eating his way on a diagonal course in both directions unimpeded. Then he found his course blocked by three famished women.

Tidge, relieved that his girls arrived safe, still felt he had been hammered by one of his father's old punches. It was one of his best, exploding into his solar plexus, dropping him to his knees where he took a mandatory nine count. His baby had a boyfriend, a boyfriend who had left his own family to be with another family during the most festive time of the year. "What kind of a kid would leave his family at Christmas?" he asked himself. Tidge didn't have an answer, at least not one that he liked. Another thing he didn't like was the fact that there would be a boyfriend sleeping in the same house as his little girl. His mind raced out of control as he said to himself: "The damned kid's got to be a juvenile delinquent or on the F.B.I.'s Ten Most Wanted list to be in military school." He cautiously approached Carol's tall, lanky red headed boyfriend with the military buzz cut as if he were about to pet the head of a giant snapping turtle he had seen sunning himself next to an old boat house two bays to the north that summer. "How come military school, Mackie?" he asked, trying to read his enemy's expression, his mannerisms. "You some kind of a bad kid?"

"In regards to your question, Sir," said Mackie, a polite smile reeking with military bearing along with a trace of mustard on the corners of his mouth. "I'm a lucky kid," he continued, his thick southern drawl more prominent than earlier and all but covering up his native Chicago tongue. "My grandfather thought a military school education was the best thing any young guy could have."

"Your grandfather," repeated Tidge.

"Yes, Sir," replied Mackie with respect Tidge remembered during his orientation at the Great Lakes Naval Training Center. "My grandfather's a strong believer in duty, honor and country. He's the family patriarch."

"Patriarch," Tidge repeated, surprised that there was more than someone besides himself bestowed with the title. "He keeps the family in line, does he?"

"Yes, Sir," said Mackie, still placing an emphasis on, Sir as his polite demeanor grew more solid by the minute. "His word's the law in our family."

Tidge turned and gave his brothers a quick glance. "I kind of like that," he said, getting the feeling that Santa Claus had delivered an additional special present early. He turned to his girls and said, "My law states that you ladies will be sleeping in Willy's studio. It's marked by a sign, Boss Turf. That's where she does her writing." He saw his daughter's nod. "You each have your own bed," he continued, "and there's the powder room down the hall." He looked at Carol's boyfriend, a faint trust emerging. "Mackie, Sir, you'll crash on the sofa in my den down here."

"Thank you, Sir," said Mackie, his drawl making Tidge forget about delinquency and wanting, instead, to send him back to military academy before he had a chance to crash on any piece of furniture near where Carol slept. Politeness only came from his late mother, Willy and her parents. He wasn't used to being called, Sir by the grandson of another patriarch.

Eating continued with Tidge's brothers grazing and picking at the platters of assorted meats and cheeses while they visited and joked with their nieces. Mackie ate like he hadn't seen food since he boarded a bus for Chicago a week earlier to start his Christmas furlough from military school.

Sleep slowly overtook the Great Room and Tidge escorted his daughters to Willy's studio. "This is your stepmother's favorite place in the entire house," he said, another touch of pride in his voice. He pointed at her Boss Turf sign. "The great American novel is being written in this very room."

Once Tidge sensed his girls' needs were met, he hustled back and forth, sometimes at a run, checking on his guests. Harold and Gert's door was closed and no light was visible. "First in, first out," he whispered to himself. Then he bounded down the stairs two at a time to show Mackie the den. "Where did you say you were from, Sir?" he asked. A quick, "Oops, Mackie," followed.

"No problem, Sir," answered Mackie. "I'm from Chicago, Sir," the answer still coated with the consistent southern drawl. "I live half way between Sox Park and the Home Run Inn."

"Where did you pick up all that ya'll stuff?"

Mackie stood at ram rod straight attention again. "Sir," he said, "I kind of picked up the accent in Mexico, Missouri," pronouncing the end of the state with an *a* instead of an *e*.

"Is that where you're military schools at?" asked Tidge.

"Yes, Sir."

Tidge had to ask. "That town filled with Mexicans, Mackie?"

A polite, serious, "No, Sir," followed. "Mexicoans, Sir." His attention hadn't faltered. "Missouri Military Academy, MMA for short, is located there, Sir. The school's been there over a hundred years. Founded in 1889."

"Oh," said Tidge, not realizing he had been corrected. Then a bolt of lightning shot through his head. The town of Mexico, Missouri jarred his memory along with the scene at the kitchen table in his Uncle Brew's apartment. You did say Mexico, Missouri?"

"Yes, Sir," replied Mackie, his politeness not wavering a fraction.

"Well, I'll be," muttered Tidge, his mind flashing so many signals at him he thought his brain had turned into a Navy Pier summer fireworks display.

"Did I say something wrong, Sir?"

"No, Sir, you did not," said Tidge, and then quickly asking, "You got enough towels?" The palm of his hand shot up. "A nod will be sufficient," he said. "You can save the sir stuff for Missouri." He headed out the door on his way to the other rooms to ask the same question and to be sure and inform each of his guests about how a septic system worked. All the while he kept repeating two words to himself, "Mexico, Missouri."

With his brothers and their wives tucked snug in their beds, he hurried back to the Great Room to help his wife. Euphoria had him by the throat. His heart raced. His brain raced. He had all he could do to squash the urge to sprint out the back door without opening it, dive into the knee deep snow and make snow angels. "Thank God," he muttered, "for Aunt Bessie's recipe. That glogg will make tonight calm and have some family members seeing Mother Ginger's children in their sleep."

Tidge's euphoria couldn't match his wife's feelings. Her mother's Eleventh Commandment for entertaining worked to perfection. She had watched their family and one extra guest devour and lay to waste her buffet. Each of her brothers-in-law, in their own unique way, paid their compliments to her. Peter, at one point, the left side of his mouth bulging and strands of corned beef, ham, turkey breast and salami extruding from his lips said, his words muffled, "Wilhelmina, this is some kind of snack." The bulge in his mouth shifted from one side to the other. "I haven't tasted anything this good since Chareese's father took me to the south side and Gladys's Luncheonette for soul food."

Once Carol's boyfriend discovered the buffet table, he consumed enough to feed the entire cadet corps at his military academy in Missouri. He had bombarded her with polite, "Thank you, Mam's", until she wanted to lead him to the spot in the woods where she and Tidge had been shot at and stake him spread-eagled to the ground.

Tidge noticed Willy in the hall between the kitchen and the Great Room after their Christmas guests had headed off to bed. "Can you believe it," he said to her, his whisper unable to contain his excitement. "They're all here, and one extra to boot." He gave her a hug. "Oh, man, this is going to be the best Christmas ever."

Willy glanced down at the floor then slowly looked up until she saw her reflection in her husband's excited blue eyes. "Were you ever a Hippie?" she asked, startling him. "I mean did you ever do drugs?" Her second question rattled him.

"What?" he asked, now feeling totally stunned.

"I'd give anything to be stoned right now," she said, continuing to surprise him. "Stoned is the right word, isn't it?"

"That's correct," he said, wanting to laugh, but not daring. "Why the jumpin' jitters all of a sudden?"

"Too calm," she said, stepping to him and putting her arms around his neck. "Something's going to go wrong. I can feel it."

"Relax, girl of my dreams," he said, tightening his arms around her. "It's beginning to look a lot like Christmas."

"I know." She began to tremble. "That's why I'd give anything to be stoned right now."

"I wouldn't know anything about this getting stoned business," he said with a smile. He brushed his lips across her forehead. "I was too busy back then growing shaggy long hair, underage drinking and trying to find all those emancipated women who had discovered the pill and free love."

Willy closed her eyes, gave a slow exhale and shook her head. "I wouldn't know. I was only a wee tot back then." She loosened her arms and stepped back, her face pleading. "Will you get me a cup of that glogg of yours?"

"For you, I can do anything," he said, looking at her questioning, his eyes asking. "I can bring it up to our bedroom if you'd like. A sip of Aunt Bessie's Swedish elixir will have you, as Mother Mary May I used to say to us kids, "As snug as a bug in a rug.""

She turned and started for the stairs. "I like your bedroom idea," she said. "Do you think you could put that glogg in a pitcher for me when you come up?"

"If Santa can bring the whole fam-dam-ily to Henry's Hut for Christmas, he can do anything."

Chapter 7

Willy held hands with the rising Christmas Eve sun, escorting it into her kitchen the way she was once presented to society at a gala debutante ball. She was a solo whirlwind infusing the aroma of a *Woods and Waters* blend custom ground coffee brewing throughout the house. Her fear of things being too calm at the end of day one didn't have the opportunity to linger. She couldn't wait to say, "Breakfast is served."

Willy's fears of having her parents relegate her intricate holiday plans to a ho-hum comparison to Christmas silver bells ding-a-linging along the S-curve of the Outer Drive view from their apartment vanished. Yesterday's blizzard eliminated all signs of ho-hum. So did hugging and kissing her mother and father, seeing their looks of approval and hearing their almost envious comments about Henry's Hut. She was elated and now immune from any pending catastrophe. If an ice storm with a loss of electric power hit in the middle of Christmas dinner, she was prepared. She felt confident and prepared for any man-made, or one of Mother Nature's, catastrophes. That's what she thought.

From almost the time of conscious awareness, Wilhelmina Schneider witnessed her parents, the consummate hostess and host, entertain guests. Now it was her turn. Her mother's Eleventh Commandment edict, *Thou Shalt Eat Drink and Be Merry Asterisk,* emerged from her childhood memory bank. Her mother's Commandment was the underlying motivation behind yellow legal page upon yellow legal page being filled with plans, schedules, itineraries and contingencies. The asterisk, a star affixed permanently to the last letter of her mother's Commandment, meant, "Guests with bloated bellies and bladders stay mellow while others bellow." Her guests settled into a mellow mode soon after arriving. A nervous hostess, plagued for weeks by a gnawing premonition that this year

Christmas and Armageddon were on a collision course, stayed nervous. Her guests had retired for the evening, too mellow.

Tidge's Swedish glogg, her buffet and the glowing asterisk preceded by hours of driving, resulted in an almost humorous collection of nodding heads. Armageddon had been diverted, hauled away to be dumped onto the mountains of rubble at the abandoned taconite mines in the Gogebic Iron Range east and north of Lake Namakagon. Even though it had been the second night before Christmas, Willy, and empty cut glass crystal cup on her night stand, slept as if she were stoned.

Star was the first creature who stirred that night. She woke up Natasha and Pauline to take her to the bathroom. The only adult creature who stirred was Tidge. He bolted to a sitting position, sweating as if he crawled out of a sauna. Gasping for air and sounding like an old steam locomotive that once hauled ore from the Gogebic Iron Range, he knew it wasn't a bad dream that woke him. He had come face to face with Santa Claus. What made him sweat was that Santa had two elves assisting him who he addressed as Moron One and Moron Two. Humper and Bean Head grinned back at Tidge from Santa's side and sang: "Tidge ain't gettin' nuttin' for Christmas."

"Damned glogg," said Tidge, noticing his own empty cut glass crystal cup on his night stand. A few hours earlier he and Willy had gone to bed after being sure their guests were settled in for the night. After they had sipped their glogg and shared whispered comments about how smooth day one with Christmas holiday guests had gone, a brief good-night kiss followed and their night stand lights were switched off. In moments they were out like their lights.

Sometime during the night, Tidge found himself burning in a special, exclusive Hell designed for patriarchs who hadn't carried out the last wishes of dying fathers. He wasn't alone. Taunting him were a familiar cast of characters from throughout his life. They snarled at him like a pack of wild dogs prowling the woods searching for something to eat. He was their entrée. Kid Scream, Uncle Brew and Chinese Fuckers with Burp Guns showed their ugly fangs. Barbara Ann, Mickey's father, Santa Claus and Humper were in the middle of the pack barking. Mother Mary May I yelped at him, her barking sounding like *can* and *may*. An adult, voluptuous Marietta Claus wearing a red bathing suit and a Santa Claus hat smiled seductively at him from her perch straddling the nose of the B-25 bomber with the name, *Sugar Claus* painted beneath her. "Sorry about dumping you after high school graduation," she said, the seductive smile enhanced by the puffy, white ball from the Santa Claus hat dangling over one eye. "I knew there had to be more in life than spend every weekend at the drive-in movie with you."

Tidge heard a subdued growl and looked to see Brother James Virgil, his favorite teacher from high school. Bro Jay-V, as Tidge respectfully addressed him, had his eyes locked on Tidge. Tidge cast a silent questioning look.

Brother James Virgil stated in a disappointed voice that matched the look on his face, "Mackiewicz, you are an amalgamation of Morons One, Two, Three and Four."

Then he heard his brothers repeating, "Do what? Say what?" They sneered and snapped then asked in unison, "Who died and made you Boss Patriarch?"

Tidge tossed and turned, kicked at the covers and twisted his pillow thinking it was the neck of his daughter's new boyfriend. Mackie didn't seem to care. He was polite, respectful, a model of military discipline stating to Tidge: "Ya'll put up your dukes, Sir." Tidge couldn't. He wouldn't. "No more dukes," he said, feeling his sweat turn to ice. Then Mackie began dancing with Marietta Claus to an even scratchier version of Kay Starr's Wheel of Fortune. Marietta Claus winked at him and said: "Wear the Santa suit, Thomas. It'll mean the world to me." She blew the white ball from her Santa Claus hat away from her eye. "My real father would also love seeing you wear it." She paused, kissed Mackie on the cheek and added: "Pretty please."

After several gasps, a shiver, a sniffle and eyes darting, he looked down to the foot of the bed and noticed that both wool sweat socks he always wore to bed in the winter were clinging to his toes. Relieved the pack of wild dogs had vanished, he leaned over, kissed Willy on the side of her neck, flipped over his soaking pillow and went back to sleep.

Willy's action plan for Christmas Eve morning sped along. She still had her concerns about the full bladder and alcohol consumption portion of her mother's Eleventh Commandment, especially after seeing her consume one Gibson after another since arriving. Willy opted to emphasize full stomachs, saying to the quiet of her kitchen: "All I want for Christmas is peace on earth and my mother somewhat sober."

Willy didn't know it, but she had exceeded her father's expectations of her learning the culinary arts. Good cooking didn't come from luck. Meals that brought on salivating were the result of preparation meeting opportunity. She had, after considerable thought, prepared several baking dishes of her culinary egg creations.

Tidge had savored each dish. He had no favorite. He smacked his lips and said, "Ah," being his stamp of approval. He also nicknamed the egg dishes, like he nicknamed most anything that was animal, vegetable or mineral. His labels, according to Willy, were gross and disgusting earning him her special nickname: "Gross pig!"

Her egg dishes sat poised on the counter ready to go into the oven of her professional chef's range. The black porcelain, six burner stove trimmed in stainless didn't wait long. She pulled open the oven door and began talking to each dish before sliding it in. Detesting her husband's insulting names, she converted them to what she called civil. "Bongiorno," she said to the Italian specialty of fennel laced sausage and mozzarella cheese, its base on top of slices of buttered bread in a baking dish. Chunks of green peppers, onions and mushrooms seemed happy and content nestled throughout the eggs. It went in the oven first and had the honor of resting on the top front of the three stainless grated racks in Willy's place of prominence. Then her tribute to her Canadian neighbors to the north followed. She used their style of bacon for her second creation. There was a touch of maple syrup added to the baking dish of eggs mixture and a thick cheddar hollandaise sauce intertwined with asparagus spears. The middle oven shelf caressed her second effort. The final dish of ham, scallions, sliced tomato and smoked salmon flavored cream cheese slid onto the bottom shelf. "Shalom," she said with a nod as the oven door closed.

Her hands became a blur as cellophane wrap peeled free from a package unleashing ten pounds of pork sausage links the butcher at "U-per John's Dressed Game and Meat Market" in Cable had stuffed for her. They began to hiss, spit and sputter the moment they hit the largest of her collection of cast iron skillets. A complacent aura settled over her kitchen thanks to a second fresh blanket of snow that had moved in during the night. She kept glancing out the kitchen window at the snow that exceeded anything she prayed for or that Hallmark could have created.

The first pot of coffee finished brewing with a series of hisses as Tidge and Paul entered the kitchen. "Good morning, poor suffering wife of Ansel Adams's illegitimate son," said Paul, his voice, like him, still half asleep.

"Good morning, Paul," she said, flashing a quick cheerful smile. "Merry Christmas Eve to you." She nodded her head twice over her right shoulder. "Help yourself to some coffee. Mugs are on the counter."

Tidge walked up behind Willy, placed his hands on her shoulders and nuzzled a kiss on the left side of her neck. "A very pleasant good morning to my lovely, energetic, efficient, sexy wife," he said giving a slight bow. "It is I, yours truly, the crème de la crème of Ansel's gene pool."

Her shoulders hunched up and she said, "Are you forgetting we have company?"

"Nope," said Tidge letting go of her shoulders. "Paul's a voyeur. Always has been."

"Tidge," blurted out Paul. "You broke your promise."

They both heard Willy laugh. "So what's new? I can get your brother to break his promises whenever I want."

"Would you share your secret with me?" asked Paul, grinning. "I won't tell a soul. Honest."

"If you were properly equipped to handle it, had the correct shoe size and could decipher a certain four letter code, I would," she said, without taking her attention away from the stove. "But you're not, you don't and you can't. Ergo, I won't. In the meantime, perhaps my husband, of questionable legal lineage would be nice enough to pour me a cup of coffee."

"I don't think he's capable," said Paul, stumped over Willy's code while he filled his mug. "You've accomplished great work with my brother up here at the Rehabilitation Institute for Obnoxious Preaching Patriarchs." He picked up a third mug, filled it and started walking towards Willy working at the stove. "Shoe sizes, codes and broken promises," he repeated, handing her the cup. "Intriguing."

Willy turned from the stove, her long handled fork pointing at her husband. "See." She took a sip from the mug Paul had just handed her and nodded her appreciation. "Even your incredibly polite brother appreciates my Mother Teresa of Calcutta efforts to cure you of the dreaded obnoxious preaching disease." She turned her attention back to the sounds and smells of her cooking. "Now I know who has the manners in your family." She didn't see Tidge stick out his tongue at her.

"When did I ever preach?" asked Tidge, as he inhaled the steam from his mug through his sinus plugged nose with a sniffle. "And, where did you get this obnoxious nonsense?"

A duet of "Oh's" echoed across the kitchen, the other from Tidge's brother, John, who was standing in the kitchen doorway catching the last part of the conversation. He was unshaven bed hair jutting out in all directions, and wearing a flannel bathrobe that looked like it had been given to him in the fourth grade. The heel of his left barefoot was scratching the top of the toes of his bare right foot.

Paul picked up another mug from the counter and tossed it underhanded to John who made a juggling catch in both hands. "Nice robe, John," he said, smiling. "I see you recycled one of Lucy's old mini-skirts when she was in grammar school." He picked up the coffee pot, walked over to his youngest brother and filled his mug.

"Much obliged," said John, his voice still heavy with sleep. He tried to inhale the vapors rising from the steaming coffee through his nose and got a snorting sound for his efforts. "Sister-in-law," he said, his eyes closed, a look of ecstasy on his face. "You are a treasure."

"I agree," said Paul, inching closer to the stove until he was looking over Willy's shoulder. "You can't imagine how wonderful it is to have someone in the family who can cook like May I." He paused and took a sip of coffee. "She's also considerate, has class galore and knows exactly when to loosen the straps on our oldest brother's straight jacket." He smiled as Tidge gave him the finger behind Willy's back and nodded his appreciation.

John joined Paul standing next to Willy. "Our brother, the Kid's favorite child and anointed patriarch of our clan, is nothing more than your basic, ill-mannered, run-of-the-mill slob and dictator who, by the way, we, his younger siblings, ignore whenever we can."

"Keep talking," said Willy. "I love every word."

"And a very Merry Christmas to you, my brothers," said Tidge with a grin, his middle finger extended again. He walked over to the stove, tried to pull the oven door open and look inside, but Willy blocked him. "Ah," he said, inhaling the aromas that escaped from the crack in the oven door before Willy's thigh had shut it. "It appears that the Wops, Canucks, and Yids are accounted for."

Willy turned and glared at him. "Your brother forgot to add that you're a gross pig who is both vulgar and insensitive." She waved her long handled fork at him. "Your vulgarity exceeds that of your father."

"Amen," echoed the off key, chimed response from Tidge's two brothers.

Tidge looked like he was gloating as he set down his mug and said, "Brothers, did you know that my loving, lovely wife has just paid me the ultimate compliment?"

Two blank stares answered back.

"She just referred to me, using her acronym, as a perfectly intelligent gentleman."

"I did no such . . ."

Tidge's right index finger went up. "I know that a gentleman never interrupts a lady," he said, acting serious. "However, this perfectly intelligent gentleman would like to present several facts to clear his much maligned patriarchal name." He could see that his wife was toying with the idea of impaling him with her large fork. "First of all, the term, Wop comes from the days of Italian immigrants coming to this country. Some had proper documentation and others did not. Those who didn't were said to be without papers, ergo, Wop." He saw his wife point her fork at him as she took several steps from the stove in his direction. Both of his hands went up, palms facing her. "I surrender," he said, continuing to back away from her. "I was just trying to clear up my good name."

"That's impossible," she said, as she turned to his brothers, her fork still pointing at her husband. "Did he learn to be rude from your parents?"

Their heads, Tidge's included, went quickly from side to side several times.

"Not from Mother Mary May I," said John, his head shaking more than the others.

"Especially not from our mother," said Paul, a look of both respect and fear on his unshaven face. His head, too, was still communicating, no. "It had to be his pal, Humper," he added. "And, if not him, there was that favorite teacher of his from Weber High School, Brother James Virgil."

"Hold it," said Tidge, his words now void of any Christmas spirit.

"All of you hold it," Willy ordered, her fork waving in all directions. "Drink your coffee." Without missing a beat of her fork, she turned, walked back to the stove and began to unwrap several pounds of sliced slab bacon. "Any arguing that will take place this holiday season will be done outside using snow balls."

"Holiday season?" asked Tidge, both eye brows raised.

"Christmas," she shot back at him, her attention focused on the bacon her husband had insisted on buying. He had spent the night before their families' arrival custom slicing the slab into thick strips the way he liked and the way his mother used to slice them for the family.

John was now at the stove looking over Willy's shoulder. "You mean you'd send me outside dressed like this to have a snow ball fight with Saint Thomas?" he asked.

Willy turned long enough for a glance at John in his way too small robe then turned back to her skillet as fast as she could to hide her grin. Her teeth dug into the sides of her cheeks the way her fork was poking at the bacon in her skillet.

John let out a long low whistle. "That sure looks like a lot of food."

"Better too much than not enough," she said, her teeth being removed from her cheeks so she could talk.

Willy's Christmas plans had contained page upon page of alternatives. She had two large bowls of eggs in her refrigerator waiting in reserve. One bowl was for scrambled eggs and the other waiting to be boiled, soft or hard, poached or coddled. Her menu had more variations than *Roget's* Thesaurus just in case anyone balked at her husband's three favorites. There were alternatives that could have been assembled faster than Tidge taking pictures out of focus when he first ventured into his new career. She was ready to assemble an omelet made with egg whites or another with broccoli, mushrooms and a low fat cheddar cheese. If the kids didn't like her original selection of egg dishes, she was ready with substitutes that had names ranging from *Chitty, chitty, bang-bang* eggs, to a *Gas House* egg, to a *Dippy* egg. She covered all bases with choices for toast and bought every type of bread in Bayfield and Sawyer Counties. If a loaf of bread contained a grain known to humankind, she bought it.

Tidge, his attention centered on his coffee and pleased that he could still feel the heat from the cup penetrating into his hands, asked, "Do you guys still think I moved up here to distance myself from you?"

"Yep," replied Paul, his answer coming faster than Tidge's question.

"We're most grateful," said John, a snorting sound coming from one nostril as he smelled the kitchen aromas. "I was impressed with the draw bridge you placed over the moat." He snorted again. "Were those sharks I saw swimming around?"

"Piranha," said Tidge, looking out the window, the glare from the sun off the snow making him squint. "A moat isn't a wall," he said, still squinting from the sun. "Bridges aren't walls either."

"That road of yours is," said Paul. He topped off his mug and glanced about for some cream. Before he could ask, he heard Willy say, "On the table."

"Thank you, most considerate lady," said Paul, then looking at Tidge. "Tomasz, I really think you followed your wife up here when she tried to run away from you. I hope she treats you like the hired help and makes you sleep in the bunk house. You do have hired help and a bunk house, don't you? You have everything else in this so-called hut of yours."

"No bunk house," said Tidge, resting his mug on the table, cupped hands still savoring the warmth, but his stomach sending out feed me messages. "Only the garage," he said, then smiling at his brothers. "Willy made me sleep out there once." Before he could continue he heard Willy say, "The coffee cakes are on the counter by the coffee maker. Be a dear and open them up before your poor brothers think that you plan on starving them."

"I am thinking that," he said, finding the six oblong, white paper bakery bags each containing a different coffee cake. "Accusing me of running away from my patriarchal duties bestowed upon me by The Kid and building a moat merits starvation."

"Enough," she said, her voice just loud enough to catch their attention.

"Did I hear someone say that Tidge belongs in a bunk house, or was that an outhouse?" his brother, Peter, added from the kitchen entrance where he stood behind John. He looked half asleep, was unshaven like his brothers, but a premature bald dome negated his ever worrying about bed hair or even barbers. His sleepy eyes popped open when he saw a mug being lobbed over John's head in his direction by Paul. John ducked and he grabbed the mug.

"Great coffee," said Paul. "Willy is phenomenal."

"Hey, guys," said Tidge, starting to go on the offensive. "I helped too. Or, I should say, my retirement account and adios bonus from La Salle Street helped. If it wasn't for that, you vultures would've had to go outside last night and forage for roots and acorns."

"Didn't I just say, E-N-O-U-G-H," said Willy from the stove, slowly spelling out the word, her back to them, hands and arms back to being a blur as the smell of sausage and bacon sizzling continued to permeate the kitchen.

"What did I say?" asked Tidge, the innocence of his question exaggerated.

"I'm talking about what you were planning on saying," she said, her voice still containing an edge. "And I'm here to tell you that you're not going to."

"Going to do what?"

"Not a thing," she said. "Well, maybe drink your coffee and get your incredibly wonderful brothers to help you get the tables set. I hear the pitter-patter of little feet and growling stomachs coming down the stairs."

"Poor Wilhelmina," said John, walking up behind her again and peering over her shoulder at the bacon and sausage sputtering in the cast iron skillets. "My brother doesn't deserve you." He turned and smiled at Tidge. "Now, Sissy, well, he deserved her. They deserved each other."

"Thank you for clearing up that part of my husband's past," she said to John without looking at him. "He seems to omit the concept of fault each time my predecessor is mentioned in our discussions."

"Willy," said John, walking back to where Tidge and his brothers were standing, "if there's anything you ever want to know about your husband's past, you just call on me, my brothers and our wives. We'll be more than happy to fill you in on the juicy details."

"You're all heart, John," said Tidge, peering over the top of his coffee mug.

"I try to be," said John, his grin almost swallowing his ears. "But I still can't imagine your beautiful wife living here in the Caesar's Palace of northwestern Winsconsin with you, Tommy Iggy Joe, the profane, preaching patriarch, and first born to May I Mary and Kid Ignacy." He made his way back to the coffee pot that had less than a sip remaining and removed it, saying, "That's alright, big brother, don't bother yourself. I'll make some more coffee." He looked at Tidge, crust still visible clinging to his eye lashes, and gave him the finger.

"And a grand and glorious Merry Christmas Eve to you too, baby brother," said Tidge, seeing that Willy's back was still to them. He smiled at John, nodded, and gave him an up and down jerking motion with his right fist. "Winsconsin welcomes you."

"Shame on you," John blurted out. "Willy, did you see the uncomplimentary gesture your insensitive husband just gave to his much younger, impressionable brother? The man should be jailed for corrupting the youth of today."

"He did the same to me last night," said Peter. "I was so distraught I couldn't sleep a wink."

Willy began shaking her head and the others laughed. "So that was you who went outside last night and began cutting down trees with Tidge's chain saw," she said.

"Tidge," said Peter, sounding hurt. "I believe that your bride is accusing me of snoring." He looked at Willy who was still turned facing them. "You've cut me to the quick. I'm such a light sleeper that even a stirring mouse could wake me up."

"Willy's not accusing," said Tidge, his smile blending in with the others. He opened a cabinet door and handed a bag of coffee beans to John. "Now we know why Chareese wears ear plugs to bed and has to call her mother at the hospital to come over and give her a whiff of gas. I bet that poor wife of yours hasn't had a good night's sleep since she married you."

Peter walked up and stood beside Willy. "I still love you," he said. "I hate your husband, but I really love you." He peered into the skillets then looked at her. "Are you cooking for an army?"

"The United States Navy," said Willy, keeping her attention on the cast iron skillets in front of her. "I'm honoring my former sailor husband." She held a long handled fork and used a back and forth system to turn the sausages and thick cut bacon strips without missing or duplicating a turn. "Have some coffee cake," she said, her order polite.

"Can I at least have a small taste?" Peter asked, his hand creeping for the nearest skillet.

Willy turned, stared at him, and raised her long handled fork. "Come one inch closer and your brothers will be referring to you as Lefty."

Peter grinned and turned to the others. "Now I know why I like your wife," he said to Tidge. "She's like Ma, only minus the May I."

Tidge looked at Peter, nodded his approval for the comparison of his wife to his mother. As soon as Willy turned her attention back to the stove, he gave Peter the same up and down closed fist gesture.

"Shame on you, big brother," said Peter as he tore off a small piece of raspberry-cheese coffee cake sticking out from one of the bags. "Do you think Mother Mary May I would've given her stock, If-you'd-like response to your request for giving me an uncomplimentary gesture?" He glanced at his other smiling brothers. "I think not."

"Come on," said Tidge to his brothers. "The queen of Henry's Hut wants the tables set." He looked out the kitchen door into the Great Room and could see the three smaller children. They were in pajamas and gathered around the Christmas tree, bodies spread out on the floor in positions that provided optimum viewing of the presents. "No touching," he said, startling them. "Just be patient and Santa will be coming down the chimney before you know it." He turned to see his brothers who had set up an assembly line process for placing red plastic dinner plates and matching utensils around the large round oak table that had been moved from the kitchen to Great Room. From the round to the rectangular they went quickly setting the long dining room table made of pine and birch that had been moved from its place against one of The Great Room's walls. Legs popped out from two folded card tables, each getting butted up to the longer table. They finished where they had started, topping off their cups with a warmer in the kitchen.

"Would you mind if I helped?"

They turned and saw Carol's boyfriend standing at the entrance to the outside door to the mud room. He was wearing leather hunting boots, heavy plaid wool pants and had on a fur lined parka and mittens secured by a leather lanyard hung around his neck. Their mouths were all open, including Willy's, no one saying a word.

"What a great morning for a walk through the woods," said Mackie, his southern drawl oozing out and traces of snow visible up to his knees. His cheeks were glowing as he rubbed his hands together. Just then, the inner back door to the mud room banged open and Carol and Carm walked in, cheeks also red, hands cupped to their lips and blowing. There was evidence of snow almost up to their thighs.

"Wow, Dad," Carol said, out of breath. She began unzipping her parka. "Do you own all this land?"

Tidge didn't answer, his face questioning.

"Just like reruns of that old Ponderosa on TV," said Carm, unzipping her parka. "Only with snow."

"Where did you three go?" Tidge managed to ask as the others' mouths worked their way closed.

"For a walk," said Carol, sounding exhilarated.

"More like a hike," said Carm, her parka in her hands. She nodded towards Mackie. "Cadet Dudley Do-Right of the Missouri Military Academy woke us up at the crack of dawn dressed and ready for some fresh air and exercise."

Carol tugged at the stuck zipper on her parka and Mackie walked over to her. "Let me help." He took a hold of the zipper when Tidge walked over to the both of them and said, "Let me." He gently eased Mackie aside. "When you've unzipped as many snow suits as I have over the years, it becomes second nature."

"I'm sure it does, Sir," said Mackie, the last word sounding as if he had been a cotton plantation owner and neighbor to Tara.

Willy turned back to the stove, closed her eyes and began to count quietly to ten.

Before she reached five, Chareese, Lilly and Lucy had found their way into the kitchen. Willy turned, smiled and said, "Merry Christmas Eve everyone." With towels insulating each hand, she opened the oven door. "Breakfast is served!"

There was a flurry of activity, children being ushered to their places before the adults sat down. Tidge's eyes scanned the kitchen and then the dining room. "Where's Martha?" he asked, concerned.

"In bed, Dad," said Carm, her eyes devouring the platters of steaming food. "That's where she's always at."

"Don't worry, Daddy-kins," said Carol, sliding as close as possible next to Mackie without being in his lap, "she'll wake up about the time gift giving starts."

"What's to worry about?" asked Tidge, finding a seat at the end of the table nearest the kitchen. "It's Christmas Eve, we're together, and things couldn't be any better."

Just as he finished, Harold and Gert entered the Great Room looking like they were going to board a ski bus to do some downhill skiing at nearby Telemark. "Guten Morgen," said Harold, seeming more cheerful than Tidge could recall and resembling an Alpine guide in his bulky knit sweater and ski pants.

"Isn't it a beautiful day," Gert added. She had on a matching sweater and pants.

Tidge seated them at the end of the long, makeshift table, helping Gert with her chair. "Yes, sir," he said, feeling better than he ever had since the day Willy accepted his offer in her classroom for a first date on New Year's Eve. "It doesn't get any better than this." Then he noticed Gert motioning to him. He walked over smiling, bent forward and heard her whisper, "Do you think I might have a teeny Bloody Mary?"

Chapter 8

The perfect Christmas they both wanted, each in their own way, purred along. Variations of mellow permeated the house, signs of bellowing absent. Inside and out, Henry's Hut looked, sounded, smelled and felt like Christmas.

To insure perfection, host and hostess, in their planning stages, expanded the Eleventh Commandment by designing a complex matrix plan of *What Ifs*. Willy's breakfast selection substitutes waiting in reserve to be called into action were only a fraction of potential alternatives available for emergencies. Had she lived in the era when Tidge's Army Air Corps jacket flew missions in *Sugar Claus*, she would have been sought out by General Eisenhower for drawing up the logistics for the D-Day invasion.

The former debutante, once battered spouse and widow turned teacher, anticipated the needs of Tidge's nieces and nephews. Their needs were her needs. She unpacked a huge cardboard box of old school supplies she had meticulously stored in a corner of Tidge's basement workshop when they moved north. Her infringing on his space was met by a mild complaint, but she explained why with a smile and then ignored him. The supplies included books for the kids along with drawing paper, colored pencils and crayons. A dollar fifty spent at a Cable sidewalk sale brought such treasures as *Rack-o, Pit* and *Uno*, table games unknown to her. Her parents, who once hosted lavish Auntie Mame type dinner parties, and being a seen-but-not-heard guest at those functions, exposed her to a sophistication that made performing the social graces second nature. A formal Christmas dinner with backdrops of Chicago's Lake Shore Drive or the shoreline of Lake Namakagon didn't matter to Willy. To her, black ties or plaid shirts, socialites or farmers' wives, limousines or pickup trucks sporting rust were all the same. Her female instincts anticipated the needs of his brothers' wives as mothers as well as her own mother. Only her role as the wife of a frustrated family patriarch gave her real concern. Everything else that could happen she anticipated. At least she thought she had.

Her fiction writing had been put on hold, replaced by a gargantuan *What If List* that seemed to have no end. "You and your family Christmas," she had said to Tidge, waving a yellow legal pad in his face. "I'm running out of pages with *What* and *If* options."

Tidge's creative photography business venture joined his wife's writing on hiatus. Digital depictions of cropped and tinted flora and fauna were shelved for almost daily trips to town, wherever her town of choice was located. Willy leaned toward Hayward because she craved the blueberry pancakes at the Moccasin Café. She shopped for most other items, including odds and ends, in Cable. On other occasions, too many for Tidge, she would nonchalantly direct her husband to head for Ashland. Her directions eventually had their pickup truck traveling south from Hurley to Woodruff and Minocqua. "But it's called the Island City," she said, defending her shopping route that turned into a scenic drive eating up most of the day along with his gas budget. "Besides, there are so many quaint boutiques to explore in Minocqua. We don't want to forget anyone or anything and ruin your special Christmas."

The trips, according to Tidge, were to, "lay in supplies for the marauding hordes attacking from the south." Whatever Willy wanted, she got even if it meant traveling a circuitous route that had them returning to Henry's Hut via Park Falls and several jigs and jogs west. Tidge had his limits saying, "I don't care what kind of award winning sausages they have in Rhinelander, we ain't goin'."

Each of their early morning shopping trips, excursions according to Tidge, started with an out-of-the-way route to the Moccasin Café, The Moc, as Willy called it. Hootchie, the ancient waitress at The Moc, waited tables using a walker to support her eighty-something legs, had two steaming cups of coffee sitting in front of them along with her greeting of, "Mornin'. Ususal?" The morning and usual were separated by the popping of chewing gum. The usual was scrambled eggs, potatoes O'Brien and the splitting of a short stack of blueberry pancakes.

Tidge sat in awe during breakfast watching his petite wife eat like

Kenny Miller's girlfriend's father. "You planning on chopping wood for the rest of the winter when we get back home?" he asked, as he watched the last bite of pancake wipe up the remaining syrup and disappear into her mouth. "Four to five full cords of logs would get us through the winter quite nicely," he commented. Then adding, "Quartered, of course."

"Just trying to keep up my strength in the event that you and your brothers resurrect that juvenile behavior that I witnessed my first Christmas Eve with you and your family." she said, a white paper napkin dabbing at the corner of her mouth. "I do pray that the Duluth television studio sport's department will opt for ice fishing highlights instead of pugilistic results."

"Oh, relax," he said, sliding back his chair and reaching into his pocket for his money held together by a wide rubber band that originally secured bunches of broccoli . "Me and my brothers never fought at Christmas when we were kids. Mom wouldn't let us." He grinned. "My dad and uncle were the ones who fought." He examined the bill and slipped three singles under his coffee cup and said: "If any of us disobeyed May I, we'd all get one of the Kid's round house, open handed swats." He smiled and shook his head. "My father was amazing the way he could control mass and speed with a heart surgeon's accuracy. His right paw would whistle through the air and barely graze the back of your head with nary a sound, not a hair mussed but, geez, did it hurt."

"So, my dearest Preaching Pugilistic Patriarch, are your plans to swat family members when they ignore your demeaning sermons?" she asked, sliding her chair out and ready to attack her shopping list. She gave her husband an uncharacteristic smirk. "Did I say demeaning or demonic?" she asked, the smirk still evident. "Demonic is a word I remove from my shelf of verbal ammunition when I feel you need it."

"Demean, demonic, or I de man," he said, returning her smirk. "Whatever works." His smirk turned to a smile and he nodded towards the door. "Time she is a wasting and I are getting anxious for you to spend me money." He ignored the grammatical usage dagger that joined her smirk.

They trudged across the street to the jewelry store where Tidge wanted to check on the custom made sterling silver pendants he ordered for his daughters. Each pendant consisted of their Sign of the Zodiac and year of birth, an easy task for the jeweler since the girls were all born in the later part of April. "My oldest," he said to the jeweler who wore a red and white Wisconsin Badger stocking cap over his ears and had a continuous, nervous sucking laugh, "is the only one of my three who has the temperament of an angry bull." He ignored the jeweler's hissing laugh without the Kenny Miller saliva shower as best he could.

The day before their guests arrived, they made one last Cable to Hayward and return circuit for last minute shopping. Tidge had never heard a wire grocery cart groan before.

"Whatever happened to the good old days of eating?" he asked, as the plastic bags of fresh vegetables and containers of perishable dairy products paraded by on the conveyor to the tune of monotonous beeps. "All my brothers and I got to eat was May I's M and C."

"Poor you," she had said, without taking her eyes off the computer screen that was flashing out her purchases along with the dollars and cents leaving Tidge's retirement account, never to be seen again.

"Poor me is right," he said, his hands gripping tighter on the shopping cart as the number of bags increased along with the bill. "Our treats were limited to dunking Salerno Butter Cookies into a glass of milk or shoveling white bread with sugar sprinkled on the margarine into our mouths until we had zits." He tried to scowl. "Most times there was no margarine."

"Your aforementioned dining delicacies and accompanying dermatological skin conditions are not appropriate for Christmas dinner," she said, her mind working to see if they had forgotten anything. She showed another burst of energy. "I'm glad you brought up cookie dunking," she said, checking to see if the items on her list found their way into the shopping cart. A bored looking teenage boy with a dated, poor version of a Beatles haircut, thick glasses and a red birth mark splotch looking like a hydrographic map of nearby Ghost Lake on his right cheek loaded the cart. "The bakery's our next stop, she said.

"Whatever happened to the baking you said you were going to do for Christmas?"

"I ran out of time," she said, pushing the grocery cart with a vengeance for the center of the automatic doors.

"How much time does it take to bake a batch of Christmas cookies," he asked, following behind her. "Mother Mary May I used to crank her cookies out in nothing flat. Beside, Cable has a bakery."

"We need more than cookies," she said, without turning, her sights set on the back of their pickup truck.

"Like what?" he asked, remembering that his mother baked more than cookies for Christmas. He missed her oat and cranberry *Kisiel* on Christmas Eve. Her *Makowiec* made with poppy seeds, raisins and nuts still made his mouth water even though it had been eons since he tasted the treat. Mother Mary May I, the lady from Ireland, could match baking with Polonia's best.

"Like what," she repeated, making his simple question sound simple. "Like everything I'll need for at least eight meals, two of which will be to celebrate Christmas Eve and my special Christmas Day feast. She stopped the cart as if she had walked into a tree, which she had done the first time they walked in the woods. Darn!" she said, turning her head to look at Tidge. "Would you run back and get me four blocks of cream cheese."

He stared at her. "That's all," he said letting out a false sigh of relief. "You mean we're not going to buy the place. How 'bout I ask Don Miller if he would sell me one of his cows?"

"Four blocks of cream cheese, please," she said, her use of the word, please lacking any resemblance of a polite request. "And hold the sarcasm while handing me the truck keys."

After the bakery, they drove to Cable and stopped to put gas in their two year old pickup truck. Tidge checked the liquor display in the gas station mart searching for ingredients for his homemade glogg. He doubted the authenticity of the lone bottle of one hundred and fifty-one proof rum on the store's shelf. The Caribbean was where run was distilled, not Phillips, Wisconsin. He bought it anyway.

As they headed east toward Henry's Hut, Tidge found himself emitting low, soft growling noises with Willy's warnings to him about being on his best behavior with the families under one roof. "My mother's nerves get frazzled when she's exposed to yelling and arguing."

He knew he shouldn't say what he said next, but he couldn't pass up the opportunity. "Mother still suffering from Lady Wrestler's Shell Shock after all of her years of slamming bodies down in the ring, eh?" he asked, tacking on the colloquialism, eh after his question. It was one of the rare characteristics about the Northwoods and being close to Canada that drove his wife insane. She had no tolerance for the butchering of the English language by any person or group.

Tidge avoided her wrath, he hoped, by stating: "I'm not going to argue with anyone, eh." His eyes concentrated on the periodic slick snow patches making blotches on the road. "If one of my brothers opens his mouth, I'll tell him to shut it. End of any arguing. End of any yelling. End of your mother's case of the frazzles before they even start. Besides, I'll be sure she's borderline comatose with my Gibsons."

"That's exactly what I'm getting at." She could feel the tension building in her. "If you're not preaching to our guests, you'll be pumping alcoholic beverages into them."

"So?"

"Sew buttons," she said, folding her hands in her lap on top of her mittens. "Has there ever been a family function where you, Mr. Self-Righteous, didn't start preaching about right and wrong?"

What's your point, love of my life?" he asked, his eyes still locked on the long jagged, dirty white strips of snow streaking under the pickup's wide tires.

"My point is that a family get-together soon has fewer members in attendance after you start telling everyone how to lead their lives."

His grip tightened on the steering wheel and he said: "Just trying to unscrew the screwed up like Kid told me to do before he died."

Tidge never forgot the scene in the hospital. Never forgot that his brothers weren't there. Never forgot what he felt was their irreverent behavior when they walked into the chapel of the funeral parlor where Ignacy Mackiewicz lay in state. What he could never forget was their looks of guilt and grief when seeing their father, three disobedient children with chocolate smeared on their mouths, crumbs on their hands and the lid to Mother Mary May I's cookie tin resting at their feet. He glanced at Willy and said: "I just wish my father would have warned me about what happens when one removes one's head from one's backside."

"You're not dealing with children," she said, tossing a quick glance his way. "The last time I saw them, your brothers and their wives were adults, adults with functioning brains. Their brains, I might add, operate on a much higher level than that of a particular family member who shall remain unnamed at this point."

He knew his wife was right. Like always. He just couldn't let go of being the only son, the only human being, with his father when he died. "I'm only doing . . ."

"Stop," she said, her voice going up an octave. "You're not God."

"I know that."

"Please be quiet and exhibit a modicum of manners while I'm trying to explain a point."

"I'm . . ."

"Quiet!"

"Yes, dear," he said, sucking his lower lip into his mouth as far as he could.

"You're always preaching about God seeing all," she continued, her voice returning to normal. "Well, Buster, you're not omniscient and most certainly not omnipotent."

"I never . . ."

A sharp turn of her head stopped him cold. "And when you're not telling your nieces and nephews, even me, about God seeing our behaviors, then you're telling us that Santa knows if we've been bad or good."

"That's right," he said, sensing the opportune time to launch his logical explanation. "I'm only . . ."

"Please," she said, her voice dropping to an annoyed whisper.

"Sorry."

"How can anybody take you serious?" She didn't give him a second to answer. "It's a mockery the way you toss God's name around."

"A mockery?" he asked. The black and white slick road still had his attention.

"Yes, a mockery," she said, her head turning as she watched the endless trees zip by the truck. "Then there's that atrocious Santa Claus costume and that silly red hat."

"Here we go again," he stammered. "There's not a thing wrong with that suit and the hat's not funny."

"You look like Snoopy fighting the Red Baron in that thing."

"I do . . ."

"Please," she repeated, this time the whisper was missing. "I know it's a family tradition of yours that you dress like a Santa Claus, but that suit makes you look like the Dutch version of Sinter Claes from several hundred years ago?"

"Who?" he blurted out, his head snapping to the right, a look of dismay plastered on his face as the truck swerved.

"See!" she said, smugness radiating from her and she loved the feeling. "Santa doesn't know all. If he did, he would have known that Santa Claus dates back to the fourth or fifth century."

He could see the growing smug look on her face out of the corner of his eye.

"He was known as St. Nicholas then. Who, by the way, was the patron saint of school-children and sailors?" Her smile continued its flashing. "God must have anticipated that you would be a real piece of work when you came into the world. My, oh, my, I'm married to an ex-sailor and an adult child." She folded her hands in prayer and said: "St. Nicholas, why did you make me the lucky one?"

"God and Santa," he muttered. "Know all and see all." His eyes found the road and he steered the truck back on the right side. "You're right about one thing," he said. He waited for her comment, but it didn't come. "You are definitely lucky to have me."

Her smile didn't budge and she said: "To show you how lucky you are I'll let you unload the truck when we get home." She acted as if she were putting an imaginary check mark on her legal pad which had been resting on her lap.

Tidge grinned and placed his right hand on her knee. Her left hand slid down resting on his. "I'm still not sure that this fam-dam-ily Christmas idea of yours is going to work," she said, as if another conversation had preceded the start of this one. "My women's intuition has been sending me more and more warnings."

"Kind of late now," he said, their pickup truck fish tailing for a moment after coming off a strip of black ice. He began singing, "He knows if you've been bad or good, so be good for goodness sake."

"For your sake I hope so."

His own sliver of a smile began to grow. "No pouting. No crying. No shouting," he said, consumed by a feeling of happiness. "Isn't it beginning to look a lot like Christmas?"

Chapter 9

Willy and her Christmas Eve breakfast received accolades that made her blush, but only for a moment. That trace of crimson was wiped away by Mackie. He had excused himself from the dining room table with an exhibition of manners unheard of from someone his age and followed her into the kitchen. "Mam," he said, standing behind her, making her jump just as she began to fill a coffee urn. "I'm sorry, Mam. But I just wanted to tell you that was the best breakfast I ever had in my life. I didn't think anything could top that so-called snack from last night. But this here breakfast sure did. I hope you don't mind, but I'm going to need another walk." He smiled. "Thanks again, Mam. By the way, what's for lunch?"

Willy loved compliments. But compliments referring to her as *Mam* made her cringe like finger nails scratching across a chalk board in her classroom. In one brief expression of thanks, she had been called Mam more times than in all her years as a grammar school teacher. Mackie had bombarded her with polite Mams from when he first stepped out of Carm's car to when he went off to sleep the night before, choruses of, "Good night, Sir" and "Goodnight, Mam" coming from the den. She had reached a point where if he had called her Mam one more time, she would've poured the hot coffee from the maroon and old gold thermal plastic urn in his lap. Now, as she watched him go back into the dining room carrying that same thermos, she turned her attention to her husband.

"Talk about a smashing success," Tidge said to Willy, as he came into the kitchen carrying a stack of plastic plates that could have passed for clean. "My brothers mustn't feed their broods at home." He tipped the stack to show Willy. "Those kids licked these clean." He set the plates down on the counter and gave Willy a hug. "They told me that Auntie Mina was awesome."

"Smashing is also an awesome word," she said, a chill in her voice and not returning his hug. She wormed her way out of his arms, picked up a dish towel lying on the counter and began polishing the stainless trim on her stove, the towel going so fast the ends frayed.

He watched her right hand work back and forth until she had jumped from the stove to the exhaust hood above it. Now the towel went in frantic circles. She had almost made the circuit across the hood a second time when he said, "Okay, what did I forget?"

She turned, her long absent laser stare glowing under full power. "Smashing is a perfect choice of words to describe your Christmas season," she said, not pleased. "Smash, smashing, smashed."

He didn't know what to say.

"At a loss for words?" she asked a chill in her voice.

He nodded and could feel the ice crystals.

"Try smashed," she said, the ice crystals solidifying into an obsidian dagger, the point grinning at him. "That's smashed as in getting my mother drunk before noon." She gave a huff, walked by him and headed for the stairs to the second floor.

"Smashed," he said to an empty kitchen. "I gave Gert a watered down Bloody Mary. Damn thing was almost virgin." He turned, zipped through the Great Room grinning and singing, "You better not shout I'm telling you why..." as he followed his wife upstairs to their master suite. He found her smoothing out the comforter on their bed that was already minus any visible wrinkles or creases. He went on the other side of the bed opposite her and began running the palm of his hand over the comforter. She stopped and looked at him. "You had to go and get my mother drunk at breakfast?"

"I did no such thing," he said to her, is voice a whisper and making the mistake of trying to anticipate what was coming next.

"The way you were feeding her Bloody Marys you could have saved all those trips to the kitchen by inserting an IV in her arm."

He didn't let her go any further. "I was being a good host, a host like you told me your father was." His whisper had become stern. "Your mother wanted a Bloody Mary. I made her a Bloody Mary, a light one, a very light one. It was so light I waved the bottle over the glass. Geez, Willy, lighten up." His face grew red and he fought to keep his voice to a whisper, but lost the fight. "I was just trying to make things perfect for you because I know how you've been walking on eggs for almost a month. There's no one who wants this more perfect for you than me." His voice returned to normal with a swallow. "Besides, didn't you make it a point to tell me about your parent's entertaining and how full bladders were good?"

"Full not pickled," she said, in a huff. "You didn't have to wave that vodka bottle over her glass so many times you all but embalmed her bladder, kidneys and brain." She began fluffing the first of four pillows on their bed. By the time she had picked up the fourth, she was beating it into submission. "Mother was so drunk she almost poked her eye out with her fork trying to get food into her mouth."

"Almost poking her eye out is not my fault." He sat down on the edge of the bed that had just been escorted into her world of super neat. "Who did you blame for Gert's poor hand eye coordination before you met me?" He leaned back on the bed, his feet still on the floor. "It couldn't have been your late ex-husband, the macho man cop. From what you told me, he would've done the sticking and added a few punches like he once did to you, the gutless bastard." He knew that he had gone too far and his apology was fast and sincere. "Sorry."

She surprised him by saying, "Accepted." She walked to his side of the bed. "And, Tidge, honey," her words accompanied by a nod that he should remove himself from the bed spread. "See if you can find a way to water down mother's Gibson later. You know she'll ask for one the moment she wakes up from her nap."

"No problem," he said, sitting up and then standing. He repeated smoothing out the wrinkles in the comforter when he started laughing. "I just hope your father survives his after breakfast nature hike with Carm, Carol and her new beau. How many times do you think he'll be called, Sir?"

She smiled. "We'll know it was one too many if that military school cadet doesn't return with the others."

"Speaking of which," said Tidge. "Is Martha alive?"

"I heard her go to the washroom not too long ago." She stepped back from the bed, pleased that the room looked presentable. "Your oldest daughter went back to bed and I haven't heard a sound since. She must really like the comfort of my Turf."

He shrugged his shoulders. "Hey," he said, holding up his index and middle fingers in a *V*. "Peace?"

"I told you before that I was too young to understand all that symbolism from your Hippie days."

The rest of the day went exactly as planned. "The kids will love it," she had said to him after his eye brows went up at what lunch would resemble.

Willy had organized a wiener roast out behind the house near the edge of the frozen lake. And the kids did love it. They sat Indian style in the snow thinking that they were so cool doing something that their friends back in Chicago weren't doing on Christmas Eve.

The male adults opted for taking their hot dogs inside to eat at the long rectangular table in the Great Room and watch a pro football game on Tidge's new big screen television.

The women tended to the needs of the kids, enjoying a different spin on the twenty-fourth of December. After lunch, with the kitchen once again spotless, Tidge announced to everyone in the Great Room, "We're going on a hay ride this afternoon." None of the kids knew what a hay ride was, and his family wasn't sure they had heard what they thought they had heard. "I wanted it to be a sleigh ride, but our neighbors who have the farm across the bay only have an old hay wagon."

"Excuse me, oldest brother," said John, a look of doubt on his face. "Did you say hay ride?"

Tidge nodded.

Peter and Paul took cautious steps up to Tidge appearing to inspect him. "It sure looks like our brother," said Paul, his eyes scanning him from head to toe.

"Are you sure?" Peter asked back.

"Fairly sure," said Paul. He inched around Tidge in a clockwise motion, eyes studying, his hands behind his back like Sherlock Holmes, mind pondering. He stopped, stared at Tidge and asked: "My good man, are you or are you not our brother, Tomasz Ignacy Jozef Mackiewicz, the preaching, profane patriarch of noblesse oblige fame?"

Peter countered Paul's move, staying a shoulder's width outside of his brother's course, going in a counterclockwise motion. "Mmmm," he repeated as he moved around Tidge at a snail's pace. "Do you know what I think, Holmes?"

"If it's not elementary then I don't want to hear it," said Tidge to his brothers, his head going from side to side.

"Mmmm," repeated Peter again. "It is elementary, Holmes, and so very obvious."

"How so, Watson?" asked Paul, his hands still cuffed behind him.

"You two guys are nuts," said Tidge, glancing first and Peter and then to Paul.

"I know this is a first," said John, not sure of what to make of his two brother's behavior. "But, I'm going to agree with my oldest brother." He looked at Peter for a moment and then turned his attention to Paul. "How much glogg did you two guys guzzle watching that game?"

Tidge laughed. "Might I suggest, Basil Rathbone and Nigel Bruce, that you start rounding up your offspring and get them bundled up. Kenny Miller's going to be here with the wagon in a few minutes." His head made one circuit from side-to-side.

"Is something wrong?" Willy asked, standing in the doorway of the mud room and noticing her husband's facial expression.

"Not a thing," said Peter, his brothers nodding their innocent agreements. "We were just talking about getting ready for a hay ride."

"Why don't you come along?" Paul asked her.

"I hear it's going to be a gay ride," said John. The three brothers cracked up with laughter and left to get their kids dressed for the hay ride.

Tidge had rented Don Miller's hay wagon for the afternoon, the fee being three more loaves of Willy's banana, raisin and cranberry walnut breads. He had convinced the Miller's teenage son, Kenny, to drive the horse drawn wagon. "I'll pay you ten bucks an hour," Tidge had said to him. "Interested?"

Kenny's face broke into a grin. A frothy drool seeped out of the side of his mouth and coursed down his chin as he shook his head up and down.

"That should give you a little extra money to spend on your friend, Mickey."

Kenny glanced away and turned quiet. Then, turning back to face Tidge said, "Mickey's dad don't want me seeing her no more, eh."

Tidge knew better than to get involved with young love. "Tell you what Kenny," he said, trying to sound like a buddy to him. "There's an extra five if you make my nieces and nephews think they're on an adventure ride."

"You don't have to do that Mr. Tidge," said Kenny, his shoulders drooping. He looked like he was about to cry. "They'll have fun." He looked at Tidge wanting to say something, but nothing came out.

Tidge beat him to it. "I'm sorry about Mickey." He had visions of her father having Kenny spread-eagled naked on the floor of the barn, standing over him with a double bladed ax. Tidge could hear Mickey's father chanting: "Fe-Fi-Fo-Doom. Never pick straw from my daughter's Fruit-of-the-Looms."

"That's okay, Mr. Tidge," said Kenny, getting them both with an extra dose of saliva. "My father doesn't want me to see her either, eh."

"Oh."

Harold and Gert opted out of the hay ride choosing to embrace the warmth of the fire Tidge stoked before heading out the door. He also refilled their drink glasses.

The Christmas guests with six children and Mackie leading the way trudged through knee deep snow to end of the drive. Curious, unsure and excited, they climbed aboard the hay filled wagon with the bald rubber tires parked on the shoulder of the snow packed road. The aftermath of the snow plow's wake had drifts towering above the wagon in some spots.

Harnessed to the wagon was, Sissy, the shaggiest sway back horse alive. The kids could have used her back for a toboggan run. The moment Tidge's brothers and their wives heard Kenny mention the horse's name; the hay ride became an instant success.

Kenny held the reins as each of the kids petted whatever they could reach of Sissy before being wrapped in blankets and buried under fresh straw. Tidge's brothers joined in the petting of the old horse, each making a comment to Sissy just loud enough for Tidge to hear.

Peter started out by petting the horse's ears and asking, "How many credit cards have you maxed out?" He stepped back looking astonished. "Nine!"

Paul followed, his gloved hand tracing the low slung depression of Sissy's sway back. He gave the horse a single pat on the rump, walked up to the horse's head and whispered in her ear, "Nice ass, Sissy." He stepped away like his brother before him only his face showed a look of sad. "Too bad that's where your warm, charming personality resides."

John concentrated on Sissy's mane. He removed both gloves, stroked the soft hair and asked the horse, "Do you have a mother and a step-sister residing in the Joliet, Illinois area? Mother gives extra milk to Santa if she hears Feliz Navidad."

Tidge never said a word. He helped Willy and his sisters-in-law climb on the wagon while his brothers burrowed deep into the straw. Even Martha joined the ride. She munched a ham sandwich on whole grain bread with mayonnaise that Willy had made for her. Mackie gave a boost to first, Carm and then Carol. He hopped on the wagon as Kenny snapped the reins. Sissy snorted, passed gas and the wagon headed west along the black top.

Gert and Harold had done their own burrowing. Harold moved one of the matching sofas on an angle capturing views of both the Christmas tree and fireplace when the others had left. Gert had no trouble sinking into the cushions, drifting in and out of her alcohol induced stupor. Harold, worn out from trudging through the snow with Mackie, Carol and Carm, opted to sit in a rocking chair next to Gert reading. He had pulled an old, worn, hard cover book from the shelves next to the fireplace, the shelves stacked with books that had been bought by Tidge and Willy at a library sale in Superior for five dollars a box. Intrigued by the title and date of the first edition he was holding, he crossed his right knee over his left and settled in by the warmth of the fire to read Washington Irving's, *Old Christmas*.

Kenny Miller guided the wagon towards Cable. Sissy clomped along County Highway M, puffs of steamy breath coming from her. Kenny, a green and gold Green Bay Packer's stocking cap pulled over his ears, was red faced, saliva starting to freeze on his chin. Assorted covered heads poked out from all over the fresh straw emitting an assortment of steam looking like smoking chimney's dotting the snow covered woods. They all marveled at the tiny segment of the Chequamegon National Forest, trees smothered under white, their branches sagging. The scene reminded Tidge of his mother's Christmas figurines from the past buried in cotton.

They had clomped along for about ten minutes when Kenny turned, his right hand pointing in that direction, and said, "That's Lakewoods Resort." Little interest was shown until Kenny added, "Injuns burned it down once, eh. Took some scalps, don't ya know."

Tidge fought the urge to climb over Willy to get to the front of the wagon and hug Kenny before his sister-in-law, the former Lucy Stooping of Cherokee heritage, started taking Kenny's scalp, Green Bay Packer hat and all.

Stocking capped and hooded heads popped up from the straw shouting questions to Kenny ranging from tomahawks, to war drums, to bows and arrows. "I wish they'd scalp you," muttered Natasha to Nathan, tossing the handful of straw he had sprinkled on her head back in his face.

Kenny kept his right arm and hand pointing in the direction of the resort as Sissy clip-clopped along like an old machine. "I was told by a friend of my aunt's cousin dat dem dare Injuns even did a war dance, don't ya know."

The questions kept coming, Kenny fielding each like an entire team of snowshoe softball players who had never committed an error. Historical records did show that the resort had burned to the ground once, back in the days of his father's childhood. The resort had been rebuilt at the south end of the large bay on Lake Namakagon only to be expanded and modernized years later joining the condominium mania that was sweeping across the country. "The same tribe that once burned it down," Kenny continued. "Well, their modern generation helped build it back." Kenny gave a snap to the reins, but Sissy kept going at her same clip-clomping gait. "Now that generation has a gambling casino."

Tidge gave a sigh and hoped that Lucy would not hold him responsible for her ancestors having undergone the *Trail of Tears*. Then Lakewoods was behind them and silence returned to the wagon. The kids, not sure of what to do on a hay ride, began to get antsy. An occasional cry from one of the kids started with Star who said: "Ma, Frankie's touching me." Another child's complaint, this one increased in volume came from Natasha. "Ma," her annoyed cry started, "Nathan's a moron of the highest order."

Tidge smiled and said to himself: "Brother James Virgil lives."

About the time Pauline finished complaining that her brother, Paul, Jr., was stuffing straw down the back of her neck, and Star carping that her brother was still touching her and poking straw in her ear, Chareese let loose. "If you want touching, your mama will touch you," she said, no sign of an army of television psychologists warning her that threats to one's children might have a detrimental effect on their growth and development. "And touch you and touch you!" Strands of straw shot up from where Tidge thought he had seen Chareese's two children, her voice elevated along with a swinging gloved hand swatting at the straw. "Touch this, and this and this!" There were no signs of her children's or any of the other children's heads. "In your father's native tongue, *Wy rezumiecie?*"

"You bet I understand," said Peter to Tidge. "And, I ain't saying, boo for the rest of the ride." Silence returned to the hay wagon.

"That's Twin Lakes," Kenny yelled out over his shoulder again, spraying only him and some unlucky straw. "One there," he said, flaunting his knowledge of the geography east of Cable and pointing his gloved right thumb. "The other's over there." His head leaned slightly towards the left, a gloved thumb twisting from right to left. Kenny pulled the wagon off to the side of the road and continued his tour guide narration endearing him even more to Tidge.

"I know both lakes are frozen over and covered with snow," continued Kenny, the straw behind him soaking up his saliva, "but under that ice lives a giant alligator gar fish." He paused before adding an editorial comment. "He's about the size of this here horse." He pulled on the reins trying to get a response from Sissy, but got puffs of steam instead and then Sissy's intestines adding more steam. "And over there," Kenny continued, his weight pivoted on the seat bench until he looked to his far left, "lives an armor back sturgeon that's the size of this here wagon."

Tidge was now kicking up his ante from an extra five dollars to a ten. "Kenny Miller," he said silently, "I hope you blow off dairy farming for a career in show business." He sat and listened as Kenny explained to his young passengers, and even their parents, that the gar and sturgeon were both very aggressive and territorial. "On nights when the moon is full and the coyotes and wolves are howling, trouble comes to Twin Lakes, don't ya know," he said, sounding like an announcer on an old time radio suspense show. "One or the other of those giant fish will get mad at the other about something. They get so violent they break through the ice." He shot his stained gloved hands out to his sides and sounding astounded said: "The ice is thicker than this. They get down on the bottom of the lake and launch themselves into it. The ice shatters with a gosh awful explosion."

"Kenny Miller, you are the best," muttered Tidge to the picturesque, snow blanketed frozen lake off to the side of the wagon.

Kenny's tale rolled on. "Once they break through the ice those two mean giants come out of the water and slither across this very road. It's like they're in a duel, a fight to the finish." He paused and waited a good five seconds before continuing. "Right on this very spot where this here wagon is sitting, eh."

Tidge watched the stocking capped, hooded and even heads covered by baseball caps and scarves disappear. They were sucked under the straw as if it had turned to muck. Tidge once found himself knee deep in muck when he got out of his canoe in a tiny, shallow bay to photograph a white flower being courted by a the largest bee he had ever seen. Now he wanted to jump out of the wagon, run up to Kenny and hoist him up on his shoulders. Before Tidge could disturb one piece of straw, Kenny continued his narration. He accentuated each word by working his voice from whispers to shouts and waving his hands as if he were conducting a philharmonic orchestra.

"Both of those nasty fish have a mouth filled with teeth as long as that straw you're buried under," continued Kenny, then going silent. Sissy's exploding intestines was the only sound the wagon passengers heard.

Kenny raised his baton for an eerie crescendo. "I'm not tryin' to scare you all, eh," he said, not meaning what he said. The baton started to carve through the icy air like Kenny's girlfriend's father's scythe annihilating a field of hay as Kenny continued: "But when those fish lose their tempers they want to sink their teeth into the other guy." There was another of his theatrical pauses, his baton stopped, poised even with the *G* on his stocking cap. "I was told by my uncle that they want to sink their teeth into is human flesh," he said, his baton beginning a series of circular motions gaining momentum. "The alligator gar," he said, stopping to wipe his chin. "Oh," he said. "I did tell you the fish looks like a giant alligator, didn't I?" There was another pause, the baton's circular motions now a blur and Kenny lowered his voice into a deep baritone. "What they love to feast on is young human flesh," continued Kenny. Then raising his voice to a cheerleader's shout, his baton crashing down, he said, "The younger the better!"

The hay quivered.

Kenny's voice turned into an instructional warning. "The gar takes his long saw tooth snout and bores into his victim, don't ya know, eh." He took a second to wipe is chin. "Either of those giants will leap off the road like a ski jumper soaring through the air, each one aching for the taste of blood," he continued, his gloved hands now folded in his lap. "My father once told me how he saw an old news reel of a boxer named Joe Louis who beat up some German guy and made him all bloody. That's what the gar and the sturgeon like to do to each other and their unlucky human victims." He smacked his gloved hands together. "Blood!"

"Dear, Lord," muttered Tidge. "Kid Scream is everywhere."

Kenny rolled on. "People who live on dis here lake tell of hearing the sound of chomping at night." He paused just long enough to let his last word soak in. "My father never told me if that Joe Louis boxer ever chomped on the German, but the vice-like jaws and the sawing action of the gar's giant snout, which I'm told was at least four feet long, make a terrible racket". Kenny let out a sneeze spraying Sissy's rump and continued. "The more they battle, the more the ice cracks and buckles. People can hear the grunts and snorts, their tails splashing waves of water over this here road, turning it to ice. The folks living here on Twin Lakes would spring from their beds to see what was the matter."

"I love you, Kenny," said Tidge to himself.

Kenny rambled on with no signs of life visible on the back of the wagon. "My father told me about his cousin who had a friend who told him there was an old caretaker back at Lakewoods who could hear those midnight battles clear back at the resort." His head turned to look back, but no one, except Tidge noticed. "One summer, when the old caretaker was a youngster. . ." Kenny stopped the wagon and turned back to look at mounds of straw concealing heads. "About the same age as you kids," he said. There was another of Kenny's theatrical pauses. "The youngster had been hiding under one of the cabins watching what the Injuns were doing to the pale faces during the fire. When he had the chance he jumped into Lake Namakagon. Hear say he swam out to tiny Buck Island to safe his scalp. To this day, he swears the agonizing screams of people having tomahawks removing their scalps sounded just like the racket those two fish make."

"Are you sure of that?" The question and the voice belonged to Lucy and she did not sound pleased.

"Yes, Mam," said Kenny, his saliva spraying him, Sissy, the straw and staining part of County M. "Did you know that Lake Namakagon means Lake Abundant with Sturgeons? That's Ojibwa." His right sleeve did a swipe across his chin. "Them dare sturgeons aren't as big as dis killer here," he said, a soothing tone to his voice. "Can't honestly say that there are any in your lake today. Maybe. I ain't ever caught one when I've been fishin'. But you kids won't have to worry if you come back this summer to visit your Uncle Tidge." He snapped his head to the left, salvia finding the road. "You'll be able to swim and have fun."

Tidge was soaking up every word while adding yet another cash bonus for Kenny. Then he almost fell off the wagon when Kenny, acting startled, stood up on his driver's seat bench and pointed to his right. "Did you see that?" he asked, acting and sounding like a sentry giving an alert. "Wow!"

"See what?" came the assorted variations of the questions as all the kids and even the adults, including Lucy, Lilly and Chareese, had popped up from under the straw and were now standing up in the wagon following the direction where Kenny was pointing.

"Only seen it once," said Kenny, the excited spray spewing out of his mouth.

"Seen what?" a mixed chorus of adult voices asked. "Where?"

"That moving hump in the ice," said Kenny, calmly inching himself back into his seat. He gave a slight jerk on the reins, Sissy passed gas again and the wagon began to move forward. "I'd better get us outta here, don't ya know, eh."

"See what?" echoed the younger voices from the straw mounds, their questions curious, unable to mask fear. "I wanna see."

"There it is again," Kenny said, jerking the reins even harder and giving a clicking sound with his tongue to get Sissy to go faster while knowing that the old horse only had one speed. "Did all of you see it?"

"See what," echoed the wagon? Even Tidge was into Kenny's adventure as the teenager continued his suspense drama. "The huge alligator gar who patrols this particular Twin Lake was on the move and heading for where dis here wagon had been parked." He gave a double accentuated click of his mouth while making the reins snap several times. "Probably thinks the wagon is the sturgeon," said Kenny. "He ain't too fond of anybody getting too close to his territory."

All of Kenny's passengers were now turned looking back at the lake, Tidge included. He felt Willy grab on to his arm and pull her close to him. "Is he telling the truth?" she asked.

Tidge put his arm around her. "Of course he is," he said, feeling relieved as the wagon appeared to be out of harm's way. "Kenny's as honest as this here snow is pure and white." He paused and pulled her to him. "His father even told me his son still believes in Santa Claus."

"So much for the truth," said Willy, easing away from him.

Tidge smiled. "You're being a skeptic, darling," he said, seriously.

"It's unbecoming of you. Don't be surprised if the feeling gets you."

"Feeling?" she asked, her skepticism growing. "You're not trying to tell me Ebenezer's out to get me, are you?"

"Nah, not him," he said, his seriousness besting her skepticism. "You'll know the feeling when it gets you." He smiled then turned his attention to necks craning and eyes straining.

"Right," she said.

Tidge continued to smile as he said to himself, "Kenny, Mickey's old man might not like you, but I think you're the greatest thing since that old Indian chief discovered Lake Namagakon." He sat, embracing his special feeling, amazed as Kenny Miller continued his tale.

"Both those monsters could break through the ice now or wait for us when we return," he said, sounding like a mother hen protecting her brood. "No need to worry," he continued. "Out of the water they're kind of slow and awkward. Don't get to close though. My father told me that he once knew a man from town, Doc Mason was his name, who had a nephew. The youngster was a little older than you kids." He inserted his dramatic pause again before going on. "Not by much though. The kid ignored all the warnings about getting too close to those nasty giants. Went to touch one to see if it was dead and, WHAM!" Kenny shouted out the word as he brought his heavy leather gloves together in a loud clap causing tiny straw volcanoes to erupt all over the wagon. Then, very softly, as if in mourning, he said, "The boy lost a hand."

The lakes were now out of view, but the passengers were still looking back. "Those two giant fish are great at playing possum," he said, sounding as if he were an expert. Then, protecting his honesty and integrity, said, "I'm only tellin' you folks what my father told me, eh."

Silence from the back of the wagon lasted only long enough until all of the passengers had turned to face forward and re-burrowed their way into the straw. Another, "He's touching me," came from the back of the wagon. Before another touching me got a chance to verbalize, Willy got the kids organized and started singing, *Santa Claus Is Coming to Town*. Just as they finished the final chorus of the song, she started them on *Jingle Bells*. The speed of the song far exceeded Sissy's hoof beats as the wagon crawled along. Tidge's nephew, Nathan, poked his head out of the straw and broke the silence by asking, "Uncle Thomas, when we get back can I plow your driveway?"

A chorus of, "Me, me, me", followed with Tidge saying, "If it's not too dark."

About that time, Natasha referred to her brother as an imbecile and Willy started the wagon's riders singing *The Twelve Days of Christmas*. They had gotten to *Drummers drumming* when Kenny turned tour guide again. He shouted over his shoulder, "Mt. Telemark will be coming up soon!" The wet stain on his worn, beige parka had doubled its jagged circumference.

Much later, after one too many partridges had been laid to rest in a pear tree, juvenile complaints started up again. The cries now included the *hitting, pulling and punching* of assorted me's, he's and she's until John's wife, Lucy turned into Grinch and threatened them by shouting, "One more peep out of any of you and I'll wait up for Santa and tell him to skip your uncle's house and give your presents to needy Ojibwa children."

Lucy's threat even turned Tidge's head. "Do you mean the Ojibwa as in the Lake Superior Chippewa, as in the Lac Court Oreilles band of Native Americans?" Then, to spice up Lucy's warning and possibly alienate himself from his sister-in-law who he sensed had Cherokee war path blood boiling through her veins, he asked, "As in the Injuns Kenny told us about earlier?"

"Who else," Lucy snapped back, causing silence to hit the wagon, heads disappearing under straw. "I know all about them. I went to girl's camp north of here on Lake Owen for several years when I was just a bit older than this antsy bunch. My father always put away some of his pay check so I could come up here. It was the best time of my life."

"I'm impressed," said Tidge. "I didn't know the Cherokee and Ojibwa hit it off."

"The only ones we don't hit it off with are you pale face types," said Lucy, just as John tried to force a hand full of straw into her mouth.

The Mt. Telemark ski resort came into view and Kenny

announced the ski hill's presence. "Dis here is where people go to downhill ski," he told his passengers, heads popping up from under the straw for a look. He snapped the reins for effect, made a clicking noise with his tongue and the horse and wagon made a clumsy, sweeping U-turn and started heading back east. They all watched the zigzag paths being cut in the Christmas Eve afternoon snow, the kids straining to take in a sight they had never seen in person. Then, when the skiers and the mountain disappeared around a curve, they started to burrow back under the straw, stopping when Kenny said: "We have a cross country ski race here every year. It's called the Berkebeiner. The race runs between here and Hayward. All the best skiers in the world are here Men and women, boys and girls and some your kids' ages race. I even enter."

"I didn't know you did cross country skiing," said Tidge, as he glanced at his watch and calculated that Kenny was going to cost him twenty plus an extra fifteen.

"Yes, sir, Mister Tidge," he said proudly. "Maybe sometime during the holidays you can bring your company over and I can give them some lessons."

An echoing chorus of, "Can we," erupted from the wagon, the adults louder than the children.

Before they knew it, straw spilled out of the wagon along with the passengers in front of the driveway to Henry's Hut. Kenny never mentioned the battling monsters of Twin Lakes on their return and no one bothered to ask. The adults shook out the blankets, fragments of straw causing hands to fan the air before being carried away by an increasing wind. There were several coughs, some spitting and a cry of, "Ouch," from Nathan, followed by, "What was that for, Ma?"

"Because you deserved it," his mother said, before adding: "Now shake hands with Kenny, thank him for the ride and wish him a Merry Christmas."

The other kids, who started to trudge through the knee-deep snow in the ruts of the driveway, were stopped by Lilly's reminder echoing out as a holler: "Did you kids forget your manners!" She pointed at Kenny. "Get back here and thank Kenny for the ride. *Kuai-kuai!* Chop-chop! Now!"

Kenny took two of the three tens and the five Tidge handed him and slipped them into his right glove. The other ten and five went into his left glove. "I'm gonna call Mickey when I get back, Mr. Tidge," said Kenny, the saliva seeming to vanish. "I love her and I'm going to buy her a nice present with the twenty dollars. I don't care if her dad comes after me with his scythe. "She's my girl."

"That's what I once thought about a girl named Marietta Claus when I was your age," said Tidge to himself. Tidge blinked and asked: "Did you say scythe, like in one of those Grim Reaper blades?"

Kenny wiped his chin with the back of his right glove, the reins held tightly in his left. "If that's what those big curved blades are called," he said, not the least bit concerned. "He's always threatening me, but I ain't the one he's mad at, eh. He knows his daughter is one of them." He paused, lowered his voice, then looking to his right and left he inched as close as he possibly could to Tidge and said without spraying them both, "Everyone knows that Mickey is one of those *PT* types."

Tidge stood with his mouth open as Kenny shook his hand and then waved goodbye to the group who had congregated around Sissy. "Merry Christmas," he said to his passengers, his head nodding that they should clear a path away from the horse and wagon. "And you kids obey your parents and listen to your Uncle Tidge. He's a smart man." There was a 'giddy-up' from him and Sissy began to pull Kenny and the empty wagon east back to the Miller farm. Suddenly, Kenny pulled back on the reins and shouted, "Whoa!" He raised his right gloved hand and looked at Tidge. "The other fifteen is for my mom!"

Tidge gave a thumbs up signal and nodded his approval.

Kenny gave a final wave with his right hand, spraying back to Tidge and the others a spirited, "Merry Christmas!"

A mixed chorus of Merry Christmases followed him, the kids jumping up and down and waving, until the wagon disappeared around a curve to the left, the lingering aroma of Sissy's intestines hanging in the cold air.

Willy's Welcome-to-Henry's-Hut snack the night before; her

lumberjack breakfast that morning and the wiener roast in knee deep snow were, according to her, mere preliminary events likened to Tidge's favorite boyhood meal of macaroni and cheese. Just before leaving for the hay ride, she had placed the necessary items for her Christmas Eve dinner on the counter tops in her kitchen. Organized stacks waited patiently to be transferred to the gigantic series of tables butted together in the Great Room.

Though not her idea of a true gourmet dinner, festive red and green table cloths quickly appeared and covered the extended tables in the Great Room. Dual pyramids consisting of lemons, limes, oranges, tangerines and mangoes punctuated with holly, pine cones and assorted candles in red, white and green were placed on the table with the assistance of Lucy and Lilly. Place settings of Willy's silver, crystal and china, wedding presents she never unpacked, cried out: "Gourmet banquet, black tie optional!" Chareese, Gert and Martha helped set the table.

The refrigerator door opened and closed so many times the refrigerator started to defrost. Oven doors followed. The microwave hummed. Corks popped from wine bottles and beer cans fizzed open. As the Christmas Eve dinner neared serving time, ice found a cocktail shaker; a ladle scooped steaming glogg into cut crystal cups and eighteen people waited.

Willy's guests stared in awe at her center piece, the biggest platter of chicken anyone had ever seen. "What's broasted?" asked Star.

Her father, without taking his eyes off Willy's special recipe for chicken, replied, "Think the best yummy in the world."

"Like Froot Loops," she asked her question complete with wide eyes.

"A million, gazillion time's better," said her father.

A whole baked ham, the bone in, and a roast round of beef acted as book ends for the chicken. Everyone but Tidge stood and gawked at the display and made no move to sit at the table and start eating. Even after Willy said, "Dinner is served," no one moved.

Tidge knew it was time. Dueling man-eating fish, scalped tourists, a farting horse named Sissy and Kenny's girlfriend, Mickey being labeled a *PT* had all of Tidge's stars in line. He quietly backed away from the others and disappeared out the mud room door. The cold grabbed at him as he cut across a short span of white yard, tracing a path plowed earlier by his nieces and nephews. He took a quick look over his shoulder, double checked to see if he was being followed by his nephews and nieces who had all volunteered to plow his driveway, and ducked into the garage. Knowing his truck was parked nearest to the door, there was no need to switch on the overhead light and possibly give him away. He hesitated then opened the driver's side door. There was a second hesitation, this pause five times longer than the first. He could hear Kid Scream in his prime yelling: "How many times do I have to tell you that there ain't no Santa Claus! Don't you ever listen?" Then he heard Willy's sarcastic question: "Are you really going to wear that hideous red relic Christmas Eve?"

Tidge replied to the two questions by reaching behind the driver's seat. His stomach churned when he felt the patched cardboard box, yellow cellophane tape hanging onto the corners for dear life. He carefully slid out the tattered box and held it as if he were holding the broken remains of his Red Ryder BB gun after Bean Head accidentally broke it, along with his right testicle, running from the police.

Tidge's work bench and the truck's front bumper provided just enough room for him to squeeze in. He and a whimpering Bean Head did more than squeeze as they wedged their bodies behind the same work bench in the Mackiewicz family garage trying to hide from the police. That long ago night now seemed like yesterday to Tidge. "Oh, crap," he remembered saying as Bean Head shot out another flashing bulb on the marquee of the Will Rogers' movie theater. A police officer had interrupted their BB gun target practice. "Run, Beanie," said Tidge, as he sprinted across the roof of Goldblatt's Department Store. Panic stricken, he slid down the drain pipe, Bean Head close behind. Suddenly, Bean Head screamed, "Ma!" Before Tidge realized why Bean Head screamed, his friend passed him in a free-fall. When Tidge's feet hit the pavement he saw Bean Head straddling a trash barrel filled with discarded florescent bulbs. Bean Head's right testicle was useless like the bulbs and Tidge's Red Ryder BB gun in two pieces.

The tattered box found the top of his workbench. Tidge thought for a moment, reached out, grabbed the metal shade of the adjustable light clamped to the back of the bench and turned it on. The florescent bulb hummed as if thanking him for the heat. His hands shook like he remembered how his Uncle Brew's continuously trembled. He lifted the lid, placed it off to the side and gazed upon a folded Santa Claus suit, the one his Uncle Brew used to wear. The suit looked worse than the cardboard box. Willy was right, but he didn't care. His hands caressed the red material, memories of his uncle, father and mother flowing from the worn red flannel through his fingertips. His entire being tingled with a sensation he never knew existed.

He removed the pieces of the suit from the box like a heart surgeon performing a delicate transplant. The pieces were as he remembered them. The beard had a tinge of yellow, the results, he knew, of age and his uncle's cigarettes and spilt drinks. There was the red hat, only shreds of a once puffy tassel visible, the hat trimmed in what used to be white fur, the trim faded, but not quite as bad as the beard. He felt a reverence as he placed the pieces of the costume on the bench alongside the box knowing he was probably the only person alive who knew the suit was worn by Santa Claus on a bombing mission over Nazi Germany. His mind, fueled by wars from decades past, generated a question that was both magical and eerie. "How could a Santa Claus suit worn by the pilot of a B-25 Mitchell bomber on a mission over Germany on Christmas Eve end up in his Lake Namakagon garage?" There was no answer.

He reached for the lid to put it back on the box and saw what looked like the corner of a manila envelope sticking out from under one of the bottom flaps. He never noticed it before. The hands of the same heart transplant surgeon lifted the corner of the business document size envelope and froze. Puzzled at never having seen anything else in the box when he had opened it before, he removed the manila envelope. As he did, a much smaller, white envelope looked up and greeted him. Underneath that envelope were several sheets of yellowed paper, lined and folded in thirds, writing on one side of each sheet. He squinted and felt bewildered. Then it hit him. He knew what the sheets of yellowed paper were without having to unfold them. "These are the letters we wrote to Santa Claus," he said, his breath visible. His fingers did a fast, nervous shuffle of the papers. "I'll be," he said, opening each folded piece of paper. "Geez, here's one from John and one from Peter and one from Paul," he said to the garage that now made him feel he was standing in a tomb. "Wow, here's mine."

Tidge's Uncle Brew always insisted that each of them write a letter to Santa saying what they wanted for Christmas. As Tidge recalled, they always got what they asked for. Uncle Brew may have continued fighting his war in Korea with *wodka*, but he still managed to sober up long enough to do his Christmas shopping and play Santa Claus. Tidge, still the surgeon, placed the letters on his work bench off to the side of the Santa Claus suit. He gave another adjustment to the pivoting extension arm of the light moving it closer to the yellowed letters. The top letter belonged to Tidge's brother John, the printing in pencil like new, eraser smudges fresh. Although the letter was filled with atrocious grammar and the spelling would never receive a passing grade from his wife, the teacher, or any other teacher from his era, the meaning and memories of John's words came racing back.

> Deer Santa
> I have tryed to be good. My mother don't love me but I tink she likes me.
> I wood like a set of Lincoln Logs for Crisamas.
> Your friend
> John M

Tidge looked at John's letter and remembered how his brother struggled with his speech as well as his behavior as a child. John wasn't a bad kid, just a free spirit who loved playing outside and who didn't want to be interrupted by being called in to eat or to even go to the bathroom. Their neighbors, the Peterson's, could attest to John's regularity with bodily functions. So could Tidge. His mother's orders were tattooed in his brain. "Thomas," she would say, making his name sound as if she had a treat for him, "please go over by Mrs. Peterson and clean up the mess your baby brother left on her front porch." His mother always referred to John as a baby when Tidge knew, by the size of his mess, that a bull moose fit him better.

Tidge fingered the letters from Peter, Paul and even his own. Peter had asked for an Erector Set and Paul an American Flyer Chemistry Set. Peter appeared to take great pains to say how he was a good boy and always obeyed his mother and father. Tidge knew that was a blatant lie and could never figure out how Santa never caught on to Peter's stealing a cigarette from his father's pack of Lucky Strikes. What was worse, Tidge couldn't understand how both God and Santa didn't know about Peter taking the cigarette and going to the same Peterson house where John had done his business, and smoke under their back porch with the Peterson's daughter, Julie. The Almighty and Saint Nick had to be aware of Peter and Julie playing *Doctor and Nurse* under the lattice enclosed porch that provided enough privacy for cigarette smoke to drift out and scientific anatomical explorations to stay concealed. They just had to know like they knew all of his bad deeds and made sure either of his parents knew, especially his mother.

Paul had taken a different approach in his letter writing, informing Santa that he had washed behind his ears every night before going to bed because he didn't want potatoes growing there. Dirt and a potato patch had been his mother's doing. Irish Potato Famine Folklore being used on Paul. He never neglected his ears. The rest of his body, however, never saw soap and water until he was a high school freshman and had to take a shower after P.E. class.

Then Tidge saw his own letter. It was evident that he would have become a successful businessman, and not a diplomat, because he got right to the point. Not only had he told Santa Claus that he wanted an H. O. gauge model railroad set, but he also gave the name and location of the store where Santa could find it if his train set didn't happen to be in stock at the North Pole. The future businessman in him included the approximate cost being sure that he quoted the top of the line model and, if by chance Santa had them in stock, he also listed miniature buildings, people and scenery. Tidge took no chances with his letter. He explained, in detail, exactly what he wanted. Then Christmas Eve rolled around and he and his brothers waited on proverbial pins and needles for Santa to arrive. They had stuffed themselves with Christmas cookies, all homemade by their mother, grandmother and aunts, and only nibbled on the traditional meal of Polish foods and delicacies. Eating would come later once Santa had left and all of the dinner would make another appearance. Mother Mary May I may have been a dirt poor child who came from Ireland, but when it came to cooking, she was the queen of continental cuisine. The lady could cook and she would have been mortified if any guest had departed her home hungry or left the tiniest morsel on their plate.

Santa made his appearance in the tiny living room of the Mackiewicz Cape Cod about the time the dinner dishes had been washed and the table set with more plates of cookies, cakes and pies. There were also bottles of bourbon, homemade Polish vodka and a gallon each of cheap wine—one red and one white. On one end of the table covered by a handmade lace table cloth were huddled matching circles of shot glasses and old jelly jars that served as wine glasses. Several stacks of his mother's china coffee cups and matching saucers, none of them chipped, graced the other end of the table. Tidge remembered that when his father started setting up chairs in a semi-circle near the Christmas tree in the living room, there would be the sounds of jingling bells and Santa Claus would enter, most times staggering, to a chorus of "Merry Christmas!" There would be a series of "Ho-ho-ho's!" and his father's reverent, borderline boisterous, "Wesolych Swiat!"

Tidge refused to believe that it was his Uncle Brew playing Santa Claus until he bid a reluctant farewell to his belief when he was into his senior year in high school. That's when his mother started showing signs of a slow growing illness that would take its own sweet, cruel time to take her. He also would never accept the fact that department store Santas wore real hats. His Santa wore the one true hat, one with a frizz of white ball on top appearing almost comical and a massive trim of fur, the white giving way to yellow beige. Other Santas smiled from magazines. His Santa, he once heard, a comment made by his father to his uncle, fought in a war.

It had been Santa's hat that had been the reason for Tidge discovering that Mother Mary May I had an arsenal of ways to teach her children respect. One weapon in her arsenal, a small, green Marshall Field's department store shopping bag, convinced Tidge to respect all likenesses of Santa even if the real one only came to his house on Christmas Eve. Marshall Field's Department Store Santa was a fraud and Tidge had let him know it. "You fat bastard!" he shouted, startling Santa, two of his elves, Mother Mary May I, other children waiting in line, their parents, other nearby shoppers and a hand full of employees. "You ain't Santa!" Tidge never got to say another word as Mother Mary May I grabbed him by his left arm, yanked him off Santa's lap with her left hand and held him airborne like a giant marionette in a snow suit. She pulled him out of the Santa Claus display section so fast he never realized what happened. The giant marionette in the snow suit, rubber goulashes kicking at air, made a four point crash landing on the polished marble floor. Tidge blinked then saw stars. He later learned that the reason for viewing a celestial phenomenon was Mother Mary May I's right hand, the one that held a small, green shopping bag with the Marshall Field's logo. Inside the bag was a jar of imported jelly from Ireland his mother had bought for Christmas. The green bag, the jar of jelly and his mother's hand found the side of Tidge's head and introduced him to manners, respect and never disgracing the family name again.

Tidge's eyes left the letters and glanced at the Santa Claus suit. Santa's hat came back into view and he knew what had to be done. He counted on Willy's Christmas Eve dinner and his family's ravenous appetites to give him time. To make his plan fool-proof, he ducked back inside the Great Room to make an appearance saying, "Sorry to be late, but nature called."

Willy's parents were the only ones who recognized his return. Harold held up his crystal cup filled with Glogg and Gert toasted him with an empty Gibson glass and her almost pleading eyes. Tidge held up his index finger, grabbed a thick slice of ham off the platter, a stainless, circular wire frame holding the giant ham upright. With the ham slice, half in and half out of his mouth looking like a grotesque, slobbering reindeer tongue, he snatched Gert's glass from her hand and was in and out of the kitchen with her Gibson in record time. "I'll be right back," he said, heading for the mud room door. "I've got to get some hay out of the garage for Santa's reindeer." As he grabbed for a slice of roast beef, six children jumped up from their seats eager to assist their uncle. "Sit and eat!" he shouted, startling everyone in the room. "Enjoy your Auntie Mina's dinner first!"

Tidge didn't miss a masticating beat. "We'll feed the reindeer after you get through feeding you," he said, slipping out of the mud room so fast he was back in the garage stomping his feet on the cement floor, the slice of roast beef hanging from his mouth. He swallowed the glob of meat as he squeezed into the space in front of his workbench again. He didn't waste a second. The small white envelope was unsealed with the sharp blade of one of his Exact-o knives and he lifted the flap. His surgeon's fingers were again at work as he removed two black and white photographs, one smaller than the other, from the envelope. He could tell the photographs were old judging from the picture of a young girl sitting on Santa's lap, the young teenage boy next to her and the way they were dressed. It could have been him at Marshall Field's. Tidge examined the snapshot. After several minutes, he turned it over where he found the following faded written words, *Sam: Nickie and Mari on our annual Santa trip from Mexico to St. Louis. Love, Sugar.* A part of the message on the back of the photograph intrigued him. He turned the picture over again. The girl in the picture couldn't have been any older than he had been when his mother had taken him to State Street in downtown Chicago that fateful Christmas season he insulted Santa Claus. They were even dressed the same. His snow suit and galoshes weren't as new looking as hers. His had been hand-me-downs from an older cousin he only saw and played with on Christmas Eve. The girl in the picture reminded him of someone he once knew, but time didn't give him the luxury to reflect. He set the first picture down and then examined the second, holding it close to the workbench light. The photo was cracked as if a spider had spun a web across it and there were small chips of the photo missing from the top corners. The picture was of a handsome man in uniform standing alongside the nose of an airplane. He recognized the plane as a B-25 Mitchell bomber. On the nose of the bomber was painted the picture of a shapely blond pin-up girl in a red two piece bathing suit who wore what looked like a Santa Claus hat. The artist's brush had accented her large cone shaped breasts with sharp points that appeared lethal. There were two words painted underneath her, *Sugar Claus.* "I'll be damned," whispered Tidge. He studied the picture, his eyes taking in every detail of the man in uniform. He knew he was a Captain from the twin bars on his shirt collar, and he wore a leather aviator's flight jacket and a Santa Claus hat with a white tassel. There was an insignia above one of the front breast pockets. His hand reached for the handle on the workbench front drawer and he pulled it open. Without looking, he took out a large magnifying glass and held it over the picture. He could make out that the insignia on the jacket and the girl painted on the nose of the plane were one in the same. And there were the same two words: Sugar Claus. "Probably the pilot," said Tidge to the empty garage. "A cocky one, I bet, judging from the look on his face." His magnifying glass worked up and down, back and forth and from side to side as he tried to make out the name on a small rectangular patch opposite the Sugar Claus insignia. Then he saw, or thought he saw, the name, S. Claus. "Holy shit!" he blurted out, feeling as if Kid Scream had hit the back of his head with one of his silent, whizzing slaps. He placed the photograph and magnifying glass back on his workbench and picked up the smaller picture again and re-read the writing on the back. "Mari? Sugar? Claus?" he asked, the questions creeping from him. "Mari? Short for Marietta? It can't be," he said, setting the picture back down. "No way," he said, his two words creeping out to join the name he remembered. "Couldn't be. Her old man's name was Wolfgang. It couldn't be." He grabbed the open drawer to steady his shaking knees. He studied the picture of the B-25, then the captain. The workbench began to vibrate as if Lake Namakagon sat dead center on an earthquake's epicenter. "The bastard's wearing my jacket," he blurted out, his knuckles white from gripping the workbench drawer. He knew all the alcohol in the world couldn't fabricate a story about an aviator's jacket two men died for, and a third trying to die. Uncle Brew's story was real. The brothers were real. He stared at the picture of the grinning older Claus brother, the original, the one and only who was wearing his jacket and the Santa Claus hat. Santa Claus fatally wounded by Messerschmitt fire and German ack-ack happened. The captain's younger brother dying in Korea happened. His Uncle Brew fighting *Chinese Fuckers* and leaving the scarred aviator's jacket to him happened. He hung on for dear life to his workbench drawer. The two photographs were side by side and he couldn't take his eyes off of them. He tried to examine the photographs with a shaking magnifying glass but it was hopeless. Trembling, reluctant fingers slid the photographs back into the envelope. He couldn't stop now. The unglued envelope flap beckoned. He took a deep breath, exhaled and pulled out a laminated piece of business size paper from the envelope. On it was written the following: *What really tests and shows the moral character of a person is telling the truth, not when it is easy and fulfilling, but when it is difficult and daring.* Under the quotation was the name of Immanuel Kant. The words had been hand written in Old English script much like the work he did. He turned over the quote and saw a brief note from his uncle, the note looking like it had been written while Lt. Jg. Bruce Mackiewicz landed his Panther on the pitching deck of the carrier Princeton. It read: *Nephew–You are to truth as truth is to you. Never stop believing in Santa Claus. -- Uncle Bruce.*

Tidge embraced the worn, cracked leather of his Air Corps jacket. Confusion swirled around him. "Did Kant really say that?" he asked the garage. "Did that guy in the picture die wearing my jacket?" Again, there was no answer from the garage. He didn't need one. He was convinced. Now he knew the reason why it had been given to him. All actions had reactions, some opposite, some equal and each with a reason. There was a reason for patriarchs being appointed and a reason for teacher-parent conferences. There was a reason behind being shot down over Korea and shooting back with a booze bottle, a reason for two brothers dying while wearing a beat-up leather flight jacket and why he now wore it. The Wilhelmina's, Barbara Ann's and Sissy's of his life were there for a reason.

Tidge heard a faint click. It was the numbers on his antiquated digital clock turning over. "Miles to go before I sleep," he muttered, as the same trembling fingers replaced the laminated quote in the envelope. What he would do next would either remove the Kid's millstone from around his neck or find it dragging him to the bottom of Lake Namakagon. "Time she is a fleeing."

He had located four of his homemade wooden pictures frames hanging from large hooks from the peg board behind his work bench. Alongside of his work bench were three stacks of cut glass, each stack in a different size. Spare matting for framing pictures in different sizes and colors also hung from the peg board. He had moved those from his basement workshop on impulse on a rare time he cleaned and took inventory. Still excited, but minus the shakes, he spread out the Santa Claus letters under the light on the work bench. Tidge, the perfectionist, centered the letters on white, matted card stock with the precision of an old time watch maker. A homemade glass cleaner and small squares of newspaper attacked the glass that would fit into the frames, the liquid cleaner spraying out in ice crystals.

Once assembled, the framed letters looked back at him from their new homes. There was no time to wrap his presents. Colored paper depicting smiling snowmen or jovial, waving Santa's was for kids, not adults who were once kids. His head began to ache as he realized he had to get into the Santa Claus suit and make his appearance on schedule even though Willy had pleaded with him not to make a fool out of himself.

"God knows and so does Santa," he had said so many times that it turned into a redundant, sour joke between them. And, now, something was telling him that both God and Santa had sent him the special three-in-one present, the special present he had waited for ever since his father anointed him patriarch. He adjusted the stained beard and fluffed at it like an aging diva defying her years. His heart raced even faster when he saw the white numbers of the clock sitting on the cluttered shelf above his work bench flip to double zero and an eight. On went the beat up red hat. He gently tucked the picture frames with the letters under his left arm, switched off his work bench light and said, "Okay, Sugar Claus, it's off we go into the wild blue yonder with your plums and Uncle Brew's red nose leading our way."

Tidge barged into the Great Room bellowing out an ear shattering, "Merry Christmas!" He stopped, looked at the startled kids and surprised adults and asked: "Are you the folks who drove all the way up here from Chicago?"

Harold and Gert nodded, Harold holding up his cup of glogg in a toast, Gert taking a sip of her Gibson, one made for her by Peter and Paul in Tidge's absence.

"Your glass is empty, Mrs. Schneider," Peter had said to her. "If you tell me what goes into one of those Gibson things, I'll be more than happy to make you one."

"Me too," Paul had said, having joined his brother.

It was Harold who had given them the ingredients and directions.

"That's all," Peter had said.

"That's all," Harold had replied.

"Wow," John had said.

"Ho-ho-ho!" roared Tidge, his greeting originating somewhere below where his tonsils used to be. His eyes bounced back and forth between the six nieces and nephews, Star and Frankie having abandoned their chairs for the security of their mother's arms. "And you must be the children I read about in a letter Mrs. Claus and I received from an Auntie Wilhelmina Schneider hyphen Mackiewicz," he continued, being sure to make the last name sound like, Mackie whiz.

"That's Mackiewicz," Paul replied, politely correcting Santa's pronunciation of the family name.

"Ho-ho-ho," retorted Tidge, his own reply more subdued. "Wesolych Swiat!"

"Wesolych Swiat!" said Chareese, holding up a cup of glogg.

Tidge glanced at each of the kids again, Star and Frankie still clinging to their mother, their heads now down beneath the gala decorated table. "Do you children know that if your parents would have driven north for a little longer, you'd be at the North Pole right now spending Christmas Eve with Mrs. Claus and my Elves?"

Two heads popped up from under the table, young eyes searching for both security and answers from their parents.

"Ho-ho-ho," said Tidge again, spying Star and Frankie, their astonished looks making his heart glow. He rubbed at the tarnished buckle of the frayed and scarred black belt around his bulging middle with his right hand. The index finger of the soiled white glove on his right hand suddenly pointed at Star. "Ho," he said, his blue eyes smiling at her.

Star looked at her mother then ducked back under the table.

Tidge's index finger shifted to Frankie. "Ho," he said.

Frankie joined his sister.

The framed pictures were still clutched under Tidge's left arm as his eyes did a sweep of the table. "Is there a little girl here who likes baby elephants," he said, then clearing his throat. "I was told her name is Martha." He looked around the room and saw his oldest daughter's head going slowly back and forth. "I have a bag overflowing with presents for her." He saw Martha's face turn the color of his suit.

Tidge was locked in the moment, the past had returned. The only difference being he was a sober Santa. "Have you all been good little girls and boys?" he asked, his head nodding up and down, the children and even the adults nodded their heads up and down. "That's exactly what Santa thought." He paused, looked around the dinner table again, his eyes doing a return trip. "Santa knows all," he said, a touch of authoritarianism in his voice. "No one can keep a secret from Santa, right Auntie Wilhelmina Schneider hyphen Mackiewicz?" He smiled at Willy. "I even remembered to pronounce your name properly this time so as not to insult the perfectly intelligent gentleman you're married to, and his wonderful family's Polish heritage."

Willy's head joined the others in a slight nod although the smile on her face indicated that she would possible end his life once their guests had returned to Chicago.

"Ho-ho-ho!" yelled Tidge, the exuberance in his voice shifting into high gear. "Time for presents," he bellowed. "Santa's got too many stops tonight to dilly-dally even though he would like to spend all evening with you." His stained beard couldn't conceal the pure happiness he felt. "Would the men of this wonderful family be so kind as to take all of the chairs away from the table and set them in a semi-circle in front of that beautifully decorated Christmas tree?" He looked at Willy. "I bet the man of the house was responsible for such tasteful decorating."

Willy gave another nod, the smile on her face changing to one that indicated that ending her husband's existence on Earth was a given. She watched as a portion of her guests scurried to the chairs, her parents already seated comfortably on one of the sofas. Star and Frankie clung to their mother's leg while their four cousins, along with Carm, Carol and Mackie were sprawled on the floor, their noses inches from the presents. Martha positioned herself next to the tree so that her near leg and hand made a reassuring contact with the gifts.

Tidge cleared his throat again. "Merry Christmas one and all," he said, a slight choke in his greeting. He noticed his stuffed recliner lounge chair was in its place of prominence sandwiched between the fireplace and the Christmas tree. Tidge pretended to adjust the lounger. His back to the others, he slid the framed letters under it. He turned, patted at his belly, grinned and sat down. "Ooooooh," he muttered. "I might have to take this chair back to the North Pole with me." He let out another relieved sigh and looked up just in time to see Paul toss him one of the festive wrapped packages and, in that instant, he felt that he was Santa Claus.

Paul continued to feed him presents, yelling out each recipient's name. Santa held out the present and a happy youngster crawled across the floor on hands and knees stopping in front of Santa, arms out, hands open and anticipation flashing from excited eyes like light house beacons along the shore of Lake Superior.

Star and Frankie were the only kids who needed coaxing. A gentle shove by their mother had them finding Santa's lap. Fear was plastered all over their innocent faces. Even after they slid off, a present clutched in a death grip in their tiny hands, they scooted across the floor back to the security of their mother's leg without looking back.

Tidge looked back. He couldn't help it. Christmas time had been different when he had been the age of his nieces and nephews. For sure, they would have never called Santa what he did that day so long ago in Marshall Field's.

Tidge, sweat starting to soak through the itching beard, continued on with the older children, asking each in a stern voice, "Have you been a good little boy?" Girl was substituted an even number of times.

Peter's and Paul's children had stopped believing in Santa Claus. Their bubbles burst by information that was Gospel passed on by obnoxious friends. Natasha, Nathan, Pauline and Paul, Jr. acted indifferent when each of their names was called out and they had to go to Santa Claus.

"I know you're not real," said Natasha, with a nervous smirk that caused Kid Scream's coffin to vibrate. She didn't see her father hold back her mother and playfully slide his hand over her mouth.

Tidge was prepared. He had waited too long, arming himself with more than his shield, sword and coat of arms. Any attempt at denigrating Santa Claus would be met with a punishment to be determined by the severity of the crime. Getting hit in the head with a jar of preserves imported from Ireland, as Tidge could attest, was one punishment not on his list.

Tidge's armament consisted mostly of items of current personal news on each of the children, his included. The items had been given to him during phone conversations he had with their parents when spelling out to them the driving directions to Cable and Lake Namakagon.

"Santa's proud of you," he said to Natasha. He cast off her skeptical look and ignored the voice of Kid Scream whispering in his ear, "Go 'head, give the smart mouth little snot nose one upside the head."

Tidge smiled. "Raising your computer science grade two whole letters is something I heard about clear up at the North Pole. I bet your parents are proud." His eyes peered into hers. "Do you know who else is proud of you?" He paused just long enough to think. "Mrs. Claus is proud of you." His eyes twinkled. "She just learned how to you use the computer we bought to speed up the routing of presents, and she admires young people like you who do well in computer science." His niece looked at him still doubting. "Santa heard that you told your parents you might want to be a nurse when you grow up." More of the doubt seemed to fade. "Did you know your father once had a girlfriend who wanted to be a nurse?"

Natasha's face showed neutral.

"Your father also wanted to be a doctor." He saw her head turn and glance at her father. "Obviously, he didn't, but he and his friend used to discuss it all the time." His smiling eyes peered into Natasha's beginning-to-believe ones. "He and his friend were at the forefront of discovering the dangers of nicotine."

Natasha glanced at her father. "Really, Daddy?"

Tidge didn't see the look on her father's face. He handed Natasha a large package, the bulging contents held in by green and silver ribbons bound in both directions. "I know all kinds of things about you," he said. He smiled. "Don't worry. Almost all of what I know about you is good."

Pauline approached Santa next, a look on her pretty face saying, "Yeah, sure, like you're supposed to be Santa Claus." She stood with her hands on her hips while Paul discretely kept her mother at bay with a firm grip on her wrist. His other hand was in an open palm position, ready to muffle any sound.

Santa held out another fancy wrapped package identical to the one Natasha had received and said: "Mrs. Claus wrapped this especially for you. She's the champion gift wrapper in this great big wonderful world we live in." His hand didn't let go of the package even as Pauline gave a gentle tug. "I bet you didn't know that your father once thought about being a farmer." He wanted to laugh at the increased size of his niece's eyes. "You might have been born in Idaho if he had continued on with his interest in agriculture. Your dad sure liked to experiment with potatoes. He got that from his mother." He released his grip on the present. "Did you know that Santa knew of a little girl who got an incomplete on her science project because her father ate her experiment?" His head went up and down several times. "It was your father's expertise in agriculture, producing wheat, I believe, that prompted the experiment." His partially hidden eyes still peered out from behind the false wire rimmed glasses. "The little girl's teacher didn't believe her student," he said, then glancing at his wife. "Some teachers find it hard to believe anybody. It's just like friends that tell lies about my not existing." He touched his chest cushioned by a pillow. "I think, therefore I exist," he said, the beard hiding his grin. "And, I know too." There was a single nod at Pauline. "That little girl's father came in and told the teacher about the unfortunate accident." Believing returned to Pauline's eyes. "Don't ever forget, Santa knows if you've been bad or good." He glanced to where Carol was sitting with Mackie and his eyes glued on him. "Santa can even read minds, he said." He smiled at Pauline. "Would you like to know who that father was?" he asked, his eyes flashing what her answer should be. "It was your Uncle Thomas," he said. "As soon as he gets through tending to my reindeer you ask him."

Pauline drifted back to where her parents sat muttering, "Oh, my, God, it's him," she muttered.

Paul kept calling out the names and Santa held out each package until he thought his arm would fall off. After the kids had their packages, a mound surrounding each, Paul started to call off the names of Tidge's sisters-in-law.

After the Great Room floor resembled an explosion in a gift wrapping paper factory, Santa got up from his chair, stifled a groan, stretched and placed his hands on the fireplace mantel. "Beautiful fire, he said. He turned and faced the guests. "Looks like Santa will have to use the door tonight to get to my sleigh. I don't want Mrs. Claus getting mad at me because I came home with charcoal on my backside." He waved at his audience and shouted: "Ho-ho-ho," and a "Merry Christmas to all, and to all a good night." Then he stopped so sudden he almost slipped on the hardwood floor. The kids giggled and he turned and went back to his chair.

Everyone was caught by surprise and the Great Room became silent. Reaching under the lounger, he pulled out the four picture frames. He carefully arranged them in a neat stack and let out a subdued, "Ho-ho-ho." He pulled the stack of frames until the top one almost touched his nose. Squinting, he said: "Santa almost forgot these." He gave each of the frames the once over, shuffling one on top of the other as if he were trying to stack eggs. "Is there a Miss Joliet here?" he asked, the top frame still touching his nose. He only waited a second for a reply and then asked: "Could that be a Mrs. Joliet?" The silence in the room became eerie. "Mrs. Schneider hyphen Mackiewicz," he said, looking at Willy. "Did you invite anyone from Joliet, Illinois here for Christmas?"

Willy's head went from side to side once. In that brief point in time, she had finalized how she would eradicate her husband from existence.

Then looking over the tops of his wire frame glasses, Tidge held a framed picture at arm's length. "Oh, I'm sorry," he apologized. "My eye sight isn't what it used to be. Is there a John Mackiewicz here?"

John came forward appearing to act like a nervous, apprehensive child. Behind his act, he was planning to join his sister-in-law, Willy in ending his brother's life.

Tidge made an attempt to disarm his brother, John. "You must've been good boy for Santa to leave you a special present. Were you?"

John nodded like the shy child he once was.

"Young man, would you be kind enough to stand next to Santa."

For the first time in his life, John obeyed his oldest brother not knowing what to expect. Then he was joined by Peter after Tidge asked: "This Julie Peterson's name must have been misplaced by one of my elves. I don't know why her name keeps coming up so much." He looked at John. "Do you suppose she was from Joliet?"

Paul joined is brothers and stood in between John and Peter. Under his breath he whispered, "If he starts preaching, I'm taking my family and heading south. Draw bridge or no draw bridge."

John whispered back under his breath, "Me too, but not until I eat."

Tidge stood stone still, his eyes shifting between his brothers and the stack of pictures. "I've got to have a word with my elves when I get back to the North Pole," he said. "First we had all of this business about growing potatoes; then we had information about nicotine and this Julie Peterson person and now a couple of women from Joliet." He paused, gave his shoulders a shrug and turned his attention back to the framed pictures."

Willy had moved and took a spot along the sofa where her parents were seated. "I have no idea," she said to the look her parents gave her.

Tidge's head nodded ever so lightly and "Mmmm," could barely be heard. He looked at his brothers. "You know what would please Santa right now?" he asked, as he handed a framed letter to each of his brothers. He cleared his throat. "Santa would like each of you to read what's in these frames." He repressed the urge not to issue a command. "Let everyone in the room hear you. Heck, we're all family." He paused. "I mean, I'm not Mackie-whiz blood, but I feel like I'm family." He paused and looked at John. "You're the youngest, you can go first."

None of them balked. When they were finished the only sounds in the room came from several muffled sniffles. Santa gave one more look around the room as if checking to see if he had missed any presents and then turned to leave.

"Isn't Santa going to read his?" asked Paul, his other brothers' faces asking the same question.

Santa looked at Paul and said, "I believe this framed letter is for your brother Thomas." He looked Paul square in the eyes, his own eyes smiling. "As you know, he's tending to my team of reindeer back in the woods. Santa wouldn't want a big old bear to eat Blitzen or Dasher." He noticed Star and Frankie scoot under the table again. His eyes made a quick scan of the room as he held up the last framed letter. "I'll give this to him."

Tidge went through the kitchen exiting out the mud room where he grabbed a strap of sleigh bells he had stashed in between the washer and dryer. He flicked off the outside flood lights and stepped outside yelling, "Ho-ho-ho," for all he was worth, the sleigh bells he had borrowed from Don Miller clanging away like joyous church bells. In a minute he had ducked inside the garage and was changing into his clothes as fast as he could without making a mess of the Santa Claus suit. He folded the suit as if he were packing it for shipment to the Smithsonian and placed it into the cardboard box. "You'd better get some moth balls for that box," he said to the empty garage.

The two envelopes he had taken from the box earlier still sat on one side of his workbench where he had placed them. "When I have time," he said to them. He went to the cab of his truck where he replaced the box. "Thanks, Uncle," he said catching a glimpse of himself in the truck's passenger side outside mirror. His fingers pulled off several strands of stray beard and the back of his hand wiped the sweat from his forehead. There was a deep exhale and he caught another glimpse of himself in the mirror. "So far, Dad, " he said to his vision, "I removed my head from my dupa like you ordered and I've been getting these funny feelings lately that I've finally found the key to the lock that's been keeping me from getting this screwed up family unscrewed. I know you're not going to be thrilled but Santa Claus and your brother fit the lock perfectly."

Tidge continued to gaze into the truck's mirror as if he were frozen in place. He had a hard time believing that he had just stood with his brothers, the four of them together united. The last time that happened was when their mother died and Kid Scream hung up his boxing gloves for good.

For eleven months out of the year, Kid Scream lived his name. He screamed. His tirades almost always directed at his four sons. At Christmas, for whatever reason, no one was spared except Mother Mary May I. Then, one Christmas day, Mother Mary May I's dispensation ran out.

Tidge and his brothers stood in shock as their father turned his anger on their mother. He had never done that before not even when he came home from Harry Dungan's Tavern. They were all in shock and Tidge could never understand what and why he did what he did.

"Leave her alone!" Tidge had screamed at his father, surprising himself, his brothers, his mother and especially his father. He was almost finished with high school, his brothers still attending St. Ferdinand's grammar school, Peter about to graduate from eighth grade.

"What did you say?" his father asked, the question coming out like an amused surprise, his hands showing signs of turning into something they had all seen many times on the Gillette Cavalcade of Sports.

"Stop yelling at Ma," Tidge snapped back.

"Oh, really, Tomasz," his father said. He opened his hands and gestured for his son to step towards him.

Tidge took a nervous step, hands clenched, tears streaming down his cheeks and started to say, "If you hit our mother, I'll . . ." He could feel himself about to lose control.

"You'll what?" said his father, still gesturing for his oldest son to get closer. His hands were like a pair of monstrous battering rams seeming to toy with his oldest son.

"Stop screaming all the time," Peter blurted out, surprising everyone and walking up to stand alongside his older brother.

"Two," their father said, an amused sarcasm coating his single word. "One for each hand." He looked at his right hand first and then his left. He looked pleased. "Take your pick, lads. You want to be first, Pietr?"

Peter didn't get a chance to pick. "You're going to need another hand, Daddy," said Paul, his voice shaking as much as he was as he flanked Tidge on his other side.

"Jeden, dwa, trzy," his father said, counting to three in Polish. "Join the crew, Pawel."

Before another word was uttered, there was a childish scream. The three of them just caught a glimpse of their brother, John, the baby of the family, streak by them and leap at their father. Arms and hands flailing, he kept screaming, "Don't yell at Mommy!" Before they could react, they saw their father, who had caught John in mid-air, drop to his knees on the kitchen floor, embracing his youngest son, repeating, "I'm sorry, Janusz. I'm sorry."

Before they knew it they were all huddled together hugging their father while their mother sat down on one of the chrome and patched vinyl kitchen chairs and wept into the floral patterned apron covering her Christmas dress. Then, when they felt they couldn't cry another tear, they heard their mother, her voice soothing and gentle, like her tender hands that had rubbed each of their shoulders as only a mother could rub. "It's okay, boys," she said, slowly and comforting. "The Christ Child has just shown his love for us."

His dad would always be Kid Scream. Names and reputations make memories, good or bad. It was only after his mother had died that his dad changed into someone else. Where his brother had joked earlier about Tidge having changed, his father's soul and will to live went in search for the love of his life.

It was a strange marriage, and an even stranger family, that Tidge remembered. But, as a kid, he thought, all families were like his. Humper and Bean Head had mothers and fathers like his. So did the Petersons. There were other brothers and sisters. Dads worked. Most moms stayed at home or went to work after dad had returned from his job. Parents drank, but none of his friends ever said they had a parent who was an alcoholic even though most of them had an Uncle Brew who they joked about. Divorce was a rarity. He and his friends only heard a rare rumor about something called drugs. Incest? Child molestation? Pornography? Adultery? Those words were hidden in the dictionary, their meanings expressed in unintelligible academic words only to be learned when children became adults. Never in a million years would he ever experience those things. Then he found himself on a Wednesday night, a stone's throw from the corner of Chicago and Michigan Avenues sitting in a Loyola University downtown campus classroom as a graduate student looking out of the corner of his eyes at the cranberry colored loafers belonging to Barbara Ann Lindstrom. His million years were up.

He saw a familiar face looking back at him from the truck's mirror. It was his, but he was different. He nodded at the image in the mirror and checked to see if all traces of Santa Claus had been removed before he went back to the Great Room. The image nodded back. He shrugged his shoulders. The image didn't. He stared into the mirror. There was no mirror. There was no truck. It had been replaced by his new, big screen Christmas present.

Tidge glanced down at both of his hands looking for the remote. It was gone. Then his screen went black, static jumping across it in a trillion white dots, followed by a test pattern in black and white with the picture of an Indian chief. The chief was holding up a pair of boxing gloves. Tidge blinked, the Indian disappeared, and he saw himself stepping into the boxing ring of the Gillette Cavalcade of Sports. "This is bazaar," he said to his garage which had now become a boxing arena.

Tidge felt himself walk to the center of the ring wearing his old Army Air Corps jacket and the bottom half of his Santa Claus suit with the faded blood stained leg. On his head was the hat that his wife detested. He blinked a couple of more times when he saw the referee. "It can't be," he said. Then he heard the referee.

"Welcome, Mr. Tidge, Sir," the referee said, ever so polite. There was a sharp crease in his black trousers and his white shirt was starched, the black bow tie perfect as if it had been tied by Myrna Loy for William Powell. "And, good luck, Sir," the referee said in a southern drawl. "You still have a little less than a day and a half to turn the key of Santa's special present."

Tidge glanced into one corner of the ring and could see his brothers. They were bare-chested, each wearing a copy of Uncle

Brew's Santa Claus pants. They didn't say a word, turning their backs to him. His head turned clockwise and another corner came into view. There sat Harold and Gert. Gert was sitting on a wooden stool and wearing her old wrestling tights, a version of a two piece sequined bathing suit that, at one time, would have been banned from most beaches. Her stomach muscles rippled and there was no sign of sagging skin. She was wearing high heel pumps and sipping a Gibson. Harold wore riding britches, knee high brown boots and a tan leather jacket. A white silk scarf was wrapped once around his neck, the loose ends dangling down his back. He wore a World War I aviator's helmet with the goggles snug over his eyes. He was sitting in Tidge's recliner from the Great Room and reading a copy of a magazine that was covered with nude women in provocative poses, all wearing high heel pumps, some of the heels six to eight inches in length. A frown of disgust would come across Harold's face and he would turn a page. Then he'd smile and glance at Gert, show her his selected open page and ask, "Would you like a pair of high heels like these?" Gert wrinkled her nose like her daughter and said, "I'd prefer a Gibson." She wrinkled her nose again and said: "Betty Page and I used to wear those all the time in the old days. Hurt our poor tootsies."

Willy was in the same corner with her parents fanning them both with a white, terry cloth bath towel. She turned, faced Tidge and held up the towel. There was an outline of a heart etched on it with the word *Patriarch* inside. Around *Patriarch* was a red circle with a diagonal line running through it.

Tidge didn't have time to question the towel as his daughters came into view. They were dressed in Karate uniforms, black belts around their waists, arms folded across their chests. Each of their faces held blank expressions as they stared at him. His head continued to turn and, for the first time, he felt fear.

In the remaining corner stood his ex-wife, Sissy and his former love, Barbara Ann. They were chatting like old friends, Sissy dressed as if she had stepped out of the pages of a Lord and Taylor catalogue. Her raven black hair was in a coiffure, he knew, that was the latest style out of Paris, Milan, or New York and the latest charge on one of her cards. He could see that she was still a fraction over five feet and another fraction over one hundred pounds. She was looking up at Barbara Ann, smiling. Her well-manicured fingers displayed a stack of gold-plated credit cards. Barbara Ann was an inch shorter than Tidge and a couple of pounds overweight to ever be competition for the Betty Page from Willy's parent's era, but she could still turn heads. Always did, especially his.

Standing along the ropes next to Sissy and Barbara Ann were his sisters-in-law. Each was dressed in a native costume typical of their heritage except each was bare breasted.

"It's time, Sir," said Mackie, the next word out of him being a resounding, "GONG!" Before Tidge knew it, each corner began to take a cautious step towards him, each in unison, a dozen stern people inching closer, Mackie one of them, but not Willy.

"Put your dukes up," said Peter, raising his hands, palms open, just like Kid Scream. Paul's and John's hands followed. "It's time you finally learned who is and who is not screwed up in this family."

Martha, Carm, and Carol stopped in front of him, just out of reach, each standing abreast of the other. On a silent cue, they took a deep bow. Four seconds later exactly, they straightened up and jumped into a ready position. "Time for an upside-the-head swat, Daddy-kins," said Carol. "You didn't think you could eat my science experiment and get away with it, did you."

"I'm going to love this," said Martha, assuming the ready position. Carm was also at the ready. "The dysfunctional family that fights together, stays together," she said.

Willy continued to fan Harold and Gert with the towel as they inched across the ring. Gert was crouched down in her wrestler's ready position stalking her prey. Harold held up the fold out page of his magazine, moving it back and forth trying to get Tidge's attention. His eyes were flashing a message that said, *How do you like these CFMP's, son-in-law?*

"What an absolutely divine Christmas," said Gert, continuing towards her son-in-law in her wrestler's position. "You are indeed a lucky young man," she said to Tidge. "You're lucky because I'm going to apply my See 'em Hold on you."

Willy moved when her parents did, staying well behind them, but flapping her towel so fast there was a breeze across the ring. Harold had returned the fold out page to his magazine and was now eyeing a picture of a naked lady wearing only six inch high heels made of clear plastic. "Would these be more along the line of what you wanted me to buy you for Christmas?" he asked, leaning over Gert's shoulder and showing her the picture from the magazine. Another wrinkled nose answered his question as Gert snatched the magazine from her husband and rolled it into a tight cylinder that resembled a small club. In an instant there was the sound of a loud pop as the magazine slapped against her open left hand like a black jack. She smiled.

Tidge could see that Sissy and Barbara Ann were still chatting amicably, girl talk being swapped. They had moved up close to him with the others and both had put up their dukes. Tidge looked at Barbara Ann, his eyes asking, why?

"Because," said Barbara Ann, her fists clenched even tighter. "You were a crap husband and a crap father who crapped all over this wonderful lady here." She nodded at Sissy, her eyes never leaving Tidge. "You deserve to get the poop pounded out of you, you pee poor excuse for a patriarch. Besides, you cheated off me on our exams."

Tidge blinked. All he could see now was himself in the truck's mirror. Sweat poured off him running down his forehead and dripping from his nose like water from their roof during a summer down pour. He reached up with the extended index fingers of both hands and began to squeegee off his forehead as if his fingers were the slow moving blades of his truck's windshield wipers. He exhaled, continued to stare into the side view mirror of the pickup truck and then wiped his hands on the sides of his pants. "I can't be the only one screwed up in this family," he said, his words echoing through the garage. "I can't be." There was another exhale as he turned and headed for the back door ready to make his re-entry into the Great Room emphatically saying out loud just before he opened the door, "Patriarchal poop or not this is still going to be a perfect Christmas!"

When Santa departed the Great Room, it looked as if it had been hit by a bombing run from Sugar Claus. Everyone had been buried knee deep in shredded gift wrap. The smaller children looked like they were back on the hay ride their heads now poking above Christmas wrapping pager as they rolled around in it, threw it up in the air and at each other.

Tidge's brothers, with subtle prods from their wives and none from Willy, armed themselves with large plastic garbage bags. They were joined by Mackie who responded to Carol's look. The quartet had the Great Room almost meeting Willy's definition of tidy by the time Tidge returned from the garage.

Willy, with help from Tidge's daughters, was putting out yet another assortment of cookies and cakes while two coffee makers poured out steam, hissed and sputtered. Mackie, after tying his garbage bag shut, pitched in to set up a tray with half dozen different liquors and a dozen cordial glasses. The sisters-in-law were trying to herd the excited kids up the stairs to the loft. The kids weren't cooperating when Tidge entered the room.

"Merry Christmas," he yelled out, unable to contain his excitement. His greeting stopped the kids on the stairs. "I talked to Santa when I was polishing Rudolph's nose," he said, continuing to walk to where the kids were standing. "He told me that you were one of the best families he ever had the privilege of visiting." His right index finger crossed the area of his heart. "And, do you know what else Santa said to me?" he asked, not waiting for an answer from anyone. "He told me that you kids were so good and so polite and such believers in him that you deserved a special treat for Christmas." He paused and drank in six different expressions of awe. "Santa told me there's still time for you and, even this entire family, to write him a letter asking for a special gift." Tidge turned and strolled back into the Great Room stopping in front of Harold and Gert. He smiled and asked, "What do you think about spending Christmas away from the city sidewalks?"

Gert held up her empty glass. "Gotcha covered," he said, taking her glass. "Harold?"

Each of the kids gave a quick look at their mothers. Before they could get a reply, they abandoned the foot of the stairs and scurried back into the Great Room just as their uncle was heading into the kitchen to refill two empty glasses.

The six kids clustered together on the floor in front of the fireplace appearing wide awake. They looked at their parents, blank expressions on their faces and wondering what a letter to Santa Claus was all about since Christmas was but a few hours away.

Tidge's daughters and Mackie joined the other kids. The bigger kids, like the smaller ones, were also trying to comprehend why a letter to Santa Claus was being put before them now. "Dad's got to be playing a game on us," said Carm, brushing her black bangs out of her eyes.

"No one's better at playing games than dear old Dad," said Martha, a trace of sarcasm still evident on everything she had said pertaining to her father since arriving.

"Oh, big sister, put a tampon in it," said Carol. "Can't you let Daddy be happy?"

"Happy," repeated Tidge, not hearing the entire exchange between his daughters as he walked back into the Great Room. "One for you, Gert," he said, handing the Gibson to Willy's mother. "And a wee touch of my late Aunt Bessie's elixir from Sweden," he said to Harold, handing him the cut crystal punch cup. "Happy it is."

Tidge looked at the families and took a deep breath. He swallowed hard and said: "If we all start writing our letters now, we can get then to Santa in time."

John blurted out, "By UPS, I hope." He grinned at his oldest brother. "That's a rocket propelled UPS I assume."

Tidge shook his head from side to side without looking at his youngest brother. "We don't need any type of special delivery, rocket propelled or even reindeer express deliveries," he said, the tone of his voice indicating he had anticipated a similar comment. "Remember, we're closer to the North Pole up here than you are at home." He looked at each of their faces and still saw puzzlement. "I understand Santa has read the *Polar Express* and will put your requests on a special schedule." He looked towards Willy who sat dumb struck like her sisters-in-law. "Your Aunt Mina has plenty of paper and pencils for letter writing. Right, Aunt Mina?"

Willy nodded and was off to the den to get the writing supplies she had bought for the kids, never imagining they would be used to write letters to Santa Claus.

Tidge walked over to his recliner indicating that the kids should stay where they were at. Reaching under the chair, he removed his own framed letter to Santa Claus written decades before. He walked back to where the kids were sitting. "Kids," he started out as if he were reading *The Night Before Christmas* to them, "once upon a time I got to write a letter to Santa." He paused even though he knew he had their attention. And, do you know what?" Six heads went slowly from side to side. "I got what I asked for," he said, his head nodding up and down in cadence with their heads.

"He even told Santa what stores he could find the presents," whispered Paul to Peter and John.

"Uncle Thomas," said Star, her soft, sheepish voice matching the expression on her face.

Tidge's look told her to continue.

"Uncle Thomas," she repeated, "I don't know how to write."

Tidge walked over to her, knelt down on one knee and took both of her tiny hands in his. "Your mommy and daddy can help with the writing. All you have to do is tell them what you want to write to Santa." Before he could say another word, Star was at her parent's feet saying: "Now you tell Santa I want..."

Tidge didn't hear another word. Before he realized, the other children headed off in search of their mothers, who, in turn, were giving the come hither eye to their respective mates.

Willy returned to the Great Room with pencils and paper and was back in her teacher mode distributing the items to the six kids. "Harold. Gert," said Tidge, as if he were addressing the children. "Care to write a letter to Santa Claus?" To his amazement, both of Willy's parents joined the kids. Without asking, Peter, Paul and John each took a pencil and a sheet of paper from Willy.

Willy came up to Tidge and asked, "Do I get to write a letter too?"

He looked at her, winked and whispered, "How many mink coats do you think you'll get?"

"As many as it takes," she whispered back, a wink following. I'll wear my pumps."

Tidge kissed her on the cheek and then they both stood in awe watching letters being composed. He took a glance at his own framed yellow letter. At the top were the initials *JMJ*. He laughed recalling how the B.V.M. nuns at St. Ferdinand's School made them use that heading on every paper, test or otherwise, that they wrote. *Jesus, Mary and Joseph* would always be with them in everything they did. He remembered that it wasn't always the case when some of his tests were returned to him having only one correct answer–his name. He had more than a correct answer now. The correct answer was Thomas Ignacy Jozef Mackiewicz.

Chapter 10

Tidge's excitement joined hands with the eerie feeling that had permeated his being in the garage after he had finished playing Santa Claus. That feeling wasn't new to Tidge. It was just stronger, at times, almost talking to him. Looking back, he figured that he first felt the weird sensations about the time he met Willy.

Willy, too, had noticed a strange sensation flowing through her about the time her feet touched the ground when first seeing Henry's Hut. She loved the feeling, embracing it, even giving it hugs like her Mitty used to give her. After Tidge exited out the mud room, his leather strap of bells echoing he had finished playing Santa Claus, Willy felt the strange sensation return and began hugging her in earnest. She picked up assorted pencils and scattered sheets of paper from the Santa letter writing exercise realizing that Christmases past never provided the magical feeling that surged through her.

Three mothers once again attempted to herd six kids toward the stairs to the second floor loft. Their efforts were met with cries of resistance, stocking feet attempting to brake on a polished, hardwood floor.

"Ma, I ain't tired."

You're tired! You just don't know it.

"Uncle Thomas promised I could wait up to see Santa."

He lied.

"Mother, Nathan is still a Cretin."

Santa doesn't think so.

"Ah, Ma, bed's for the little kids."

It's also for big kids like me.

"I want my *blankey*."

If you don't get up those stairs, I'll give it to Santa.

"I'm hungry."

The food's all gone. Your father and your uncles ate it all.

Lilly was the first to lose her patience. Her warning was so loud it startled a family of voles sleeping in Tidge's pile of romantic leaves. "No bed! No Christmas presents under the tree tomorrow morning with your names on them!" she shouted, arms spread wide and making sure none of the children got outside of her reach. "Make the wrong choice and bamboo will replace fudge brownies and Santa."

The reluctant kids trudged up the stairs with a maximum of dragging, kicking and the stomping of feet.

"If I hear one more stomp, your mama will show you real stomping," said Chareese, as she zeroed in on the unlucky children bringing up the rear.

Tidge's brothers watched their wives follow the herd as if they were Santa's elves corralling his reindeer. Mackie and Tidge's daughters fell in behind the parade hoping to be of some help as Mackie counted cadence. "Hup, two, three, four, he ordered, his left foot hitting the floor on hup and three.

When mothers, daughters, Mackie and the children disappeared around the corner three fathers sprinted out the front door. They plowed and stumbled, high stepping through the knee deep snow of the unplowed apron to their cars. In minutes, they were back at the front door, stomping their feet on the door mat, the bear paying no attention to them. Traces of snow clung to their pants, socks and shoes as they sought the warmth of the house.

Tidge closed the front door behind them and noticed three towers of more presents blocking his brothers' faces. "Looks like UPS uses more than rockets."

Paul set his presents at the base of the Christmas tree. He began blowing on his hands then rubbing them together saying to Tidge: "Brother, your letter writing idea was brilliant." His bald head glowed red from too much Swedish glogg washed down with beer and his brief exposure to the icy Christmas Eve night. "Where did you find those letters?"

Tidge shrugged. "I guess Santa planted them out in the garage," he said, turning his head to take a quick check to see if the front door was shut tight. Another glance showed the second floor landing minus human life. "If it worked for our Uncle Brew when we were kids, I got the feeling it would work up in Winsconsin." He looked at

John. "Right, Janusz?"

John blew on his cupped hands his eyes giving his approval.

"It was more than brilliant," said Peter, as he knelt down and positioned his load of presents next to Paul's. "For the first time in my life I saw my kids get as excited as we used to on Christmas Eve."

"Me too," said Paul. "I thought my kids' eyes would pop out of their heads." He gave Tidge a serious look. "Did you or the ghost of Uncle Brew cast a spell over us?"

Tidge shrugged his shoulders.

"I hate to say it," said John. "But, I noticed a feeling I've never had before the moment I first set foot in this here mansion of yours, Tomasz."

"Me too," said Peter. He looked seriously at Tidge. "Paul was right when he said your letter writing to Santa Claus was more than brilliant. It was like some kind of a hypnotic spell took over my kids."

Tidge shrugged again. "Don't all patriarchs possess magical and hypnotic talents?"

"Patriarchs need to do more than pull rabbits out of hats," continued Peter, changing the mood. "You'd be in deep do-do right now if any one of us couldn't come up with the presents our kids requested in their letters to Santa." His cupped hands appeared glued to his lips.

"Forget the kids," said John, looking relieved. "I got a glimpse of Lucy's letter, and the one item she asked Santa for was the one item I had hidden under the spare tire." He simulated wiping his forehead with the back of his right hand.

"Mine was under the front seat on the driver's side," added Paul. "It was buried with all the crap the kids have stuffed under there since the last time I washed the car."

"My wife's was under the front passenger seat," said Peter.

John walked over to where Tidge stood holding his hands, palms forward, toward the warmth of fireplace then put his arm around his shoulder. "Tomasz, you have been called brilliant, lucky and even possessing magic." He paused turning his head and grinning at his two brothers who were standing behind him. "Nice accolades." He tried not to laugh. "But, oldest brother and so-called family patriarch slash dictator slash preacher slash royal pain-in-the-dupa, do you realize this is the first time any of your family members paid any attention to you?"

Tidge shrugged again, looked at John and flipped him the finger. He nodded for Peter and Paul to join him and John by the fireplace. "Just before the Kid went to that great big boxing ring in the sky," he said his voice solemn, a tone his brothers didn't know existed, "he ordered me to remove my head from my rear end and unscrew this screwed up family. Man, I had no idea how screwed up you guys were."

"Us, screwed up?" asked Peter sounding surprised. "Surely not me," he continued. "Perhaps the rest of you, but never me. Heaven's, have you forgotten that my name is Peter and I am the rock that the Kid and Mother Mary May I built their family on?"

"And, not me, the oldest?" asked Tidge.

Peter's head went from side to side. "May I and the Kid would never construct a foundation made of doubts."

'True," said Paul, his own head going from side to side feigning disbelief. "A Thomas foundation is a disaster waiting to happen."

Tidge's right hand shot up. "Pietr," he said. "The reason May I and the Kid named you Peter is because you were born with a massive erection that startled the maternity ward nurses. Too bad you never grew another inch after infancy."

"Right on, brother," said John to Paul. "Poor Julie Peterson must have gotten a most pleasant surprise on her honeymoon after all those years of playing *Doctor and Nurse* with Pete under her porch."

"You also got a surprise," said Paul, smiling and looking at John. "You were the most surprised human being on God's green earth after you discovered that gift your mother and daughter duo from Joliet gave you."

"Okay," said John, both hands raised for them to stop. "You guys are rattling sacred bones in the old family closet. John's eyes zeroed in on the fireplace. "At least I experienced life in the fast lane," he said, recalling that brief era in his life marked by stupidity mixed with pleasure.

"Did you ever get milk with your cookies on Christmas?" asked Tidge.

Peter and Paul grinned at John, Peter saying, "You're the first person I ever knew who got a shot of penicillin as a Christmas present.

The entire time the four brothers talked, Gert and Harold sat unobserved by the fireplace in a tranquil stupor respecting Gert's special Commandment. Their eyes clicked open when they heard what they interpreted as a jocular conversation between Tidge and his brothers.

"If I may," said Harold, politely, startling the four brothers. "I would like to contribute a pertinent observation or two concerning your intellectually stimulating conversation."

The Mackiewicz boys sheepishly made their way to the sofa where Harold sat with Gert. His right knee was crossed over his left and he held an empty glogg cup between his thumb and forefinger as if he were at a formal tea party. "Gentlemen," he said, sounding almost apologetic. "Mrs. Schneider and I were not eavesdropping on your conversational topic concerning. . ." He paused then said: "In my native German, I believe the expression for screwed up is *vorkorkst*.

"Harold, darling," Gert interjected. "You're making our dear son-in-law and his siblings blush on Christmas Eve. Shame on you," she said, her admonishment unable to defy her smile.

Harold nodded at Gert. "I apologize, gentlemen," he said, another nod given to his audience. "Matters pertaining to family are private and, more often than not, are best kept locked up, as John so succinctly stated, with the family bones."

"No need to apologize, Harold," said Tidge, a touch of warmth still evident on his cheeks. "It's Christmas, we're all here as a family and, because we're family, we want everything to be right with the world. Unscrewed is the way our late father dreamed of seeing his family."

"Nicely stated," said Harold. "My own late father had similar thoughts about the status of his beloved Germany somehow becoming unscrewed." He glanced at Gert who nodded her agreement. "I didn't recall a single citation in the book I read today while you were on your hay ride that pertained to magical spells, dysfunctional families or the size of one's member at birth." Harold's eyes twinkled.

Four sets of cheeks ignited with a whoosh of flame.

"Harold," said Gert, playfully slapping him on his thigh. "A little decorum. We're guests, remember, and I don't believe Washington Irving's delightful story, *Old Christmas* you were so engrossed in this afternoon delved into dreams." She looked at Tidge and his brothers. "I never know what to expect from him. He can be such a naughty boy at times."

"Naughty, but well meaning," said Harold, a wry smile easing the tension in Tidge and his brothers. "Had Washington Irving been alive today, he would have used you, dear son-in-law, as his Squire."

Tidge and his brothers cast a confused look at Harold.

"I couldn't help but notice, Thomas, how you were perceived with deference and regard during gift giving and your letter writing activity," said Harold.

"I wasn't aware of that," said Tidge, heat still emitting from his cheeks. "What I know and truly believe is that Santa and the Almighty are pretty smart guys and they work in mysterious ways." He gave his brothers a nod. "I also believe that they think those gifts you three guys brought in might need a bit of rearranging under the tree. Your kids will be up early, eager and looking. That is if they have any of your genes."

Eloquently stated, Thomas," said Harold. "As a child in Germany, I, and all children received gifts on Christmas Eve. Not from *der Weihnachtsmann*, Santa Claus, but from the Christ child."

"Mr. Schneider," said John, keeping his curious interruption polite. "I never knew you were born and raised in Germany."

"Don't feel like the Lone Ranger," said Tidge, looking at Harold. "I just thought Willy's grandmother was born and raised there. I didn't find out until Willy and I got engaged."

Harold, a look of melancholy saturating his face, glanced at his wife and then back to the others. "I believe I may have alluded to the fact earlier that my mother was born in Switzerland. Her father was Jewish. My mother and father met when he was on holiday in Switzerland." He smiled. "They fell in love at a chocolate shop in Berne." A reflective pause took over. "Mother and I came to America about the time the war's outcome looked bleak for the Third Reich. It was my father's idea. His well thought out plans made what could have been a precarious trip easier for mother and me. His plans were also his orders. *Mien vater* was an officer in the Luftwaffe. An *Oberleutant*, Senior Lieutenant, I believe. My mother being Jewish never mattered to my father. He adored her. Hitler and his followers didn't have the same perceptions of the Jews as my father did. He would have been executed by a firing squad if my mother's true lineage ever got out."

Harold seemed to be in another world. "One memorable overcast day when no one flew, he had a rare day's pass and came home. Normally he was all military, all business. But he talked to us in a whisper that day even though he was in his own home. My mother and I were shocked to find out, in my father's opinion; the war wasn't going well for Hitler and his cadre of psychopathic clones. Rumors of dissension among high ranking officers had been heard. My mother tried not to cry as she listened even though she knew the inevitable. When he showed us the documents we needed to get out of Germany, to travel, she broke down. He had money for us. Everything was mapped out. We were to take only what my mother could carry in her purse and what wouldn't show bulging from our pockets. I even wore extra socks and underwear. Thank God it was still winter. We removed family pictures from ornate frames and concealed the pictures in the linings of our heavy coats. Besides two shirts, I also wore two sweaters." Harold held up both arms in the fashion of making a muscle. "I looked like a real he-man," he said. "Like a Charles Atlas." His arms went limp. "My father assured us we would be together after the war. Father had a brother living in New York. Poughkeepsie. It was another fragment of information Hitler didn't know about that would have gotten mein vater executed. Father's voice got lower than a whisper when he told us to follow his orders explicitly and not to show any fear of the SS. Mother and I were both scared, but we followed my father's orders and, almost three months later, we were looking at the Statue of Liberty. Unfortunately, the reunion with father never took place. We learned later, that on his way back to the airfield that same day he bid us auf Wiedersehen, weather reports had the heavy fog lifting. Allied fighters strafed the military vehicle in which he was riding. Mien

vater and three other pilots, along with the driver, were killed. What
was ironic is that on our last Christmas together father had a twenty
four hour pass for that day. He told my mother and me about an
incident that happened to him during a combat mission against allied
bombers the day before. It was Christmas Eve. He was very sad,
almost distraught, after telling us about making a dive toward an
enemy plane and, just as he fired his guns, he thought he saw Santa
Claus flying the bomber."

"He thought he saw what?" asked Tidge, his knees almost giving
way as he grabbed Pete by the shoulder.

"Santa Claus," said Harold, his hushed voice reverent. "Mother
and I thought he was joking. My father always liked to joke with us.
But we could tell that this was no joke. He shot at Santa Claus. He
was sure his gun fire hit the plane, saw some of the damage, but got
engaged with another plane and never saw any smoke or flame or
evidence of a plane going down."

"Geez," said Tidge, gawking at Harold. "You did say Santa
Claus, didn't you?"

Harold nodded then glanced at Gert. If by some invisible signal,
he changed the subject, saying: "Thomas, your letter writing activity
was the finest experience I've ever had at Christmas in my life. It was
most certainly something I never experienced in Germany as a boy."

"Thank you, Harold," said Tidge, still leaning on Peter, his knees
not shaking as much. He saw Gert's empty cocktail glass and
Harold's equally empty glogg cup. He also noticed a yellow legal pad
on Harold's lap. "Writing a letter to Washington Irving telling him
how much you enjoyed his Christmas novel?" asked Tidge, nodding
at the legal pad on Harold's lap.

"A letter to Santa Claus for my wife if you must know," said
Harold. He went to take a sip from his empty glogg cup. Holding it
at his lips he tipped it then looked inside.

Tidge felt relieved, but still shaken, after the topic of conversation
shifted away from Santa's possible annihilation through the gun
sights of Oberleutnant Werner Schneider's Messerschmitt, to letter
writing. In three short steps, two to politely take Harold's cup, and
one to step back before heading for the kitchen, Tidge said to his
father-in-law: "I think you might need another taste of my Aunt

Bessie's Swedish Make-A-Man-Mellow-Potion. It'll put a nice finishing touch on your story of growing up in Germany."

"Most thoughtful of you, Thomas," said Harold, his sophisticated demeanor unchanged. "I'm more than mellow thanks to you and my daughter, your wonderful families and the young cadet," he said. "His military bearing reminds me a bit of my father those many decades ago."

Tidge was in and out of the kitchen, the cup refilled, nestled in a red and white napkin pressing against Santa's smiling face. He handed the cup to Harold.

"Thomas, you are most definitely, as your sibling mentioned earlier, a host with the most," said Harold, taking the cup with both hands. He took a careful sip from the steaming cup of glogg. He looked at Tidge and the others and said: "I do believe that I'm closer to embracing the true spirit of Christmas than I have in my entire life." His right arm shot up at a forty five degree angle and, from his sitting position, his heels clicked together and, in his most polite and conversational voice said: "Hiel, der Weihnachtsmann."

Harold's tribute to Santa made Tidge realize Gert also had an empty glass. "Please excuse my poor manners," he said to Gert. He bowed and politely removed her glass by the stem. "Harold's story of Santa being shot down on Christmas Eve really gave me a jolt. At first I thought he was playing some kind of mind game with us."

"My dearest Harold does not play mind games," she said her voice almost a warning. Instantly, a perfect cover girl smiled flashed at Tidge. "The only game my husband has ever taken delight in playing has been Charades."

"Did I hear you say Charades, Liebchen?" asked Harold in a burst of enthusiasm. He placed his hand on his wife's knee and looked at Tidge and his brothers. "When Gert and I used to entertain with great regularity, before we both retired from our chosen professions, we played a parlor game called, *Can You Top This.*" He gave Gert's knee a gentle tap. "We combined Charades with an old television game show. Remember, my love?"

"Indeed I do," said Gert, her own enthusiasm joining that of her husband's. "We never knew what to expect from our guests."

"I don't think Georgia O'Keefe had as eclectic and varietal group of friends and associates as Mrs. Schneider and I," said Harold. Then he and Gert broke into knee slapping laughter.

"Who in the hell is Georgia O'Keefe," asked John in a whisper to his brothers, getting a shrug from Paul.

"A famous painter," said Tidge.

"A painter you'd like," Peter said to John. "Chareese's father has some of her works. Told me she was rumored to have run with a kinky crowd in New York City and around Taos, New Mexico. Maybe the Joliet duo knew her."

Before John could retaliate they heard Harold say, "Our friends were so very creative." He smiled at Gert then gazed into his glogg cup for a moment before looking at the others. His cup was empty. "I think the game would be a most delightful way to add to the merriment of the season."

"I agree, darling," said Gert.

Tidge held up Gert's empty glass for her to see. "Before the games begin," he said, starting to walk towards the kitchen, "I think one of our main contestants needs another glass of Christmas cheer, with an onion of course." He stopped and turned back to Harold. "Oops," he said, walking back and taking Harold's newly emptied cup he said: "We mustn't forget the memories of Aunt Bessie's Sweden and your mother's Switzerland."

Tidge disappeared into the kitchen as the wives, his daughters and Mackie started tip-toeing down the stairs. Each of the mothers held three letters to Santa Claus while Carm and Martha each had a letter in their hand. Carol held two, one for Santa from Mackie and the other from her to the same address. Wives, daughters and daughter's friend joined the others filling up the spaces on the sofas and the semi-circle of kitchen and dining room chairs that had been set up earlier for Santa's visit.

Willy, after picking up the left over writing supplies and packing them away, had disappeared into the kitchen. She knew pastries; coffee and liquors guaranteed continued feelings of an Eleventh Commandment's edict for mellow. Then she saw her husband with a gin bottle in his left hand, his right on the cap and her own mellow turned to mush.

"I wonder what visions those kids will be seeing dancing in their heads tonight," he said to Willy, an empty stem glass and an equally empty cut crystal punch cup eagerly waiting to be refilled. Tidge didn't realize his wife hadn't responded to his comment. He watched her attack several stacks of white bakery bags and boxes along with a tower of holiday painted cookie tins brought by their sisters-in-law. Tidge was in his glory as he rambled on. "The kids are probably dreaming of Kenny Miller scaring the crap out of them." He cracked the seal on the Bombay Sapphire gin bottle, one of a half dozen Harold had brought. "Maybe they won't be dreaming. Not with all the sugar they crammed down their gullets. They'll be tossing and turning all night." He paused looking pleased. "Honey, if this ain't Christmas, then there was never a miracle on Thirty-Fourth Street. Man, oh man, what a wonderful life."

Willy never looked up. Her growing nervousness wouldn't let her. Her hands were a blur. Cookies appeared out of nowhere turning three ornate silver trays on the counter in front of her into creative, mouth-watering masterpieces. "I'm sure that gin bottle will contribute to my mother having a wonderful life."

He ignored her comment by not smiling when he placed the cap of the gin bottle on the counter. Ice clinked in the polished metal cocktail shaker. "Didn't James Bond want his Christmas cheer shaken and not stirred?" he asked, just as one of the two coffee makers, the one used for decaffeinated coffee, ended its cycle with a long hissing and sputtering sound. Gibsons, my darling, will not prevent our family members and single stray guest from hearing the silver bell tinkle on our Christmas tree when a certain angel," he stopped, pointed the cocktail shaker at himself, nodded and continued. "Me. I'm that certain angel. I earned my wings on that pile of leaves behind our house before our company arrived, just in case you forgot."

"Wings?" she asked. "I don't remember seeing any wings. Come to think of it, what leaves are you talking about?"

"The pile of leaves behind the back deck that made you announce to the residents of Bayfield County that Santa Claus was coming to town." he said.

Willy tossed an indifferent look at her husband. She saw curious mixed with excited and tempered with caution as she watched him refill her mother's glass. Her own trepidations began to vanish when she noticed him pour some ice water and juice from the cocktail onion jar into her mother's glass.

"I'm trying," said Tidge, noticing his wife's scrutinizing look. "The onion juice makes Gert's drink a Dirty Gibson." He came over to her and kissed her on the cheek. "No need to worry," he said, beaming. "The Santa Claus suit has been laid to rest and we're more than half way home." He gave her another peck on the cheek. "I have a feeling that there will be no creatures, big or small, stirring tonight." He held up Gert's glass. "Not even a spouse."

Willy's contingency back-up plans pleased her because she didn't need them. She anticipated almost every want and need of her guests along with a plan to funnel her tense nerves into the marble hot tub in their master bedroom. If an oversight did occur, luck or Tidge stepped in. Mackie, for example, didn't drink coffee, but loved hot chocolate. She bought two cans of mix thinking of the children. Mackie's surprise arrival as Carol's guest and boyfriend didn't upset Willy. Mackie's needs dovetailed those of the children's. Peter's wife, Chareese, had opted for hot spiced hard cider. Tidge's late Aunt Bessie came to the rescue just the way she had decades earlier when she met, fell in love with and almost saved a very handsome Bruce Mackiewicz from self-destruction.

Tidge and his brothers never forgot how Aunt Bessie's glogg turned Mother Mary May I and the Kid into a pair of grinning deaf mutes who lost the use of their limbs. "Too bad Aunt Bessie and May I died before you had a chance to meet them," he had said to Willy one afternoon as they took a break from cleaning, decorating and organizing. "The two of them had one thing in common," he continued, as Willy listened, sipping a cup of decaffeinated tea as Tidge gulped down a half a can of diet root beer. He belched and said, "They were both incredibly loving human beings."

Tidge surprised Willy with a cup of glogg on their first Christmas together. He had resurrected his aunt's recipe from memories of a young boy eavesdropping on adult conversations. Trial and error led him along an exploratory path of markers filled with grimaces, spitting, grins, purple tongues and the loss of one or all of the five senses. He brewed and fine-tuned his potent concoction following a directive from his favorite teacher from high school, Brother James Virgil who said, "Perfect practice makes perfect, you moron."

Willy's initial cup of glogg, actually about one third of a cup, saw her grimace as her tongue and lips turned purple. A second sip made her feel warm all over. By a third of a cup she had turned into Mother Mary May I with a running nose even though she had never met her.

The morning before Harold and Gert arrived; Tidge placed his enameled kettle on the stove, lined up his ingredients like a squad of Marines awaiting inspection and lit the back right burner on the stove. The kettle was the same one Mother Mary May I once used to boil their soiled diapers in.

Tidge began the process of perfection. Two gallons of cheap burgundy found the kettle. The rest of Aunt Bessie's recipe followed. A bottle of grain alcohol joined the burgundy as a substitute for Swedish Aquavit. The Aquavit seemed to disappear from local liquor store shelves in Bayfield and Sawyer counties about the time deer season drew near. The clear, highly flammable liquor wouldn't appear again until spring.

Tidge knew his wife feared only one thing when it came to her plans. "Please, no glitches," she had said to him when discovering his intent to make glogg. "I don't want a house full of comatose zombies sprawled out all over."

"There's no glitch in glogg," he had replied, while searching the cabinets under the sink for his enameled kettle.

When Tidge heard about Chareese's request for cider, he said to Willy, "Tell Peter's wife that glogg is just northern Wisconsin's version of spiced cider. In the Northwoods the locals use a combination of blueberries and blackberries for coloring. It makes the drink more festive looking. Chareese will love it."

Tidge poured, mixed and stirred away at his kettle all morning. He added a bottle of one hundred and fifty-one proof rum to the now slightly steaming purple mixture. Next he cautiously dropped in his late Aunt Bessie's secret spices. He unleashed raisins, unsalted almonds, cardamom, a couple of cinnamon sticks and citrus peels all measured in the palm of his left hand. The secret ingredients, given birth in a little village outside Stockholm and brought to America by Bessie Sorenson, disappeared under the sinister looking liquid. He stirred and simmered, simmered and stirred, his stained, long handled wooden spoon savoring the moment.

Chareese, after enduring a nine hour ride through a blizzard, sat mesmerized in front of the great room's fireplace. A cut crystal cup of steaming hot glogg warmed her hands while the vapors drifted up and into her nose. After her second cup, she was convinced Lou Rawls was singing, *Oh Holy Night* to her, his lyrics drifting from the flaming logs.

Chareese repeated her two cups of glogg during the lunch time wiener roast the next afternoon. She ended up sitting very somber Indian style in the snow so close to the open fire that her eye lashes got singed. She didn't seem to mind. Something was troubling her. She looked at the flames and asked: "How am I going to tell my parents I'm Swedish?" She continued to stare at the flames. "And that Lou Rawls is too."

The breezy cold of the hay ride brought her back to the world of the living along with a ravenous appetite and a thirst for the biggest, coldest beer she could find. Chareese hated beer.

Tidge's heart and something else told him that this was the Christmas he had yearned and prayed for. Uncle Brew's Santa suit, the discovery of four old letters and the contents of several envelopes all but put the special in a special Christmas. A stocking trimmed fireplace, a magnificent Christmas tree looking as if it had stepped off the cover of one of Willy's issues of *Country Living,* her sweet table and his glogg embellished the special.

"No Gillette Cavalcade of Sports," he had said to himself after what he imagined in the garage changing out of the Santa Claus suit. He knew what had happened at other family Christmases after his father had died. He wasn't about to allow disaster to grab this Christmas by the throat. If disaster tried to get down his chimney, he would stuff as many logs as he could into the fireplace.

Willy's experience with a Mackiewicz Christmas disaster happened only once. It was during her first Christmas with Tidge. They were living together with Tidge spending time between his Norridge apartment and her Lake Shore Drive condo until his lease ran out. Christmas Eve was to be with his brothers and their families. Paul hosted the night.

Willy smiled the entire evening. She laughed, played with Tidge's nieces and nephews and enjoyed small talk with his sisters-in-law. She also heard shouting and arguing coming from the kitchen. Tidge and his brothers had made themselves scarce, but they weren't out of mind. Elevated language fueled by glogg and laced with vulgarities guaranteed that.

Willy's smile vanished about the time she left the party and got into Tidge's car. With her smile gone, her sense of speech went on strike. It was a quiet drive to her reserved parking spot in the condo's enclosed garage.

Tidge, with more on his mind than Christmas, escorted Willy to the front door. The silent ride didn't seem to bother him. Conversation was for old people and women. He had planned to spend the holidays with Willy at her place. He also planned to propose to her on Christmas Eve.

Tidge's insides felt like discarded Christmas trees being fed through the crushing high speed blades of a shredder. He had wanted to ask her to marry him after their first date on New Year's Eve. Cold feet brought on by ugly memories of a brutal divorce that left him almost destitute had, for a rare time, his brain engaging before his tongue moved. It was his friend Humper who put Tidge's new found passion into perspective.

Humper, who had married Jumbo Jugs Janice Koester a week after graduating from Weber High School, said to him over a beer at their old neighborhood haunt, the Sunset Inn, "Get to know her first. Get to see what's inside her suitcase, sort through her belongings."

Tidge wanted to laugh. His ex-wife had been right about one thing. Looking at Humper made him laugh. Sissy's interpretation of laughing in no way was connected with humor. Hers was a vicious, almost evil connotation in no way related to friendship, respect and, most certainly, not love. Humper in no way resembled a psychotherapist, but here he was psychologically analyzing his friend's exploding feelings of love, devotion and death 'til us part.

"Janice married me because she couldn't stand her parents," said Humper. "How does your new love feel about her mommy and daddy? I know damn good and well how you felt about your old man."

Tidge took a sip of beer and nodded, his expression telling his friend to continue.

"Janice's old man was like your uncle, the guy who gave you that pilot's jacket with the holes and stains. The one you've got on now."

"Her old man had a problem with the sauce?" asked Tidge, knowing it was one he didn't have to ask to get an answer.

"So did her mother," said Humper, pausing to take a sip of his beer. "Her mother was a nice lady until she drank. "Then. . ." Humper's head went from side-to-side a look of anguish filled his face. "Her mother would rub her crotch up against the nearest male she could find."

"She didn't," said Tidge carefully.

Humper's head went up and down once.

"Geez!"

'Nothin' happened, my friend," he said, starting to smile. "It almost did, in their house, under a sprig of plastic mistletoe dangling from a hall entrance hanging light." He laughed, gulped his beer down and slid the glass to the edge of the bar. His index finger gestured to Andy the bar tender for two more. "I had a little accident if you know what I mean." He laughed again. "After I got home and I was cleaning up I thought about those pictures of your mom you showed me once." He toyed with the Michelob beer coaster in front of him. "Remember how Brother James Virgil used to refer to us as morons?"

Tidge grinned.

"I felt like a moron. I really did. Here I was in love with this incredible girl and it dawned on me that I didn't really know much about her. It took an episode under the mistletoe at Christmas during my senior year for me to step back and think this love stuff through in detail."

Andy placed their beers in front of them saying: "Two beers for two steers."

Tidge, trying not to smile, said to Humper, "You must've done some heavy duty thinking if you made Janice a June bride."

"My analysis didn't take long because both Janice and I agreed that we would put distance between us and her family."

"Are you telling me to back off?" he asked, the fingers of his right hand stroking the pilsner glass.

"No way," replied Humper, his own fingers tracing the rim of his glass. "You wouldn't do anything I told you. Never did." He let a roar of laughter, his hand slapping down on the bar. "You wouldn't go over to find out how far the old Yule log was in," he said. "I had to get Beanie to do it."

They both laughed.

"Tidge, if your heart tells you to pop the question, pop away," said Humper, his slightly tilted lips turning into a grin. "Just don't let that little head of yours control the big one like you did once-upon-a-time."

Now he was ready to pop the question. Before his proposal formed the first word, her foot came down and Willy popped him instead. Her tiny high heeled pump landed hard, spiked heel first, on Tidge's head. He listened without blinking and without breathing. The beautiful lady's string of sentences earned his respect and frightened him to death. She had done her own analysis of his baggage.

"Wilhelmina," he said, trepidation in his voice and his defenses up, out of habit, like his boyish arms that once tried to ward off his father's not-so-playful jabs. "My days of shouting are over. No more arguing. I promise. I'm putting jolly back in the season, permanent, just for you."

Tidge knew the days of a band of brothers doing battle were history. If they weren't, he would be looking for another fiancée. Battered and bruised, scraped, scabbed and scarred, he picked himself off the Gillette Cavalcade of Sports' canvas and popped the question.

She accepted. "I meant what I said about you and your brothers arguing," she said, her eyes glued to the engagement ring. The marquee cut diamond set in a simple platinum band with two tapered baguettes had cost Tidge his life's savings. "One more fight at Christmas and you're history, Buster. And, I keep the ring. Didn't one of your brothers' fiancées do that?"

That Christmas Eve they both got what they had wished for.

The moment her guests arrived, starting with her parents, Willy's sensitivity level heightened as did her ability to hear words that remained unsaid. It didn't make any difference who said or was about to say a word. If the word seemed incendiary, she would glide to the source with a cheerful holiday smile and snuff it out, usually with food or drink. In the Northwoods, she had learned that Smokey the Bear warned, "Crush it, break it, drown it, use it. Only you can prevent forest fires." Crush, break, drown and use it she did, to perfection.

As their contented, weary, mellow guests settled in after putting the children to bed, Willy anticipated each of them making a trip to her sumptuous dessert table. Her anticipation was led by Mackie.

"He's definitely not shy," Willy said to herself. She smiled as Tidge's brothers circled the table of assorted sweets. Then her smile vanished as she saw what she didn't want to see. Her mother and Martha had gone into the kitchen. Agonizing moments later, they emerged into the Great Room chatting like longtime friends, giggling and smiling. Each sipped a Gibson. Willy dug for her list of alternatives buried somewhere in her organized mind. Pages flapped; fanning the burning logs in the fireplace so furious they let out a, WHOOSH! "Thomas," she said, her tone so cheerful that if she smiled any harder her cheeks would shatter, "why don't you show everyone the pictures you're planning to put on exhibit and hopefully sell at a few art fairs this summer." She felt a line of cracks working their way across her cheeks. "You must have close to a thousand."

He did not want to drag his collection of pictures from his workshop but he knew her request, like almost everything she ever suggested to him, had a logical reason. Her reason usually end with, "Or else." His artistic fascination with capturing Wisconsin's flora and fauna through a camera lens had nothing to do with her request. He obeyed then held his own breath.

His sisters-in-law gave their overwhelming approval to his black and white, cropped enlargements. There were miscellaneous, "Ah's" sprinkled in with nods and some, "Oh's" as they passed around his first stack of pictures. Each picture was matted and framed, a grainy charcoal affect he experimented with grabbing everyone's attention. Other stacks exhibited tin type prints for antiquing and a hazy, fog aura he used to create, what he felt, a spiritual essence. The pictures worked their way around the room. Nods continued with and without sound effects.

Tidge was ready for what happened next. Willy wasn't.

John looked at a framed picture then looked at Tidge. He looked back at the framed picture, holding it at different angles, his lips twisting back and forth, the tip of his nose appearing to get lost in his eyes. "Is this a picture of a cow with horns tied on her head?" he asked, his face beet red, an empty glogg cup on the floor by his feet along with several crushed beer cans. "And, what's with the red ribbons on the horns?"

Tidge could hear Kid Scream whispering in his ear. "Go 'head, give the obnoxious little squirt one of my upside the head specials."

Tidge laughed as he stood next to John. "That ain't a cow, you city slicker," he said, smiling. "If you look close, you'll see it's a bull."

"Looks like a cow to me," said John, trying to goad his brother into using an outburst of creative profanity.

"A bull," said Tidge, sounding like he majored in animal husbandry in college. "In the immortal words of Mother Mary May I, if you'd like, I'll have Kenny Miller come over and explain his rationale for tying red ribbons on the horns."

Willy's contingency plan wasn't cooperating. Suddenly she felt like one of the tourists surrounded by fire and marauding savages at the Lakewoods Resort Kenny Miler had described earlier. She thought she heard Kenny say: "Some of those poor folks, I heard tell, ended up on a heap of charcoal big enough to cook all the brats at the Stone Lake Cranberry Festival." She shuttered, blinked and heard John's voice.

"Looks like a cow to me who just might have an identity crisis," said John. He pawed at the hardwood floor with his right stocking foot.

Willy blinked again and saw her husband.

"Exactly," said Tidge, his hands clapping together. "You saw it right away. Little brother, you are an artistic genius. How would you like to move up here and be my partner?"

No one in the room said a word. They looked at John. Then they looked at Tidge. A repeat of their hay ride visit to Twin Lakes anticipating an attack by either a gar fish or a sturgeon, each fish carrying a tomahawk and looking for a scalp was about to commence.

"Me?" asked John, confused. "I saw it?"

"Yep," said Tidge grinning. "After Thanksgiving, your sister-in-law and I walked over to the Miller's farm to thank them for an enjoyable Thanksgiving. Kenney Miller gave me the idea. He thought putting human traits onto whatever grew, growled or lived on their farm or in the woods would add a touch of humor. The kid's a genius."

"Me?" repeated John again.

"We'll talk after you have another cup of glogg," said Tidge. He picked up the empty cup at John's feet along with the crushed beer cans and headed for the kitchen while the pictures continued to make the rounds.

"I did?" Tidge heard John ask again.

"You did!" shouted Tidge over his shoulder as her shuffled across the hardwood floor of the Great Room to the kitchen. "On Winsconsin, On Winsconsin,"he sang softly. If he was going to carry out his plan to send John outside for a walk in the woods searching for Paul Bunyan's ox, Babe and decorate the beast's horns with red ribbons, John would need at least two more cups of glogg.

Paul examined a framed, matted picture and asked: "Is that small shack up in the trees a high rise outhouse?"

"Tree stand," said Tidge after returning with more drinks. He knew that Paul never saw a real gun. "It's what many hunters use when they go out to shoot deer." He shrugged his shoulders. "Geez, someone even fired shots and me and Willy when we were walking through the woods. The idiot must've thought we resembled Bambi and her mother."

The room turned very quiet, most of the faces asking if they had just heard that two family members had been mistaken for Disney characters and could have ended up as assorted broiled cuts on dinner plates.

Tidge didn't seem to be concerned that he had shocked his guests.

"Those large metal hooks you see on that limb between the two trees are for hanging the deer when they're dressed," he said. He looked at John. "That's where they clean them so the meat doesn't spoil." Tidge was on a roll. "Me and Willy thought we might end up on one of those things." He had the upper hand and loved the moment. Then a perfect Christmas got an unexpected jolt and Willy's contingency plans were nowhere to be found.

It was Martha who walked toward her father said: "My, Dad, but aren't you the knowledgeable, smug one." Her comment lacked any signs of Christmas spirit.

Both Willy and Tidge looked questioning at Martha. "Smug?" asked Tidge, ignoring Kid Scream's remark about having his granddaughter put up her dukes.

Martha held a cocktail glass in her hand and looked at Gert. "Thank you for introducing me to these, Mrs. Schneider," she said to Willy's mother. "The onion enhances the taste of the gin, don't' you think."

Gert nodded.

"And the gin, Dad, enhances my ability to embrace the new you during this enchanting holiday season.

"I'm still the old me," he said. "You don't need a Gibson for that." He managed to force a faint resemblance of a smile. "And the holiday season you referred to is still the Christmas season."

Willy's mind flipped through page upon page and legal pad upon legal pad of plans. She found nothing. "Why was I so stupid as to think she wouldn't pull another of her wedding reception stunts," she said to herself.

Martha inched as close to her father as the night of the wedding reception when she told him, bile coating every word, that she hated him. "Dad, I'm sorry. I truly am. I totally forgot that the season is Christmas."

Tidge smiled at Martha and asked: "Has Santa Claus been good to you so far?"

Martha took another sip of her Gibson, smiled at Willy's mother again and said, "Couldn't be better, Dad." She pursed her lips for a moment feeling the bite of the gin. "So far your man with the bag has been more than generous."

"So far," he repeated, unable to keep from letting out a tiny laugh. "For sure you haven't changed." His laugh climbed to chuckle status. "You're still the same lovely, excited child who used to sleep with her Christmas presents."

Martha drained her glass and glanced over to Gert who came to her side as if she were Martha's lady-in-waiting. She took the glass from Martha and walked toward the kitchen like royalty departing her subjects, an elegance that reminded Tidge of old movies he had seen starring Grace Kelly before she departed for Monaco. "It's Christmas, Dad," said Martha. She smiled, her smile the effect of the Gibson. "Your child is still excited, although a few pounds overweight and she's a happy camper. I believe camper is the correct term up here in God's country." She gave her father a hug then stepped back. "How did Santa Claus ever manage to find this place?"

Tidge smiled. "Martha, have you forgotten from your excited little girl days that Santa knows all?" He watched her smile turn into the little girl grin that melted his heart. "May I ask you something?" he said, looking and sounding like a father.

"Ask away," she said. "You're the Patriarch."

"I've been called that and similar several times since everyone arrived," he said. Before he could ask his question, he saw Gert.

Gert came up to Martha like a graceful model working in a Bloomingdale's cosmetic department, a Gibson in each hand. Martha took the drink from Gert, gave her a toast gesture, emptied half the glass, and looked at her father. "Is it true that patriarchs can say what they want?"

He shrugged. "I guess." He shrugged again. "They can say anything as long as it' Patriarchal."

Martha plucked the onion from her glass and popped it into her mouth, the toothpick still attached, the red cellophane like frilly top visible between her lips. "Is there such a word as matriarchal, Dad?" she asked, removing the toothpick from her mouth.

He nodded.

Good," she said, looking pleased as the toothpick slid back in her mouth. "Dad, I think this excited child matriarch might love you."

Before Tidge could reach for Martha, Harold was standing in between them. He put an arm around each of their shoulders.

"Love," he repeated, almost unable to contain his happiness. "This is wunderbar," he said. Harold beamed like the glowing beacons of Lake Superior light houses out in the bay off Ashland that greeted iron ore boats decades past. "What a marvelous category. Wunderbar!"

The entire room heard the word, wunderbar repeated. This time it was being sung. *"Wunderbar, wunderbar."* By the time everyone in the Great Room did a double take, they were hearing, *"Let us drink Liebchen mein in the moonlight benign..."*

All heads turned to the staircase where Carol stood, her hands in Mackie's hands, her eyes glued to his as he continued singing as if he were the reincarnation of Howard Keel singing to Kathryn Grayson in *Kiss Me Kate*. *"Here am I. Here you are. Why it's truly wunderbar."*

Tidge and Martha looked at daughter and sister and her boyfriend, both stunned and said, in a duet, "He sings?"

Harold radiated joy. "Love is such a beautiful category for, *Can You Top This*," he said, leaving Tidge and Martha and, in several effortless strides stepped in between Carol and Mackie like an experienced chaperone. He began singing, *"Wunderbar..."*

Chapter 11

Harold hummed *Wunderbar* as he rejoined Gert and said: "Liebchen, the time seems most appropriate for Can You Top This."

"Tempus fugit," she said, giving him a loving smile and patting the seat cushion next to her.

Carm followed Harold. Carol led Mackie by the hand and trailed her sister. Harold Schneider had churned up their curiosity earlier with something called a parlor game during their Christmas Eve morning hike. Harold had set the pace, his short legs appeared to Goose Step a kicking path through the snow as Mackie, Carol and Carm puffed to keep up. As he pranced through knee deep snow, Harold expounded non-stop like a sophisticated magpie about his wife and daughter. His marriage, according to him, "A joy of our dream come true."

The three young people absorbed every word Harold said. "My wife and I hosted grand, lavish parties in our co-op overlooking the Oak Street Beach." Harold then explained to his three hiking companions the difference between a condo and a co-op, elaborated on formal social functions and the meaning of black tie optional. Parlor games are what caught the trio's attention.

The three young hikers never heard of a parlor, Mackie stating: "I think my grandmother had one, but we were never allowed in it. I was warned that it was for company only."

Carm, Carol and Mackie stayed glued to Harold as he continued to cut a path through the snow like the plow that scraped County Highway M clear after Mother Nature left her calling card. Harold's pace turned their breath into an icy cloud while his enthusiasm painted a contagious picture of a life they had only heard and read about. By the time the hike ended, Carm, Carol and Mackie felt they knew Sophie Tucker, night clubbed at the Chez Paree, did lunch at

Henrici's and had Tony Bennett join them at their table at the Edgewater Beach Hotel.

Harold softly whistled Wunderbar as he embraced an inner glow watching his three hiking companions arrange their chairs in front of him and Gert. "Ah," he said, sounding pleased, "I'm so glad three of my favorite *kinder* could join us." He smiled at Gert. "Lovely youngsters, aren't they my dear?"

"Indeed lovely," said Gert.

Tidge's philosophical logic tried to deduce his father-in-law's enthusiasm for an operetta song and a party game. The more Tidge deduced the more confused he got. Why had two of his daughters and a south side of Chicago guest via a military academy in, of all places, Mexico, Missouri, taken to his father-in-law like he was a special magical elf sent by Santa himself? Any party games to Tidge, except the games of strip poker he played with Barbara Ann, were alcohol induced exhibitions giving adults a license to act like kids.

Harold's whistling Wunderbar caused Tidge's deductions to splinter off in a million different directions. Tidge kept deducing until he found himself shadow boxing in the middle of the old Chicago Stadium's boxing ring. He could hear the blare of the Stadium's giant, gold pipe organ high above in the rafters. Al Melgaard, the organist, was playing, *Wunderbar* after an introduction of, *Stormy Weather*. Popping flash bulbs of the ring side press photographers caught his every punch. Then the organist changed his selection to, *All I Want For Christmas Is My Two Front Teeth* and Tidge thought he saw Kenny Miller's girlfriend's father, leaning against the organ, his shoulder leaving an indentation in the side of the massive instrument, his eyes shooting lightning bolts.

Tidge blinked and saw Martha standing by the staircase leading to the second floor of Henry's Hut. He walked over to her and said: "Would you get your tired, old, beat up father a glass of Aunt Bessie's glogg?"

"Your wish, tired, old, beat up father, is my command," she said, giving him a deep curtsy.

He watched Martha head to the kitchen, his mind in a dither and his deductions still splintered. Then he saw Willy standing in the entrance to the kitchen. She was smiling, but Tidge knew she wasn't smiling. Upturned corners to mouths were smiles to most people. Not Willy. She smiled with her eyes. "Oh, boy," he muttered.

Willy sensed trouble. Apparent civilized dialogue between a father and daughter, civility missing from Martha's verbiage to her father for years, made no sense. So did smiles from her husband to his daughter and her smiles to him.

Martha walked out of the kitchen with a cup of glogg for her father and a Gibson for herself. As she passed Willy she asked: "Didn't you just love my father in that Santa Claus suit? He was so real."

Willy leaned against the kitchen door entry for support. She knew she heard exactly what Martha said. What caused a siren to go off in her head was the meaning behind, "He was so real."

"Contingency! Contingency! Contingency!" screamed Willy's siren. She flipped on the selection switch labeled with a bold *C* and shifted into her hostess mode. She edged towards Tidge and Martha playing the role her mother had taught her. "Eleventh Commandment it is, mother," she said to herself, her contingency fire extinguisher strapped to her back. She was both nonchalant and vivacious as she walked up to the end of her still festive Christmas table. Her nervous hands smoothed, straightened and rearranged every inch of the table until she was at the opposite end and nearer to her husband and Martha. Her ears strained to hear the father and daughter conversation. Willy's right ear was drowned out by her father's animated explanations of a parlor game and his love of Sigmund Romberg. Her left ear had trouble filtering out the gibberish Tidge's brothers were discussing about someone or something called a quarterback.

"Does time heal, Dad?" asked Martha, surprised at both her and her father's tranquil, sensitive demeanor."

"Time brought you up here for Christmas," he said.

"More like curiosity."

"And how many Christmas presents are under the tree with your name on them," he said, trying not to grin. "I saw you sneaking a look. And, so did Santa, Missy."

She twitched her head attempting to get several strands of her long black hair out of her right eye. "Perhaps you haven't totally changed, Dad."

Those were the first words of the father/daughter conversation Willy heard. She inched closer. Her hands continued to organize, reorganize and then completely alter the entire arrangement of the pastries and liquors on her Christmas table. Her ears strained harder. Then she heard, "Not totally. Your stepmother can attest to that." Willy's stomach went into a free fall, her hand waved and forks and spoons magically transformed from a straight line to a uniform arc display. Then she heard Martha say, "Well." The mention of, "Quarterbacks," by Tidge's brothers, blocked the rest of the statement. Her father saying, "Pantomime," followed by both her mother and father clapping their hands together and laughing, took care of the rest of Martha's comment to her father.

Willy watched Martha take a sip of her Gibson. She watched her pluck the onion from her glass and place in her mouth. Willy swallowed her feeling of frantic. Trying not to stare, she saw Martha look at her empty glass and heard her say, "You've definitely mellowed."

Red paper napkins found themselves being alternated with green paper napkins and then being rolled with a white plastic cutlery.

Willy wondered if a miracle was happening. "My husband the dreamer," she said to herself, still not fully believing. "The big, little kid who never let go of believing is finally being rewarded." She didn't want to believe what was telling her to believe. The man she loved was getting his prayers answered. His faith and his unwavering belief in Santa Claus and God had finally come to fruition. A father and daughter were burying the hatchet and not in each other, not like a dramatic Kenny Miller had explained during the hay ride.

Willy's hopes of getting through a long holiday with so many people under one roof without a disaster continued to grow. "High hopes," she said to herself, realizing she had been infected by her husband's own pie-in-the-sky optimism. "High hopes," she repeated, adding music to her wish. For the first time since Tidge dropped his idea for a family Christmas on her, she felt nothing could prevent the perfect Christmas from taking place. She had worked too hard, expected the unexpected, preparing until a blanket of her plans spewed out the window of her writing room forming a gigantic cover of mist over a tranquil Lake Namakagon, just as the first rays of a summer sun greeted her each morning. "I've got high hopes," she continued, singing to herself as she watched Tidge and Martha.

The Christmas party, like the parties Willy remembered in her parent's sprawling, Gold Coast apartment, became more mobile. Guests clustered in small groups, then moved like nomads. A tribe went from kitchen to Great Room. Brothers congregated in the mud room. The only ones who hadn't folded up their tents were the tribe in front of the fireplace: her mother, the customary Gibson in her hand, and her father, his emoted descriptions still enthralling Carol, Carm and Mackie. Tidge's two daughters and Mackie hadn't budged, appearing to hug every word, even the ones in German. Howls of laughter emanated from them.

Willy's hopes climbed higher and her silent singing continued as she carried on with her role as hostess. More cookies were rearranged, plus cake, pie and brownie slices were consolidated. Newer, more creative designs with the rolled napkins took shape as another problem went ker-plop.

Relationship between father and daughter now appeared so ideal Willy could visualize an article about them appearing on the cover of *Time* with a caption, *Mack and Marty—A Living Nobel Peace Prize.* She knew perfection carried a price. Pipers had a way of showing up with hands extended out, palms up. Little did she realize she would be the one placing the price of admission into the Piper's sweaty palms.

Tidge looked lovingly at his daughter. "When are you planning to head back to Chicago?" he asked.

"Now, if you want," said Martha. Her father's question caught her off guard, giving her a feeling of sad surprise. The sad and surprise parts were slightly contorted by the affects of her Gibsons.

"No. Not now," he said, realizing how easy scars can tear open by even the most innocent of questions. "I meant we could talk about this love and change stuff day after tomorrow."

"I'm kind of enjoying it now," she said, feeling more comfortable with her father than she could ever remember.

"I was just thinking that our topic of conversation doesn't seem to fit in too well for Christmas Eve," he said, proud of himself for sounding more like the father he always wanted to be. "You can remember how your grandmother wouldn't allow anything but the spirit of Christmas in her house." He began to smile and added, "That also included keeping Christ in all holidays like the Fourth of July and even Ground Hog Day."

"I remember that." She noticed that there was a feeling of really wanting to be with her family for Christmas in the Northwoods. "Grandma was quite the lady and I think she would have really liked being here." She smiled and added, "And being called, Mam by Mackie."

"Yes, she was quite a lady," he said, a vision of his mother, her long red hair down for Christmas. He smiled at the mental image of a mother, Mother Mary May I, transforming into a ravishing beauty. She was a queen for a day. "Your grandmother is looking down from Heaven right now as proud as any grandmother could be of her first grandchild. And, yep, you were also right in saying that she would have really liked being here, especially being called, Mam."

Too many smiles from her husband and stepdaughter finally got the best of Willy. She could only take so many problems going ker-plop. She walked toward them, her smile chiseled in ice and fighting the fear of having it fall to the floor, a billion crystals melting into a miniature Lake Namakagon. "May I freshen your drinks?" she asked.

Father and daughter looked at each other, laughed, and in unison said, "If you'd like."

Willy shook her head from side to side. "If there were ever two peas in a pod," she said, turning and walking towards the kitchen reluctantly giving into tear ducts spilling out happiness.

"Dad," said Martha, feeling way too serious, "why a family Christmas gathering way up here in God's country?"

"Why not?"

"It doesn't make sense to me," she said. "Eighteen people plus you and your wife living under one roof for several days, sounds kind of insane to me."

"We'll talk day after tomorrow," he said, nonchalantly. "No hurry."

"Dad, are you trying to hide something from me?"

He pointed at himself without saying a word. Just then Willy returned to them, a cup of glogg in one hand and a Gibson in the other, each drink cradled by paper napkins with a modern picture of a jolly, cherry cheeked Santa Claus that Tidge despised.

Santa and God smiled at each other knowing that a perfect Christmas would continue to unfold, Santa saying: "That Sinatra fellow's song will certainly help solidify this Christmas Eve as the best one of our boy, Tidge's life." Santa smiled, took a puff on his tarnished meerschaum pipe that he hid from Mrs. Claus and said to God, "Those old letters partially hidden in the box under that beat up old red suit that was supposed to belong to me was a stroke of genius."

God looked at Santa saying, "Our boy was looking for a panacea, but I don't do panaceas. Those old letters in that poor excuse for a cardboard box was my way of paving the way for him to find that special gift he's been dreaming and praying for." God paused, a perplexed look radiating from him. "Remember his mood swings with that Red Ryder BB gun?" he asked. "I had to give that poor kid an extra spiritual dose of TLC to prevent him from strangling his poor friend, Bean Head." God paused. "Oh, my, Bean Head. What a demeaning name." There was a sigh. "And, speaking of demeaning names, I don't even want to get started with Humper."

Santa, giving his bowl full of jelly a gentle rub, said: "At least you placed a couple of clues for our lad to find before he might think about jumping into that old diaper pail of vile glogg stuff."

God smiled. "The darned letters were there all along. So were the two old photographs. I only added that atheist philosopher's quote to jump start our boy's sometimes stagnant mind. Why he waited all these years punishing himself when all he had to do was to lift up a flap and take a look is beyond me. But, Mr. Kringle, as you well know, there are way too many of those human beings who want things handed to them. It's like my saying, 'I have your special gift, are you ready for me to give it to you'?" God let out a sigh. "All you need is to believe."

Santa also sighed. "Along with a little love," he said. A subdued laugh came from him, his belly barely jiggling. "At least our boy didn't say, 'If you'd like'."

"Amen to that," said God. "Now, if we can just keep our boy's lovely wife from resurrecting her bad Christmas experience with that sad, sick, late husband of hers, tomorrow will be a most joyous day.

My wife likes to say it will be peachy keen."

God nodded and added, "It will be even peachier if we can also get those two wannabe operetta singers to stop with the *Wunderbar*."

Willy's apprehensions, coupled with her novelist's collection of creative scenarios, vanished along with her contingency plans. Even dialing 9-1-1 got shelved.

Witnessing Tidge's angry outbursts at his brothers the first Christmas Eve she spent with his family almost ended their courtship. She found herself immersed in an impenetrable hooded cloak that night. There was a warning painted across the front and back of the cloak in mammoth red letters. *Get Out While the Getting's Good!*

Willy had been conditioned to equate anger with brutality. Her conditioning came at the hands of her late husband in the form of physical abuse. She could've gotten out back then. She should've gotten out. She didn't. Now the time for getting out was good. The warnings on her cloak flashed out that message.

There were no warning messages the night of the Parent-Teacher conference when she first saw Tidge, just gentle eyes and the father of Carol Mackiewicz wearing what Willy's mother would have exclaimed in dismay: "Judas Priest, how could any self-respecting person be seen in public dressed like that?"

Gentle eyes, a unique sense of humor, evidence of manners and even signs of old fashioned chivalry almost made her forget what Carol's father was wearing when she first saw him. A beat up brown leather jacket with a patch of a semi-nude female above one breast pocket, faded jeans and sneakers was not what good impressions were built on. He did have a hint of the trappings of what she had been told made a gentleman.

"A real man is a gentleman," her father had said to her more times than she could count. "A real man treats a lady like a lady should be treated." She recalled the twinkle in her father's eyes when he added, "Provided the lady acts like a lady."

Willy could never remember her mother ever being treated less than a lady. She could never remember her father dressing inappropriately. Her parents thrived on making a good impression wherever and whenever. Then she saw Thomas Mackiewicz, father of her favorite eighth grade student, Carol and good impressions lost out to gentle eyes.

Those same eyes later showed up at his unannounced visits to school. She knew that no parent checked on their child as much as he did. Good impressions wore different covers. Carol's father's cover was certainly different. Their first date New Year's Eve left her with more than good impressions. Good kept getting better and better until Willy knew he was what she had always dreamed of. Then came their first Christmas Eve together and she experienced her dream arguing vehemently with his brothers.

Willy suddenly found her doing something out of character. She cast off her cloak with the Get Out... warning signs and did something she heard Tidge mention in stories about his family. She put up her dukes.

Willy had only known what could best be described as mostly funny drunks during her life. Her parents were funny, many times hysterical with laughter. Most of their friends and social acquaintances were the same. As a child, Willy witnessed raucous, hysterical laughter on a weekly basis when her parents entertained.

Her first husband, Robert Jones rarely laughed. Raucous didn't fit his persona. Alcohol fueled violence did.

Being tossed about like she once tossed her homemade sock doll, Grizelda was a confusing new experience for Willy. Cocktails were equated with comedic behavior. She never felt pain dished out by a drunk before. Her first taste of drunken violence and pain came less than a week after her idyllic honeymoon to Cancun. First instincts told her the slaps and punches punctuated with shouts were her fault.

The honeymoon over and day one of her first beating history, a different Robert Jones came home bringing her flowers and candy. He also presented her with excuses and apologies. Even tears joined his pleas for forgiveness. "It'll never happen again," he had promised. But the beatings and apologies came like clockwork until she feared the sound of his key in the front door to their apartment. Each day she vowed never to let her husband beat her again. Her vows, however, were too little, too late. Her duke's way too inadequate.

Willy's parents questioned her bruises from the start. She had excuses, a million of them, explaining the ugly shades of black and blue colors that couldn't be hidden by make-up. Her own clumsiness headed the list. It was Gert who said to Harold, "I think our little girl is in trouble." Harold agreed.

Thanksgiving had just passed the baton to Christmas when Harold, the diminutive, polite man, approached Officer Jones one evening after his son-in-law's beat had ended and he was coming out of the station on Grand Avenue. Robert was surprised. Harold, being his incredibly polite self, said to Officer Jones, using vocabulary, most of which went over his son-in-law's head, and in a soft voice: "Violence only begets violence, Robert." Then, using is native tongue, asked him if he understood: "Verstenhen Sie mich?"

Officer Robert Jones clenched his fists. The part that didn't go over his head was a polite warning complete with, please: "Robert, *bitte* refrain from unleashing any more physical punishment on my little girl." He nodded at his scowling son-in-law and, in a voice so soft and polite, several fellow officer friends of Robert Jones thought Harold might be effeminate: *Anderenfalls.*

Officer Jones and his four fellow officers around him never grasped Harold's, *Or Else* warning. Robert, who towered over Harold said, "First of all, you half-pint, arrogant Kraut piece of crap, what goes on between me and my wife is none of your goddamn business. Second of all, threaten me again and I'll show you real physical punishment." He turned to his concerned fellow officers and said, "Come on guys, I need a beer. I'm buying."

Harold felt his son-in-law's shoulder bump into his chest, but he had been ready, feet planted wide apart, weight kept low. It was his son-in-law who did the bouncing. Harold gave Robert a look he had never experienced. None of his police buddies had ever experienced seeing a mixture of revenge and pending doom coated with a sophisticated smile. The Gestapo from Harold's youth would have been pleased.

Robert Jones drank with his buddies. Then he went home and took out his frustrations on his six week pregnant wife. The frustrations produced a miscarriage. Make-up and clothing couldn't conceal that. After two days in the hospital, her room filled with flowers and cards courtesy of her husband, she went home. The flowers stayed behind along with the spirit of Christmas and her discarded present.

The following day after Robert left for the station, giving his wife a kiss on the cheek and another of his hugs filled with empty apologies, Wilhelmina moved in with her parents. Like her grandmother and father before her fleeing approaching mayhem, she took what she could carry.

Harold hired an attorney and they waited for Officer Jones to claim his battered wife. Robert Jones, came, he saw, but did not conquer. What he saw besides Harold and his attorney was a retired police captain and close friend of Harold and Gert. The captain was still connected to the highest echelon of the Police Department. Officer Jones left looking like a whipped, wet puppy. The spirit of Christmas was absent from his soul. On the inside he was seething and preparing for payback time.

There were flowers and written apologies to Wilhelmina. The flowers and apologies departed faster than they arrived, Gert taking great pleasure in escorting them to the trash. There was no payback. There was no alimony. A divorce was made final.

The career of Officer Jones began to fade and, gradually, his drinking buddies slowly vanished until he was the only one seated at the bar of his favorite haunt, Lucky's. A month later, Lucky's and his luck were in the past. A fully clothed male body was hoisted out of Lake Michigan by the Chicago Fire Department. The body, wearing a police officer's uniform and dressed for inspection, was minus a hat. The human remains had been accidentally hooked by a fisherman trolling for Coho Salmon near a Water Crib. Robert Jones was laid to rest with full police department honors. He even received a fifteen second sound bite on the evening news that brought a wry smile to

Harold Schneider's face.

Harold did more than explain *Can You Top This* to the others. Love was his theme, love and a wild card. He picked the groups who would perform together based on his astute observations amassed since arriving. A litany of orders, camouflaged as smiling dignified suggestions, followed. They were accompanied by a pointing index finger that jumped from group to group. He even jotted down lyrics to dated songs that were popular before some of them were born.

Harold had turned into an anal retentive Broadway director with an overinflated ego. This was the final rehearsal before opening night. He bombarded his actors with a barrage of reminders. "Lest not we forget, devoted thespians, out in the audience will be Santa Claus and God himself."

Tidge wanted to blink, but couldn't.

"Are there any concerns?" asked Harold. He ignored their waving hands saying, "Das is good." His eyes scanned his apprehensive cast. "Remember," he said, as he began to pace back and forth, taking three short steps in each direction before doing a precise pivot like a member of a German youth drill team. Completing a pivot, he paused, stared at his cast, held up his extended right index finger and stated, "Eins! The old will play young." There was a pivot, three more steps and his middle finger joined the index. "Zwie! The young will play old." Another pivot and three more steps saw the ring finger on his right hand join the other two extended digits. "Drei!"

His rapt audience jumped.

"Love is our central theme," said Harold, his pacing continuing. "Vier." He clapped his hand several times in rapid succession. "Come. Follow me," he ordered.

Mackie and Carol were the first to perform. Harold insisted that the wide staircase be the backdrop for each of the performances. All Carol knew about Jeanette MacDonald and Nelson Eddy was that they were in old movies and that she thought their acting and singing were horrible.

According to Harold's directions for role reversals, Carol wore Mackie's fur hat and he had on her scarf over his head. They began to sing the lyrics Harold had written down for them, but by the time they got through the first four words of, *Indian Love Call*, Carol's singing was so bad that the only, *Calling you* they heard was the audience booing. Carol looked like she wanted to cry.

Mackie surprised the audience by snatching the fur hat from Carol's head and put it on over the scarf he was wearing. He took both of Carol's hands in his and began to sing in a voice that would have brought a nod of pleasure from Nelson Eddy.

Their audience was stunned. Peter whispered to Tidge, "That long, lanky red headed dork can definitely sing."

"And he'd better keep holding both my little girl's hands and nothing else unless he wants to become a member of the Vienna Boys' Choir," said Tidge back to his brother.

"He's singing," said Peter. "And, acting."

"I'll be the judge of that," said Tidge.

Harold stood alongside of Tidge beaming. "The young man is magnificent," he said.

"I'll be the judge of that."

Their audience passed judgment giving Carol and Mackie a standing ovation, Harold's the most rousing of the group.

Carol and Mackie took a deep bow then jumped up and down like the younger children had done earlier when Santa gave out presents. Mackie, however, was not finished. He pulled down the ear flaps of his fur hat, stood at attention for a full ten seconds and then began marching in place. Carol, standing next to him, a befuddled look on her face, watched. With head held high, chest out and shoulders back, Mackie broke into a chorus of *Stout Hearted Men*.

Harold, unable to control his emotions, began marching in a circle in front of the staircase. Mackie's original syrupy southern drawl became a vibrant tenor and he knew every word to the song. Harold joined in singing as he continued to march. After Mackie finished, his right fist thrust into the air and the applause had quieted down, he said, "I'd like to thank Mr. Schneider for supporting my career change." He bowed in Harold's direction. "My pursuing a medical degree has been replaced by music thanks to you." Harold bowed back and scattered applause came and went. "I'd also like to thank Sigmund Romberg for his inspiration."

"Who in the hell is that?" John asked Paul.

Paul shrugged and said, "Probably some guy from that military school."

Tidge joined the two performers and presented Mackie with one of Willy's centerpieces that he had removed from the dining room table. "From an adoring fan," he said, playing his new role as master of ceremonies, as Mackie took the centerpiece made from real pine branches. "That fan has definitely been blest with incredible bad taste."

"Thank ya'all," said Mackie, his southern drawl back, thicker than ever, as he blew kisses to the audience. Carol took him by the hand and pulled him from in front of the staircase, whispering in his ear, "You big showoff."

Harold had also written the lyrics and prepared a simple choreography for Chareese, Lilly and Lucy who were to be the Andrew Sisters singing, *Don't Sit Under The Apple Tree.* They started in total synch not knowing which one of them was Patty, La Verne, or Maxine besides having only a vague clue as to who Patty, La Verne, and Maxine were. They began to sing, got through the title and a verse that dealt with walking down Lover's Lane and bogged down as if they had fallen off Kenny Miller's hay wagon into a snow drift that paralleled Lover's Lane.

Harold had scribbled the lyrics on a green paper Christmas napkin using a similar colored pencil his daughter had provided for the younger children. Chareese, Lilly and Lucy couldn't make out a single word. Finding the snafu funny, they kept returning to the song's beginning once Lover's Lane ended. Their audience soon tired and their clapping turned to booing. They still received a standing ovation while Tidge presented them with another centerpiece saying, "Same fan. Same bad taste."

Martha and Carm were next. Harold had explained to them that they would be doing the *Sisters* number from the movie, *White Christmas.* They almost made it through the first stanza of the song when descriptions highlighted by, *You rag, Grow up* and *Baby bitch* had them standing back-to-back, arms folded across their chests. There was no applause. No booing. Their father, however, presented them each with a sprig of holly saying, "Beautifully done. Now don't go and stick yourself with your bouquets."

Harold cornered Tidge and his brothers explaining to them that they would be harmonizing like the Ink Spots singing, *You Always Hurt The One You Love*. The four Mackiewicz brothers surprised even Harold with a near perfect rendition. The surprise would have been greater had Harold and the others been able to read what lay buried behind the facades of four facial expression.

Tidge knew he hurt his daughters and that his actions, especially with Barbara Ann, caused pain he tried to avoid, but failed. In the end, he hurt the ones he loved and he vowed he would never hurt Willy.

Hurting special loved ones had no boundaries, no restrictions and no limits. John crushed Mother Mary May I. He never intended to. His realization came too late and her death took away his opportunity to apologize.

Mother Mary May I was on the receiving end of more hurt from Peter and Paul. Divorce and broken engagements weren't meant to hurt her, but they did and her two sons didn't know how to say, "Mom, I didn't mean to hurt you. You're the one who shouldn't have been hurt at all."

"You young men were brilliant," said Harold, after witnessing their performance. "I thought I was sitting in the Empire Room with my dearest wife listening to the real McCoy. Where did you learn to sing like that?"

"From our parents," said Peter. "It was their favorite song."

"Even though it was an oldie to us kids, it would always be a brand new hit to our parents," said Paul.

"It was on an old scratchy 78 phonograph record," said John, suddenly turning sheepish. "I broke it."

Peter let out a laugh. "Yeah, John thought it would make a great toy when he discovered it would spin along the kitchen floor. And it did spin. The only problem was the base of the kitchen stove met the record. Something had to give," he said, continuing to laugh and narrate. "The record lost, and the Kid walked in about the time we all heard the record crack. We all thought that John would get a matching crack for his butt. He would've if May I hadn't stepped in to protect her baby."

Paul joined in laughing. "You might say that John was a slow learner. It wasn't too much later that he discovered how those old phonograph records would sail like a Frisbee. He was bouncing them off our bedroom wall. Man, did they shatter."

Tidge joined in. "He would have been safe from bodily harm if he didn't use May I's favorite Bing Crosby Christmas records for his new toy. Shatter's a great way to explain what happened to White Christmas and Adeste Fidelis."

John's head went down and he mumbled, "Mother Mary May I never got mad at anything we did. At least that's what I thought. She pulled me away from those old records so fast I thought my arm would come off my body."

"Geez," said Tidge, stopping his laughter. "I experienced similar pain after she hauled me off of Santa's lap in Marshall Field's after I called him a fat bastard. At least you didn't get hit upside the head with a jelly jar."

John's head continued to hang down. Then, possibly fortified by way too much glogg and beer, and exhilarated by memories of his mother and daughter fling, he made a decision that was even dumber than breaking his mother's favorite Christmas record. He sauntered up to Gert, stopped and stared giving her the once over. His lips pursed and then he verbalized his dumb decision. "I got twenty bucks that says your See 'em whatchamacallit wrestling hold is all hearsay," he slurred, the twenty dollar bill brushing the make-up off of the tip of Gert's nose. Before anyone could blink, Gert had politely set down her Gibson on the floor alongside her chair, gently plucked the twenty dollar bill from John's hand with her right thumb and forefinger, smiled and nodded.

No one remembered what happened next. A speeding bullet, a powerful locomotive and seeing Gert and John go totally out of focus joined several collective blinks. A hush hung over the Great Room. When all eyes refocused, John lay dazed on the Great Room floor looking up at the ceiling, Gert on top of him. His body resembled a grotesque knot and all of his limbs pointed in directions contrary to their intended direction. John's nose was pressed so close to his crotch he could count the number of teeth in his zipper fly.

"I give! I give!" John kept screaming in pain while Gert, seeming to be lost in the past, continued to use her four limbs to apply pressure to John's limbs, his eye lids now being scratched by his zipper. "Uncle!" shouted John. "Uncle!"

Harold tapped his wife on the shoulder and said, "Liebchen." He held her cocktail glass under her nose. "The young man did say uncle."

Gert looked lovingly at Harold, relaxed her grip, took the glass, slowly exhaled, smiled and took a sip of her Gibson.

Harold placed his hand on her shoulder. "Keeping with the spirit of Christmas, I do believe it would be generous of you to return the young man's wager," he said, a slight nod accompanying his request.

John didn't move, couldn't move. All he could do was stare at his crotch and whimper.

"Was that the famous See 'em hold?" asked Tidge, his verbal awe matching silent faces.

"That it was, dearest Thomas," Gert replied, adjusting the waist band of her one hundred percent wool, designer slacks that had ended up half way down the crack of her dimpled behind. "Never failed me once," she said a touch of pride in her statement.

John lay in shock looking up at the polished log ceiling beams through the V of his spread crotch trying to determine what loose end of his anatomy to pull on so he could start to untie himself. He decided to wait and study his twisted strands in detail. One wrong pull and he knew there wouldn't be enough uncles to call on for help.

The others in the Great Room ignored John, his wife included. They clamored around Gert hoping she would relate to them more of her career as a professional wrestler in the early days of the sport.

Gert had made sure that no one could top her when it came to playing, Can You Top This. The others listened like a group of adoring hypnotized fans to Gert's professional lady wrestling experiences.

John, still on the floor, tried to determine if his left limbs were left and his right limbs right. He was convinced that Gert had transformed his body into a geometric figure that would make it impossible for him to ever engage in anything but visual sex. No one seemed to care except Harold. He looked down at John, his face radiating understanding and released the twenty dollar bill. He watched it land on John's chest and began singing, "Wunderbar."

Chapter 12

The first item on Willy's list for Christmas Day, underscored with three heavy, pink ball point pen lines, stated: *First Up Christmas Morning*. That's what she thought coming down the stairs. She let out a gasp when she saw it. Nothing escaped Willy's sight when it came to the order of Henry's Hut. She could put the eagle nesting in the woods near Henry's Hut to shame when it came to who had the best eye sight. The Great Room wasn't how she left it Christmas Eve when, along with Tidge, she did her double check just before he turned out the lights.

Willy tripped and stumbled when she saw it. Her slippers skidded and her list went flying with two steps to go. She managed to grab the hand railing preventing her from landing in a heap at the foot of the stairs.

"Oh, my," she said, her voice hushed, as she struggled to regain both her balance and composure. She picked up her list and pink pen then inched into the Great Room. Stopping, her nose wrinkling, questioning, she asked the object of her attention: "My, my, what's this?"

A cozy fire popped and crackled a Merry Christmas to her. That wasn't what startled her. Off to one side of the fireplace, by Tidge's recliner, stood the drop leaf table Tidge used to stack magazines, unopened mail and any other items made of paper that could be piled. Willy stood like a giant icicle hanging from the eaves dead center over the front entrance ushering in the spring thaw. She glanced at her list. "You're such a sneak," she said, referring to Tidge. There was no check mark alongside one of the many sub-headings on her list, this one stating: *Remove Clutter from <u>HIS</u> table*. The drop leaf table top had clutter, but not Tidge's piles of anything resembling paper he could stack. This was organized clutter.

"You think you're so clever," she muttered, an empty drinking glass and an equally empty dessert plate rimmed in tiny Christmas trees receiving her comment. The plate showed remnants of what looked like cookie crumbs and powdered sugar. There was also a red, trimmed in gold, folded, cloth napkin, one reserved for her Christmas dinner The glass appeared to have been filled with milk. She took a cautious look around and whispered her husband's name. "Thomas," she said.

No answer.

She repeated his name again.

The fire wanted to reply, but could only crackle and pop.

She took another look at her Christmas Day list of things to do. Item number three, after sub-parts two with making the Great Room neat, had been completed. Her fourth item, *Special Christmas Breakfast,* also received a triple pink underscore. She left the drop leaf table as is, the urge to pick up the plate, glass and napkin no longer important. "Cute touch, my darling husband," she said, passing by the table, the strange sensation she had experienced the day before going through her as she entered her kitchen domain. She came to a dead stop. "Oh, dearest God," she said, trying to catch her breath as she looked out the kitchen window into the backyard. She wanted to cry. During the night Mother Nature, Irving Berlin and Bing Crosby teamed up to present a stunning sequence to *White Christmas.* Ansel Adams, with her husband as his lackey, couldn't have captured the beauty that overwhelmed her. Tidge didn't exaggerate when he told her that their guests would be up to their backsides in snow. Neither did he fabricate a picture of a deer in their yard. Three punctuated his picture. She eased nearer the window and saw the eagle. He soared overhead making lazy circles, his large white head brilliant and bold in the cold, clean air. She drank in the wintery scene, her creative brain soaking up the beauty and filing it for a future writing reference.

Where Christmas Eve morning had her dealing with the shenanigans of her brothers-in-law and husband, she now had her kitchen domain to herself. The whirlwind whirled. Somehow, a white apron stayed white as did the towel she had draped over her left shoulder for wiping hands. She was all business except for stealing a sip of coffee. When she pulled away from her professional cook's range to get her coffee cup situated on the counter top, she glanced into the Great Room. Her, "Oh, my," was muted as she witnessed the sight of six pajama clad children. Five wore white sweat socks. Star had on a pair of Rudolph the Red Nosed Reindeer slippers, the noses aglow. The six nieces and nephews were sprawled on the floor in front of the Christmas tree that appeared to have twice as many gifts under it than the day before.

Hopeful eyes searched the display of gifts. Imaginations tore open the gift wrap while excited feet polished the hardwood floor at the edge of the area rug, nary a word spoken. Tidge would have loved the scene. Santa did.

Willy's front teeth dug into her lower lip at the sight, and she fought the urge to join the children on the floor. "Empty milk glass indeed," she said in a whisper. "Do you really expect me to believe that?" The six prone bodies inched in different directions, heads moving, curious hands wanting to touch, but not touching.

Willy did her own inching back to her stove. Finishing touches still needed to be put on a breakfast befitting a logging camp. There wasn't a logger alive who would not have devoured her breakfast. Stacks of blueberry pancakes joined artistically arranged slices of French toast on two identical platters. She had used French bread, the slices cut on a diagonal, each sprinkled with a liberal coating of powdered sugar. Her Belgian waffles needed a separate plate. She didn't have one big enough and pulled out another platter from the cabinet above her stove, this one having dimensions that would accommodate a ten point buck. Tidge's politically incorrect egg dishes had been put to rest. Replacing them were chunks of grilled ham off the bone from the Christmas Eve dinner. With all of her culinary skills, she could never get the hang of a carving knife, and slices became a variety of slabs, slivers, chunks and hunks.

Skillets sizzled but respected her wishes not to splatter. Various sized strips and chunks of sautéed beef and ham replaced bacon and sausage on a silver serving platter. Willy had even put together a plate of cream cheese and thin filets of smoked salmon. These were surrounded with paper thin slices of red onion and tomatoes, the ones that survived her knife. Capers punctuated her one adults-only selection. That dish was joined by a basket of assorted bagels. A second basket, the wicker handle wrapped in silver trimmed green ribbon complemented her plethora of toasted breads. Three bowls of different homemade jams she had purchased at an American Legion Fund Raising Pancake Feed were clustered together next to her bread basket. A silver spoon lay in waiting alongside each bowl.

Six ravenous kids, real maple syrup rimming their lips, were eating like said starving lumberjacks when their mothers entered the Great Room. "Sorry we didn't wait," said Willy, enjoying the sight of her cooking disappearing into hungry mouths. Her head gave a nod towards the window. "They're going to need all the strength they can get today."

"Oh, my" cried the trio of mothers, spellbound by another winter sight that all of the Christmas cards of all of the Christmas seasons in history couldn't replicate. A chorus of, "Merry Christmas," filled the kitchen.

Tidge and his brothers, groggy, hung over and eyes peering through crusted slits stumbled into the kitchen. "Merry Christmas," each mumbled.

Just then Carm, Carol, and Mackie banged into the mud room after another morning walk. 'Merry Christmas," said the two girls wrapping the arms of their icy parkas around their father.

"Merry Christmas," he gasped, pulling away and finding himself no longer a captive of sleep.

"Gawd, Sir," said Mackie to Tidge, sounding in awe. "The snow's up to our rear ends." He paused still catching his breath. "Talk about a white Christmas." His breathing started to catch up with his talking. "We hiked your drive," he continued. Boy, those ruts are deep."

"I see you didn't lose my two daughters," Tidge said, his eye lids trying to pop open, the reluctant crust hanging on. "I don't see my father-in-law. Did you lose him in one of the ruts?"

"No, Sir," Mackie said. "He slept in." Mackie looked out the kitchen window. "Gawd, Sir, there's that giant bird still circling around up in the sky. It's bigger than the pigeons in downtown Chicago. I bet it's got to be an eagle."

Tidge caught Willy's eyes and he gave her an I-told-you-so look. Then he said: "That's definitely an eagle, Sir Mackie. Big sucker, ain't he?"

"Yes, Sir."

Tidge reached up and patted Mackie on his fur hat. "I'd be careful if I were you," he said, his eyes fixed on the hat. "I think that eagle's mistaken your hat for his Christmas meal. Be careful the next time you go out," he warned, glancing out the window. "You and that hat could end up being carted off to a nest the size of a Holiday Inn on the top of a pine tree so high your nose would bleed," said Tidge, no smile on his face. "The nest is just east of here. Not far from where Kenny Miller lives."

Mackie went to the kitchen window and stared. "You're not making up a story about a Holiday Inn, are you, Mister Tidge, Sir?"

"You keep wearing that hat and you'll find out, Mackie, Sir."

About the time the daughters-in-law were placing napkins on their laps and Tidge and his brothers were inhaling the steaming vapor from their coffee mugs, all eyes turned to Harold and Gert. They came down the stairs into the Great Room looking like members of the Royal Family. Gert's hand rested with a touch of sophistication on Harold's forearm. They were wearing matching beige slacks, cordovan penny loafers and blue blazers, his, a double breasted model and hers, single. Both sported a gold coat of arms over the breast pocket. They wore white turtle neck sweaters. Harold's was wool and Gert's cashmere. There was a gold Christmas tree pin on the neck of her sweater with emerald stones as miniature ornaments.

All Tidge could think of doing was to bow and give a sweeping motion with his right arm directing them to their place at the dining room table. He curtsied and said to Gert in a whisper so Willy wouldn't hear, "Bloody Mary?" Gert gave a courteous nod. "How 'bout an eye opener, Harold?"

Harold also nodded and said, "You wouldn't happen to have a cup of that warm, sapid ambrosia called Swedish glogg handy, would you?"

"Handy's my middle name," said Tidge.

After breakfast, the wives tended to the kids. The return of stomping, thundering stocking feet heading to the loft rumbled through Henry's Hut with minor vibrations causing the snow plow blade to clatter on the cement garage floor. The men, including Mackie, cleaned the kitchen and washed the dishes. Harold and Gert sat in front of the fire holding hands, her Bloody Mary and his second cup of glogg within reach.

Peace and a crackling fire were soon replaced by a Great Room filled with children and adults, all wearing their Christmas finery. Flavored coffee choices that included French vanilla, hazelnut and chocolate mocha waited for the sipping. There was also a thermos of hot chocolate. The coffees and hot chocolate were joined by plates of cookies and assorted pastries. The faint strains of *Hark, The Herald Angels Sing*, one of a thousand songs in Tidge's collection of Christmas music that played from waking up to bed time, drifted throughout the house.

Willy also served two trays of sliced fruit cake even though Tidge warned her upon learning that part of her menu. "No one eats that brick hard, recycled reindeer manure," he had said. Her laser look had him apologizing and accepting that part of her menu. He even, like good patriarchs do in such situations, took a slice from each tray when he knew his brothers were watching. They followed his lead and Willy looked pleased. Any desires Tidge entertained of mocking her fruit cake disappeared when he heard her say, "Did you know that the first letter in fruit and cake are two of the four critical initials for a happy marriage?"

The only response came from the three sisters-in-law who had no clue as to Joan Crawford's fetish for high heel pumps.

Chareese convinced Lilly and Lucy to try a cup of the blueberry and blackberry hot spiced apple cider that had shooed away all feelings from her body on Christmas Eve. "It's made with Swedish berries," she explained to the other two. "You do have more," she asked Tidge, her eyes pleading.

"I sure do," said Tidge, glancing at the glogg simmering in sinister innocence on the kitchen stove. He took their requests with a smile and returned with three steaming cut crystal punch cups. "Don't get too close to the fire," he warned. "Swedish glogg is highly combustible. I've heard that Santa uses it to put his sleigh into passing gear when he's behind schedule."

The semi-circle seating arrangement in the Great Room took place again in front of the Christmas tree that appeared to have grown during the night. Adults found their seats joining Harold and Gert, coffee mugs, glogg cups and beer cans in hand. The kids, all traces of breakfast washed from their faces, had returned to the floor as close as they could get to the myriad of tempting packages beckoning to them. Santa himself may have been missing, but he made his presence felt by the mounds of gifts spilling out from under the tree.

"Before we get started," Willy announced, "Dinner will be served at four, appetizers at three thirty." She couldn't get herself to mention cocktails. Drinking, she knew, would go on all day, and she prayed that her mother would not fall asleep at the dinner table. It wasn't the sleeping that concerned her. Gert could fall asleep, fork in her hand, looking at whoever she was seated next to and no one noticed. When she began to snore the entire world noticed.

Tidge stood alongside his wife beaming. "Kids and adults," he started any signs of his being related to Kid Scream missing. "It's time to check and see if what you asked for in your letters to Santa last night is what he brought for you while you were dreaming of sugar plums."

"Was Santa really here last night," asked Star, her own eyes as big as the beacon that guided the three Wise Men.

"Did he make popcorn on the fire?" asked an equally wide eyed Frankie. "Did he? Did he?"

Tidge nodded, a smile being added. Before he could carry on with the lore of Santa Claus, his brothers started calling out names and packages were sailing across the room in a million different directions. Somehow not one of the missals scored a direct hit on the statues of Santa Claus, the Infant Jesus, Frosty the Snowman, Uncle Mistletoe, Aunt Holly, Suzy Snowflake and the miniature replica of a leg lamp. Kids and adults gouged out ragged chunks of gift wrap from their packages as if they were a marauding band of black bears attacking garbage at the town dump. Kid Scream's appraisal of Christmas gift wrapping and unwrapping couldn't have been more accurate.

As fast as the festive gift paper hit the floor, Tidge's brothers and Mackie were there scooping it up into plastic garbage bags. Willy had her world of neat, but the kids were cheated out of their chance to bury themselves in the paper, roll around on the floor in it and then hurl it at each other.

"Well, ladies," asked Tidge to the female guests, "did Santa bring you what you asked for in the letters you wrote to him last night?"

Hands, wrists, ear lobes and necks went on display showing sparkling presents from the men in their lives. Tidge's daughters were thrilled with the custom made pendants he and Willy had given them.

"Look at the cool charm bracelet Santa bought me," chirped Pauline, four gold charms depicting her name and the names of her parents and brother inscribed in Chinese.

All jaws dropped, however, when Willy appeared wearing the full length mink coat that Tidge had brought her for Christmas. She had briefly worn it when her parents arrived, but this was the first time they all saw her wearing it under perfect conditions.

Willy had played her role as hostess when they arrived, doing battle with swirling snow, escorting her guests and indoctrinating them to the Northwoods. Now the perfect hostess had become a quick-change artist adorned in her luxurious mink coat. The room turned respectfully silent. Suddenly, Gert sat upright, eyes wide as the disposable white paper plates that were used for the sweets and appeared to be choking. She grasped at her throat as if trying to tear it open with her fingernails to let in air. A minute before she had been crying softly, tears of a mother's proud happiness for her daughter. Then her tears vanished, wiped away by coughs and gasps.

It was Tidge's brother, John who came to Gert's aid. He gave her a hard slap on the back, watched and waited for a second, then changed tactics. In a moment he was behind her. Gert was out of her seat, long legs spread out, feet kicking, loafers sailing as John applied what he thought was the Heimlich Maneuver. After one near rib cracking squeeze, the lime wedge from Gert's Bloody Mary shot from her mouth and bounced off the fireplace screen. In the time it took John to get her feet back on the floor and in her seat on the sofa, Gert had pulled down her sweater, pulled up her slacks and had her feet in her loafers. She looked up at John and, out of breath, said, "If I were still performing, I'd incorporate your hold into my repertoire." Her composure fully returned, she said to John, "Of course, with your permission, young man."

John gave her a blush that hadn't appeared since he was a child and lost his two front teeth in a collision with a fire hydrant. He never forgot the incident. During Christmas Eve and Christmas that year every one of his relatives wanted to see the gap where his teeth used to be. They all drove him to his room where he hid under his bed after being asked too many times about wanting his two front teeth for Christmas. He hated his three brothers that Christmas. They had pulled his sled too fast. He loved that part. Love switched to fear when they whipped the sled by the rope attached to the front. Screams joined John's fear as he was propelled into a giant, skidding arc on the snow packed street in front of their house. His brothers laughed, but not for long, as the sled bounced up the hidden, snow covered concrete curb and went head on into an equally snow covered fire hydrant. John and his sled followed the laws of physics, John's momentum ceasing when his face hit the iron hydrant.

Now John joined his brothers who were wrestling the T.V.'s remote from one another while the sisters-in-law fawned over Willy's coat. By the time all of the ladies had tried on the mink, stroked the pelts and did a pirouette or two, Tidge thought there would be a pile of fur scattered across the Great Room floor. His brothers, laying aside the remote for a moment, made Willy the center of attention. Each took a turn taking her by the hand and escorting her around the perimeter of the Great Room while Harold and Mackie sang a duet of *A Pretty Girl Is Like A Melody*.

After gift giving and the adulation focused on Willy, the men turned their attention back to the remote and Tidge's big screen TV. Appetizers at three thirty were at least one Christmas Day football game away and already salivating aromas emanated from the kitchen.

Harold and Gert continued to chat in front of the fire when they saw Tidge emerge from the kitchen. They both held up empty glasses. In less than a minute, Tidge returned with fresh drinks for his in-laws. Then he heard Paul say to John, "Wouldn't you have thought that our new and improved brother and patriarch would have considered our imbibing needs?"

Tidge didn't waste a second. "The three coolers you guys decimated since you got here are still on the back deck, restocked and waiting," he said, a glance towards the mud room door accompanying his answer. "Red cooler has the imported beer, white cooler the domestic and the blue one bottled water, diet and regular soft drinks and juice boxes for the little kids."

Paul shrugged his shoulders. "Pick your country," he said, as he headed for the back deck.

John and Peter camped in front of the television. "How many channels did you say you got on this thing?" asked Peter, as he opened his belt several notches. "The game's a colossal bore."

"As many as there are," Tidge informed him. "I still haven't figured out how to work the darned thing although I did stumble on a channel once that sold women's lingerie. They used sexy, live models. I never could find it again."

"Really," said Peter.

Before he could say another word, he heard Willy yell from the kitchen. "This is Christmas!" Her reminder was followed by, "Surely it's *A Wonderful Life* or *Miracle on 34th Street* is playing."

"Okay," said Peter. "Looks like we continue watching the game."

Christmas dinner was a thing to behold. Willy outdid herself again while Harold and Gert sat beaming with looks that only proud parents can own.

Willy's center piece was a roast turkey, the biggest she could find pushing the scale near twenty eight pounds. On each side of the gigantic bird was a stuffed pork crown roast, an apricot topping adorning one crown and raspberry on the other. She had made three kinds of dressing, her traditional sage stuffing roasting with the turkey, a double batch of one made with corn bread, apples and raisins that filled the crown roasts, and then an oyster dressing. If there was a way potatoes could be prepared, Willy found it adding her interpretation of garnish touches to each. She even made

Lyonnaise potatoes for her father, his favorite. Mackie tasted the Lyonnaise and said to Harold, "Gawd, Sir, I never knew potatoes could be so good." Then he almost lost a hand when he reached across the table to scoop up a second helping.

Harold smiled and asked, "Cadet, may I pass you the Lyonnaise?"

Tidge and his brothers looked at one another and grinned. As if on cue, they replied, "If you'd like."

Tidge had tried to discourage his wife from serving vegetables by saying, "Kids hate vegetables, my brothers hate vegetables, and I despise them." She had three kinds. She also served orange halves each stuffed with a raw cranberry and orange filling soaked with Grand Marnier. Those were a hit with Gert, John, Carm and Carol. Tidge's two daughters sat at the table giddy and giggling then started crying when they noticed Gert take the last two stuffed orange halves from the serving plate.

Tidge insisted on two kinds of gravy. "Be sure and make plenty of mushroom and plenty of giblet. I'll do all the slicing and dicing." He did. But she made three, adding a plain packaged turkey gravy saying, "Some of the children might not like giblets or mushrooms."

"Then let 'em starve," he had said, while slicing fresh mushrooms.

All of the wives and Tidge's daughters had pitched in. Too many chefs, in this case, did not spoil a thing. Chareese did her deviled eggs that had an essence of Chicago style hot links. Lilly prepared crispy egg rolls served with bowls of sweet and sour sauce and hot Chinese mustard. Lucy catered to the kids. She prepared a platter of peanut butter and jelly sandwiches for them, the crusts removed and the sandwiches cut into triangles. Mackie ended up eating half the platter before it found the main table.

With the men still camped in front of the television and the kids busy playing with new Christmas presents, the women continued to put the finishing touches on Christmas dinner. Cranberry and pine scented candles flickering from four centerpieces made from pine branches, pine cones and an assortment of lemons, limes, oranges and dark red apples made them forget how beautiful the setting and meal had been the night before.

Paul looked at Tidge and asked, "Do we get to do this again next year?"

Tidge acted so nonchalant he hated himself. "Sounds like a plan to me," he said. Inside, he kept asking himself, "Did I just hear Paul ask what I thought he asked?"

It was after dinner, after the cleanup and the kids bundled up and outside in the yard screaming off dinner in a massive snowball fight with Mackie, Carol and Carm, Willy decided to let down her guard. "Honey," she said to Tidge as the fire was beginning to burn down and drowsy eyes added to the decor of the season, "Would you pour me a cup of your glogg our sisters-in-laws seem to be enjoying?"

"Are you sure?" asked Tidge.

She smiled.

A *Christmas Waltz* circulated throughout the house in three quarter time while Gert's Eleventh Commandment, asterisk and all, purred along as predicted. Mellow, as commanded, followed orders and continued pressing down on adult eye lids.

Tidge's fire, he had dubbed delightful each time he added a log, burned like a giant pacifier. Martha seated on the floor at Gert's feet, sipped a Gibson and let the fire do her talking. Carm, Carol and Mackie had left the kids outside building an igloo sat on the floor off to the side of the fireplace watching the flames act out their own unique version of a *Night Before Christmas*. Harold, still dignified, quietly hummed, *Wunderbar* to Gert who didn't hear a note.

What was once an igloo behind Henry's Hut now resembled a chunky snowdrift after Nathan and Paul, Jr., being playful, pushed their sisters on top of it. Playing got replaced by scared stiff after they had to dig out Star and Frankie from under the snow.

Energy spent and the Eleventh Commandment's asterisk swallowing up the six children, there was no need for stomping up the stairs. Frankie got carried up by Mackie while Star buried her face in her father's chest and purred like an overgrown kitten. The six nieces and nephews were snuggled into their makeshift beds in the loft without a whimper. Not a one of them stirred except Natasha who said to her brother, "When I get home I'm going to give your friend, Vincent a piece of my mind about his telling us there's no

Santa Claus." She pulled up her covers till they were just below her lower lip. "He's a bigger Cretin than you are."

Sleep set in and so did the ghosts of Christmases past. They rubbed their chilled, grey hands together and called on Aunt Bessie.

The next morning, a dreary grey sky made the day old snow look less than Christmas card fresh. Tidge had taken Willy's place in the kitchen. His coffee, as usual, was the best of his culinary efforts. He managed to convert eye appealing leftovers from Christmas dinner into a breakfast that almost all of the animals in the surrounding woods would make a face at and hold their noses. By the time platters of his breakfast sat staring back at puzzled family members, he had incinerated a variety of meats. "It ain't burned," he had said to his brothers while they watched dark smoke emanate from the cast iron skillet. "The bacon's crispy." His pork sausage patties resembled a cross between miniature hockey pucks and charcoal briquettes. Crinkled and curled up pieces of ham and beef were coated with a blackened crust with the appearance and taste of roofing shingles. Every yolk of every egg was broken before it splattered into too much smoking grease.

Tidge looked at Paul and Peter who were up early and pitched into help. "Don't worry guys," he said, a soiled towel over his shoulders unable to conceal the grease splattered front of his white Loyola sweatshirt. "It's pretty hard to screw up toast." Then they all looked at the black cloud rising out of the four slice toaster. "Scrape off the black crap," he said to Peter and Paul who could only gawk. "That's what May I used to do."

"We remember," said Paul, making a face. His growling stomach kept telling him that burnt or not, awful tasting or not, it was food and he needed to eat it.

John appeared in the kitchen entrance and made a face. "What's burning?" he asked.

"Nothin'," replied his brothers.

"Smells like your Santa Claus suit," said John, turning and glancing up at the polished logs spanning the Great Room to see if there were any signs of their being singed. He joined his brothers to help and accidentally dropped an open carton of orange juice on the floor.

All the creatures who had stirred were up. Three were not. Martha slept late as usual, Gert was incredibly hung over and Willy was nowhere to be found. Seventeen confused people, including Tidge, sat at the dining room table configuration studying what was piled and teetering on several platters staring menacingly at them, daring any one of them to take a chance.

"Your Aunt Mina made this especially for your last breakfast," said Tidge. "She calls it Gobbledeegook. She got the recipe from Julia Child. Honest. It's' your aunt's favorite." His right index finger crossed at the area of his heart so many times he almost wore the *L* in Loyola off his sweat shirt.

The mounded blob Tidge incinerated, scraped, broke and scalded sat perched upon layers of toast and jam. The toast, black side down, three types of jam plastered on each piece, were stacked four high. They were buried under a mixture of eggs and breakfast meat. "Honest," continued Tidge, "it's called Gobbledeegook."

The platter's Gobbledeegook resembled something that had belched from the bowels of a ready-mix concrete truck, a brownish black streaked tint to the chunky cement that should have been served from a wheel barrow. "You aunt's not feeling well," said Tidge, trying to divert the attention away from breakfast. "I think it's the Flu or something like that. After she made your breakfast she took some high powered medicine and went back to bed. She's sleeping like she's curled up on a bed of straw in Santa's reindeer stable up at the North Pole." He swallowed hard, lifted a large serving spoon, swallowed hard again and transferred a serving of Gobbledeegook to his paper plate. A wet grease stain turned the paper plate into a useless, soggy disk with a white rim. Sixteen others followed.

The only accolade given for breakfast that morning was from John who said: "It doesn't matter what it's called or how it looks. Willy's Gobbledegook ate good."

Peter gave a nod of approval that was followed by and echoing belch and a glare from Chareese. "Gobbledeegook always does that to me," he said, defending himself.

"Excuse the pigs the hogs are coming," said Paul. The kids laughed. The wives didn't.

Harold covered his mouth with his napkin then said: "Gobbledeegook is indeed, as you Americans say, a meal that sticks to your ribs. I won't have to eat again until we get back to Chicago."

Deck the Halls wafted throughout the house as Tidge, Peter and Paul cleaned up the dining room table and the mess in the kitchen. Three mothers were back in the loft putting laundry in backpacks, planting books and travel games in easily accessible locations for the trip home and straightening up the loft. John aided Harold bringing Gert's luggage down the stairs.

Mackie, Carol and Carm had taken the kids outside behind the house for what was to be a snowball fight. Snowball's got side tracked for lessons in close order drill taught by Mackie. Left, right and about-faces soon mushroomed into demonstrations of hand-to-hand combat. Paul, Jr. volunteered to be the enemy then wished he hadn't. Mackie had him over his back with a flick of the wrist faster than what Gert did to John. The boy's eyes were barely visible from under the snow. The rest of them clamored to be the next enemy assailant almost tearing Mackie's trousers from his body. "Teach me," said Natasha, pushing ahead of the others, ice forming on her braces. "The next time my idiot brother picks on me will be his last time. Stupid ignoramus," she sputtered, almost doing an imitation of Kenny Miller."

The kitchen cleaned and not quite spotless displayed a tower of Styrofoam cups for coffee standing next to one remaining coffee urn and a stack of small paper plates. Next to the plates was a meat platter stacked with assorted cookies, pastries, bagels, dinner rolls and various grain breads defying the laws of gravity. Joining the cups, plates, coffee urn and baked goods were several large, stuffed plastic garbage bags standing at attention by the mud room door. Each bag looked as if it would explode.

"Whoever invented paper plates and plastic things to eat with should be sainted," Tidge said to Paul, a damp, soiled dish towel around his neck, a wet stain visible on his sweat shirt.

"Amen to that, brother," said Paul, a matching towel, his streaked with dirty stripes, draped over his right shoulder. A wet stain crept out from under the towel on his shirt.

"Never used those things when Wilhelmina was growing up," said Harold from behind a pair of Air Force style sun glasses as he stood in the kitchen entrance. "Wish I had." He poured coffee into a disposable cup for Gert. "Indeed a great invention." He picked up a small paper plate, paused, looked at Tidge, looked at the platter, then looked at Tidge again.

"Whadda you need, Harold?" asked Tidge.

"Would you happen to have a pair of serving tongs?" he asked, his eyes peering at Tidge from over the tops of his glasses. "And, perhaps, two aspirins. I believe that my wife may have also been attacked by an influenza strain."

Tidge folded his upper lip over the top of his lower lip and gave half a nod. "Kind of like your daughter."

With a blueberry muffin bending a flimsy paper plate in his one hand, a cloth napkin over his forearm and a steaming hot cup of coffee in the other, Harold excused himself and headed back up the stairs. Two aspirins, wrapped in a green paper napkin as the background for Santa's smiling face, accompanied him in his trouser pocket the uplifting lyrics to *Caroling Caroling* climbed the flight of stairs with him.

John looked seriously at Tidge. "He's quite the guy, ain't he?"

Tidge nodded.

"So is your mother-in-law," said John. "Strong too!"

The brothers laughed.

John thought for a moment and looked at Tidge. "Last night when I was in and out of my contented cat nap I thought I heard your wife say something about your mother-in-law had to testify before some kind of U. S. Senate committee. Some senator from Tennessee wanted to hold her responsible for juvenile delinquency in our country because of her pin-up pictures?"

"I heard that too, but not last night," replied Tidge. "Geez, you guys know as much as me."

Paul laughed. "Did you remember your wife falling asleep with her head on her mother's shoulder?"

"Kind of," said Tidge.

Paul continued laughing. "When I woke up from what John calls a cat-nap, I heard her give a combination huff and laugh. Then I saw a blank expressions absorb her huff and laugh. She folded her arms across her chest, teetered from side to side, almost falling over, but thanks to you, big brother, you caught her and she remained on her feet. I heard her say, 'Thank you, my darling husband'."

"I don't remember that," said Tidge.

"I didn't remember anything you guys are talking about," replied Peter.

"What I do remember," said Tidge, breaking into a grin, was filling glogg cups for your wives and mine and her saying, 'Oh, host with the most, our lovely natives and Joan Crawford need a refill and some new CFMP's'."

Paul and Peter gave each other the same questioning look then looked at Tidge. "What's with your wife and those initials she keeps bringing up?" they both asked in unison.

Tidge shrugged. "What I vaguely remember is filling up Harold's cup with glogg and saying, Prost, to him," said Tidge, smiling. "The next thing I knew I woke up in the middle of the night because of this wild dream."

His brothers' expressions told him to continue.

"I was with Harold. Only he wasn't the Harold we all know, he was Harold as a young teenager. And, guys get this. We were with his father."

"The German fighter pilot?" asked Paul.

"The very one," replied Tidge, putting up his hands. "Honest, I saw him." His expression asked if he should continue and his brothers nodded. "Harold and I were riding piggy back in his father's Messerschmitt."

"Messerschmitt?" asked Peter.

Tidge nodded. His father plunged his plane into a steep dive and headed for what looked like a B-25 bomber. I couldn't believe it. If that was bad enough, I couldn't believe what I saw next."

"Don't tell me Santa Claus was in that bomber?" asked John. "I mean, I lied about liking your Gobbledeegook, but don't ask me to eat this story too."

"Honest," said Tidge, his heart beating faster. "I saw Santa Claus at the controls of that bomber. Then Harold yells out, 'Vater, don't shoot at Santa Claus again!' and his father pulls up, banks the plane, and the next thing I know he's maneuvering the Messerschmitt through a canyon of buildings. We zip under the Chicago El tracks and land in front of a bookstore on Wabash Avenue. Harold says to me, 'What do you think?' I look at Harold and don't know what to say. Then I hear Harold say, 'You're the best, mein vater,' and pats him on his parachute shoulder harness. 'Thank you for the ride,' he said, unbuckling his own parachute harness. I looked for my harness and discovered I didn't have one. Then I hear Harold say to his father, 'Now, it's time to toil for my daily bread. I'm up to my neck in grunt work'."

"Grunt work?" repeated Peter.

"Yep, grunt work," said Tidge. "Then I heard his father say, 'Son, when you get the opportunity send me some of those magazines of yours. The men at the base need a morale booster what with the failed attempt on Hitler's life'."

"Oldest brother," said Paul, looking skeptical. "Were you doing shots and beers last night the way the Kid and Uncle Brew used to do?"

"Only glogg and a sip of my Martha's Gibson when Willy wasn't watching," said Tidge.

"I'd put a cork in the bottle if I were you," said John, grinning.

"Maybe I will after I tell you what woke me up out of my dream," said Tidge smiling. "I watched Harold climb out of the cockpit, lean against the fuselage for support and say to his father, 'I'll do what I can for the war effort, Vater.' "Then he gives one of those Hiel Hitler salutes and says, 'Remember, no shooting at Santa'."

Tidge and his brothers now sat quietly, the Harold Schneider Messerschmitt episode blowing in a northeasterly wind headed for Michigan's Upper Peninsula, trying to figure out where the time had gone. It was December the twenty sixth, but they weren't letting go of the twenty fifth or any of the other days in the Northwoods. They weren't letting go of blizzards, hay rides, a horse named Sissy, writing letters to Santa Claus, gourmet dining and embracing feelings they hadn't enjoyed since they were children.

Paul broke the silence saying: "I know I heard what I heard last night," as the brothers sipped the remains of breakfast coffee that had the consistency of the cutting bar oil Tidge used in his chain saw. "Big brother, your wife was being funny when she mentioned how her father made a million bucks, wasn't she?"

"He did make a bunch," said Tidge, a smile on his face. "But he made his dough bringing in advertising revenue for the so-called men's magazines back then. He didn't sell the magazines or act as the photographer." He paused, looked into his coffee cup, made a face and continued. "The pictures in the magazine, according to Gert, were pictures of women who were ahead of their time posing in their underwear or less, giving provocative looks at the camera. Gert once told me that most of those pin-up girls back then had to work other jobs to pay their rent. Most of them worked as waitresses or store clerks."

"Were any of them ever *Playboy* centerfolds?" asked John, turning his interest from his coffee to the conversation.

Tidge laughed. "Centerfolds came later," he said. "Back then, according to Willy's mother, women knew how to make a man's imagination imagine. She said to me in that husky voice of hers: 'Thomas, the female's anatomy, although flawed, is still a thing of beauty. We women know how to use those flaws to our advantage. Of course, we couldn't do it without a male's fertile mind creating mental images that suited his particular need'." He took a sip of his coffee, grimaced and let the liquid slide back into his cup. "I don't mean to change this intellectual subject, but did any of you understand a word my wife said last night?"

"Not I," said Peter, the mood turning serious. "She sounded about the same as our Uncle Brew in his prime." He smiled. "Now if she were wearing that funny Santa Claus hat you wore Christmas Eve, maybe I would have been able to understand a word or two."

"Who cares," said John. "All I want, Tomasz, is for your wife to give my wife the recipe for those orange and cranberry relish things soaked in that expensive orange flavored booze that we had for Christmas dinner." John stopped, shook his head, then said to Tidge, "Your mother-in-law almost went after me and two of your kids with another of her See 'em holds when she thought we were going to take the last of those orange halves. She snatched them up so fast she made Carol and Carm cry."

"I'm not concerned about my kids crying," said Tidge, his eyes dancing. "I'm just hoping my wife doesn't remember anything about last night." He glanced at his brothers. "If she doesn't, this will be the best Christmas of my life." He paused. "If she does, you'll hear me crying all the way down in Chicago."

It was the best Christmas I've ever had in my life," said John.

There was a, "Me too," and a "Me three," from Peter and Paul.

"Guys," said Peter, seriously. "I don't know about you, but from the moment we drove up to this mansion of our brother and his incredible wife in that blizzard I got the strangest feeling going through me."

"Me too," said Paul, looking at his brother.

"Count me in," said John. "Weirdest sensation I ever had."

Tidge smiled. "Weirder than what the Joliet duo used to give you?"

John nodded. "Way weirder, guys," he said, his voice showing a reverence. "Like supernatural or something out of science fiction. Heck, don't ask me to explain, because I can't."

"This was a great Christmas," said Peter, giving a nod to Tidge.

"My kids will be talking about this trip when they're older than the Kid and May I," said John, then giving his cup a slight push away. "Thanks to the preaching patriarch here," he said, nodding at Tidge, "my little girl wants me to put a fireplace in our house so she can make popcorn. Wants me to buy one of those long handled, rusted corn poppers you used. Where in the hell did you get that relic anyway?"

"The State of Wisconsin has almost as many flea markets as it does pine trees," said Tidge, grinning at John. "There are all kinds of treasures scattered around this state." He paused and flashed a smile at John. "If you'll continue to address me as Patriarch, you'll each get one next Christmas."

"Don't forget the recipe for the orange halves," said John.

"Not a one of our kids will ever forget this Christmas," said Paul, returning the mood to serious. "I know I won't."

"At least the kids were in bed when Willy had one too many cups of glogg and got herself pillaged by Eric the Red," said Tidge. "Aunt

Mina would have never looked the same to them had they listened to her speak in some strange Viking tongue." He began to laugh and started slapping the top of the kitchen counter with the palm of his right hand. "She made the Kid, his na zdrowie games at Harry Dungan's and coming home with his bundles look like a rank amateur."

They were all laughing, John finally saying, "Can you imagine Mother Mary May I finding out that Dad really didn't work in a meat packing company, but was selling dirty pictures he took with his old Polaroid." He shook his head and started laughing. "He could have cut off all the heads he wanted and no one would have cared as long as there were bare boobs and bottoms staring back." They all chuckled except Tidge.

"Mom would have thrown him out of the house so fast he wouldn't have had time to scream," said Peter.

"Maybe not," said Tidge, remembering. "She was our mother and mothers, well, are sometimes more than just mothers."

"Are you trying to tell us that Mother Mary May I would have condoned the Kid taking dirty pictures?" said Peter, fragments of his laughter lingering. "The only pictures of a female she allowed in the house were the Blessed Mother. Remember the calendar the Kid brought home with the pin-up girl on it?"

Heads nodded and collective grins answered his question. "That poor girl's sexy grin changed to terror when she found herself being squeezed to death by May I and headed for the garbage can."

Paul stopped laughing long enough to say, "The Kid snuck out that night and pulled her out of the garbage can and hid her in the garage." He saw the looks his brothers were giving him. "Hell, if he hadn't, I would've. Besides, I knew the Kid's hiding places."

"All of them?" asked Tidge, not wanting to hear what he didn't want to hear.

"I think I did," said Paul, a shrug following his answer. "I knew where he hid things in the garage that he didn't want May I to see. I can't believe that he would be brave enough or even plain stupid to try and hide contraband in her scared domain surrounded by crucifixes and a rosary hanging in every room." Paul began to chuckle. "I bet we were the only house on the block with a holy water font inside our front door."

Tidge's mood shot from somber to hilarious as he said, "Wrong!"

His brothers all looked at him like he had taken one too many swats upside the head from Kid Scream. "You're kidding," said Paul.

Tidge's head went from side to side. "I kid you not," he said, making the sign of the cross. "You guys remember Michael Constantine Beanos who lived on the corner by us," he said to his brothers. "We all called him Bean Head."

The three brothers nodded, Peter saying, "His mother was Italian and Roman Catholic and his father Greek Orthodox."

"Bean Head showed me where his mother and grandmother placed holy water fonts at both the front and back doors in their two story apartment building."

"None in the basement?" asked John.

"One there too," said Tidge. He got up from his chair and stretched. "I'll tell you the details once I go to the potty." He left his white lie in the kitchen with his brothers as he walked to the stairs. A glance over his shoulder told him it was all clear and he sprinted up the long stair case taking the steps two at a time. Stopping at the bedroom door to their master suite, he took a look around to see if anyone was near. He gave a cautious tap on the door. "Willy, honey," he said in a half whisper. "Are you okay?"

There was no answer. He repeated the process, the knock a little harder, his voice no longer a whisper. There was still no answer. A third try produced the same results. "If you're interested," he said, trying not to sound annoyed, "your company is leaving. It would be nice if the lady of the house was there to wish them a safe trip home. You know the classy, mannerly thing to do." He tried the door handle and found the door unlocked. A look inside produced no sign of his wife. He shrugged his shoulders and walked back to the stairs leading down to the great room. Then, changing his mind, he dashed back into their master suite and stuck his head in the dressing area of the closet. No Willy.

He saw his sisters-in-law and the nieces and nephews coming down the hall, all of them bundled up for the long ride home. "She's still sound asleep," he said, his body blocking the bedroom door. "I'll give her your good-byes later."

Outside, standing in front of the garage in his flight jacket, his breath visible as if birds could perch on it, he dispensed hugs and explained away Willy's absence. "Oh, well," he said, a blast of icy wind digging at the back of his bare neck over the top of the leather collar, "that nasty influenza bug has incapacitated more than one hostess at an inopportune time."

"I can understand," said John's wife, as she got Star and Frankie situated in the back seat of their Jeep. "That bug had me flat on my back over Thanksgiving." She looked inside the Jeep and yelled, "Hit your sister one more time and I'll show you what Santa's dungeon up at the North Pole looks like." She backed out of the car, looked at Tidge and said in a whisper, "You did say you're pretty close to the North Pole."

Tidge, stern faced, nodded.

"I just got over a bout with the flu," said Paul's wife, checking in the back seat of their Suburban to see if Paul, Jr.'s seat belt was buckled. "All I did was sleep. I was so lucky to be able to be here." She continued to talk as she walked around to the other side of the car. "Last week at this time I couldn't get out of bed." She stooped down, leaned inside the Suburban, half of her body disappearing and they heard, "Sit still and stop acting like a couple of morons."

"And a very Merry Christmas to you, Brother James Virgil," thought Tidge.

More hugs followed punctuated with final exchanges of "Merry Christmas" and a round of handshakes from his brothers. Each said the exact same thing that came in the form of a question, a dream and a wish: "Christmas here again next year?"

"Of course," said Tidge, his hands searching for warmth in the tattered pockets of his jacket. "Why would it be anywhere else?"

Doors slammed shut, engines turned over and a series of final waves appeared from inside the three vehicles. Tidge waved back and took several steps off to the side to allow his brothers' cars to plow their way to his road. He watched the three car caravan plunge through the snow packed driveway, tires spinning. As the final car disappeared over the rise, he wished with all of his heart that he could latch on to their tail lights and drag each one of them back. For the first time in his life, Tidge felt himself fight back tears at seeing his family leave.

He walked over to Carm, Carol and Mackie who had Carm's car packed. "You guys leaving your sister behind?" he asked.

Both Carol and Carm looked at one another, Carol saying, "Martha's taking a couple of vacation days. She can take her sweet time getting back."

"I have a group study session tomorrow," said Carm. "We prospective lawyers have a test to pass called the BAR, and I'm not talking about the bar where Grandpa used to hang out."

"By the way, Daddy-kins," said Carol. I think we're going to run back inside and take one last check to see if we have everything."

"Be my guest," said Tidge.

"I think I'll help them, Sir," said Mackie, turning and catching up with the girls.

"Sir," muttered Tidge, as he walked back in the house and saw his in-law's luggage aligned at the bottom of the stairs as if Harold were anticipating a military inspection from Mackie. He glanced up and saw Harold at the top of the landing, one arm supporting Gert around her waist and the other reinforcing the loop she had through his other arm. He watched them get half way down the stairs when he said, "Good morning, Gert." His voice showed way too much exuberance for Gert who stopped, leaned against the banister, and put her left index finger to her lips. "Sorry," Tidge said in a whisper. "A mild Bloody Mary for the road?"

"Be a dear," Gert managed to mumble, her eyes hidden by her sun glasses, "Would it be too much of a burden to get me a cup of just tomato juice and two more aspirin?"

"My pleasure, said Tidge, his voice softer than a whisper."

Before Harold could help his wife to the front door, Tidge was back with her order.

"Anything else?" he asked, still maintaining his hushed voice.

Gert's hand made a slow gesture that resembled that she was fine.

Tidge gave a knowing smile. "Let me get these for you," he said to Harold giving a nod toward the luggage.

Harold nodded back his appreciation. "Thomas, you continue to be a most attentive, accommodating host. A vanishing art, I fear." He paused, put his arm around Tidge's shoulder and said, "I firmly believe you are the Paladin of Christmas. And, if you'd be so kind, extend my appreciation to your youngest sibling for assisting me earlier with the bulk of our luggage."

They headed to the garage, Tidge lugging Gert's tote bag, a large handbag made of genuine alligator. In his other hand were two designer shopping bags with the Bloomingdale's name, Christmas presents almost spilling out.

"Bed rest and not emotional interruptions of good-byes is the best medicine for Wilhelmina," said Harold, believing influenza was the culprit. Gert managed to move an index finger indicating she agreed with her husband. She hung on to Harold as they gingerly shuffled along the path cut through the snow by Tidge's brothers and their families. Their car was in the garage waiting for them, warm and free from snow.

From behind their sun glasses that did more than protect them from the hazy sun reflecting off the snow, they extended their love and thanks for, in Gert's subdued words, "An utterly divine Christmas."

Harold followed with a, "Here, here," and a firm grasp of his wife's arm. He removed his sun glasses with his left hand and looked Tidge in the eye. "Thank you for treating Wilhelmina with love and, above all, respect. You are a true gentleman, Thomas." He paused. "My father would have been most intrigued to see you wearing that Santa Claus suit Christmas Eve." He replaced his sun glasses and shook Tidge's hand as Gert took her first two fingers, kissed them and showed them to Tidge with a nod. "He would have been intrigued even more with your jacket." Then Harold escorted Gert to the car, opening the door and helping her with her seat belt. When he closed the car door he turned to Tidge. "Maybe I just might take you up on your offer to help me set up my bookstore. Your volunteering your services for what you refer to as grunt work is much appreciated."

"Yeah, Harold," said Tidge, feeling a slight trembling in his knees. "That grunt work will get you when you least expect it."

Harold walked to the driver's side door, opened it and said: "I could use a partner like you who appreciates old books."

Tidge felt a shortness of breath. "Old books?" he repeated, at first not understanding what his father-in-law was talking about. "You mean our library?"

"Exactly," said Harold. "And, Thomas," he continued, appearing shy. "I hope you don't mind, but I took the liberty of packing the book I was reading while the family enjoyed your hay ride. I want so much to finish that wonderful story."

Tidge gave his father-in-law a questioning look.

"The Washington Irving story, Thomas. You have read it?"

Tidge hadn't, but nodded.

"It reminds me so much of what took place in your lovely home this Yule," said Harold. Then quickly adding: "I shall return it upon completion. I hope you don't mind."

"Harold," said Tidge. "Why don't you keep the book? Maybe you can showcase it in your new bookstore." He smiled and winked at Harold. "Books are like sex, Harold. You can't put the good ones down."

"Thomas, you are priceless." There was a look of admiration radiating from him visible with even his sun glasses on. "You and I are very much alike."

Tidge had no idea what his father-in-law meant. "How's that, Harold?"

Harold didn't bother to lower his voice and said, "Both of us have experienced the real test of the wedding vows in our lives."

Tidge's head went up and down in a cautious slow motion as he thought for a moment. Then he sent out a probe. "You mean, the for better or worse stuff?"

Harold nodded. "More like the entire vow," he said, as he slid his sunglasses down his nose so his red streaked eyes were visible. "You're like me, Thomas. You believe. I believe."

Tidge tried to understand. "So, you think a couple of believers from different generations can work together?"

"Give it some thought," said Harold, taking a glance inside the car at Gert who sat nursing her tomato juice and waiting for the aspirins to kick in. "Regardless of my wife's unfortunate habit which we have both lived with for way too long, I never stopped loving and caring for her, and I've never stopped loving Wilhelmina. She is still my pride and joy to this day." He got one leg inside the car, stopped and looked seriously at Tidge. "I made damn good money," he said, the pride in his voice matching the swelling in his chest. "I gave my family the best." He slid his sun glasses back into place.

"I'm sure you did," said Tidge, enjoying the feeling of satisfaction that he finally got to know his father-in-law for the first time.

"I walked away when the walking was good," continued Harold. "I never once got messed up with anybody in that business. If you know what I mean." He stopped, his right hand finding the ignition key. "You've heard the old expression, I'm sure."

Tidge shrugged his shoulders. "Which one is that?"

"You don't defecate where you sleep."

"Harold, shame on you," said Gert softly.

Harold became even more serious. "I could never be a disgrace to my little girl."

Tidge stooped down, leaned forward and surprised them both by giving Harold a hug.

"Wunderbar," said Harold, after Tidge straightened up. "When my mother and I came to this country we didn't speak the language and didn't know where our next crust of bread would come from. I worked hard in school and even harder when I got the job that would make me, my mother and Gert comfortable. If American men wanted to see pictures of smiling women in their underwear, who better than I to provide those smiles?"

Before Tidge could say another word, Harold started the car and reached for the door handle. "Hope you'll have us again one of these years."

"How 'bout next week," said Tidge.

He watched Harold give him a two fingered salute touching his forehead and then close the door. Harold's window opened. "Next week it is."

The window closed and Tidge made his way to the back of the car to give Harold directions for backing it out and get it into position so he could ride the ruts plowed by Peter, Paul and John.

Harold swung the big Lincoln around as if he were a child playing with a toy. Tidge stood off to the side and waved as the huge sedan lumbered over the slight hill of their eight acres, another set of tail lights he wanted to grab and not let go. "Wunderbar is right on, Harold," he said, his steam covered words lost in an increasing north wind.

Two cars remained looking like lonely snow covered bookends. One car was packed and ready and the other minus a driver who hadn't been seen since Christmas night. Her stepmother hadn't been seen either. He started back to the warmth of the house when he saw Carol, Carm and Mackie coming towards him. They were kicking at the snow, pretending to ski as they shuffled along the driveway and laughing out of control. "And what's so funny?" he asked.

"Nothing, Dad," said Carm, trying to curb her laughter, but failing.

"We're just expressing the way we feel about having had such a great Christmas," Carol said, then bursting out laughing. "Can we do this at Easter?"

"Sure," said Tidge, wanting to join the laughter, but not knowing the cause of their laughter. He looked at Mackie who was biting his cheeks, his usual red complexion now blazing. "And you, Sir, would you like to come back at Easter?"

Mackie couldn't talk he was laughing so hard, and Tidge's daughters had tears streaming down their cheeks.

"Off with you three," he said to them. "And drive carefully. I don't want to hear renditions about your comedic behavior resulting in a relative of Bambi's mounted on the front of this car as a new hood ornament."

"Thanks, Dad," said Carm, her arms around him giving him the type of hug he remembered before divorce came into their lives.

"Any old time," he said to her, hanging on so she wouldn't see him fighting back the tears. "You're welcome here whenever you want."

She released her grip on him and he could see that tears had replaced the laughter. Carol stepped in next and gave her father a hug every bit as hard as her sister. "Take care of my favorite teacher."

"Consider her taken care of."

There were more tears when they broke their hug, the tears unable to mask the love in their eyes. "Like I said to your sister, don't be a stranger." He looked at Mackie. "And, Sir, that goes for you."

Mackie shook Tidge's hand. "Thank you for your generous hospitality, Sir." He smiled. "And, Sir, I really appreciate that present of your picture of the cow with the horns tied on her head."

They all laughed and Tidge said, "Be gone." He flicked his wrist as if shooing a bug. "You just might get back to Chicago before dark."

He watched their car disappear like the others and, for the first time, felt the cold and questioned his sanity for standing in snow almost up to his knees and freezing. "You own a parka, dummy, why aren't you wearing it?" he asked aloud. His one last look at the faint glow of the car's tail lights disappearing lasted only a second before he started jogging back to the welcomed warmth of the house.

Two things were on his mind as he stomped his shoes clean on the mat by the front door. The other of the two was Martha. He knew she would stay snuggled in the warmth of her bed until hunger drove her in search of anything that resembled food. His first concern was Willy.

Tidge knew he had placed her in bed and she was sleeping. At least she was when he carried her up the stairs. He had waited until the other drowsy family members and guest had yawned their way to their rooms. When the last, "goodnight" was heard and the final door clicked shut, Tidge turned into Rhett Butler. He lifted Willy off the couch where she had been sleeping and carried her up the staircase. Unlike Rhett who didn't stumble twice and bump Scarlett's head against the banister both at the bottom and the top, Tidge got Willy into their master suite. There was no crescendo of music. That was replaced by Willy stammering and asking: "Why does Aunt Bessie hate me?"

Tidge laid a goose down comforter across her fully clothed sleeping form. He bent down, kissed her on the cheek and whispered: "All I want for Christmas is you." He headed back down to the Great Room and the end of an almost perfect Christmas.

Tidge felt the confusing, eerie feeling in his heart and soul when he returned to the house after saying goodbye to Carm, Carol and

Mackie. His Christmas wasn't over. More giving and receiving stood patiently in line. Martha headed up the line. Willy was behind her.

The warmth of the house gave him a feeling of being wrapped up in his wife's mink coat. He walked into the kitchen blowing in his hands. There was still coffee left and he poured a cup for himself to help thaw out his fingers. He found Willy's cup then postponed the idea realizing he had no idea as to where she had disappeared. What he surmised was that she would be suffering from the Queen Mother of all Hangovers. Where she was suffering was his unanswered question. "Fear not my Christmas angel," he said to the kitchen's four walls. "Your man will make everything better once he finds you."

As Tidge took a sip of his coffee, he glanced out the window. "What the," he gasped, as coffee sprayed from his mouth like Kenny Miller's exuberant saliva. He stared at the sight of Willy wrapped in her mink coat, sitting on a stack of pier sections at Lake Namagakon's frozen edge.

"There you are," he muttered to the image outside. A relieved sigh saw him getting up and going to the mud room where he pulled on his Bears stocking cap being sure his ears were covered. He grabbed his parka off one coat hook and his jacket off the hook next to it. On went the jacket, the parka over it and he walked back into the kitchen and poured a mug of coffee for Willy. He was out the back door his boots tracing one of the jagged paths through the snow cut earlier by his nieces and nephews.

"Good morning, Queen Glogg," he said, holding the steaming mug under her nose. He could see her eyes fixed on a snow buried Buck Island. "Tis I, your friendly chipmunk, Alvin, bringing you a hot mug of coffee," he continued with a slight bow. He paused then presented the mug to her. "Bernie the Saint Bernard couldn't make it with his keg of brandy. He's hung over from lapping up too much glogg last night."

Her bare hands slid from her coat pockets as if they were in pain and she took the mug, caressing it without a word.

"You're quite welcome, Your Royal Gloggness," he said, an intentional touch of sarcasm coating his comment. He brushed off a small area of snow next to her and set down his coffee cup. He placed his hands under the collar of her mink and felt the warmth of the back of her neck. "Feeling any better?" He thought he felt a shrug of her shoulders as his fingers began to knead at the tightness in her neck. "There was an item I saw on my big screen television this morning while watching the news," he said, softly. "It was a fascinating story about this lady residing on Lake Namakagon who gave a Christmas speech that cast a spell over her audience. Do you know anything about it?"

"You're not very funny," she said, her voice soft and calm surprising him.

His fingers continued their gentle massaging. "Well, not as funny as the news anchor said you were." he said, increasing the pressure on his fingers as he worked them into the nape of her neck. He felt her push back against his fingers. He waited for her to respond but she didn't, sitting as if she were frozen to the stacked pier sections. "They showed a film clip of you cracking up your audience in the beginning when you stole a line from an old comedian, Henny Youngman and said, 'Take my screwed up families. Please!' They loved that line. Then they fell asleep."

Her head pressed back against his hands. "Hold that for a minute longer will you, Alvin," she said. "And try keeping your lips sealed for the same amount of time."

"It is done, your majesty," he said, as he took his thumb and index finger and pretended to zip his lips shut.

They both stared at the tiny, picturesque Buck Island, a natural channel separating it from the Miller's property, a larger inlet forming a curving bay from their property line.

Tidge released his grip, picked up his cup and took a slurping sip, the slurp designed to annoy her. "Speaking of the news," he said, setting down his cup. "Have you seen today's special edition of the Stockholm Gazette?"

"Your minute's not up," she said, her eyes still frozen on the island.

"Their reporter not only raved about your comedic talent, but thought you were, how did he phrase it, seductively radiant adorned in your mink and CFMP's." He paused, took another slurp of his coffee, the gurgling sound louder and longer than before. "Also, the critic's review in this week's *Trading Times* said, and I quote,

'Wilhelmina Schneider hyphen Mickiewicz's performance put the perfect icing on the Christmas fruit cake'."

She turned, looking at him, her tired red eyes beginning to pool. "I really ruined it, didn't I?"

He moved his cup in tiny circles watching the snow melt and then freeze a few moments later. "Excuse me, your majesty, if I may be so bold to ask, me, your humble servant, Alvin, but, what are you doin' New Years, New Year's Eve?" His hands slid inside her coat collar and started massaging her shoulders again.

"I'm sorry," she said, sounding remorseful.

"For what?"

"For turning your dream and everything we worked so hard for into shambles," she sniffled.

His fingers dug into her shoulders and he felt her cringe. "I told you, you didn't ruin a thing. All of our guests, from oldest to youngest, not including Sleeping Beauty inside," his head nodding towards the house, "said this was the best Christmas of their life. Mine too." His fingers dug deeper. Thanks to you, the family's unscrewed."

"But, I . . ."

His kneading fingers stopped her. "I talked with Harold this morning before he and the Gibson poster girl headed back for Chicago and everything they said about this weekend could be summed up into one word."

"Oh, God," she moaned.

"No, but in the same category," he said, a smile starting to form. "I believe their overworked word was, Divine."

She looked at him not believing.

He crossed the heart area of his open parka with his right hand and then his left. "It was divine this, and divine that. Our daughter was divine. Heck, I even made their divine category."

"You're not just saying that."

He crossed his heart again, this time twice in each direction. "I'm serious. Why would it be anything else? How could it? They never heard a word you said."

"Tidge, honey," she said, the look on her face pleading. "My heart, soul and splitting headache are in no mood for any more of your sick form of levity."

"I'm not joking," he said, defending himself. "Both mom and dad were sound asleep. Most amazing thing I ever saw. Two people, eyes wide open, drink glasses in their hands, sitting poised and attentive and snoring. Well, your mother snored. Your father was a sophisticated snoozer.

Willy's head dropped down, her chin buried inside her coat. "God, I didn't even say goodbye to them."

"They understood," he said. "I blamed your horrible manners on the Flu." Tidge laughed. "The only goodbyes Gert said were to me and to the Bloody Marys. None for her this morning, I might add, only tomato juice and two aspirins for the road."

Her head tilted back forcing her neck against his fingers. "I bet your family thinks you married a screaming lush, the product of an alcoholic mother and a smut peddling father."

"No way," he said, his enthusiasm returning. My family loves your parents. They loved them so much that they're all coming back next week for New Year's Eve." His fingers pressed harder.

"Say you're joking about New Year's Eve," she said, her head retreating back into her coat.

"I'm joking," he said, trying to reassure her. "Your parents, however, want to come back for Easter provided Gert's hangover is gone."

She looked at him out of the corner of her eye trying to generate her laser look. The beam gave a sputtering flicker before shutting down. "What was in that glogg?"

"You'll have to visit the cemetery next time we get back to Chicago and ask Aunt Bessie." He laughed and waited for her to respond, but she didn't. Changing the subject he said, "Before he left, your dad told me he might take me up on my offer to help him start his bookstore."

Her head poked its way up from the luxurious fold of her collar like a cautious, shy turtle coming up for air in the lily pad patch between their pier and shore during late summer. Her eyes were barely visible. "Daddy really said that?"

He nodded. "And like I just mentioned, they can't wait to come back."

"How could they?" she asked. "I embarrassed them to tears."

Tidge playfully pushed her head down into the folds of her collar. "How could you," he said. "They were both under the control of the asterisk of your mother's Eleventh Commandment, especially your father. Harold really liked the glogg."

"I guess I also liked it," she said, the sound of her voice making her head echo. "I liked it so much that I'll never take another sip as long as I live."

"If it wasn't for my late Aunt Bessie's recipe and addressing our guests in a Viking dialect, the party would've broken up early," he said, his grin returning to a smile. "Then my brothers could have gone to bed with their spouses and received a thank you for their gifts from Santa."

"I think I'm becoming a little leery of your hands on my shoulders," she said, her head beginning to roll in a circle.

His fingers continued kneading, this time more gentle. "You know that bookstore your father mentioned," he said, his words softer than his massage. "The one he wants me to help him get started." He heard a cross between a purr and a moan come from her. "Did you know he's thinking about making it an adult bookstore?"

Her head popped up from the collar, her eyes on fire. "That's not the least bit amusing, you perverted pig."

"Your dad's not going to be selling girlie magazines in his bookstore," he said, trying to reassure her that he was only joking. "He did mention in passing that part of his plans were to add a trendy bistro to the bookstore. He said something about specializing in Gibsons and serving glogg during the Christmas holiday season."

"Thomas Ignacy Joseph, I'm torn between loving and hating you." She leaned in his direction and put her arms around his neck. "I apologize for making a spectacle of myself."

"What spectacle?" He held her tight. "Spilling glogg down your chin, slobbering all over yourself and falling asleep on your mother's shoulder is not making a spectacle of yourself." He let her go, stepped back and looked at her. "At least the children were all snuggled up in their beds dreaming of sugar plums when Kenny Miller showed up with Mickey to wish everyone a Merry Christmas. I think those two kids really enjoyed your explaining to Mickey the subject of why to wear high heel pumps while rolling in straw in her father's barn."

She pushed away from him like a shot, "They didn't!" she shouted. "I didn't!"

"What can I say," he said, his teeth digging into the sides of his cheeks. "Kenny stopped slobbering on himself and picking straw out of Mickey's hair when he heard you recite your version of the alphabet. Poor kid never knew it started, C-F-M-P."

Willy launched herself off the pier section. Both fists were clenched. "You'd better be joking if you know what's good for you."

"Okay," he said, bending over and picking up her mug that she sent flying into the snow. He stood up and handed it to her. "I'm joking. Kenny and Mickey were never here. Besides, I cleaned up the straw that fell out of Mickey's underwear after she left."

"Thomas Ignacy Joseph!"

He backed away from her. "By the way, your eyes can use a tourniquet and some sleep."

She leaned back against the pier section. "Do I look that bad?"

He stared at her for a moment and said, "In one word, yes."

"Feed me first and then I'll go to bed."

"Geez," he said, shaking his head once from side to side. "A man's work is never done." He turned and motioned for her with a wave of his right hand to follow him. She walked in his footsteps staying several steps behind him. As they got close to the back steps, he turned and said: "While I'm at it, I'd better wake up my daughter and feed her too if I know what's good for me."

"Oh, poor baby," she said, from behind, reaching down for a handful of snow and shoving it down his bare neck. Before she knew it, he had wrestled her into the snow. "My coat," she cried out. "You're going to ruin my mink!"

"I'll buy you another one," he said, pinning her down in the snow, his knees against her shoulders, a snow ball in his left hand, the flakes falling onto her face. "Say you're sorry."

"For what," she said, trying to kick and slap him. "Let me up."

"I only let good girls up." More snowflakes drifted onto her face. "*PT's*, on the other hand..."

"You're going to ruin my coat!"

"Say you're sorry."

"I'm sorry," she said, feeling his grip loosen and wiggling out from under him. Just as she turned a powdery snow ball caught her on the back of her hair. "You jerk."

"I love it when you get mad." He came up behind her and brushed the snow from her hair and shoulders. "Are you okay?"

She put her head on his shoulder and held him, the sound of a far off snowmobile interrupting the moment. "I'm fine," she said into his jacket. "How about you?"

"He gave her a nod. "I'm fine. Shouldn't I be?"

She burrowed her face into his chest and shoulder, the patch of Sugar Claus on his jacket rough against her face. "I don't know," she said. "I just thought you might be worn out from playing the role of the new and improved you for four days."

Tidge laughed and tilted her chin up. "New and improved?" he asked. "Is that like changed, overflowing with love, honesty and perfection, like a real live Patriarch who just unscrewed his family?"

"Your family didn't need the unscrewing," she said, pointing at him.

"Are you trying to tell me that I'm the one who was messed up?"

"Not much to tell," she said, seriously. "If I were you, I'd have another one of your Christmas letter writing activities and send one off to your buddies, Kris Kringle and Yahweh asking, no pleading, for them to unscrew you. She reached up and removed his arms from around her shoulders, turned and walked up the back stairs stomping the snow off her mukluks.

"I am unscrewed," he said, following after her as she entered the mud room. "At least I think I am." He got along side of her. "When Harold and I talked just before he left, he told me that he and I were alike." He put his hands on her shoulders.

"Alike," she repeated, pushing his hands away. "Now I really am hungry," she muttered, taking off her mukluks and placing them in the rubber boot tray by the kitchen door.

"Not so fast," he said, reaching around her and placing his hand on the door knob. "We're alike because we're believers."

"Believers," she repeated. "You and my father might be believers, but what each of you believes is entirely different than what the other one believes in." Her nose wrinkled. "Besides, my father's not screwed up."

Tidge ignored her remark. "You know that I believe in you and in us." He waited for her to agree, but all she did was place her near hand on top of his hand that was on the door knob. "I believe in God and I believe in Santa Claus." He waited for her to comment, but she didn't. "Your dad, well, he believes in your mom, although not in her Gibson intake, and he believes in you. He also believed in giving you and your mother the best."

She began to place pressure on his hand. "You're asking me to believe that you and my father are alike?"

"Asking isn't necessary" said Tidge. He looked at Willy with all the love a man could have for the girl of his dreams. "Your dad and I believe. In support of my case, I believe therefore I'm unscrewed."

"Did I just hear the cry of the Loon?" she asked.

"Geez, I wonder how many naughty, sarcastic little girls Santa had to put up with when he made his deliveries?"

"Only one," she said, removing his hand from the door knob.

"One?"

She opened the door leading to the kitchen and felt the warm air engulf her. Smiling she said: "Only one who wears black high heeled, patent leather pumps, the CFMP model endorsed by Joan Crawford."

Chapter 13

Willy felt relief and a sense of security being inside and away from a snarling northwest wind snapping its nasty jaws as it pouted and pounded on the mud room door. Her frozen, bare hands, growling stomach and a headache being pummeled by reindeer hoofs appreciated the warmth of Henry's Hut. She hoped that food, aspirin and a cup of coffee without a rim of ice on the cup would end her husband's illogical comparison between himself and her father. It didn't. There was also a surprise sitting at the oak table in the kitchen.

"Hi, kids," said Martha, looking bright eyed and chipper in her white terrycloth robe and printed cherubic Santa sweat socks, a heaping plate of steaming food in front of her. "I appreciate your closing the door. So do the owners who aren't heating the outside."

Tidge and Willy stared.

"Great leftovers," said Martha, piercing what looked like Lyonnaise potatoes with her fork. "That microwave oven of yours works like a charm."

"Heating the outside," repeated Tidge, starting to smile. "I wonder where you heard that before."

The potatoes found her mouth and Martha did a slight wave of her hand, the one holding her fork, indicating that her father and Willy should join her at the table. She made a sound that indicated the potatoes agreed with her then wiped at her mouth with a paper napkin and said: "What kind of games were you two kids playing in the snow?" she asked, her fork toying with the next selection of food on her plate. "Would you teach me how to play that Believing and PT game you were shouting about out there?" she asked, her fork spearing a slice of roast beef. "And what's with all this C-F-M-P stuff I heard periodically during Christmas time? Is that some kind of game that people up in Wisconsin play to wile away the winter months?" She glanced at Willy, her bright eyes even brighter. "Like an offshoot of your fathers Can You Top This game?"

Tidge and Willy continued to stare, stunned, pushing the chill from their bodies.

Martha placed a slice of roast beef on her plate and then stabbed a chunk of ham. "If I had to wait for you two to finish wrestling in the snow, I'd starve to death," she said, scanning more selections for her plate. "In the immortal words of my late grandmother, if you'd like, I'll re-heat breakfast for you." Martha smiled at her still staring father and stepmother. She got up from her chair, tugged at the ends of her robe belt pulling them snug and walked to the microwave, Santa smiling from her socks. "After all that Christmas cheer last night and winter games this morning, you two should be famished." She paused and looked at Willy. "No offense, dearest Stepmama, but you look like hell."

"I feel that way," said Willy, as she eyed the packages of food on the counter.

"Heating the outside," repeated Tidge, as he set two more plates and plastic utensils on the table. "Coffee, dearest Stepmama who looks like hell?" he asked. He removed two cups from the wooden peg cup rack on the counter and filled Willy's cup. Then he drained the last of the pot with a bouncing motion, managing to squeeze out a third of a cup for himself.

Willy watched Martha put several packages in the microwave, "May I help?" she asked.

Martha smiled, paused and said, "If you'd like."

"Oh, brother," said Tidge.

Willy cupped her hands and put them to her lips. She began blowing into the cup. It was a trick the former debutante learned from Tidge after her first encounter with a frosty morning in the Northwoods. After several more warm puffs, her hands began a rubbing motion as if she were applying her favorite pear scented lotion. She squeezed her eyes shut blocking out a filament of sunshine that was fighting its way through the late, grey morning. "I'll put the leftovers on several platters after you finish heating them," she said to Martha, as her focus shifted to the cluster of bulging plastic garbage bags at the entrance to the mud room. Her nose crinkled.

Tidge saw the crinkle. "I'll take them out later," he muttered.

The microwave let out a series of beeps and Martha popped open the door. "Will one of you please tell me what all of that yelling was coming from the yard?" she asked. "Geez," she said, sounding like her father. "Do you two argue and roll around in the snow every day?" she asked, failing at trying to be serious. "All that yelling about believing this and believing that," she continued as she juggled the hot packages of food, letting them roll out of her hands to the counter top. "Geez, Dad, but you were certainly agitated." She gave her father a look of disapproval. "Very unbecoming behavior of a Patriarch," she scolded. "What would your nuclear family think?"

Tidge shrugged. "Your stepmama, as you call her, doesn't believe that her father told me that he and I were alike because we were believers."

"Alike," gasped Martha. "You and Mr. Schneider?" Her eyes bounced back and forth between her father and Willy. "Alike," she said, now pondering the comparison. "I don't think so." She looked at her father. "A believer," she continued, her eyes not leaving him. "That you are. If it wasn't for you, there'd be no Santa Claus."

"And no Cinnamon Bear, as in Paddy O'Cinnamon, no Marshmallow World, no Uncle Mistletoe and no family Christmas in Winsconsin," snapped Tidge.

Martha grinned at her father. "You are definitely a believer, Dad," she said, her eyes twinkling. "I don't know what else you believe in." She paused and looked at Willy. "Yes, I do," she continued. "I know you really believe in this lady right here."

Willy blushed. "Thank you, Martha," she said, giving her a hug. "But, after my behavior last night, I don't know why."

"What behavior?" Martha asked, genuinely not understanding.

"Because your stepmama got incredibly sloshed last night," said Tidge, smiling. "Stink-o, Pie-eyed, Blotto in the grotto, Hammered." He paused. "I think that about covers it."

"Geez, Dad," said Martha. "And here I had the impression that you really changed."

She gave a shrug and sat down. "Stepmama, would you like to join me for breakfast?"

"I'd love to," said Willy, pulling up a chair alongside Martha.

They both placed their selections on their plates as Tidge stood and watched; wondering if this was really a part of his special Christmas gift. "May I join you beautiful ladies?" he asked politely. "Or have I been relegated to dining alone in my basement workshop?"

"Oh, don't be so melodramatic, Patriarch Believer," said Willy, while scanning the open, steaming packages. "You don't have to exile yourself to the basement. Your den is a good place."

Martha let out a laugh and held up her hand for Willy to give her a high five. "Good one, Stepmama."

"Not funny," said Tidge pulling up a chair alongside of his daughter.

"Your father was partially right," Willy said to Martha as if Tidge wasn't in the room. "The last thing I remember about last night was this morning when your Uncle John and my father were struggling with my mother's luggage carrying it down the stairs. I jumped out of bed to help, but I didn't get beyond the jump before I fell back, crawled under the covers and prayed for death." She placed down her fork on the table and started to cry.

Tidge slid off his chair and was at his wife's side in an instant. He placed his arm around her shoulder and said: "I thought I told you that Henry don't allow no stinkin' tears to be served with leftovers in his hut." He gave her shoulder a gentle squeeze. "What child is this who cries at Christmas?"

"Mom," said Martha lovingly, placing her hands on top of Willy's. "Don't cry." She smiled at Willy. "The entire family was, in my father's loving, understanding and sympathetic words, blotto, pie-eyed, stink-o and just plain plastered last night. I know I was. So, why are you crying?"

Willy sniffled. "Because I went and ruined your father's dream." She dabbed at her eyes with her paper napkin.

"Poo-poo on Daddy's dream," said Martha, giving a glance at her father. "Last night you made my dreams come true by giving my father back to me. I don't know how you did it or if you did it. All I know is that I had the most beautiful sensations all night that I had a father again."

"Are you sure it wasn't being introduced to Gibsons by Willy's mother," said Tidge, his eyes radiating love for his daughter.

"The Gibsons helped," said Martha, gently taking the napkin away from Willy and dabbing at her own eyes. "Whatever, it was a perfect Christmas for me and, I think, for everyone else."

"I don't think my brother John thought it was so perfect," said Tidge. He gave Willy another gentle squeeze. "Can't blame him after your mother almost inserted his head into his butt demonstrating her famous wrestling hold," he said. He kissed his wife under each eye tasting the salt from her tears. "And, if you must know, Christmas wasn't totally perfect for Pete's wife either."

Both Willy and Martha looked at him as if asking the same question, Willy's tears gone, but not the sniffles.

"Chareese wanted to take some of the leftover glogg home for her parents, but the only thing left in the kettle were chunks of spices and purple citrus peels," he said, returning to his chair. "She told me she wanted her parents to experience the feeling of being Swedish."

"Liar," mumbled Willy, as she gave Martha a look that indicated her father was off in his dream world.

"I'm serious," he said. "I told her I'd mail Aunt Bessie's secret recipe to her."

"Liar."

"Not I," he said, keeping a serious expression on his face. "My Aunt Bessie contributed to Christmas perfection from the beyond."

"Your Aunt Bessie almost killed me," said Willy, still feeling her head pounding. "You and your so-called perfection."

"My brothers thought this was a perfect Christmas, bar none," he said. "They ate themselves into a coma each time they sat down and, collectively, drank all the beer there was in southern Bayfield County. "For a moment there, I thought I'd have to get in the truck and drive all the way to Oneida County to buy more beer. Now if that ain't perfection then I don't know what perfection is."

"Dad," said Martha, her own expression at her father identical to Willy's. "Stop beating perfection to death."

"I'm not. . ."

Martha put up her hand with the fork in it and pointed it at her father. "May I finish?"

"If you'd like," he said, laughing.

"Thank you," said Martha, her fork finding a sliver of ham, the ham finding her mouth. She swallowed, smiled and looked at Willy. "My father, the Patriarch and Crown Prince of Perfection has spoken.

"Ignore him," sniffled Willy.

"I did."

Tidge rolled his lips under and looked at Martha. "Okay, Miss Smarty Pants, I can see that this conversation isn't going anywhere, but, if you like driving along snow covered roads in the dark with no signs of human life, then you'd better finish stuffing your face and get ready to motor. You might still have daylight by the time you get around the Wisconsin Dells."

Chapter 14

Lyrics to, *Baby, It's Cold Outside* filled the kitchen after Tidge had switched on his Christmas music. Willy's mood changed instantly.

"I think the three of us should dine by a delightful fire," she said to Tidge. "A few minutes of daylight won't matter that much." She nodded at Martha and then looked at Tidge. "Are believers capable of building a fire for two hungry ladies, both beautiful and one shivering?"

"A warming fire courtesy of yours truly, Smokey the Bear, he's Alvin's half-brother, coming right up," said Tidge smiling."

Martha and Willy scooted off their chairs and, with plates, utensils and napkins in hand, headed for the Great Room. "Be a dear," Willy said to Tidge over her shoulder. 'Before you burn Henry's Hut down, would you be so kind as to bring in the platters of leftovers for your first born and me?"

Tidge followed them both with the platters of wrapped packages and set them down on the woven throw rug in front of the now cold fireplace. Less than twenty four hours earlier, the rug's blended brown colors lay buried under the assorted, greens, reds, whites, golds and silvers of Christmas wrap. The last of a supply of wood from the night before waited.

Tidge knelt in front of the hearth constructing a pyramid of sticks and scrap wood over a crumbled ball of shredded gift wrap he found wedged in the mechanism under his recliner chair. He added several more pieces of kindling wood on his pyramid structure and then searched for the elongated decorative brass wooden match holder. "Come out, come out wherever you are," he mumbled, as Bing Crosby's words to, *Adeste Fidelis* filled the Great Room.

"Ah, ha," exclaimed Tidge, when he spied the match container peeking out at him from behind the popcorn popper. He looked at the match and then looked at Willy and Martha while continuing to laugh.

Willy's head dropped down and she sighed. "Don't you know that both Smokey and Alvin say that a loon shouldn't play with matches?"

Martha let out a giggle. "Is that what you call my father?" she asked. "A loon?" Her giggle turned to hysterical little girl laughter. "A loon," she repeated. "That's too cool. As my baby sister and her friends would say, that's awesome, even epic. Any more names for dear old Dad?"

"None that I'll tell you while old what's-his-face is listening," she said.

"Very funny," said Tidge, his face minus a smile but glowing. He held up the match stick and looked at the two women in his life. Then, from out of nowhere, he asked" "Do you think Smokey, Alvin, Santa and God would have approved of Humper and Bean Head having a fart lighting contest in Bean Head's basement after Mass Christmas Day?" He waved the match stick back and forth. "And with this same type of match," he said, then striking the match and lighting several sections of the Christmas paper. Appearing pleased, he blew out the match and strategically placed it in the smoking kindling unaware that his wife was staring at him.

Willy sat in silence a dumbfounded look on her face while Martha wrestled with the plastic wrap covering a ball of dressing from the pork crown roast, the package orange in color. "What kind of contest?" Willy asked in disbelief.

"Don't pay him no mind," said Martha, pleased that the package unwrapped. "Daddy's friends were all retarded. I heard that story at least two dozen times before."

"Well, I never heard it," said Willy. She paused. "And I don't think I want to. How disgusting."

"A fart lighting contest is not disgusting," he said, in all innocence. "It's not even retarded." He shot a look at Martha. "Actually, it was a scientific experiment," he said, looking at Willy. "I bet you would've given them each an A Plus if they had been in your class."

"Where did you and your friends learn about such things?" Willy asked, her disbelief growing. "Maybe your family and not just you were screwed up," she said, pausing. "Your father must have been hallucinating when he was on his death bed." She tried to shake her head back and forth but it still hurt too much. "Did your family associate with the families of your friends?" she asked, sarcasm flowing from her like the tears before. "As in contaminate them."

Tidge scooted back to the fireplace and stacked two smaller logs on his pile of kindling, the pyramid having collapsed. Satisfied, he scooted back to kneel alongside of Willy. "No, my family was not a bad influence on Humper's and Bean Head's families. Families had nothing to do with what we did and everything to do with what we did," he continued, no trace of a smile, only the glow remaining.

"Oh, boy, lucky us," said Martha, tasting the dressing and giving a nod of approval. "Stepmama, we are about to be honored with my father's digressing on family values. I believe the term *noblesse oblige* is about to descend upon us."

"Manners, my first born," said Tidge to Martha. He turned his attention to Willy. "We grew up being taught respect and believing in same by those families who have just been mocked by a member of the younger generation," he continued. "We were the last generation that was seen but not heard by our elders." He stared at his fire, enjoying seeing it spread. "But, being seen and not heard didn't mean we didn't hear. We learned quite a bit from an adult world that exiled us from their presence." He watched the growing, lazy flames lick at the two spindly logs.

The sound of the crackling flames prodded Tidge to retrace his route again. He dropped one of three logs split in quarters on the fire. An eruption of sparks shot up. The other two logs followed with the same effect. "Warm enough?" he asked.

Willy didn't respond, her attention having turned to satisfying her stomach.

"Great fire, Dad, "said Martha. "But, could you cease with this family stuff." Her fork toyed with the food on her plate. "If I may be so bold to ask, when are you and your lovely wife going to explain the other half of your Believer and PT game?" Her laughing eyes danced, shifting back and forth. "Were you referring to Kenny Miller and what he said after the hay ride?" she asked, a fork full of roast pork finding her mouth.

Willy's eyes clicked.

Tidge gave a questioning look.

"Please, Dad," said Martha, sounding disgusted. "You males have been using those initials since the alphabet was invented when you couldn't get your way with some poor, innocent female." She smiled. "I heard what Kenny said to you about his girlfriend, Mickey after he dropped us off from the hay ride."

"You heard!" he shot back.

Martha swallowed the pork, dabbed at the corners of her mouth with her napkin and said: "Most of us heard Kenny's command of the alphabet." She glanced at Willy. "By the way, Stepmama," she said, a coy smile peeking out from her napkin. "When are you going to share with me the meaning of those initials you bandied about this Christmas season?"

Just as Willy started to turn a dark shade of pink, the sound of Brenda Lee, her country twang filling the Great Room from the speakers, began rocking around the Christmas tree.

...later we'll have some pumpkin pie and do some caroling.

"Oh, no," Willy said, appearing in shock, the pink turning to pale white. Her paper napkin went to her mouth. "Oh, no," came a muffled cry.

"Honey, what is it?" asked Tidge. He was at her side ready to perform the second Heimlich maneuver of the Christmas season.

"I'm sorry, Mom," said Martha, her knife, fork and plate being pushed aside. "I didn't know that four lousy letters would upset you. I really didn't."

"Tidge looked at Martha, his eyes bulging from his head. "Mom," he repeated.

"Darn it all to Hades," Willy said, appearing as if she would burst into tears again.

"What is it?" asked Tidge.

Willy looked at Tidge and then at Martha. "The pie," she said, flabbergasted. "I forgot the pumpkin pie."

Tidge and Martha managed to comfort Willy after her realization that she flubbed both her Christmas Eve and Christmas Day dinners.

"Pumpkin pie's a Thanksgiving thing," Tidge said to her. "Between Norma Miller's and the one you baked, I thought I was turning into a pumpkin." He smiled lovingly at his wife.

"Mom," said Martha again, sounding as if that was the only name she ever used to address Willy. "You served three kinds of pie plus a couple of Polish pastries I can remember eating as a kid at my grandmother's house. There wasn't a soul here who even thought of pumpkin pie."

Willy reached out and stroked Martha's cheek with her left hand, her fork still in her right.

Tidge breathed easier even though the strange feelings he had experienced several times during Christmas had returned. He didn't need those feelings to tell him that Christmas wasn't over. It couldn't be. Everyday would always be Christmas to him. This Christmas, however, still had one small, but intricate part waiting to be positioned into the puzzle to make it special.

Tidge walked Martha to her car, dragging his feet as if he were wearing snow shoes. He was carrying most of her belongings. Two large plastic bags containing Martha's Christmas gifts and wrapped packages of holiday food were clutched in both of her hands as she followed her father.

He knew he had been blest with a magical Christmas. His mind, heart and soul told him that. So did the parcel wedged under his left arm, his left hand carrying her duffel bag and a large tote bag, his right latched on to her suit bag that was draped over his shoulder. He set down her duffel and tote, her suit bag going on top of it along with his parcel. His bare hand brushed snow off the door handle and he lifted the latch. He looked inside the car for a minute then turned to Martha. "What do you use to clean snow off your car?" he asked.

"The wipers" she replied, as if he had asked her a dumb question.

His right hand went to his pants pocket and he pushed the remote button twice. The middle door of the garage went up. He was in and out with a long handled broom before the door motor stopped humming. Snow got pushed and brushed in several directions until Martha's car windows were cleared and clean to his liking. "Now you can see where you're going," he said, sounding like a father. "I'll put your things in the back seat." He placed the duffel and tote bags at one end of the back seat and laid her garment bag flat across the rest of the seat. His parcel was placed on floor behind the passenger seat and her two plastic bags wedge behind the driver's seat. He turned, rested his hands on her shoulders and stared into her eyes as if he were a hypnotist. "Thanks for coming."

"Thanks for having me."

"You made my Christmas," he said, looking at her as only a father who adores hi daughter can. Then he kissed her on the forehead.

"Am I forgiven for being such a screaming bitch at your wedding reception?"

He hugged her knowing his daughter loved him. "You had to get a few things off your chest, that's all."

She pulled back from him just a hair. "I think there were more than a few things on my chest."

He laughed. "A few were ample."

"I can't believe that your wife, her parents and even your family said one word to me over the holidays," she said, her eyes downcast. "They acted as if I never threw a juvenile tantrum at your wedding."

"Oh, they witnessed," he said, smiling at her. "I think maybe God and Santa Claus heard a word or two. Humper most certainly did."

"What a wonderful friend you have, Dad," said Martha. "Mother despised him and I've had a crush on him all these years. He'll always be Missa Billys to me."

"Baby elephants can have that affect on little girls," he said, then gesturing for her to get into her car.

"So can new moms."

He clutched her mom comment to his heart. "Don't forget the directions I gave you for getting to the Interstate," he said, stepping out of her way. "You might just make it before it gets too dark. Come to think of it, the way I remember how you drive, you'll be in Chicago before it gets dark." He ignored her thumbing her nose at him.

"Dad, thank you for a Christmas I'll never forget," she said.

"I'll never forget it either," he said, knowing that after she got home she would realize just how unforgettable this Christmas would be.

"Dad, one question before I head south," she said, her car door still open.

"Shoot," he said.

"Why is it you're standing out in freezing weather without a coat?"

He gave a macho shrug. "Who needs a coat in this balmy sunshine?"

"What happened to your beat up leather jacket you always wear?"

There was another shrug. "The jacket's fine," he said. "Don't worry about it."

"I'm not," she said, then closing her door. Her window rolled down part way. "I'm just worried about you coming down with a case of double pneumonia or freezing to death."

"I'll be fine," he said, unable to take his eyes off her smiling face, the smiling face that once belonged to his little girl. He felt the emotion building but, thanks to Kid Scream's boxing lessons, he didn't cry. Patriarchs weren't allowed to cry. "Don't you know that a family leader is immune from freezing to death?"

"Why is it that I love you?" she asked, putting her hand on the gear shift.

"Because I'm *P* for perfect, *T* for terrific and because I've always loved you," he said. He swallowed hard and barked silent orders to his tear ducts warning them not to let loose. His upper and lower lips pulled in. He watched as she turned away, rolled up her window, and put her car in gear. She didn't hear him say, "God, but I love you," as she drove off, her car fish-tailing on the snow and bouncing out of one of the ruts before he saw her get it back under control.

He walked back to the house still oblivious to the cold weather and finding it hard to believe that Christmas with the whole fam-dam-ily was over.

He stood inside the front door, his back pressed against it, his eyes seeing only the staircase. His thoughts were on Martha and how they had hugged Christmas night before she had gone to bed. They had shared that night. Sharing and talking were two things that eluded them for way too long. They had never had a conversation between them like the one Christmas night. Then, again, he had never been drunk with his daughter before.

Their conversation, he remembered, came in snippets. Each snippet slurred.

*** "A dad and his first-born have a lot in common."
*** "We're responsible types who tell the truth."
*** "We believe in Santa Claus."
*** "My mother didn't."
*** "Marietta Claus did."
*** "Who?"
*** "Dammit, Dad, you were never around."
*** "I wasn't around in the eighth grade because you weren't born."
*** "That's why I was angry with you."
*** "Brother James Virgil never said life would be easy."
*** "Dad, you're forcing your paranoia with family leadership on me."
*** "I don't force. Not even boyfriends."
*** "There is this guy."
*** "Is he a prince charming?"
*** "He kind of reminds me of you."
*** "Can't wait to introduce him to Wisconsin supper clubs."
*** "Supper clubs?"

It was her laugh he now clutched to his heart as he continued to stand with his back against the front door. He felt his daughter hugging him. There was his hug back. Then the patriarch lost his fight.

He tasted his tears. The Christmas he had wished and prayed for what seemed forever poured from him. His tears flowed along with the four letters he and his brothers had written to Santa Claus during what they thought were happy, carefree years. The trickling streams meandering down his cheeks contained the old picture of the pilot and his plane with the pin-up girl, Sugar Claus painted on the nose. A second picture of the little girl on Santa's knee had reminded him of

Marietta Claus from the eighth grade, but he knew that couldn't be. He shivered and said to himself, "On second thought."

More tears followed in the form of the laminated quote attributed, he thought, to Immanuel Kant. The plastic laminate was now propped up on the corner of his desk in his den next to Willy's graduation picture from Loyola. Those two memories along with his framed letter to Santa Claus and the pair of black and white photographs from another lifetime were now his most valuable possessions. His most valuable, his jacket, on the other hand, was now behind the back seat of his oldest daughter's car heading for Chicago. His back pushed against the front door as his chin found his chest and his hands covered his face.

Tidge had wrapped his jacket like a Christmas present. He placed it in a plain bag, and then folded the bag like a nondescript parcel. He had enclosed a letter explaining why he had given the jacket to her. It was the longest letter he had ever written in his life. More than the single page notes he wrote to his parents or the two pagers to Humper when he was in the Navy. It was longer than the ten pages he had written to Barbara Ann after they had parted ways. This letter to Martha, a combine of Confession, Love, Life's Lessons, Warnings and Humor, he thought, would prove to her how much she meant to him. Knowing his daughter the way he did, he felt she probably wouldn't discover it until sometime in May. By June she would have figured out that the family leadership torch had been passed to her.

Dual fists gouged at his eyes trying to dry them. He pushed himself away from the door with a sniffle and started into the Great Room. "Willy!" he called out.

There was no answer.

He called out her name again. "Willy!"

There was silence again.

The Great Room was empty and neat looking, a dying fire the only evidence that someone lived there. "Willy," he called out again. Silence greeted him as he walked into the kitchen. He looked out the window, but only saw the stack of pier sections. No Willy. He turned to leave the kitchen and almost jumped out of his skin.

Willy was silhouetted in the kitchen door clad in her mink. The coat was opened just enough to expose samples of a naked thigh and a touch of cleavage. She stood in a model's pose, one black patent leather pump, the right one, at a forty five degree angle. The other pump was extended a shoe length in front of the other, turned on an angle and her weight barely on her toe. She cocked her right eyebrow, her left arm extended, palm open. There was something in her hand that looked like a small packet.

"Look what I found while you were saying goodbye to your daughter," she said, a different type of laser beam projected at him.

He glanced, took several steps towards her then changed his focus to what she held in her hand. "That no good, red headed son of a bitch!" he blurted out.

"Are you sure?" she asked, handing the condom packet to him. "I found this in between the cushions on the sofa."

"If that lanky Mam and Sir Shitbird was screwing my little girl under our roof, I'll drive to Chicago and castrate him."

"Only one way to find out," she said, heading for his den.

They found another condom packet under a throw pillow on the couch where Mackie had slept. Tidge was incensed. "I'm not driving to Chicago, I'm flying."

"Wait here." She turned and walked across the Great Room, her high heels clicking on the hardwood floor as she headed for the stairs.

He was pacing the floor in the Great Room when she came back down the stairs. "What's so funny?" he asked, as she stood at the foot of the stairs, her hands in the pockets of her coat.

"Guess what I found in my sanctuary," she said. "That's the same sanctuary where you isolated and protected your three daughters from the amorous advances of Don Juan Mackie."

"I'm not going to castrate him," said Tidge. He smiled. "I'm going to kill Cadet Lance Romance."

Willy's hand opened displaying three more packets.

"That bastard was doing all of my kids."

"I kind of doubt that," said Willy, her words having trouble getting out, "I found all kinds of those packets up stairs."

"You what?"

She reached into the slit pockets of her mink coat and pulled out several more of the same foil packets in both hands. "Found four under our pillows. Mom and Dad had one under each of their pillows."

His eyes looked up to the polished beams of the Great Room, pieces to a puzzle dropping neatly into place.

"I bet if we looked into the bedrooms your brothers and their wives used, we would find a bunch more." She paused, and then broke out into laughter. "There was one in the loft where the younger kids slept."

Tidge walked to the sofa and sat down. He leaned back and stretched out, his head resting on the back cushion, his eyes zeroed in on the polished beams. "Those devils," he said softly. "Those no good devils."

"Whoever wanted to play a practical joke on you sure did a wonderful job," said Willy, enjoying her husband's mood swings.

"Carol, Carm, and that long, lanky red headed son of a bitch," he said, his head barely rolling from side to side. "That's who played the practical joke."

"The kids," she said, surprised as she joined him on the sofa. "Not your brothers?"

"Those darned kids." He broke into a grin then explained to her how they had gone back into the house when he was saying goodbye to Harold and Gert. "They came out laughing hysterically, wouldn't tell me why. I got two hugs and a handshake, all three laughing their heads off. They set me up. Those devils set me up."

Her smile turned into laughter as she sat down next to him and placed her hand on his knee. "Gee, and I thought Santa knew everything." She paused, still smiling, giving his knee a squeeze. "Do you think God saw it all?" Her laughter was out of control.

"Very funny," he said, getting up, his mind racing in a dozen different directions at once, not knowing where to go. He walked over to the floor-to-ceiling windows and looked out at the frozen lake and snow covered trees as the sun was getting lower, just resting on the tree tops across the lake.

"Excuse me, Santa," he heard Willy say. He turned around and saw her standing by the sofa in the same pose she had greeted him earlier before the Great Condom caper, as it was later called.

"I heard that Santa only comes once a year," she said, her tongue tracing her upper lip. "Is there any truth to that?" The front of her mink coat fell open exposing just her.

He smiled, his eyes drinking her in, almost leering as he slowly walked to her singing softly, "Here comes Santa Claus. Here comes Santa Claus."

Chapter 15

Drowsy and wrapped in each other's arms, her mink coat over them, Tidge yawned and said to Willy: "If I didn't eat my daughter's science experiment, all of this would have never happened."

Willy let out what resembled a purr and said in a voice succumbing to sleep, "Gee, a mink coat in exchange for moldy bread." A contented sigh was followed by a sleepy, "I like the way you think, Looney Loon."

Tidge felt the pins and needles on his right side and shifted his body that balanced precariously from falling off the sofa where he and Willy lay intertwined. The big screen television sat silent, an unwelcome intruder. There was a chill on his bare back side, but he didn't care. His love for his wife had soared out of sight.

At first, he felt a touch of pride thinking he had fit together the hodgepodge of fragments and pieces that had answered his prayers and created his perfect Christmas. He was still baffled by the explosion of events that took place during the four short days of the fam-dam-ily Christmas visit that made his perfection possible. "A handful of condoms?" he thought. "Aunt Bessie's glogg?" His mind picked up speed, the following questions firing out of him like tracers from a B-25's turret guns: "Kenny Miller and *PT*'s? Immanuel Kant? Who was Marietta Claus's real father? Did Oberleutant Werner Schneider's Messerschmitt shoot at Santa Claus?" The fragments and pieces started to become more hodge than podge resembling the holes in his jacket. He was too tired, too in love to care. "Santa," he mumbled, his words barely audible so he wouldn't wake Willy. "You do work in strange and mysterious ways." Just before he succumbed to sleep he muttered, "Oops, and you too, God. Sorry."

Willy recognized the noise without even having to open her eyes. The constant, rhythmic vibrating punctuated with sputtering and intermittent periods of silence meant only one thing. Tidge was snoring. Her elbow nudged at his ribs and his sputtering turned into several gasps for air. There was another nudge, this one harder, but with the same reaction. She started to roll over and felt him blocking her. "Just a smidgen more," she thought, pushing against him as she positioned herself to playfully blow in his ear. She heard the tell-tale sound. Looking down at the floor she saw his bewildered look. "I'm sorry," she muttered. "I didn't mean to wake you that way, sleepy head."

"Sofa hog," he muttered, sitting up and rubbing at his eyes.

"I intended to wish you a good morning," she said, wiggling under her mink coat. "Then I discovered it's really good evening."

"Evening," he repeated, his curved index fingers still trying to erase the sleep from his eyes. He looked at her as he propped an arm on the coffee table where he sat wedged, a mumble asking, "As in night?"

She purred out a simple affirmative reply. "Sleep well?" she asked.

"Nightmares," he said, his arms wrapped around himself for warmth. "Did we just have eighteen visitors here for a perfect Christmas?"

"Depends on your definition of perfect," she said, her hand then covering a yawn.

"I don't think perfect includes the love of my life and lover unceremoniously shoving me off the sofa," he said, making a face at her. He began to shiver.

"If you're so cold, why don't you get up off the floor and put on a sweat shirt or that leather jacket of yours," she said, her lips barely visible from under her coat.

"I would if I could."

"Meaning?"

"Meaning I don't have it." He saw her sit up, the mink covering her front."

She stood up her arms going through the sleeves of her coat as if she were putting on a hospital gown to go into surgery. "You don't have it?" she asked, standing up and almost crushing his hand that was on the floor next to the sofa. "I hope you're talking about the sweat shirt."

His head went slightly from side to side as he got up off the floor. "I don't have the jacket," he said, sounding sheepish. He turned away from her and put on his pants. "I gave it to Martha."

"You did what?"

His head turned back and he was looking into the eyes that could go from sweet sugar brown to angry molten red in a nanosecond. He saw shocked compassion. "I gave the jacket to Martha." His lips rolled in then returned to normal. "She doesn't know it yet, but she has it," he continued, his lips rolling in and out again as he pulled on his sweater. "She also doesn't know that she's now an heiress of sorts. Kind of young to be a matriarch, but not that young that she can't start learning."

"You gave it to her, but she doesn't know she has it?" Her eyes closed and her head went from side to side. "And she has no idea she's a matriarch?" Her head continued to go from side to side. "Oh, oh."

"What's this oh, oh business?" he asked, confused at not getting his wife's support for his decision. "What dumb thing did I do now?" His mind jumped back twenty four hours when he prided himself on making one of the greatest decisions of his life. His greatest was asking Willy to marry him.

The image of Martha standing at the foot of the stairs Christmas night, their slurred conversation punctuated with hugs and two sets of teary eyes told him he did the right thing. After she had gone upstairs and everyone was in bed, he sat in the kitchen using some of the left over paper and a colored pencil from when the kids wrote their letters to Santa. It took him hours and more rewrites he ever knew existed to get his words right to his daughter. In his mind he felt his daughter would love the surprise, another Christmas present. Hiding the jacket in her car, he thought, was a touch of genius, logic to the nth degree.

Now he tried to explain to Willy his rationale, the *Whys* and *How Comes* of his act, hoping she would understand. He ended his explanation to his wife by saying, "Heck, you never did like that tattered and charred beat up embarrassment in the first place. It was like a second Santa Claus suit to you."

Willy stared at Tidge oblivious to the goose bumps on her exposed back side. She walked around the coffee table and stopped when her toes touched his.

Tidge opened up his arms expecting his wife to give him a hug.

For the second time in her life her tiny fists began to beat on his chest. "But, you loved that jacket," she said, the tears coming harder than when he had surprised her with the news he had bought Henry's Hut. "You believed in that jacket and the stories behind it." She began to gasp, fighting for air; her fists still a flurry being absorbed by his sweater.

"Geez," he said, not comprehending. "It's a lousy old jacket. The darn thing's falling apart."

Sniffles relied to his comments as her fists dropped to her side. "That jacket gave you the strength and determination to keep believing that your cherished Santa Claus would eventually bring you your special gift." More sniffles followed. "And he did bring it!" Her statement was followed by a hic-cup, several sobs and then her wrapping her arms around her husband's neck. "You and that jacket made this Christmas special for everyone."

"Do you think you're giving too much credit to that jacket?" he asked, a soothing tone in his voice that made her tighten her arms even more. "All I know is that I kept believing and that Santa and God and, maybe, with a little bit of help from that jacket a Captain S. Claus once wore, would bring me my gift." He hugged her back not letting go. "I just felt it was time to pass the torch, to bring someone else on board, to use an old Navy expression, someone who would keep the true spirit of Santa Claus alive." He paused, released his arms and looked into her eyes. "Please tell me I did right," he said. "Tell me I got an A Plus in your grade book."

"I don't have my grade book with me," she said, releasing her arms, reaching out and taking his hands in hers. "If I did, I'd probably give you an *I* for Incomplete," she continued, a sniffle acting as a period. "That *I* can also stand for Idiot," she said, a bumpy sigh punctuating her statement, eyes downcast. "I'll change your grade after you hear from the new matriarch." She paused and looked way too serious at him. "And, love of my life, man of my dreams, you will hear from her."

Chapter 16

The only evidence remaining from the Martha / Jacket incident were faint red welts on Tidge's chest. With a mutual nod and Willy saying, "I've got icicles from my heels to the nape of my neck," she did a quick three hundred and sixty degree turn. "See 'em?" she asked.

He grinned. "Hah," he said. "I thought you knew that my brother, John was the only member of this family who was a fan of lady wrestling." He held out his hand, she latched on and they vacated the Great Room and headed for the stairs.

Tidge, never one for wearing matching ensembles since leaving La Salle Street and the stock brokerage business, opted for convenience. He pulled on a pair of paint stained white sweat pants, a maroon and gold spotted Loyola University logo on the right thigh. A De Paul University t-shirt with holes under both arms went on next followed by a faded purple bulky knit ski sweater, a white wildcat and an embroidered Northwestern over the left breast. The moths who Willy had told him wouldn't want any part of his antique Santa Claus suit had found a source of comfort food in his sweater. He slipped into a pair of white sweat socks; both heels worn out and a hole in one toe, and then jammed his feet into ankle high lamb's wool lined slippers. He crushed down the heels as he shuffled over to Willy in a combination walk and force-the-slipper-on technique.

After hanging up her mink in the protective garment bag she stumbled on in the corner of her closet, Willy slipped into a pair of white flannel pajamas decorated with tiny bear cubs and pine cones. Her feet became warm and toasty once inside her matching pair of lamb's wool lined slippers, the heels appearing off the store shelf new.

Tidge kissed her left ear lobe as she slipped into a matching quilted robe and asked, "What color wine would you like for news watching?"

"Surprise me," she said, as she tied the robe's sash into a perfect bow. "A snack would surprise me even more."

Tidge made them both turkey sandwiches on white bread with mayo and lettuce, a heavy dose of salt on his. They sat on the sofa in front of the television eating and taking sips of a Merlot, each not enjoying what they thought was a too dry taste for sliced, cold turkey. Tidge clicked on the remote. His thumb found the button combination he wanted and a commercial for a nebulous franchise pizza parlor in Superior, Wisconsin came on the screen. He pushed the buttons and stopped when he saw an old movie he recognized as *Miracle on 34th Street*.

Willy's elbow was ever so gentle against his rib cage. "We've had a perfect Christmas," she said, a relaxed, drowsy warning creeping into her voice. "Let's not go into overkill."

Tidge laughed, his thumb pushing down and the channels changing. "Would you want me to search for, *It's A Wonderful Life*?"

A crinkled nose replaced her nudge this time and she said, "News, thank you."

Channels continued flying by. "How 'bout *A Christmas Story*?" he asked.

"News, thank you."

"*White Christmas*?" He grimaced. "Ouch," he said, after feeling her elbow jam into his ribs. "What was that for?"

The next morning they sat in the kitchen eating breakfast. Besides the Christmas tree and the decorations, there was no visible evidence that eighteen people had spent four days with them. Neither was sure of how to deal with the quiet that was broken by Tidge's periodic slurping of his cereal.

"Okay, Sinter Claes," said Willy, pushing her coffee mug away.

"That's Dutch," he interjected, his cereal spoon half in his mouth. He smiled, removed the spoon and gave it a lick.

"Very good," she said, giving him a sympathetic pat on the head. "I hope you show the same enthusiasm for cleaning up after the small invasion that overran our home."

"What happened to the spotless house we cleaned yesterday after we finally got rid of Martha?" he asked, seeing the day he planned in his workshop being altered. "I thought that passed your white glove inspection."

"That was merely a surface cleaning," she said, then indicated with her index finger that he should follow her. "Now we check to see if nary a soul was left behind."

Before he knew it, Willy had reached in between the stove and the counter top and was holding up a child's white sweat sock between her thumb and forefinger. Her other thumb and forefinger pinched her nose shut. "When was the last time this was washed?"

"That's beyond washing." He took a large plastic bag from under the counter, shook it open with several snaps, and held it out for her. "Garbage," he said, nodding toward the bag.

Later, satisfied with the kitchen and the aroma of a pine scented cleaner permeating the room, he followed her index finger into the Great Room where he discovered a child's left sneaker stuffed between the cushions of one of the matching sofas. The laces sported so many knots they looked like his late mother's rosary. "I'll put this in the garage," he said, as he watched her pull the cushions from the other sofa. "In a week or so I'll deodorize it and give it to Morty for mailing."

His hand traced a deliberate circular course under the cushions of his recliner chair. A look of satisfaction replaced his grumpy disposition as he held up a quarter and a dime. "Keep your hands off," he warned, the coins placed on the drop leaf table next to the chair.

Willy was on her knees reaching behind the new television cabinet. When she removed her hands each held a black, patent leather pump by the heel. She extended her arms out in front of her so Tidge could see her discovery. Then she started spinning the shoes by the heels and began to sing: "If you've got the money, Honey, I've got the time."

Tidge dropped the dust rag and aerosol can of duster spray he was using and started towards her. "Are those your new ones or the tried and true Joan Crawford endorsed ones?" he asked, reaching out for her while his other hand went for his back pocket. "I seem to have left my wallet in my other pants. Do you take *I. O. U.'s?*"

"That's what they all say," she said, then concealing the shoes behind her back. "After we finish cleaning I'll check your credit references."

"Figures, he said, picking up his dust rag and spray can. Getting on his knees, he began spraying and wiping the drop leaf table both under and on top. Stopping, he leaned forward and wormed his hand between the table and the chair. He scooted back and held up a half-eaten kolachke. "That's not like Santa to waste food," he said.

"Oh, sure, blame Santa," she said, a slight touch of sarcasm to her comment. "You set up that whole Christmas morning cookies and milk charade. Admit it."

"I don't know what you're talking about," he said, then putting the remainder of the kolachke in the garbage bag. "Honest. I really don't." He didn't.

"Right," she said, as the cleaning progressed. After wiping up various sized sticky hand prints that had stuck to everything in their home that had a surface, they both continued to search behind, under and in between every item in Henry's Hut. Remnants of Christmas wrap that escaped his brothers and Mackie found the garbage bag. So did another sweat sock and one foil condom packet that Willy had missed after discovering the caper.

After a day of wiping, washing, dusting and mopping, Willy's home soon returned to her interpretation of neat. "Is Commodore von Schneider pleased with her command ship's appearance?" he asked, plopping down in his recliner. His dust rag and spray can lay exhausted on his lap. "Would the Commodore like to go below deck to see if any of my brothers' children have stowed away?" He ignored the parade of wrinkles marching up and down her nose.

They enjoyed a light early dinner of still more leftovers leaving their dirty dishes in the kitchen sink, vowing to wash them before they went to bed. Tidge took a couple of wine glasses from the cabinet above the sink and they moved from the kitchen to one of the sofas by the fireplace. He uncorked two bottles of wine that had been opened for Christmas dinner, but had gotten lost in too many beverage choices. He held them up for Willy saying, "Take your pick."

They sat in silence in the Great Room mesmerized by the colored lights and a swarm of enchanting, glistening ornaments on the Christmas tree. They gave each other a warm smile noticing the clumps of too much tinsel rearranged earlier by the little hands of Star, egged on by Frankie and Paul, Jr. "Any more thoughts on what everyone said about doing this again next year?" he asked, sounding mellow.

"I'm still thinking," Willy mumbled. She snuggled closer to him. "But first, I'm thinking about an idea I had for a novel about Christmas."

He swirled his wine around in the glass looking pleased. "Sounds interesting," he said. "Can you tell me what it's about?"

"It's not about having our families back again next year."

"Oh." He took a sip of wine and could feel the start of a mellow feeling. "Okay, what did your cum laude mind come up with?"

She gave him a serious look. "If you must know, it's about a family who gets together at Christmas and watches their children light farts."

His hands went up, a roar of laughter bellowing from him. "And you taught my daughter!" Then he looked in dismay to see part of his wine being soaked up by his sweater and sweat pants.

"Yes, I did teach your daughter," she said, her head going slowly from side to side several times. "Among other things, kind of like I'm assuming your Brother James Virgil tried to do with you, I taught her manners and how not to spill wine all over her."

He rubbed at the blotch of wine stain that disappeared into the faded purple color of his sweater but not the white of his sweat pants.

Willy looked at him and wrinkled her nose. "I'll make you a deal."

He rolled his lips inward and waited.

"If you promise to take that heinous glogg recipe back to the cemetery where your Aunt Bessie is resting in peace and sprinkle the torn pieces over her grave, I'll give serious consideration to a repeat of this madness next year." She saw him start to open his mouth and her right hand went up. "I want several guarantees."

"Whatever you want," he said, crossing one leg over the other hoping to blot up the wine stain on his sweat pants. "Name it."

She got right to the point. "My first guarantee, besides the glogg funeral, is that we put to rest all parlor games. *Can You Top This* is history."

"Agreed," he said, his right index finger being raised. "But you have to tell Harold and Gert." He tried not to smile. "Especially Harold," he added. Somehow he's going to request another platform for his singing Wunderbar."

She nodded. "Second, you will escort your three brothers through the woods to the Miller's farm. There they will be indoctrinated and educated by Kenny Miller about the difference between a cow, a bull and a deer. That includes, buck, doe and fawn." There was a twinkle in her eyes. "Maybe they should each be forced to milk a dairy cow."

"Sounds fair," he said, a smile forming. "Do you want Mickey to be there with Kenny so she can demonstrate to my brothers the fine art of removing straw from her underwear while the Creature from the Black Lagoon sharpens his scythe?"

Her nose crinkled. "Third," she said, ignoring his comment involving Mickey and her father, "I want you to rent a villa in the Caribbean." She thought for a moment. "Maybe two weeks," she said. "Perhaps three," she said, her suggestion preceded by a too long pause. I'm not quite sure. Late February or March seems like a good time. Don't you think?"

"I think."

"I think so too," she said, sounding pleased. "That's about the time of winter when most people up here are getting that shack happy disease you once mentioned to me and becoming addicted to brandy Manhattans. Be sure and get some brochures before that happens."

"I will." He kept looking at her, feeling better by the minute. "Does my Sugar Claus have any other wishes?" What was left of his wine started swirling around and out of his glass again. "Geez."

"One other thing," she said a look of disgust on her face.

"This isn't about the Santa Claus suit, is it?" He knew he sounded as if he were pleading, but didn't care.

"The suit can stay."

She was so nonchalant the way she cast aside his greatest fear that he wanted to both scream at her louder than his father ever did to him and hug her at the same time. Then he calmed down. "What's the one other thing?"

"Prepare yourself for when your daughter calls to express her feelings about a certain surprise Christmas gift given to her by her father, Thomas Ignacy Mackiewicz, also known as, The-Hypocrite-Coward-and-Man-I-Love-Mackiewicz," she said, pronouncing his last name, Mackie-whiz, the way she did when they first met. Then she switched on a look that was more than serious. "And, my darling husband and once screwed up patriarch of a perfect, never screwed up family, mine included, she will call." There was another pause. She didn't like ultimatums, but this was one time she felt she had no choice. "If you raise your voice one teeny tiny bit when your lovely daughter, Martha calls, there will never be another family Christmas in this house for as long as I'm living here. And, this here stepmama plans on out living you by at least twenty-five years."

"I'm not known as Mackie-whiz, the calm, collected, cool logician for nothing."

"You promise you'll be nice to her?"

"I promise."

"And, if you break your promise and I get Kenny Miller to fix you up with Mickey's mother as part of our divorce settlement, you won't think unkindly of me?"

"Never."

"The future of family Christmases in this house is now in your hands. Mess up with Martha and you'll find out what it will be like to be damned by a whole fam-dam-ily."

"Does that include a certain young man attending the Missouri Military Academy in Mexico, Missouri?"

She nodded.

"Really, Mam?"

Just then the phone rang. Two concerned looks responded to the initial ring. The second ring saw Willy give Tidge a nudge. A third ring produced an annoyed look. "Mackie-whiz-the-Coward," she uttered after the fourth ring, as she answered the phone. "Of course he is," she said. "It's too cold and dark for him to be outside in his shirt sleeves. Only someone minus a brain would do that." She listened and smiled.

Tidge watched her head go first up and down and then from side to side. Then he saw her frown. There was a smile, her eyes rolling, and her nose twitching before another smile took over. The parade of expressions continued on each making him more nervous as he tried to piece together the other side of a long distance phone conversation.

"Love you too, my beautiful daughter," said Willy. "And a Happy New Year to you." She held the phone out for Tidge. "It's your heir apparent matriarch." She gave him a smile.

Tidge put his hand over the mouth piece. "Did she sound mad?" he asked in a whisper, suddenly seeing future family Christmases drifting off in every direction except towards the North Pole.

"How could your heir apparent be mad?" she asked. "She just got a beat up leather jacket from Santa Claus and a letter of sorts written by a crazed member of the Mackie-whiz clan."

Tidge knew Willy was right. She was always right. His stomach chewed on itself the way it did when conflict faced him, when danger was eminent. It was like the first time he and Willy took their second hand, beat up toboggan for a test run down their rut road after their first Christmas in Henry's Hut.

"Hey, how dangerous can it be," he had said to Willy? The two of them looked, fascinated and excited by the slight slope of the road that cut through the trees and ended at County M. They had purchased the battered wooden relic at a Catholic Church bazaar on an exploratory journey to Woodruff during a mid-July Sunday. Tidge and Willy discovered the meaning of danger on the toboggan's maiden voyage. "It ain't no more than a bunny hill," he said. Those were his last words before he uttered, "Oh, shit," upon seeing the world's biggest, meanest tree in their path after the toboggan hit a rut, veered off the road and took a vertical four foot drop. As Tidge discovered, the tree didn't budge and danger didn't waste any time creating a collision. He had rolled Willy off the toboggan a moment before it came to a dead, crunching stop thanks to the tree's massive trunk. She escaped, laughing like a lunatic, buried in a snow drift. "Oh, shit," Tidge said again, his right leg sprouted a new angle that right legs shouldn't have. He hobbled around the house wearing a crotch to ankle cast on his right leg for six weeks feeling both empathy and sympathy toward his brother who had lost his two front teeth decades earlier.

Tidge exhaled and watched Willy return to her seat on the couch, her eyes fixed on the charred portable phone. "Oh, shit," he said.

"Well," she said, waiting to hear every detail after he had talked to Martha for a full thirty minutes, all but a fraction of those minutes coming from him. For Tidge, any phone conversation over, hello-goodbye and a brief message wasted his time. His daughter introduced him to a new communication skill. So did his wife. Listen or else.

"Well water," said Tidge, after he pushed the end button on the phone, the "n" and "d" letters having been burned off along with digits one through three. His effort at being flippant failed and he sounded like he was in a trance as he began regurgitating the conversation.

"She got pulled over by a State cop outside of Edgerton," he said, his voice a whisper, the monotone drone of his words lacking any signs of emotion. "The cop gave her a warning ticket. I bet she went into her crying mode and struck a sympathetic nerve with the cop, it still being the Christmas season. Martha's a real pro at that with her driving record. If the cop was a young, good looking stud like yours truly, I bet she gave him her phone number."

Willy's eyes rolled. "Get on with it."

Tidge related Martha's details. "She found a parking place on an icy side street a block from her apartment and unpacked her car. Two trips in the dirty, slushy Chicago snow carrying her garment bag, Christmas presents and cross between a beach bag and purse she calls a tote bag got her up the stairs to her second floor flat."

He knew the old brownstone in Lincoln Park on Belden down the block from John Barleycorn's Pub. He had driven by it several times after Martha had moved in, after she had shunned his offers to help her with the moving. Years earlier, he had taken Barbara Ann to

Barleycorn's for hand holding to recorded classical music and Roquefort topped hamburgers while making vows he knew he could never carry out.

Tidge continued. "Martha never touched any of the things she brought home until today. Miss Van Winkle had the day off and slept late," he said, his narration continuing in almost a whisper. "At first she thought there had been a mistake. She knew she had opened all of her presents when she was here, faster than all of the little kids, her the consummate Christmas wrap shredder. Then, sometime around noon today, in the quiet of her apartment she tore open my little surprise."

Willy's eye brows went up. "Little," she repeated, matching his whisper.

"Staring up at her from its cradle of torn Christmas paper was my, you-know-what," he said. "I guess curiosity took a slap at her, kind of like my father's not-so-playful love taps. Dismay then popped up. She told me she just stared at it trying to make sense of why she had the jacket."

"That comes as no surprise to me," said Willy. "At least she could stare. I thought I lost my eyesight when you told me what you had done."

"Geez, had I known I would create more commotion than Santa's notorious bombing run over Germany during Christmas Eve of 1944, I would have driven down to Chicago. Then I would have taken my daughter to a formal Christmas Tea at the Drake Hotel and made a grandiose presentation."

"You never took me to a formal Christmas Tea at the Drake or any other fancy place," said Willy, a tiny pout forming.

"Poor you," said Tidge, wanting to laugh but not able. "Your father probably owned the Drake once-upon-a-time." He stared straight ahead. "Martha then told me about a series of questions she presented to her bedroom walls."

Willy sat stone faced, no crinkles, wrinkles, raised eye brows or laser stares evident.

"The kid's very intelligent," he said, looking proud. "Smarter than me and my come lousy degree from Loyola," he continued. "She asked her bedroom walls great questions. Didn't use very lady-like language from what I could gather from our chit-chat. For awhile I thought I was listening to Kid Scream." He paused and gave Willy a serious look. "If Martha becomes a parent someday, her language guarantees her a place in your Hall of Fame of not-so-perfect parents."

"Get on with it," she said, her lower lip making a slight roll over the top of her upper lip.

"Her questions didn't provide any answers," he said. "Martha couldn't figure out why her father would leave his pride and joy in the back seat of her car." He glanced at Willy. "Then she saw my multiple page note or, as she referred to it, not very reverently, my blankety-blank epistle."

Martha's language stunned him. "Daughters don't talk like that to a parent," he said. "Maybe to mothers, but never to fathers."

Tidge and his brothers would have never used four letter words of one syllable to either of their parents. The fear of bodily harm, even death had that affect on them. He glanced again at Willy trying to garner sympathy, forgiveness or, at least, a glimmer of understanding for his action. None came.

"I'm glad four hundred miles separated us during that phone call," he said. "My first born was upset. I half expected a repeat performance of her showdown at the O.K. Corral Room in the Ambassador East at our wedding."

"Didn't I warn you that your little girl might be a tad on the upset side," she said, an accompanying look reinforcing her words.

He nodded. "I guess she was angry enough to take my blankety-blank epistle and perform a Biblical miracle by turning it into a crushed paper ball. Then the blankety-blank paper ball soared across her bedroom and exploded against her radiator." He glanced at Willy, his look asking if he should continue.

A silent yes gave permission.

"Wrinkled sheets of my finest prose fluttered down redecorating her bedroom. That's when not very lady-like language in the form of very creative blankety-blanks got attached to every page." His sad, sensitive eyes asked, "More?"

She nodded.

"Martha referred to me as a mean-spirited, selfish coward," he said, pointing his right index finger at the center of his chest. "Me, mean-spirited?" He didn't wait for a response from Willy. "Boy, oh, boy, did she ever use the descriptive adjectives and colloquialisms with those blankety-blanks of hers."

Willy's eye brows went up a fraction.

"Her Grandma May I would not have been pleased."

Willy's eyebrows went up a second fraction.

"Can you believe that she screamed at me saying: 'You never loved us, you bastard. You abandoned us. You abandoned me, you son of a bitch'."

Willy's eyebrows slid gently back in place.

"She even went so far as to blame me for Sissy's credit card balances. Told me I was a self-centered tight wad, used a bad word after centered. Told me I hadn't changed after all. Then she reiterated her frustrated curses and ended up telling me how she buried her face in her hands and cried. She cried most of the afternoon."

"She told me," said Willy, in her subdued whisper.

Tidge could visualize his daughter, her tears drying up about the time the first signs of sunset melted off her bedroom window that hadn't been washed since before she moved in the apartment two years ago. He didn't miss a word of her litany as he continued to tell Willy what she already knew. "She repeated phrases earlier, all similar in content, adding, 'I believed you. You told me to believe and I believed. You told me to be truthful. You told me to trust and I trusted you, you fucking bastard'."

Willy only thought she could feel her husband's pain. She said nothing, her eyes unblinking, her lips sealed.

"Oh, man, talk about insanity," said Tidge, his blue eyes trying to show that he was alive.

The only sign of life Martha's eyes showed after reacting to her father's written attempt at an explanation was blazing anger. She went to her kitchen, took an open can of diet cola from her refrigerator, the can opened just before she left for Lake Namakagon, and took several frustrated gulps. Choking on her last gulp, she coughed and found a stream of flat cola running down her chin to be absorbed by her turtle neck sweater. She blotted at her neck and chin with a dish towel that hadn't been washed in two weeks and muttered, "Damn." She set the can on her kitchen table and sat down on the one chair she owned, a cane back rocking chair that her Grandma May I once had in the corner of her bedroom. Her grandmother used to sit and knit when her husband was glued to his television watching boxing.

The cola's caffeine rammed into Martha's super-charged emotions. Her hands choked the rocker's arms. "Damn you," she yelled. She rocked forward, stopped and realized she was acting the way she remembered how her scary grandfather acted. The rocker finished the return trip. Martha sat and stared. Childhood memories marched by. The bruised and the ugly marchers were joined by a legion of laughing, giggling jump-up-and-down, roll-around-on-the-living-room-rug-hug-daddy ones. The rocker started forward and froze. Martha blinked, blinded for a second by what she thought was a flash. She sat and stared for what seemed forever into the tiny opening of the cola can. There was another flash, this one bringing calmness to her. She saw herself with her father at the foot of the stairs Christmas night. Too many Gibsons that had dulled her senses that night couldn't erase her memory. Martha heard every word her father spoke to her that night, the biggest word, the one that set her off, was now the one responsible for her calm.

"Believe," Martha had whispered, making the word sound like both a spiritual question and an order. She got up from the rocker and went back to her bedroom. The jacket was where she had left it, still in its torn Christmas wrap cradle. She picked it up and held it out in front of her. Two small jagged slits in the leather, one above each of the breast pockets, caught her eye. She sat on the edge of her unmade bed lightly stroking the cracked leather. Gradually, the fingers of her right hand traced one, and then the other slit giving her a feeling that she couldn't explain. She saw three more holes in the front of the jacket. They were more like round punctures. Something compelled her to turn the jacket over. She did and discovered matching holes in the back, almost in line with the ones in the front. Curious fingers spread the jacket open. That's when she saw dark stains around all the tears in the lining. Her fingers traveled to each of the holes and the two slits, respectfully sliding into each. She knew her father had done the same thing. Anyone named Thomas had to poke his fingers into those holes. Her inspection continued going from back to front. She examined the worn faded insignia on the breast pocket. The smiling female wore a bathing suit Martha or her sisters would never have been caught dead wearing. Martha, however, would have died to have her figure. The Santa Claus hat the smiling female wore seemed silly and out of place. The words around the insignia were still legible and didn't make sense to her. "Sugar Claus?" she asked herself. Curious fingers turned to even more curious hands as the urge to put on the jacket overwhelmed her. It was way too big for her. Tiny hands and wrists rattled in the frayed cuffs, her slender arms lost in the baggy sleeves. A feeling she couldn't explain seeped into her pores. She found herself down on all fours crawling on the ugly, stained oak floor of her bedroom searching for the epistle. The crumpled pages were scattered along one wall, a single ball finding its way under her bed. She apologized to each page as she picked them up, her hands ironing out creases of her father's explanation into smooth sheets. She sat on the floor, her back against the chilled outside wall and read the letter again. It still didn't make sense. A third reading created more questions. How could adults who were about to die use their last moments on Earth talking about believing in Santa Claus? How could her father's uncle find sobriety long enough to give his nephew the jacket and relate the sad, but magical, story attached to it? How could one person, her father, face disappointment upon disappointment and keep on believing that what he believed would happen, would actually happen? Answers began to trickle out of the jacket. Every act, every action had a reason, that's what his epistle said. She could feel the jacket embrace her even more and she embraced it back. There was a realization welling up in her saying, that in a unique sort of way, her father's way, she was special. She had been chosen, handpicked. She had been given what few people in the world would ever experience. Another human being believed in her, believed in her enough to trust that she could, and would be able to take on responsibility when it confronted her. She knew what her grandfather's last words to her father had been, those words both gross and amusing, like the Wicked

Witch costume from the Wizard of Oz she wore during Halloween when she was a child trick or treating. The words of her grandfather were orders. So were the words, she assumed, of a Captain S. Claus as he lay dying on the concrete tarmac of an R.A.F. air strip in the south of England receiving the Last Rites. "How could his final words be about Santa Claus?" she asked herself.

Trusting and believing, Martha knew, could be expressed in a myriad of ways. Like her father, she had been selected as the new master link in a family chain. Her father's Uncle Bruce had been picked to wear the jacket of one dead hero by a second dying hero. Few people knew that her father's uncle was also a hero. The Navy Cross and a Purple Heart found in a small night stand next to his stained, soiled bed after he died were kept by her father. Now she was the one who would wear the old leather jacket with the faded insignia. Once it dawned on her, the rationale behind why she had been chosen, a docile humility closed the door on her anger and hatred. If life threw a challenge at her, she would take on that challenge. Like her father, there would be no excuses. And, as her father had instructed her at the foot of the stairs as they stood forehead to forehead just before they hugged and she staggered up to bed: "Never, ever call Santa Claus a fat bastard."

Tidge gave his shoulders the weakest of shrugs and said to his wife after relating the phone conversation, "That's all there is, there ain't no more."

All Willy could do after releasing her grip on the heels of her pumps she had set in her lap was dab at her eyes with the cuffed sleeve of her robe. She reached across the sofa and touched his arm. "Are you going to be okay?"

"Never better," he said, not looking that way.

"Are you sure, Santa baby?"

"Slip into those pumps and I'll really show you how sure I am."

"You are okay." She broke into a smile and gave him a wink.

Just then, the phone rang again and both their expressions turned identical, twin cases of annoyed. "Who can that be now?" he asked.

"Answer it," she said, giving him another wink. "I'm heading up to our boudoir." She puckered her lips for a second then said, "I have to get our room comfy and cozy for Santa's visit."

Tidge sighed and picked up the phone. "Hello," he muttered. There was a pause and a smile.

"Humper, you silly bastard, Merry Christmas and Happy New Year," said Tidge, grinning. "You're late as usual, but it's good to hear from you."

Willy stopped at the foot of the stairs. "Excuse me, Mister Alvin," she said, "I hope you won't keep Mrs. Claus waiting. I heard rumors floating around the woods that she has a surprise for you." She turned after seeing the look he gave her and walked up the stairs singing, "Silver Bells, silver bells, it's Christmas time in the Northwoods."

Tidge smiled and started relating his family Christmas to his best friend from boyhood. Episodes of growing up with Bean Head and Brother James Virgil made the telephone lines laugh. "I wish Brother James Virgil would've told us how tough life really would be when he was beating his noblesse oblige into our moronic heads," he said, repressing emotions that were several decades old.

(Pause).

"No, Bean Head was Moron One, I was Moron Two and you were Moron Three. Zamboni was Moron Four until he got kicked out of school and joined the Marines."

(Pause).

"No, you never did tell me."

(Pause).

"No kidding.

(Pause).

"Your old man was in World War II with the Polish Army fighting for the British?" he asked, his mind starting to whirl. "At an air base in England? Are you shittin' me, Humper?"

(Pause).

"A B-25? No shit!"

(Pause).

There was a faint reply of: "I heard that," coming from the second floor.

Tidge ignored his wife's remark. He then related to his friend the story about his father-in-law's father, the Luftwaffe pilot, shooting at Santa Claus over Germany on Christmas Eve. "I'm not kidding. My father-in-law told me how upset his old man was when he came home for a twenty four hour pass to celebrate Christmas."

(Pause).

Tidge nodded in awe and said: "Your old man really saw Santa Claus getting the Last Rites?"

(Pause).

"Oh, man, Humper, you ain't gonna believe when I tell you about the travels of my World War II Army Air Corps jacket that you used to make fun of."

(Pause).

"Now you can make fun of my first born, the one you used to baby-sit."

(Pause)

"She has the jacket."

(Pause).

"Whatever your old man told you wasn't made up. I'm now convinced of that."

(Pause).

"Do you remember that tall girl with the German last name? Claus. The one with the nice set of sugar plums. The one I had a crush on all the way from the eighth grade at St. Ferdinand's until just after you and I graduated from Weber High. Then she dumped me and you married Janice."

(Pause).

"I swear to God I think I know who her real father was."

(Pause).

"I know this sounds farfetched, but your old man may have watched him die on the ground at that air base in England."

Their conversation seemed to end before it started as Tidge looked at the portable phone in his right hand for what seemed like an eternity before he cut the connection. The faint sound of his wife's voice from upstairs startled him.

"Oh, Santa, are you coming to bed? Mrs. Claus has a surprise for you."

Tidge didn't say a word. He was beaming as he got up and started for the stairs, the strains of *Silent Night* following him. He knew that there would never be another Christmas like this. Perfection is, well, perfect and even Santa Claus and God can't get better than perfect. His father's three orders in the form of a crippling millstone were sitting somewhere on Lake Namakagon's frozen surface buried under the snow. With the spring thaw the debilitating stone with its etched orders would rest fifty feet down on the bottom of the deepest part of the lake. "What greater present could a person ever get from Santa Claus," he thought. Then he heard his wife again, her voice louder.

"Mrs. Claus is waiting!"

He didn't answer. As he got to the foot of the stairs, he stopped, reached out wide to grasp both polished oak hand rails, and then took the stairs two at a time. When he got to the top he could see what looked like flickering candle light coming from the open door of their master suite. Three strides had him to the door where he stood, his mouth open and knees starting to shake.

"Do you like?" she asked, sitting on the bed covers in her robe, her knees tucked under her and her brown eyes dripping sugar.

Tears began to well up. He couldn't help it. The room danced to the swaying beat of more candles than he knew existed. Dancing in the candlelight were all of his mother's religious figurines nestled in cotton, every available space from dressers to night stands filled. Three empty cardboard beer cartons were stacked next to the bedroom door where he stood as if he were one of the figurines. Tears dripped off his cheeks like the spring melting snow from the roof of Henry's Hut. He looked at Willy finding it hard to breath.

"I had Cadet Mam bring them up from your den and hide them in my closet before he left," she said, the sugar flowing. "You can't have perfection and your special gift at Christmas with your mother suffocating inside old cardboard beer cases tucked away in your den closet."

Suddenly his days in Boot Camp at Great Lakes washed over him.

He snapped to attention, saluted and said, "Seaman Recruit Alvin reporting as ordered Sugar Claus." The candles glowed, the golden flickering radiating from their eyes. "Can I have my surprise gift?" he asked, his tears being shoved aside by a smile.

"Can you," she repeated, one cocked eye brow joined by the other. "You may if you think you can."

www.ingramcontent.com/pod-product-compliance
Lightning Source LLC
Chambersburg PA
CBHW020259120726
47904CB00001B/268